W9-AVL-340

ENDANGERED

Jordan dared not look back. She cleared the branches obstructing her path, pulling the leafy limbs back. Yancy might have cared for her but in the wrong way. He had betrayed her, too.

Stop, she told herself. Can't outrun him. Jump behind a tree, plant your feet and shoot. But these tree trunks were thick, the shrubs low. No cover. He had a gun, too. She felt naked.

At least she was familiar with the area, or had been once. But everything seemed changed since the days she had hiked here; grass and shrubs had shifted since she and Seth met secretly. If only Jordan could make it two miles out to their old meeting place. . . .

Black Orchid

SIGNET

 ONYX

DON'T MISS KAREN HARPER'S
CAPTIVATING NOVELS

☐ **DARK ROAD HOME by Karen Harper** Attorney Brooke Benton comes to the Maplecreek Amish community to escape the stalker who terrorized her after her last murder case. But the homespun Amish frown on her worldy ways. Daniel Brand returns to his Amish people after years in the outside world to find a good Amish wife. But when a mysterious hit-and-run driver kills four Amish teenagers, Brooke and Dan plunge into an investigation to find the killers and find love. (187253—$5.99)

☐ **RIVER OF SKY** When Kate Craig's husband died, the St. Louis riverboat captain left her only a legacy of debts, a battered old riverboat, and a plot of land up the Mississippi. Worse, he had betrayed her love and trust. Kate takes up her husband's trade to recoup her fortunes and win her independence. But two of the riverboat passengers are men as different as day and night who pose another challenge to Kate. (184904—$5.99)

☐ **PROMISES TO KEEP** It is the first Christmas after the Civil War in Lockwood, Ohio. For Amanda Wynne so much has changed, leaving her heart feeling as bleak as the dreary winter. But then she receives three unexpected visitors at her house for the holidays, and Amanda discovers that everything is possible for those who dare to dream. (182529—$4.99)

☐ **THE WINGS OF MORNING.** "A lively, satisfying 19th-century romance ... that moves from the remote Scottish island of St. Kilda to Victorian London and finally to the wild paradise of Sanibel, Florida ... admirable research, lively prose, and an epic-scale plot make this a sturdy bet."—*Kirkus Reviews* (180658—$5.99)

☐ **CIRCLE OF GOLD** From frontier America to Britain's ruling class—a stirring saga of a beautiful and indomitable woman caught up in the surging tides of history and the crosscurrents of duty and desire. "Superb!"—*Los Angeles Daily News* (403819—$5.99)

*Prices slightly higher in Canada

Buy them at your local bookstore or use this convenient coupon for ordering.

PENGUIN USA
P.O. Box 999 — Dept. #17109
Bergenfield, New Jersey 07621

Please send me the books I have checked above.
I am enclosing $_____ (please add $2.00 to cover postage and handling). Send check or money order (no cash or C.O.D.'s) or charge by Mastercard or VISA (with a $15.00 minimum). Prices and numbers are subject to change without notice.

Card #_____ Exp. Date _____
Signature_____
Name_____
Address_____
City _____ State _____ Zip Code _____

For faster service when ordering by credit card call **1-800-253-6476**

Allow a minimum of 4-6 weeks for delivery. This offer is subject to change without notice.

Black Orchid

by

Karen Harper

A SIGNET BOOK

SIGNET
Published by the Penguin Group
Penguin Books USA Inc., 375 Hudson Street,
New York, New York 10014, U.S.A.
Penguin Books Ltd, 27 Wrights Lane,
London W8 5TZ, England
Penguin Books Australia Ltd, Ringwood,
Victoria, Australia
Penguin Books Canada Ltd, 10 Alcorn Avenue,
Toronto, Ontario, Canada M4V 3B2
Penguin Books (N.Z.) Ltd, 182–190 Wairau Road,
Auckland 10, New Zealand

Penguin Books Ltd, Registered Offices:
Harmondsworth, Middlesex, England

First published by Signet, an imprint of Dutton Signet,
a division of Penguin Books USA Inc.

First Printing, December, 1996
10 9 8 7 6 5 4 3 2 1

Copyright © Karen Harper, 1996
All rights reserved

REGISTERED TRADEMARK—MARCA REGISTRADA

Printed in the United States of America

Without limiting the rights under copyright reserved above, no part of
this publication may be reproduced, stored in or introduced into a
retrieval system, or transmitted, in any form, or by any means (electronic,
mechanical, photocopying, recording, or otherwise), without the prior written
permission of both the copyright owner and the above publisher of this
book.

PUBLISHER'S NOTE
This is a work of fiction. Names, characters, places, and incidents either
are the product of the author's imagination or are used fictitiously,
and any resemblance to actual persons, living or dead, events, or locales
is entirely coincidental.

BOOKS ARE AVAILABLE AT QUANTITY DISCOUNTS WHEN USED TO PROMOTE
PRODUCTS OR SERVICES. FOR INFORMATION PLEASE WRITE TO PREMIUM
MARKETING DIVISION, PENGUIN BOOKS USA INC., 375 HUDSON STREET, NEW
YORK, NEW YORK 10014.

If you purchased this book without a cover you should be aware that this
book is stolen property. It was reported as "unsold and destroyed"
to the publisher and neither the author nor the publisher has received
any payment for this "stripped book."

*For Don
and our Florida friends
and all those with
sunny winter dreams.*

Orchids come in all shapes, sizes, and colors—except black. A black orchid would be a freak of nature. If one were ever found, it would become expensive, exclusive, even endangered.

My orchids are none of those things, though they may just change your life. You will enjoy their priceless beauty at reasonable costs, so please give us a visit.

—Jordan Quinn, Owner
The Orchid Tree Shop
Fifth Avenue South
Naples, Florida

Chapter One

Southwest Florida
January 11, 1994

Her feelings ran deep and sure out here. They had never included fear or even foreboding—until now.

Jordan Quinn stopped to survey the view. Islands of trees dotted the blue-green grasslands of the Everglades. Everything seemed normal, so what was the icy prickle along the nape of her neck? Shoving back her spill of copper hair, she sucked a steadying breath deep into her lungs, then sighed. She jostled her backpack to shift her load and, watching for snakes, picked her way across the spongy soil.

Maybe that distant sound made her so uneasy, she thought, squinting into the sun. A droning hum like a mosquito became the buzz, then roar of a motor. An old white one-engine prop plane circled, dipping its inner wing. Then, to her amazement, it swooped low at her, like an old-time stunt plane.

Despite the billed cap she wore, Jordan shaded her eyes to glare up at it, and as it passed, she shook her fist. She knew they could see her; someone was leaning out with binoculars. Two men aboard, she could tell that much.

At first she had assumed it was the plane used by

the Endangered Panther Research Team, but that one was newer and painted blue. Her husband was on their staff so they would have recognized her and just wagged their wings as they had once before. Perhaps these men were illegal hunters. Or it was just some jerk's idea of thrill riding, like the tourists and locals who roared around out here on their swamp buggies, airboats, and ATVs, scarring the land and scaring the animals.

Right now, damn them, they were scaring her. The plane circled, then dived toward her again. "Idiots!" she yelled but ducked instinctively. That crazy scene from Alfred Hitchcock's movie *North by Northwest* darted through her mind: Cary Grant fleeing a low-flying plane flown by people trying to kill him.

The plane's next swoop blasted hot air at her; this time the wheels missed her head by about twelve feet. Jordan scrambled away, then ran. It came around, lower, at her. She zigzagged now, not daring to slow to look up and back. If she hit the ground, they would miss her, and on their next pass she could make the trees. At least they didn't have hunting rifles, or did they?

Jordan threw herself down as the tall grass whipped and thrashed around her. Her heart pounding, she squinted up: no numbers painted on the plane.

Bent over, keeping low, she ran for the hammock where she had been headed. Things in her backpack jogged in rhythm with her steps. She darted erratically until she was close enough to the tall trees that the plane dared not dive at her. Still running, she glanced up and back to look at them again.

Just then the earth moved under her feet.

She stumbled and gasped. She hit the ground, face-down, her feet plunging into a limestone solution hole the grass had covered. Feeling herself sliding, she thrust both arms stiffly to her sides to grab something. Her knees, shins, then stomach scraped a hidden ledge, slick with damp grass at the lip. She bit her tongue. Her baseball cap was yanked off, then her sunglasses. Clawing the shrinking surface, she spread her legs and dug her toes into the slick rock. Her boot wedged against something.

She stopped skidding.

She hung suspended, her breasts, shoulders, spread arms, and head above the edge of the hole worn away by water puddling in the porous rock bed. The plane buzzed her but not as low, then circled higher.

She clung, trying to decide whether to risk one big lunge up or try careful, tiny movements. Her chin had raked over the grass, not sawgrass with its razor-sharp edges, but she tasted blood. Her backpack felt like a lead weight. Maybe no one would find her if she slipped clear in. She'd seen these pits with bones of animals from who knew how long ago. All she needed was a cottonmouth or diamondback down this one.

Grunting, sweating, she inched, shoved, and clawed her way up, straining and balancing, the way Dad had taught her in one of his numerous wilderness survival lessons years ago. At last, she rolled onto the bulk of the backpack, panting, staring up at the now empty sky. "Thank God," she whispered. They had just been joy riders, sick bullies wanting to scare her.

She dropped her backpack and moved her limbs. As far as she could tell, she was bloodied only where she'd bitten her tongue and scraped her elbows. She washed her face and sponged her arms with a Handi Wipe. She felt bruised and sore, but darned if she was going to return to her car. She had just set off for her day in the Glades.

She brushed off her jeans and khaki shirt and took a steadying swig of water from her canteen. Rehooking her arms through the straps of her backpack, she retrieved her sunglasses and her dad's old fishing cap. Watching each step, she went on, limping a little, perspiring, though this was the cool, dry season of the year.

Only a few ponds dotted this part of the Everglades today, but in the saunalike summers and autumns they became part of the shallow water her Seminole friend Mae called *Pay-hay-okee*—"river of grass." Her original goal of the small, elevated area of hardwood forest called a hammock lay just ahead. Beyond other, distant hammocks dappling the horizon, two huge ranches shared boundaries with the Big Sawgrass Seminole Indian Reservation and various government land preserves.

As always, she felt a coolness and expectant hush as she entered the vaulted, pillared cathedral of living green. At the fringe of forest, she leaned against a tree until her heart and breathing quieted. The sweet silence of soughing breeze greeted her. Among the leafy trees, the bald cypress stood like bleached skeletons of primeval fossils, cradling their orchid and airplant bounty in bony arms. Automatically searching for them, Jordan looked up. She never took so much as cuttings or seeds of the native bromeliads or rare orchids unless she had written permission: it was just the search and discovery that mattered, for she had a booming business with such plants she cultivated in town.

She soon lost herself in the lush splendor, photographing the pale green umbrella *epidendrum* and purple-spotted dollar orchids dangling from stalks over her head. She walked in deeper, and there, with a big

cowhorn orchid on either side as if to guard it, was
what she always hoped to find, an endangered orchid.

Like a white frog flying in midair, the rare ghost
orchid displayed its fragrant flower from its leafless
stem. She clicked through all her extra film. As her
camera began its buzz through automatic rewind, she
jumped at the sound of a woman's scream.

Who was that? She leaped behind a tree trunk, then
heard yelping dogs, a man's shout, the distant crack of
a gun, the screech again—no, it was not quite human.

Maybe the research tracking team was shooting a
panther with their tranquilizer dart, she thought. But
more likely she had heard an illegal hunter with his
dogs. That plane might have been a spotter for them,
trying to scare her out of the area. Though fines and
jail terms for harming a Florida panther were severe,
no one—private owners, park rangers, or Seminole—
could police all the land.

Though frightened again, she couldn't just ignore
someone in need. And she wasn't going to stand by
while animals that had every right to this land were
harmed. She'd found out the hard way that potential
problems were best handled by confrontation, not
flight. Steeling herself, she cut straight through the
heart of the hammock, then emerged in the grasslands
again. From here the sounds of the hunt were unmistakable, but she felt immensely better when she recognized, parked at the edge of the next hammock, the
balloon-wheeled yellow swamp buggy of the panther
team.

She slowed her pace, careful where she put each
foot. She'd never seen a capture. Lawrence had described it, but never invited her along.

She plunged into the next hammock, following the
jumbled noises, men's shouts, too. She'd just stay

back, she assured herself, and watch from a safe distance.

The two men had to talk loudly to be heard over the noise of the plane's engine.

"I can't believe she went just the opposite way you wanted," the pilot yelled at his passenger.

"She's braver than I thought, but it won't matter in the end."

"At least she got outta that hole."

"That one maybe," the passenger muttered and shoved his side window open wider in the old Cessna to stick his binoculars out into the rush of warm wind. "But I'm going to make her need me."

"Wha'd you say, chief?"

"I said, don't call me that. Head back to the airstrip," he ordered, pointing and gesturing. "We don't want the team on the ground spotting us."

As the plane tilted and banked again, the passenger shook his head in dismay. He'd told his man watching her to page him if she went near her old apartment, but he should have asked to be warned if she was near the scene of the hunt.

"Good thing you had me paint over the numbers on this baby or she could of read them, low as we got," the pilot yelled. "There'd be hell to pay if she could identify us later."

The passenger bumped his binoculars against the window as he pulled them in. "Hell to pay anyway," he said, his voice so low the pilot shook his head and pointed to his ear.

He ignored him and pressed his forehead to the glass, frowning down at the writhing trails all-terrain vehicles and swamp buggies had made like random worm tracks through the sweep of blue-green earth.

He would like to have everyone banned from all this land, so only his people could use it.

As Jordan crept closer to what she knew now was an official capture, examination, tagging, and release of a panther, her pulse pounding in anticipation. Finally, she was getting close to the heart of Lawrence's work.

He was a consulting virologist for the team, and his passion these last years had been a study of the rare panther's apparent immunity to a feline AIDSlike virus, and in turn, a possible cure for human HIV. It was worthy, thrilling, secret work. She admired him for that, even though in the process he had shut her out of his life.

There it was. In the distance, draped loose-limbed on a branch of a gumbo-limbo tree forty feet above her, was the beautiful, furious focus of Lawrence's obsession. It bared razor-sharp teeth, its deep brown eyes narrowed, its tail whipped as it protested human interference in its private affairs.

Jordan carefully stepped closer. She knew that no Florida panthers on record had attacked a human being, but Lawrence had mentioned how one of their mountain lion cousins out West had mauled and killed a female jogger the year before.

She bent low to keep the cat in sight. Even from here she could tell the animal looked sedated; the tranquilizer dart gun had begun to do its work. She saw the cat's head loll. The jaws dripped saliva and merely emanated muted outrage and defiance at being chased and treed by dogs, now gone strangely silent, she realized.

Jordan could not see the men waiting under the tree, but she knew pretty much how this was done, like anyone else who read the local papers or watched

TV. From time to time outraged citizens or animal conversation groups protested the drugging and testing of the big beasts, especially after a pregnant cat had been accidentally killed during her fall from a tree into the net.

Jordan held her breath as the big cat shifted and sprawled onto the branch, putting its head on its paws. Then it toppled toward what must be a waiting net.

She gasped as it cracked limbs and sent leaves drifting. The men gave a muffled cheer. Hoping to see how they handled the cat on the ground, she quietly crept closer, parting thick foliage. Still, she could see no one. The men were no doubt kneeling around the cat to weigh and measure it, draw blood, then affix the radio tracking collar and tattoo its ear for identification. Jordan didn't want to startle them, but—

Her foot bumped something, and she glanced down. A man's body, sprawled, open-eyed. *He looked dead,* she thought. She sucked in a gasp and froze. Two more men lay beyond, stone still, their backs to her.

Her skin crawled. She knew the man at her feet. He was Brent Rymer, the head panther team veterinarian. She'd met his wife and kids, blond twins, pretty little girls. She noticed that no blood stained his clothes or skin, yet his eyes were open, unfocused, staring up unseeing at her. Saliva slid down his cheek. Even uglier, a radio collar was clamped around his neck, and his right ear was marked with a blurred number.

And ... what was it? Some sort of short, painted spear lay broken across his body.

She pressed her hands to her mouth to stifle a scream. If this was the team, who were the men with the panther? Crouching over Brent to feel for a pulse, she heard a car start somewhere nearby. It was too close to be the team vehicle on the far side of the hammock. She half straightened and peered through leaves in the direction of the sounds.

Three black-haired men wearing bright patchwork shirts, bandanas loosely tied around their necks and big-brimmed hats slammed the back doors of a white van. She could not believe what she saw. Those looked like local Indians. Seminoles had done all this?

She realized now they must have taken the cat. That's what they had worked together to put in the back of their van. But how had they come here at the same time as the team?

She took a few steps and squinted, trying to read the license number. The plates, like the van, were mud-spattered. She glanced at her camera, then cursed herself for being out of film. The men got in, and the vehicle pulled away, bumping over rough terrain. Around the tree the cat had climbed she could see three silent, sprawled tracking dogs and another body—a man.

She hurried back to the others; yes, she knew these men, too. She bent to touch the pulse in Brent's neck again. Slow, weak, but he was alive.

She looked around. She had never felt so alone. The thick leaves seemed to crowd in on her. She began to tremble as icy shivers cooled the sweat on her skin. Act now, she told herself. Help these men.

That's when she realized the spear by Brent's body was a traditional Seminole dart gun, painted with their sacred panther. She's seen one something like it years ago, in the possession of the first man she'd ever loved. Seth Cypress, now the leader of the Seminoles.

Chapter Two

On the Big Sawgrass Seminole Indian Reservation, Mae Osceola pulled her van into the small, crowded parking lot near her house and hit the brakes hard. Her own dust cloud caught up with her as she opened the door. She was late, because she'd had big business today, and had been speeding almost all the way back.

The circular compound of clustered wooden buildings made up not only her family home but those of her two married sisters, Ada and Betty. However many were here today, she'd try to keep this discussion quick and calm.

Just last week one of her husband Wilson's old aunts had come to complain that she had caught her granddaughter ordering underwear from a Victoria's Secrets catalog with money Mae had paid the girl for sewing the traditional, floor-length skirts to sell in her shop in downtown Naples. Yet here, waiting for her, were three generations of tribal women willing to sew Seminole designs for cash so their families could hit the Burger Kings, Kmarts, and malls of southwest Florida. Silently, Mae blessed her childhood friend Jordan for lending her the money to make all that possible, even though their husbands had been against it.

"*Che-hun-ta-mo!*" she greeted the women as she

walked toward them in the circle of chickees. They sat or stood in the shade of the large, traditional open-air chickee made of cypress poles supporting the slanted, palmetto-thatched roof over a raised wooden floor. She sank on a blanket among them with paper and pencil poised on her knee. More or less in order of age and clans, the women sat or knelt beside her to sell their finished projects, the older women barefoot, the younger ones in Reeboks or Nikes. Mae spoke to them in English or Mikasuki, depending on the age of the seamstress.

She felt her tension begin to uncoil: the unique beauty of the varied wall hangings, placemats, sundresses, skirts, purses, tote bags, and men's and boys' shirts always awed her. In vibrant, dancing colors the geometric precision of the patterns spoke to her heart as did the glories they represented: lightning, trees, crawdads, clouds, birds, arrows, feathers. To outsiders, these wonders created on Singer sewing machines might look random or repetitive, but, like life, Mae knew it took hard work to grasp the underlying patterns.

"Oh, oh—big thunder on the horizon," she heard Ella Jimmie whisper. Slowly, the buzz of conversations ceased. Mae looked up, expecting to see Wilson glaring at them.

But another truck had jerked to a stop in a cloud of rolling dust on the road that passed the compound. You might know Ella had recognized Seth, Mae mused, even though he got out of their father's Ford pickup instead of his own. As Seth slammed the door and strode closer, another unmarried girl, Mary Tiger, stepped slightly forward to arch her back against a post and prop one foot on it at her knee.

Seth might have been divorced for over a year, Mae

thought, but he now poured his passion only into his new job of caring for the tribe—that and spending time with his nine-year-old son Josh, who lived with his mother at her family's camp on the other side of the reservation. Of course, lately their youngest brother, Frank, had been taking up Seth's time, too, and for all the wrong reasons.

So, Mae thought, Ella had been right about his mood. She could tell by the stretch of his long stride and the set of his broad shoulders that he was angry about something.

He lifted one hand briefly and called a greeting in Mikasuki to the women, addressing only the elders by name. As Mae went to meet him, he took her elbow and steered her toward the truck.

"What's wrong?" she demanded. "Wilson hasn't been thrown from his horse or something, has he?"

"No, but I want you to ask him to cover Josh's baseball team practice tonight for me. I'll be back to coach the game tomorrow. I'm going out to my Glades camp. Frank and some buddies are coming out to bring my truck from the shop, where they're supposedly working on it and take Dad's back. As a matter of fact, as usual, Frank's late with my truck."

Mae only nodded. That was Frank, the black sheep like the whites always said. The boy was eighteen to Seth's thirty and determined he was not going on to any white man's school the way Seth had.

"Sure, I'll have Wilson cover your baseball practice," was all she said.

"*Sho-na-bish,*" he replied as he opened the pickup door and climbed in. How tired he looked, she thought, strained, older than his years. Little crow's feet perched at his eyes because he never wore sunglasses on the reservation; a furrow ridged his high, wide forehead. Right now his dark, deep-set eyes were narrowed, his thin lips taut. A little vein ticked at his bronze temple near the thick black spill of hair he usually kept better trimmed since he moved often in the world of white government to protect Seminole rights and serve as spokesman for tribal tourism. He seemed coiled, like *co-wah-chobee,* the panther of their clan, ready to spring. All he needed was trying to father Frank on top of everything else, when the kid resented it.

"See you!" she called brightly. "Anything I can do, just let me—"

Seth jerked the truck away. Despite the drifting dust, Mae stood staring, shaking her head.

"Brent! Brent, wake up. Can you hear me? It's Jordan Quinn, Brent, Lawrence's wife. I called for help. Hang on. Help is coming."

Although the four drugged men—one of whom she did not know, evidently the dog handler—did not respond, she kept talking to them while time dragged on. Marc Chay, head of the panther team, had picked up her frantic radio call at their headquarters and relayed it through 911 to the police and medical emergency people. But that had been over twenty minutes ago.

Again she hurried among the injured men, sponging their faces with the last of her Handi Wipes and water dribbled from her canteen. It was so eerie how their eyes, with hugely dilated irises, stared without seeing, like zombies from the old horror flicks her sister Lana and brother-in-law Chuck used to scare her with when they baby-sat for her.

"Please be all right," she pleaded. "All of you, wake up."

Touching their carotid arteries on their necks, squeezing their limp hands, she kept her frenzied pilgrimage from man to man. Leaning this close over them, she saw that each had been hit by a small, single dart still embedded in their backs or necks. She fought her instinct to pull out the short things, apparently fletched with some puffy plant seed substance and shot from the blowgun broken over Brent's body.

Drugged, collared, and tagged, just as they had intended for their feline prey. The rational world seemed tilted upside down. She had always felt so at home in the Glades. Now everything had been somehow violated. She felt desperately afraid these men might die, and she could do nothing to save them. She hadn't felt so panicked since everyone had dragged her and Seth apart years ago.

Were the Seminoles so angry at the panther team that they would do this? After all, the team's goal was to save, not destroy the precious beasts. She wished Mae was here to ask, or even Seth himself. But the mere thought of seeing him, facing him again, made her stomach do cartwheels. They had last met that day Seth came in full Seminole costume to the opening of Mae's shop. Despite the years they'd been apart, despite the fact she was married to someone else, the impact of his presence had almost swamped her senses.

Jordan's head jerked up at the sound of a car engine, more than one. Then a siren. She ran from the hammock to motion the men in.

Three police cars, two from Naples, the other a Florida Highway Patrol. Brakes squealed, car doors opened, then slammed.

"This way," she called and started back into the canopy of trees.

"Tape this whole area off for a crime scene and find a safe spot for the MedVac choppers to land," a voice commanded.

She sucked in a deep breath. Help was really here; the burden of these men's lives wasn't on her shoulders anymore.

"Jordan!" the same man behind her called. At first she didn't stop, for Marc had probably given these people her name. But the voice sounded familiar, and she turned back. "When I heard you needed help, I came as fast as I could," the man said, hurrying to catch up to her.

It was Yancy Tatum, someone she'd known since childhood, now a detective on the Naples police force. He was the only officer not in uniform; how could he look so sharply dressed, cool and collected out here? Tall, muscular, and ramrod straight, he came toward her, whipping off his opaque sunglasses. Even in the shadows, his uncovered blond hair, slicked straight back, gleamed pale gold.

Years ago Yancy had been what her grandmother described as "sweet on her." And she wasn't sure he'd really gotten over it. Even after returning from a career overseas in the Marines, he'd never married, and when Jordan had run into him in town, he'd looked her over so intently that she'd made up excuses to be quickly on her way. She had certainly never told him that she and Lawrence were living apart. Now, for the first time in years, she was glad to see him.

She gestured, leading him deeper into the trees, talking back over her shoulder. "Yancy, it's good to have someone I know in charge. They've been shot with some sort of narcotic, maybe the same stuff they used on the cat they caught."

She knelt by Brent's body. Yancy followed, bending

over, his face close to hers. But at first he studied only her, his eyes narrowed as if nothing were amiss. Then he straightened to scan the area as if her words had just sunk in. "A wild panther? Where is it?"

"The same men who did this took it—drugged, just like this. Oh, I hear a helicopter."

Everything began to blur by her as the scene soon swarmed with medics and more police. Voices, questions, the metallic snapping open of medical bags. Somehow reporters and cameramen got in from the other side of the hammock and began shouting questions and taking pictures. With her back to them, Jordan leaned against a tree until the police herded them out. Now that her part was over, her legs began to shake worse than ever. She tried to keep calm as the four drugged men were finally put on stretchers and carried to the two medical choppers for the flight to Naples Hospital.

"These dogs are dead. Darts in them, too," she heard someone call out. "Must have hit them with the same dose as for the men and the big cat. At least it's wearing off the men."

"You're gonna have to wait for your first murder-one case, oh you-who-would-be-chief," someone else said to Yancy.

She saw him glare at the man and motion him away. She was even grateful when Yancy put an arm around her and guided her to his car through the increasing bustle of investigators looking over the site. She leaned her head back against the passenger headrest while he turned on the engine and the air and ran up the windows.

He turned to her, his face intent and earnest. His nostrils flared and he sighed. "I'm thankful I can be here for you, Jordan. Lucky I was on Alligator Alley when the call came in. You were very brave and smart about this. If you need me for fallout or anything else, I'm always a phone call away in Naples."

She nodded. "I've got my car off 830 at the edge of the Milford Ranch. The Milfords are my clients—I put in a tree orchid garden for them." She sat up straight. "Yancy, if I need to make a statement, I can drive to your office for it later. I got to go tell my husband about this. He's a team consultant."

His smooth, tan forehead furrowed in a frown. "Yeah, I know, but I heard somewhere you were— well, separated. Listen," he added quickly, as if he was sorry he'd mentioned that fact, "if you can, I'd like to take a basic statement here, while everything's fresh in your mind." He fished a little black leather notebook out of his shirt pocket and then ran his hand over his hair to make sure it was still brushed straight back from his tanned face.

Even out here, she noted, where the Everglades could strip men down to nothing, Yancy Tatum reeked Marine Corps macho from every pore. She almost expected him to break into the "Halls of Montezuma" as he had once when he was home on leave after a deadly bomb blast at his barracks in Beirut. Gossips on Lokosee said Yancy had a lot of making up for since his daddy, Clem, was still in prison over in Immokalee for getting caught running drugs.

"Now what's this," he asked, "you blurted over the radio about Indians? We've got the dart gun, but exactly what did you see?"

She didn't answer at first, realizing what she had to say could churn up all the Seminole-white animosity she'd hoped was buried forever. Suddenly she remembered that, when they were kids, she used to be kind of afraid of Yancy, partly because he was so devoted.

He'd beaten the crap out of a guy from Chok once who had tried to get fresh with her. And, although she hadn't been there to see it, Lana had told her years after that Yancy had absolutely gone berserk, smashing his fists into a tree trunk, when he heard about her and Seth.

"Jordan, you're not going to hold out on me, are you—because of your bleeding heart for those Seminoles? I know who owns that Patchworks shop next to yours and who her brother is."

She sat up straighter. Would people never let the painful past just be in the past?

"I have no intention of holding out, Yancy. And all that's long past and has nothing to do with anything now. It's just I can't make a positive ID, because I only saw them from behind and that was at a distance."

"How far away?"

"I'd have to go back and show you and have you pace it off. All I know was, I saw three dark-haired men, dressed in traditional Seminole garb and hats like they wear a lot, who evidently put the panther in a white van and took off. Obviously, there was also a driver, but I didn't see him or get the make or license. I heard their voices once, but it was just a little cheer when they caught the falling cat, not words."

"You're doing great," he said, reaching over to give her knee a quick pat. "Just tell me what you remember—time, how you got your arms and chin scraped . . ."

She described everything, from the time she spotted the plane. He said he'd ask to go up in the traffic-control plane soon, just to check around the city airport for a small unmarked one like the one she'd described. He took a lot of notes, occasionally interjecting calm questions or assuring her he would help her any way he could if this got sticky. It was when he nodded at the cluster of cameras focused on them through his side of the car, though from behind the yellow tape, that she realized what he meant by sticky.

"Oh, no. I saw them, but I thought your men cleared them out. How did so many get out here so fast anyway?"

"I know they haven't been your favorite folks since your Seminole problem. But I understand—I really do," he said, when he saw her glare shift from the media to him. He reached over to take her hand. "If you want me to keep them off you, I will, but they'll dog you if you don't give them a short statement. Listen, let's go back to the scene first and you walk me through everything. Just a quick word to the press, then I'll run you to your car and follow you to make sure you get home safe."

Her first instinct was to protest, but he was acting helpful and professional. She would look silly if she refused a simple ride to her car. "I'd appreciate the ride, but I'll be fine after that. You don't have to follow me anywhere."

"Sure, whatever you want," he told her and surprised her by squeezing her hand.

She pulled back gently. It scared her to realize what she had to do when she got out of here—even before going to tell Lawrence what had happened to his friends today—but it absolutely had to be done. For the first time in eleven years, she was going to call Seth Cypress. She had to warn him about what had happened before this mess got splattered all over the TV and newspapers.

Yancy's commanding voice interrupted her agonizing. "Listen, you steer completely clear of the Seminoles, at least for a while, hear me? Hey, you're not gonna faint, are you, Jordan?" he asked, leaning so close at her shocked expression she could smell garlic on his breath.

"No," she said, shifting away, surprised he seemed to have read her mind. "I've been through worse and might again, but I'll handle it."

"Damn good credo." He gave her a bright smile as if to buck her up, but she knew he'd have a fit if he realized what she was planning. "You just remember," he said, squeezing her shoulder, "if you need anything, call me, 'cause my motto's *Semper Fi.*"

Seth had been at his rural campsite for over an hour when Frank, driving Seth's truck, finally came barreling in much too fast. Frank braked so sharply the truck fishtailed.

"Trying to make up for lost time?" Seth asked. He nodded to Danny Jumper, a cousin, sitting in the passenger seat as if he were riding shotgun. Which in a way he was, because Seth saw he had a rifle propped between his legs. Both boys wore black T-shirts they sometimes used under the Seminole patchwork ones, and they had red bandanas knotted around their necks. Both looked sweaty, as if they had run rather than driven out here.

"You two been off hunting?" Seth asked, propping his hands on the window frame of the passenger side. He frowned when neither boy answered him. Danny finally shrugged.

"Told you, Danny," Frank said after he killed the engine, "he don't do much but order me around and ask white lawyer questions." He opened his door, got out and sauntered forward, stopping across the hood from Seth. He tossed Seth's keys to him in a high arc.

Danny got out more slowly, giving Seth and Frank a wide berth as Seth strolled around to face Frank.

Seth gritted his teeth when he saw Frank's sullen glare. "The look on your face," Seth said, "I guess I should be happy you showed up at all. I don't mean for us to start arguing again."

" 'Course I showed up. The *micco* commands, the warriors obey, right, Danny?" Frank called over his shoulder to the other boy. "It's just, see," he added, turning back and lowering his voice, "somebody but you might have official tribal business, too, you know."

"You? Such as? If you're not willing to work at herding with Wilson, I hope your official business was looking for a job off the res."

"Money—that all you care about? How about the honor of this tribe? You think you're being so smart doing things the white man's way in a white man's business suit, but some of us are real sick of getting shoved around, know what I mean?"

The smart, sarcastic mouth was something Seth was used to. The kid had turned really bitter two years ago after he'd been jumped and beaten up by some white kids when he'd gone in full Seminole garb to give a dance at a Civil War reenactment in Fort Myers. Before Seth could control himself he reached out to grab Frank's upper arms. He was tempted to shake some damned sense into him, but he loosed him, shoving him back against the truck.

"I've got a good notion to just let you and the buddies you run with make a mess of your lives. Maybe you'll need a lawyer when you get locked up for something."

"Sure, thanks, I'll know who to call," Frank said, flexing his arms as if to shake off Seth's touch. "Every-

one makes kid mistakes at my age, right, like you did
with that white woman?"

That was like a fist to the belly. Any mention of
the biggest mistake of Seth's life still stunned him. But
sometimes he thought that the hard lesson he'd
learned with Jordan was what made the elders really
trust him. Last year he'd been the youngest man ever
elected tribal chairman of the Sawgrass Seminoles. He
was certain it had been because he'd survived the Jordan catastrophe and come out fighting, not because
he'd earned a law degree.

"Look, Frank, yeah, I know what you mean. I care
big time about our lands and ways being violated, like
you said. Matter of fact, it's obvious from the plane
ride I took today that cowboys on one of the local
ranches been breaking down our fences again. They're
using our grass and water, and this is the dry season.
So I'm gonna have to decide whether to sue, just protest, or what."

That got Frank's attention. The Seminole herds
were important to the tribe's purse and their pride.
Their brother-in-law, Mae's husband, Wilson Osceola,
was herd foreman.

"So we just rebuild the fences again?" Frank demanded, crossing his arms over his muscular chest,
though the sullen look on his face did not soften. "I'm
sick of that kind of stuff. We should do what our
ancestors did—hit 'em with a raid. That'll teach
them."

"Frank, we don't go on any damn raids anymore.
You want to do something to help the tribe right now,
take some bales of barbed wire out to Wilson."

The sun was in Seth's eyes, but he caught the sneer
on the boy's round, handsome face turn to a smug
smile. Frank's dark brown eyes glinted as he glanced

over Seth's shoulder. Seth spun to look at Danny, who hastily wiped a smile from his face. Seth slumped inwardly: there were factions in the tribe who didn't support him, but why did it have to be his own kin?

"Get on out of here, both of you," he ordered. "I got my own thinking to do about tribal concerns bigger than you and your little band of braves goofing off."

Frank looked like he wanted to say something else, but he took the set of keys Seth dug from his jeans pocket and sauntered to their dad's truck. The two boys climbed in. The wheels spit broken shells as they took off.

Chapter Three

Jordan slammed down the receiver of the pay phone at the toll booth on Alligator Alley. Seth's secretary had said he was not in his office and was not able to return calls until the next day, but if he came in for his messages she could pass one on. Jordan didn't leave her name because tomorrow could be much, much too late.

She got back in her car. If he might come in for his messages, it meant he was somewhere on the reservation. She didn't want to drive out there but she owed it to Mae and her tribe, she told herself. But her stomach knotted even tighter as she took the turn toward the Big Sawgrass Seminole Reservation instead of heading back toward town. She never came out here unless invited, and then only to see Mae and her family or on crowded powwow days.

Again she checked in her rearview mirror to be sure no police cars were following her. A white car had turned off on this road, and she kept an eye on it. Unfortunately, she had lied to Yancy to say she was heading straight home, but at that point she had just planned a phone call to Seth.

The white car was still behind her. But just past the Big Sawgrass Grocery, when she turned through the gates toward the village of wooden and cement block tribal buildings, she saw the car hesitate at the gates as if it were lost. She breathed easier when it did not turn in. Probably curious tourists.

She concentrated on what was ahead and not behind her. The old bingo hall looked like a humped airplane hangar with its temporarily empty runways of parking lots of charter buses and tourist cars. These days most of the big action was off the reservation in the new gambling palace that funneled money, if not power, to the tribe.

She ignored the arrows pointing visitors toward the tribal headquarters building set in the cluster with the rec hall, school, and old BIA building. Just beyond where the basketball court and baseball diamond met the grassy powwow grounds, she headed for Mae's compound on the looping road. The alligator wrestling pit blurred by; the health center; the Big Cypress Baptist Church, which Seth and Mae belonged to, but their parents had never joined; the new cemetery, forced on people who were no longer permitted to leave bodies of their departed on scaffolds at distant points in the Glades as their ancestors had done.

She passed mobile homes, chickees, every conglomeration of houses the Seminoles used, strung out along and off the road in clusters they called camps. They might be a tribe, but at heart the Seminoles were fiercely independent and kept their distance.

Luckily, she saw Mae in the yard, talking intently to a man—her husband, Wilson, not Seth. Wilson was always quietly polite, but Jordan knew he didn't approve of Mae's friendship with her. The Seminoles were a tribe in which the women had a lot of power, but Wilson didn't want Mae cosigning papers with banks and working in town at her own shop. He would have preferred, Jordan thought, to have Mae pregnant again, hawking patchwork potholders from a pickup on some back road. If he knew Mae was secretly on the pill, he'd probably sleep only with his horse.

She rolled down her window and waved. Wilson nodded and stood his ground while Mae hurried over. "What're you doing out here?" she asked, her sleek ebony eyebrows arched with curiosity. Mae had a broad face and wide forehead, but most models would kill for her straight nose, full mouth, and slanted cheekbones. Her slightly upturned gold-brown eyes could sparkle with approval or nail you to the wall.

"On your way back from finding flowers? Want to come in for supper?"

"I'll explain everything later, but I have to talk to Seth. His secretary said he's not in his office, and she doesn't know when he'll be back. Please," she said, gripping her friend's wrist when she put her hands on the car and just stared openmouthed in at her. "It's very important, or I wouldn't ask—after everything that's happened."

"He's out the dirt road, then to the right the first shell road. At his little camp by the canal. But I wouldn't disturb him. He wants to be left—"

"Thanks, Mae. I have to," she said and drove on.

She'd just explain to Seth what had happened, she assured herself, then go tell Lawrence in case Marc Chay hadn't called him already. Actually, Lawrence might be just as surprised to see her as Seth, because since she'd moved out nearly a year ago, she seldom went back to the condo except to see the cat.

She gritted her teeth as she drove the rough, pot-holed road, remembering how her family had had a fit that she was the one who had moved out. She'd never told them it was part of her and Lawrence's yearlong, unwritten agreement. To build their separate futures, he had showed her in black and white—his elaborate computer printouts of their financial statements—what they must do.

She had to expand her jointly owned business, and he needed to pursue the big breakthrough that would allow him to get more grants from pharmaceutical firms, universities, and private investors. He was thrilled to be getting ever closer to findings how the panthers fought off feline AIDS, which might lead to something even bigger. So how could she cause him problems during that tense time? One year, he had asked, just one year more and they could both go their separate ways.

Besides, he'd reminded her, she had gone deeper into debt to underwrite Mae Osceola, when the tribe had denied her friend a low-interest loan for a shop in Naples. If she and Lawrence split their assets early, he had told her, it would mean withdrawing all support for Mae, and Jordan could not let Mae down. She understood Mae's dream and her lack of cash.

Jordan had never exactly been poor, but she had felt poor. Before she was born twenty-eight years ago, her father had done seasonal fishing supplemented by clam rustling and gator skin poaching. When she was just a baby, he inherited the sports-fishing fleet of four boats from a friend in Key West. But she'd heard the tales and seen the small, now derelict house on Lokosee Island where her parents had raised Lana, who was sixteen years older than Jordan. They had built a bigger, better house on Lokosee, but even with a steady income the family had continued to live frugally.

Until she'd gone away to college, partly on a scholarship, Jordan had never had what Lokosee kids called store-bought clothes, though she'd had one yearly back-to-school outfit proudly picked from the Sears catalog. Instead, along with Lana's three kids, Jordan had clothes Lana had sewn for her, cleverly designed and beautifully made, but she felt like a doll Lana was dressing.

She'd felt the same about Lawrence in the early years after they married—that he was trying to make her what *he* wanted. She had resisted to become a small businesswoman and her own person, but would she ever be free of him, any more than she was ever really free of Seth? Her heart began to pound, and she gripped the steering wheel harder and turned onto the shell road. She hoped Seth had someone out at his camp with him, so she wouldn't have to face him alone. Now she wished she'd asked Mae to ride along.

About two miles out, she saw a pickup truck speeding at her with two guys in it. Both of them—young men—craned their necks and gawked, but when she realized neither was Seth, she just moved over to get past them and drove on.

Finally, quite a ways off the road, shaded by a cluster of coco plums and sweet bay, she spotted a small, traditional chickee. Beyond it, sun glinted off one of the straight-as-a-die canals the Army Corps of Engineers had dug years ago when the government thought it could control the Everglades.

She looked around but saw no one, though a truck was parked there. She unhooked her seat belt and stood up in the open door of her car, propping her elbows on the sun-warmed roof to survey the flat area. Unless Seth was sleeping under that tent of mosquito netting on the chickee's raised wooden platform, he was not nearby.

Yet she felt she was being watched. She jerked her head around to glance down the road. No one in sight.

"Anybody here? Seth? Seth!"

His name felt forbidden on her lips. It was so long since they had met at their hiding place in the Glades near her father's hunting lodge. Seth would run to her from the little chickee they had made with tree limbs and thatch, his arms outstretched, his bronze face lit with the whitest smile.

"Hello? Seth!"

She slammed the car door loudly, hoping the sound would carry. He'd always had good ears, though he had not heard his father's approach that time he tracked and found them twined in each other's arms on their little mattress of soft kapok down.

Kapok down. That was it, she thought—that white fluff those narcotic darts from that Seminole blowgun had been fletched with today.

Her heart beat harder as another memory struck her. Seth had been so proud that time his father—a tribal medicine man, an *ayikcomi*, they called him—had given him an heirloom dart gun. Had it been exactly like that one broken over Brent's body, painted with the panthers of their clan?

Jordan stopped walking and gripped the strap of her shoulder purse with both hands. Maybe she should not be here. She'd better just leave a note and head home.

She glanced into the chickee. Not one modern thing in it, no furniture, phone, calendar, photos, TV, stereo, or appliances like at Mae's, though she knew Seth had another house on the reservation. A few items— bread, bananas, a six pack of 7UP, and a jar of peanut butter—dangled in netting from the cypress rafters, out of reach of raccoons. Her nostrils flared at the scent of fragrant, almost invisible smoke drifting from a pile of smoldering leaves in a small clearing just beyond. Someone, she realized, had just been here.

She turned quickly away. She'd get some paper from her briefcase in the car and put it in writing to him. She really didn't want to face him even after all this time. But, looking up, she stopped short and gasped.

Seth sat on the trunk of her car, elbows on spread knees, chin on his hands, just watching her, as if he was deciding what to do. His bare feet rested on the bumper. His eyes burned hotter than the sun.

"Oh. You startled me."

She walked slowly closer, expecting him to say the same, give some greeting. But he kept silent, and that unnerved her even more. "I didn't see you," she added.

"I know."

His voice seemed deeper and rougher than she remembered; he looked bigger, too. Gleaming water beaded on his sleek, bare upper torso; it spiked his thick ebony hair to his forehead and lean cheeks. Damp, dark jeans molded to his long legs and thick thighs. Had he been swimming in that canal, or had he been sitting in the smoke? He emanated the tart scent of it. Burning bay leaves—that was it. The Seminoles believed bay was strong medicine, but she could not recall for what.

"I saw Mae a little while ago," he said, "so you're not here about her. What do you need me for? You look—bad."

"Thanks a lot," she said, trying to keep her voice light. But his comment stung, and that annoyed and scared her. She tried to tell herself it didn't matter what he thought—not after all these years. Yet she glanced down at her torn, dirtied clothes and brushed at smudges on her shirtfront before she felt him staring again and stopped. Her palms and breasts tingled. She lowered her hands to her shoulder bag and held it tightly again.

Clearing her throat, nervous about how he'd take all this, she took the plunge. "Seth, I'm here to warn you about something. I guess this is your private retreat, so I'm sorry to just burst in like this. But the police are looking for four men from the tribe, and I thought you should—"

"What men? Why?" He slid off the trunk and came toward her. Though he had been lean and lanky as a young man, his chest and arms were broad and solid now. He looked angular, austere, almost menacing. From his left shoulder to his left nipple, he still bore a thin white scar from an old barbed-wire fence cut she had bandaged for him long ago. For one crazy moment, she wanted to reach out and touch him, but she took a step back.

"I don't know the men's names," she said, "and didn't see their faces to be able to identify them, but I wanted to tell you what happened."

The air between them seemed to seethe with drifting smoke. It stung her nostrils even as she explained what had occurred in the Everglades hammock.

He frowned out at the far horizon, then at her, his gaze narrowed accusingly under the slash of thick eyebrows. "And you had to identify them as Big Sawgrass Seminoles, of course, even though you weren't close, can't even say if they were old or young. Didn't see their faces—"

"Seth, I said I recognized their looks and shirt designs," she protested, narrowing her eyes to glare at him. His sarcastic tone really hurt, but what had she expected?

"Great. Just great." He smacked a hand on his thigh, then ticked things off on his long fingers. "I'm sure that will be enough for a police lineup, indictment, and conviction of someone from the tribe. But Seminole men would not be doing such a thing and for sure not in ceremonial costume."

His face looked carved from stone, but his voice quavered. Suddenly, she wondered if he was only reacting to what she said or to her, after all this time. It shook her deeply that she was finding the logic of her message entwined with her painfully buried emotions for him. She had to control these feelings with reason.

"What if they wanted to make a point," she demanded, "a public protest about whites tampering with the panthers? Seminoles have had their protests before, as you well know."

"Some protest," he insisted, his voice mocking, both fists stiff down at his hips as if he were trying to control himself, too. "That's making a real public statement, out there where they evidently drugged those men before they knew what or who hit them, and then they took off before anyone could get any publicity."

"How do you know all that?" she asked, fighting to keep her voice from rising. "Maybe when the men come to, they can identify those Seminoles."

"But can you?" He pointed at her, but with a fist, not a finger. Still, she held her ground, though she suddenly added physical fear to her jumbled emotions. She recalled all too well the strength in those arms and how his temper could surge from one passion to another.

"You said you didn't hear them speak Mikasuki," he argued.

"Or English either. Forget I even tried to help, just

forget it. I'm sure you'll hear it somewhere else from someone official you'll have to believe." She turned and walked away, but he followed, keeping up with her effortlessly.

"You said the van was white. What make or year?"

"I don't know. It was splattered with mud."

"And the license plate? Was it one of our special Seminole Indian ones?" he questioned, pointing over at the truck parked nearby.

At least, she thought, it wasn't a white van. The man was so defensive she almost wondered if he knew something about this whole mess. Or was it the fact that she was the messenger that had set him off? She used to be so attuned to his moods, but now she had no idea how to read him. "If you want to know, the license plate was mud covered, too."

"When it hasn't rained for days?" he goaded. "With dry dust only on the roads?" For emphasis, he scuffed the dirt on the edge of the shell road near her car.

"Then what about the blowgun with the panthers on it?" she demanded, her voice rising. "For sure that's Seminole."

For a moment he looked as if she'd hit him. He blinked; his voice faltered at first. "A few are in museums or private collections," he said, his tone suddenly subdued. "Bottom line, there is absolutely no motive. We've given permission for the panther work and even let them come on our land."

Again, he pointed his finger for emphasis the way she'd seen him do in TV interviews. He'd probably learned that in law school, because Seminoles hardly ever gestured. In so many ways, he had changed and yet the mere impact of his presence still stunned her.

"Look, Seth, I came out here to do a good deed

for—for Mae's people, and I don't appreciate this grilling as if I'm a hostile witness."

"But you are, aren't you? At least to me. Still hostile?"

"Yeah, I guess I am. And really sorry I came."

He put one arm on the roof of her car to partly block her in against it. "I appreciate your warning, honestly. It's just I'm very personally protective of— the whole tribe."

Even through her sunglasses, his intense gaze held hers: she glimpsed again the very soul of the man she had once known and loved before everything went so bad. They breathed in unison, not moving, but she felt his closeness as if no time had passed at all. His power—and the sense she yet possessed power over him—even to annoy and argue—terrified as well as thrilled her.

"I've got to go now." When he didn't budge, she ducked smoothly under his arm and opened the car door. She tossed her purse in, got in, then fumbled in the stupid thing for her keys while he closed the door and stood back, with his arms crossed over his chest.

She found the keys, dropped them, leaned over to retrieve them, then jingled them like bells trying to grasp the right one and get it in the ignition.

Then before she could stop herself, she mouthed the words, "See you."

He didn't answer, hopefully had not heard or thought she meant anything by it, because she was nothing but relieved to leave him—and their bitter past—in the dust of her rearview mirror.

Jordan saw she was doing over forty-five as she turned onto Pine Ridge Road. How had she gotten this far into town and didn't remember one darned thing about the drive? She slowed in the rush-hour traffic made worse by the snowbirds and tourists heading out for twilight dinner specials. Mingled relief and regret flooded her after that volatile interview with Seth—some reunion after all these years. She had not been prepared for the torrent of conflicting emotions unleashed between them. She wondered if they'd gotten all of that damned-up passion out of their systems now, but she'd have to see him again to know. At least, she'd cleared her conscience about warning the Seminoles. Now she was anxious to talk to Lawrence about the attack on his friends today.

She turned onto the street that circled the Venetian Bay Village Club a block from the Gulf of Mexico, one of the more upscale areas in the new Naples sprawl. She gazed across the exotically landscaped, manicured lawns at the six-story, cream-colored stucco condo with the wraparound, screened lanais. No one used the porch furniture on theirs anymore since she'd moved out. Even on cool days like this, Lawrence kept the AC on and ignored the gentle breeze; he didn't want dust clogging his computer, he always said.

She pulled her car under the carport next to his. Maybe Lawrence knew more about the injured men than she did now, for surely Marc had called him. As soon as she told him her side of the story, she'd head over to the hospital, maybe sit with some of the wives or offer to take care of Mrs. Rymer's twin daughters while she stayed with her recovering husband.

"This is *your* idea of lux living, Lawrence, not mine," she muttered, gazing up at their windows as she walked toward the building. He liked the posh, densely populated location, the heated pool and Jacuzzi, the view of yachts coming and going on the web of waterways below, and looking down on others— not that he took the time to enjoy all that anymore.

"How ya doing, Ms. Quinn?" the condo association's young, crew-cut gardener, Max, called to her from down the hall as she punched the elevator button. "How's the business? Got any more extra tree orchids? I'll put them up in the palms out by the pool."

"Sure. And maybe a Vanda for that fiancée of yours?"

"Better skip that," he called to her with a grin and dismissive wave. "I come up with an expensive flower like that she'll think there's something I'm not telling her and give me the third degree." He laughed as the elevator doors closed.

The elevator glided up to the fourth floor. Deeply exhausted, she leaned against the wall and fanned the smell of stale cigarette smoke. She felt weird ringing the doorbell, since she still had her key. When he didn't come, she used it and went in. Maybe Marc had picked him up after all. Lawrence had forgone jogging months ago so that wasn't where he was. And he would have gone hungry if she didn't keep the place stocked with frozen food, so he hadn't gone out for an early dinner. Lately, she would have let him starve if it hadn't been that she admired him and hoped— not just for financial reasons—he would somehow succeed in his medical quest.

And, she had to admit, she kept the kitchen stocked with food so their pet cat didn't starve. The gray-and-white male longhair had started out as Lawrence's cat Mike, but she and Mike had bonded several years ago when Lawrence got so busy he worked evenings and half the night, too. She'd secretly renamed the cat Micco, or "big chief" in Seminole. At least the cat didn't just ignore her, then on rare occasions turn on his bright beams to bathe her in the limelight for a few moments of his time, as his master had. She had wanted to take the poor thing with her when she left, but it was Lawrence's cat, after all, and he'd drawn the line at that.

"Lawrence?" she called, still standing in the tiled foyer. "Have you heard about what happened to the panther team? Did Marc call?"

The silence struck her as strange. Micco always came running to rub her ankles; the soft whir of the computer fan was a muted constant, but not now. She heard no sound of a shower running—no sound at all but the hum of the AC that made it much too cold in here. She walked over to turn the thermostat way down. Goose bumps peppered her skin.

"Micco? Here, kitty, kitty!"

Lawrence must have absentmindedly shut him in somewhere when he stepped out. She opened the foyer closet door and peered into the darkness. She glanced in the kitchen, opened the pantry door, then hurried down the hall to the two bedrooms, one of which Lawrence had taken over for his work. She stood in the door of his office and gasped.

Even in the dimness of Lawrence's office, Jordan saw nothing was left other than the furniture. No computer, no files, backup tapes, or books. No microscope or centrifuge or metal boxes of specimen slides. The drawers of his empty filing cabinets were ajar or open. The shelves lay bare of all but dust, the phone and fax. Only his printer was on his denuded desk, swept clean of its usual stacks of printouts, reports, and faxes.

The place looked like it had been thoroughly ransacked.

Chapter Four

Afraid for her husband, Jordan raced through the condo, turning on lights, looking on the other side of the bed, behind the large chairs. Nothing in the living room was disturbed, but his things in the bedroom were also in some disarray. Lawrence was gone.

She returned to his office. Trembling, she reached up to slant the vertical blinds to let in fading daylight. She stared at the desk and the shelves, her mind grabbing and discarding possibilities. Then she saw a single piece of paper lying in the tray of the abandoned printer. She pulled it out and stared down at its one line of print:

JORDAN, I'M LEAVING FOR GOOD. LOVE, LAWRENCE

She read it again. She wanted to scream, cry, and laugh, but she only stared at the words. I'm leaving for *good—love,* Lawrence? But they had decided on their split so long ago, and Lawrence had been adamant about keeping this condo.

Once again panic energized her. She rushed across the room to slide the closet open and looked behind the hanging garments. He'd taken a suitcase, her old one, not his new one. Had he been in such a hurry he didn't notice, or had he just wanted hers because it was slightly bigger? She ran to their—lately, his—bedroom; it had a few drawers pulled out, several polo shirts dropped. He had certainly been in a hurry.

But why? The long, lighted walk-in closet seemed to have holes in it: clumps of his clothes had been carted off, hangers and all. But some were still here, including his two best suits. Was he planning to come back for them?

Suddenly she thought of the gun. Marc had helped him pick it out. It would be under Lawrence's side of the bed if he hadn't taken it. She kneeled down and felt for it. Yes, it was there, small, metallic, and cold.

"Micco. Micco!"

But she knew now he'd taken the cat. Still, she looked in Micco's favorite hiding places. His too-dirty litter box was still on a plastic sheet in the office bedroom closet. She hurried into the kitchen; his food and water dish were there, so Lawrence hadn't thought to take those—or any cat food at all, she noted, banging open and closed the cupboard doors to check on what she'd bought last time. She saw that big burlap sack of dried letaria leaves was still under the sink, making the enclosed area smell faintly musty and minty. It was a Glades plant related to catnip that Lawrence had brought home for Micco awhile ago. She sneezed again and again and hugged herself hard.

"I can't believe it," she whispered. Lawrence was absentminded, yes, but—well, maybe he had just scooped up Micco on his way out as an afterthought. And where had he come up with the many boxes it must have taken to move his things? When was he coming back for the rest?

But his car was still downstairs. He must have rented a truck or had someone pick him up. She could call the rental dealers. Max or the neighbors could have seen him loading it, talked to him. Why had the note sounded so final when he was obviously coming back for his car and other things? She decided she would run downstairs and put her Club steering wheel-locking device on his car. He didn't have a key to hers, so when he came back for another load he'd have to call and at least talk to her.

And she had thought this dreadful day could not get any worse.

Yet as she stood there, fighting for control, she felt a funny lightening of heart to know it was really over and she could move ahead to finalize things. Yes, maybe Lawrence was leaving her for good. But something seemed so wrong about his method and timing.

"He's got to contact me, tell where he's gone," she assured herself, leaning against the kitchen counter. She shuddered once, then began to shake harder. Nerves, nerves from everything. But she had to act, not just feel. She was going down right now to put that Club on his car and talk to Max before he left for the day.

The doorbell rang. "Thank you, God," she cried and ran to answer it. She pictured him standing there with more boxes to fill in his arms; he'd seen her car and figured she could get the door for him. "At least now we can talk things out. Lawr—" she began as she yanked open the door.

Marcus Chay stood there, his handsome, oval face smiling at her. Of compact build, he was exactly her height. He wore one of his expensive Hong Kong-tailored suits, but his silk tie was loosened and his sleek black hair looked mussed across his high forehead. His almond-shaped eyes always tilted up when he smiled, but his face became serious as he took in her expression and appearance.

"Is Lawrence staying with you for a while?" she blurted. "Did he send you for more things, or to tell me where he is?"

He shook his head once in surprise. "Lawrence? Isn't he here? I just came from the hospital, thinking you two might want an update on the men who were hurt."

"Oh. Marc, it's a bad time for me . . ."

"May I come in? You look like you need a friend." She shook her head hard but swayed on her feet. He moved swiftly, cupping his hands under her elbows, turning her, putting an arm around her shoulders. He walked her inside and closed the door behind them.

"Jordan, what is it? May I help? Were things just too much today out there at the site of the attack? You are my people's—the team's—heroine now, you know."

His words flew so fast past her, she couldn't grasp them. "We were just about to end things officially," she tried to explain as he walked them to the sofa and sat beside her, solicitous, leaning slightly toward her. "But I have no idea where he's gone," she went on. "Lawrence—he's cleared out. He took his work but left me—I mean, after I left him first."

For the first time he looked alarmed. He bounced off the sofa and took several steps around the room to survey it. "Gone? You mean, really *gone*? With his work? That can't be."

He always spoke at a quick pace, but he sounded as frenzied as she felt. Then he seemed to grab hold of himself. He sat back down on the edge of the sofa, looking dazed.

"Lately," he said, speaking more slowly, his gaze not on her but still darting around the room as if searching for something, "Lawrence has been getting close to some kind of breakthrough, and he has been distracted. Maybe he just worked himself too hard— had some sort of temporary breakdown, but I don't think so. Or he actually made the breakthrough and double cr—that is, took off to meet with a sponsor or secret colleague. Jordan," he said, appealing to her again, "if he's left anything behind at all, let me have it to take in to work. We can go through his things there to give us a clue. You know, to where he's gone. Jordan?"

She swiped away sudden tears. He pressed a monogrammed, white handkerchief in her hand. She used it, heaving in huge breaths to keep from plunging into hysteria.

"Jordan, believe me," he vowed, "I will do whatever I can to help you. I can take a careful inventory, go through his belongings for you, if you like."

"I guess. But not right now," she faltered, but her mind was racing. "I don't mean," she said, quickly changing the subject, "to be so selfish. How are the injured team members doing at the hospital?"

He looked annoyed for a moment, maybe resentful of her not taking him up on his offer to help. He stood to stride across the room as if to survey the bookshelves before he looked at her again. "Our people," he explained, "came out of their drugged states slowly, just as the panthers do. So they are staying in for observation tonight. The doctors believe they will mend completely, except it will take laser surgery to remove those tattoos on their ears."

It annoyed her he was still obviously looking for something. "At least they didn't get an overdose, like those poor dogs. I guess a man would weigh about as much as a panther, so the dose would be the same."

"Exactly. The darts were coated with the same substance our tracking team uses, a heavy tranquilizing but not immobilizing drug, a mix of ketamine and acepromazene."

She nodded as if the terms meant anything to her. "That drug is hardly what the Seminoles used to use with dart guns," she told him. "I saw it with my own eyes, but I can't believe they did it."

"Maybe these are very modern Seminoles. I am going to check if we have had a theft of those drugs at the lab." As he spoke he walked out into the dining room, then through the kitchen; she could tell by his voice. She got up to keep an eye on him.

"Our people," he went on, "were taken by surprise. They can give only vague descriptions of their attackers, so your identifying those Indians is doubly valuable."

When she walked out to meet him, he was peering down the hall. "I just cannot believe he is gone and all his work, too, that's all," he explained, looking a bit sheepish at last. "What do you know about him keeping copies of his work?"

"But—wouldn't he have copies at the lab?"

"He was so careful—paranoid about not losing anything—about people maybe breaking in there. So, as far as I know," he went on sounding suddenly very annoyed, "everything was here."

"I can't believe that. I didn't know."

"But you may know more than you think, and I'll help you." She could tell he wanted to click on a light in Lawrence's office, but he took her elbow and guided her back down the hall to the living room. "For one thing, I can try to trace his steps through his contacts in cyberspace. Perhaps one of the pharmaceutical firms he had contacted offered him their lab facilities, a place to stay to finish up. If I may be of any help, I—"

"I do need to talk to the gardener and some of the neighbors who might have seen him loading his things. If you could just stay here a moment to answer the phone in case he calls—"

"Of course. I'd be happy to."

"And I'm telling you, Marc, he has cleared things out of here. I'll be right back."

"Then I will fix something to eat so you can keep up your strength," he insisted, walking her to the door.

"Oh, I couldn't eat," she called back over her shoulder as she hurried out into the hall.

"You must. I will take care of everything."

This, she thought, as she took the steps instead of the elevator, was not the Marc she and Lawrence had first known when he had moved to Naples. He had always been polite, even somewhat shy and ingratiating, but now he seemed—grasping.

Two years ago, twenty-six-year-old Marcus Chay had arrived to work on the panther team, fresh from the University of Michigan with twin doctorates in computer science and feline physiology. Lawrence had found Marc's dissertation on infected cellular DNA in domestic cats endlessly fascinating, while Jordan had studied the man himself, the first Asian American she had ever known personally. He had seemed such an introvert, painfully grateful for their friendship and hospitality.

Independently wealthy from inheriting his parents' restaurant in Detroit, Marc had bought a condo on the beach and showered her and Lawrence with gifts in return for their hospitality: elegant Cantonese home-cooked meals, porcelain vases to set off her rarest orchids, enough silk to have matching robes made, and tickets to Tampa Bay and Miami pro football games. Those games were some of her last happy memories with Lawrence, even though Marc was always along.

Lately, perhaps because of his six-month stay out West working with the Idaho Cooperative Wildlife Research Unit studying mountain lions, leadership of the panther team had been rotated to Marc, and that, she realized now, must have given him more confidence and control of the panther work here. Or, quite simply, she realized now, there was entirely more at stake in what Lawrence had been working on then she had realized, work Marc was responsible for—or thought he owned—in some way.

She sucked in a breath of air; the condo, even with Marc there, made her feel constricted, claustrophobic. Downstairs, she roamed the grounds looking for Max. She finally spotted him out by the pool house, putting his hedge cutters away. She motioned him over to avoid having to face people she knew sitting poolside with evening cocktails. John and Mary Hawkins looked happy, so normal, discussing their day calmly, probably sharing plans for the evening to come.

"Max, you didn't see my husband moving some things out today, did you?" she asked the moment he came in earshot.

Still coiling the long orange extension cord, he came over in big strides, his usually tanned face serious now. "No, but I saw the van. I know it was his stuff being loaded in the back because the wind caught some of it. Who else would have labeled diagrams of wildcats and photos of them eating leaves? I chased the papers—one was columns of letters and numbers, too—and gave them back."

"Back to Lawrence?"

"No, like I said, I didn't see Mr. Quinn." He heaved the electrical cord over one muscular shoulder and propped the other dirty fist on his frayed, cutoff jeans. He took off his aviator-type sunglasses and stuck one earpiece in his mouth, as if that were his deep-thinking pose.

"The one I saw," he recalled, squinting and cocking his head at the memory, "was some guy who must of been helping him. Kind of Hispanic-looking, I don't know. It was when I was going to start cutting the grass around by the waterway. Then I found a fire anthill I had to pour poison pellets on, so I didn't really stand around watching. Then, after the van was gone, a lot later, I did see the garage guys bring his car back from getting a tune-up or something, but they just left it and didn't go up to see him or anything. Say, is there anything I can do?" he asked, searching her face again. "You look really funny—kind of strange, I mean."

She said she was fine and made a mental note to check whether someone from the garage really had his car out for a checkup or not. She questioned him about the van—a dark blue Dodge Ram, he said; the license plate—Florida, one commemorating the NASA Challenger disaster, but he couldn't recall the number.

She deflected his questions, thanked him. She forced herself to wave to the Hawkinses, who were motioning her over to have a drink with them. She walked into the carport to move her safety lock Club to Lawrence's car, then recalled she had neither set of keys. She smacked her palm on her forehead and started back to the elevator.

Everything spun through her head as if she'd jarred something loose: seven years and no farewell, just ex-

ploded remembrances to commemorate the Lawrence
and Jordan Quinn disaster, like that spacecraft, blowing up sky high.

Upstairs, she walked in to smell something cooking,
but Marc was not in the kitchen where rice steamed
on the stove and the microwave made its cooked timing buzz. Feeling shaky and sick, she went down the
hall to the office, then to the master bedroom. She
found Marc with his back to her, kneeling, going
through things on the floor of the closet.

"Marc, what are you doing?"

He jerked up and bumped his head on a garment
bag making everything in the closet sway. "Oh, Jordan, just thought I'd be sure there was no clue here
to help you find him. If I'm going to have to go on
without him, I need all the help I can get."

"Yes, but . . ."

"I was watching from the window to be sure you
were all right," he said, getting hastily to his feet, "but
I got some stir-fried rice and frozen vegetables together. What did that boy have to say?"

She opened her mouth to ask him if Lawrence
might have known anyone from work who looked Hispanic and had a blue van with a Challenger license
plate. But suddenly, as the microwave bell dinged, the
smell of food thudded like a rock in the pit of her
stomach. She raced past him to the bathroom,
slammed the door, and held hard to both sides of the
basin to make the world stop tilting.

Chapter Five

"Ever see an old, primitive Seminole dart gun looks like this?" Yancy Tatum asked Seth in the tribal chairman's office. As the sun sank lower, reddish rays speared through the vertical blinds. Tatum thrust a rough sketch of the dart gun across the desktop. "Panthers on it for tribal good luck, right, chief?"

"Chairman's the proper title, Detective."

Although they had known each other years ago, they made no pretense of good-old-days camaraderie. Bad blood had been between them from the beginning. Looking back on it all now, Seth figured it was the only way a cracker kid like Yancy from a poor family could have someone to look down on. A couple of Seminoles new to the white man's school like him and Mae made a good target for the Tatum boys. But it excused none of Yancy's early bully attacks. And it sure as hell didn't justify his bigoted—if more subtle—attitude that seeped out like septic tank fluid under his aura of authority now.

Struggling to control bitter resentment, Seth went on to explain the role of the protective, sacred panther. He even told him some of the Seminole creation story, then summed it up. "So that's one of many reasons I'm convinced the Seminoles would never harm a panther or those who are trying to save them from extinction. We've even let that research team tag panthers on our land. The Seminoles don't want *co-wah-chobee* to be hurt any more than we want the Everglades ruined by outsiders."

He paused, looking at Tatum, hoping he got the point. "As for that dart gun," Seth added, "yeah, I've seen one or two around like that over the years. Strictly antiques that are never used, but I'll look into it. If I could see that one, I could probably tell if it was a reproduction or not. The County Museum has one that, like a lot of things, should be given back to the tribe for the living museum we're going to build."

"Not likely for a while—your getting the gun back I mean. It's evidence in a crime. But you've got lots of big plans for the tribe, huh? As far as I can tell, you people don't see cooperating worth a damn unless you're pulling whites in to pay for something. Fakey alligator wrestling, gambling, selling patched shirts. Got a museum with weapons on display planned next?"

That tirade and tone didn't deserve a reply, Seth decided. He only stood and stared down at Tatum, forcing his fists to stay on his desk as he leaned across it toward him. "You'd better get going if you don't have anything but insults to offer, Tatum."

"I'm offering next time you're in town on tribe or lawyer business, stop by and take a look at the dart gun, or I'll wonder what you're hiding," he said. He shoved his chair back away from Seth before he rose, but evidently realized retreat was the best tactic. Seth followed him to his police car to be sure he didn't harass anyone else on the way out.

"Anything you learn from asking around—like I'm going to have some officers come out here to investigate," Tatum added brazenly, though he kept hightailing it for his car, "we'll expect a call. Those days are gone when you Seminoles can get away with holding your own courts and dishing out punishment at secret ceremonies."

Seth crossed his arms over his chest and clenched his fists under his armpits to keep from slamming Tatum right onto the hood of his car. Fortunately, Tatum seemed in a rush.

"We'll get those four Seminole mystery men," he vowed, sticking his head out the window. He didn't meet Seth's eyes until he had jammed his sunglasses on and Seth could only see his own reflection in them. "Like I said, I'll want to follow through on what our mutual friend Jordan told me. She's cooperating fully with me," he called back as he pulled away. Seth saw Tatum reach over to hit the revolving bar lights on the squad car as if to warn all Indians on their own land to get out of the way.

He was suddenly so furious he almost pulled one of those *Terminator* moves, throwing himself on the roof of the car so he could smash through the windshield and then smash that superior sneer off that bastard's face.

But he turned away and sprinted for his truck in the side parking lot. His mind was in turmoil as he drove toward his place. Jordan's description of the dart gun and then Tatum's rough sketch of it—he had to know for sure his was where he kept it. And if it wasn't ... and if the attackers of the panther team possibly had been Seminoles, he knew who might have access to his antique gun.

He passed his parents' new double-wide mobile home they had bought last year with a low-interest tribal loan. Yet his mother felt trapped inside the place—like living in a tin cocoon, she said—and they did most of their cooking and living outside.

His single-width mobile home was at the edge of a narrow strip of pinelands so he could see out his door and windows to the prairie beyond. It flourished yet with ibis, deer, and ducks, but it had once been home to black bear and panther, which had been hunted almost to oblivion. He was not going to let the same thing happen to his people.

He'd left no lights on inside or out. It was dark, no moonrise yet. On a hunch, he reached up and groped in the notch of the big palmetto for the extra door key. It was there. He left it and used the one on his key ring. Frank knew where to find the hidden one, but that had never worried him until now.

He walked around his cypress picnic table and unlocked the door, going through the kitchen and living room to the narrow hall to the single bedroom. He felt along the wall for the light switch and clicked it on, blinking at the brightness.

This room, like the whole place, was small and spartan with his waterbed and pegs along the walls for extra clothes; his good suits for trips to Gainesville, Tallahasse, or Washington were the only things on hangers; he had the clothes closet full of old files and piles of things he needed to sort through. Since Paula had told him she was marrying Clay Jumper—someone who was *really* Seminole and didn't do big-shot kissing up to the white man, as she'd put it—Seth had lived here instead of in the house he'd built on the fringe of her people's compound. Other than the basics—and toys and books for Josh when he visited—he'd done little more than camp out here.

He had thought about mounting the old dart gun on his office wall, but it was valuable, and he worried

that the two berry juice-stained panthers might fade
even further in the light. And, he had to admit, he
didn't like being reminded that he had not become a
medicine man, as the panthers had once decreed in a
dream his dad had. But after all, *co-wash-chobee* was
also guardian of the law.

From the floor of his closet, under his old cleated
baseball shoes, he dragged out his first toolbox, the
one he'd had from the years putting himself through
law school working half time on a construction team
in Gainesville. These days, deep tribal pockets would
send a bright, ambitious kid like him clear through
college and grad school—if only they could keep him
in high school first.

He opened the box and fumbled through his cache
of boyhood treasures, trying to think when he'd had
the dart gun out last. He'd shown it once to a few
friends since he'd lived here, his brothers, too. And
Frank that day—yeah, he remembered that Frank held
it with silent reverence.

He dug down past a small, plastic baseball plaque,
then a snakeskin sheath holding his first battered skin-
ning knife he'd give to Josh someday. It lay partly on
a wrinkled, faded black-and-white photo of him, Mae,
and Jordan someone had taken when they first knew
each other. They looked short, skinny, and happy.
He'd forgotten that was here—and really forgotten
that he'd drawn a ballpoint X across it that smeared
against his thumb as if it were fresh ink.

But the dart gun and its black bear fur case were
gone.

He smacked his fist into the closet door so hard he
cracked the wood. "*Hal-wuk*!" he cursed. "He—they
couldn't do all that."

*   *   *

Click. Jordan listened for the first voice on her telephone answering machine.

"Hi, Jordan. Lana. Uh, the time is eleven-thirty-ish a.m. I've got something so great to tell you, kid! I'll be in town tomorrow, so I'll find you then."

In a rush, as an afterthought: "Don't bother calling me at home, 'cause it can wait. Don't you dare breathe a word to Mama. I have something I'm excited about, so I can tell her in my own way. I haven't even told Chuck yet. Bye."

Click. "Jordan, hon, it's Mama. I guess since you haven't called lately to tell me different, you're still living like some gypsy over the store instead of home in that pretty condo where you should be. Hon, when most marriages get a little rocky, it's the man who moves out for a spell till things get patched up."

"Give it up, Mama," Jordan whispered, picturing her mother as if she were there to argue with.

Arlene Hartman was an imposing woman, not in height or size but in the impact of her presence. Though just five feet, her body was lean and firm, so she seemed taller. Her voice might be praline sweet, but it could cut like steel, and her periwinkle blue eyes could glint glacially. Arlene wore her silver-blond hair in a French twist to emphasize her elegant facial bones and taut skin. She dressed mostly in shades of beige or soft blue, but on her, Jordan thought, even muted colors looked stunning and strong.

"I have to bring Grandma into town to see her eye doctor about the cataracts tomorrow," Mama's voice went on, "so we'll stop by for a little chat. You might know, she wandered off again today, but I can't bear to tie her up or lock her in. Liddy Tatum found her clear down by their place, so you know how far she walked."

Yancy's mother, Jordan thought. The two women had been friends for years. Grandma Hattie, even at age ninety-three, hadn't forgotten they had started out as poor as the Tatums.

Click. "Jordan—Lana again. I saw on the evening news my little sister's a local media star, but what a way to get publicity for the shop. Now seriously, I've told you a million times not to take those orchid walks out there alone, a young, attractive woman like you. Mama will have a conniption if she sees it."

Click. "Jordan!" Mama's voice again. "I saw you on the late-night news about finding those men on the panther team, and I can't believe you're not home yet. Thank heavens, Lawrence has more of a desk job and wasn't out there to get shot with some awful dart. You might know it was Seminoles. I don't know why you had to keep Mae Cypress what's-her-name-now as such a close friend after everything, and—"

Blessedly, the machine whined shrilly, out of tape, although Mama was probably only getting started. Jordan sat with her head in her hands, listening to the sudden silence, wishing it could lull her brain to sleep. Long after midnight, she sat in her small bedroom above her shop, too emotionally bereft and physically exhausted even to roll into bed.

After she'd convinced Marc she wanted to be alone tonight, she had gone door to door to talk with the condo neighbors, but no one had seen anything of the van beyond what Max had told her. Lawrence was such a loner no one would be checking up on him. But she had learned something from one neighbor that had corroborated Max's observation about Lawrence's car. A service station man had returned it late in the afternoon, just before she arrived, so she could check on that tomorrow. Now why would Lawrence take off on a day he knew his car was in for a tune-up or something?

Not sure what to do next, she had returned to her apartment just in case Lawrence had left her another message here. But no, all she had recorded was Lana and her mother. Then another strategy hit her. After Sally had left the shop at five today, a phone call or E-mail could have come from Lawrence downstairs in the shop, if that's where he'd expected her to be. She forced herself to her feet and went out onto the back steps. In the long, narrow yard behind the shop, the glass roof of the greenhouse gleamed in moonlight. She could feel her plants breathing through the open vents, however closed in they were, and that comforted her.

Inside the shop, she wove her way past the wrapping shelf with its big bolts and sleeves of colored paper, around the cash register counter and through the banked displays of moss-bedded or hanging plants. She stopped to inhale the foresty fragrance. Street lamps and the headlights of a car going slowly by silvered the interior, so she did not turn on the lights.

She felt for the computer ON switch and then the monitor's; she skimmed the E-mail, but it was all business. The letters on the monitor screen seemed to sway before her aching eyes. She reached over and hit the button for phone messages.

"Jordan Quinn of the Orchid Tree Shop? This is Michelle Merwyn."

Jordan's head snapped up. The movie actress Michelle Merwyn? She listened intently as the message went on. Yes, that rich voice with the little lift at the end of her sentences, even that tremolo of suppressed humor that made her romantic comedies so delightful.

"Ms. Quinn, I've always thought that word of

mouth is the best endorsement there is, and a neighbor at the next ranch, Sarah Milford, just raved about the orchid garden you did for them. We adored it when we saw it. I'm visiting my father at the SunRay Ranch now, and we would love to discuss with you the possibility of your doing an extensive airplant and orchid garden, probably out by the pool. I swear, those flowers of yours look and smell so good, I would swim in them instead.

"And so, if you would be so kind as to call me, you and I could do lunch in Naples and discuss everything. Then you could come out to the ranch later and plan something very special. I'll be here for the next couple of weeks before I go back to L.A. to begin a new film, so here's the unlisted number ..."

Jordan fumbled for a pen and scribbled it down in the dark. It was *the* Michelle Merwyn. Lana, fan of fans of every film ever made, would-be actress of the century, would be thrilled. And it sounded like a wonderful business opportunity to make new contacts. Wait until she told Law—

Reality crashed back in on her. Lawrence didn't care about her victories or sorrows. Lawrence had deserted her in every way, and worse, her love for Lawrence had left long before he had. Hunched over on the desk, her face in her hands, she finally surrendered to tears.

Then she heard someone rattling the front doorknob. She stopped crying, stopped breathing. All was darkness and silence. Her heart starting to thump, she checked the front door and peered out into the street as a police car went slowly by. It made her feel safer. Perhaps she would call Yancy Tatum in the morning and tell him what had happened with Lawrence.

From the window, she thought she saw a flicker of

light across the street in the second-story law offices. No, nothing now. She was seeing and hearing things, that's all, as if reality had been swept from her control.

The luminous clock in the back room said ten after four as she went outside, locked the door, and trudged upstairs, shivering. The night arched black and vast above her.

"You just don't understand me!" Frank shouted when Seth asked him where he'd been before he'd picked up his truck for him yesterday afternoon. Sunrise was spilling light through the trees; he'd finally tracked Frank down at his little camp on the pine prairie fringe of the reservation. Luckily, his buddies weren't there as well.

"I just asked a simple question, Frank. Let's try another one. Did you take that tribal dart gun Dad gave me years ago?"

"Why accuse me?" Frank demanded, facing Seth squarely. At his feet, spread on a blanket on the thin grass, was his meager breakfast of corn bread and *sofkee*. "You think I'd take anything of yours? That white woman years ago rubbed the red right out of your skin." He rubbed his hand up and down his own arm, his face derisive.

Seth fought to keep his temper in check. "We're not talking about me, brother. All that's in my past."

"Oh, sure. That why I saw her yesterday—supposedly just Mae's friend—driving out to your private camp when you told me you wanted to be alone? I think you're the one hiding something."

Seth felt his muscles go rigid. He fought himself to keep from taking on Frank. "Look, Frank, I—"

"Besides," the boy interrupted, "you think I'd harm *coo-wha-chobee*? But that's the next thing, right? You think I took the gun, I attacked those guys, and took the cat? Naw, it's not the panther team guys I'd like to take on," he said with a defiant sneer and sniff.

"Meaning me?" Seth said, stepping closer and tapping Frank's left shoulder with his right knuckles. The boy backed up several steps, then held his ground so he wouldn't be pinned against a slash pine. "But first, all I'm asking is, did you take the old dart gun out of my closet?"

"No way," he insisted, looking Seth straight in the eye. "But I know you won't believe me."

Seth thought he was lying, but he hoped to hell he wasn't. The last thing he wanted was to alienate this kid. "If you're telling the truth, I believe you," he said, trying to sound conciliatory. "If you're not, I'd be stupid enough to want to protect you. But I may not be able to. You've gotta learn we can't just play by our own rules, or everybody suffers."

"Suffers, yeah. Tell me about it. But see, I told you straight out, and you didn't believe me. Just get out of my face." He raised his voice again as he shouldered past Seth hard enough to bounce him back. He started for his truck, but Seth grabbed his arm and spun him around.

"Frank, I know the whites hurt your pride when they jumped you that time. But I don't want you to get more hurt doing—"

Before he could react, Frank swung a fist. It smacked solid jawbone, snapping his head back. Seth staggered a few steps, stunned. As he did, Frank bent his knees and jabbed, stiff-armed again, a glacing blow off his shoulder. Seth ducked and lunged, slamming his shoulder into Frank's flat belly so he made a woofing sound, then a grunt. Locked together, they went down onto the pine needles, thrashing for position, advantage. Despite Frank's flailing fury and youth, Seth outweighed and outmaneuvered him, pinning his arms over his head.

"Frank! Frank, listen to me. I'm on your side. We need to work together, not pull the family apart. All right, you didn't take the dart gun, but I want you to help me find out who did, before someone ties us to that attack."

The sudden transformation in Frank's face scared him. Seth sensed it wasn't because he claimed to believe him, or because he had temporarily bested him. For a moment that defiant expression looked as if it would crack and shatter. Frank's taut facial muscles slackened, erasing all emotion. His wide eyes seemed to stare beyond or within, that same dead look he'd had for weeks after the white kids beat him so badly. He seemed almost limp when Seth stood and hauled him to his feet.

"See," Seth said, patting his shoulder. "Fighting's no good. You okay?"

Frank squared his shoulders and shuffled over to the spokes of the fire to scuff dirt on the low flames. He picked up his brimmed hat off the ground and, head down, walked slowly to his truck without a word or look back.

Fingering his jaw, Seth stood staring at him. What had he accomplished if Frank had slipped back to moping silence? Their parents would have a fit. Worse, he knew in his gut that Frank had taken that damned dart gun.

Chapter Six

"The things I've seen I just can't tell you," Hattie Hartman, Jordan's paternal grandmother, announced again as Jordan poured more coffee for the three of them in the small sitting room above the shop. Jordan had described finding the panther team in the Glades yesterday to Hattie and her mother, but she had not mentioned Lawrence's departure yet.

"Since the panther team is actually working for the government, maybe the FBI will get involved," Mama mused.

"What's the name of that gray-haired boy who's president right now?" Hattie asked.

"Bill Clinton, Grandma," Jordan told her.

"That's the one, Bill Clinton," Hattie said, her cloudy blue eyes alive in a face as wrinkled as cypress bark. "Arlene, Bill Clinton hasn't been fishing with J.J. yet, has he?"

"No, Mama. J.J. passed two years ago, and you're thinking of Eisenhower or Nixon in the old days. Lana's husband, Chuck, has the boats now."

"I'm thinking of that gray-haired boy, Bill Clinton! I've seen him in the moving pictures or somewhere. No, it was on TV when you weren't watching that boring weather channel. She thinks," Hattie told Jordan earnestly and reached over to tap her arm, "that

Hurricane Donna is coming again, and she's got to warn J.J. out in his boat or lodge or wherever he's gone off to this time."

That reminded Jordan of Yancy's advice on the phone when she'd called him first thing this morning, leveled with him, and asked for advice about Lawrence's disappearance. "Jordan, wherever your husband's gone off to, give it time," he had advised. "We can't act for a couple of days yet with a rational adult gone. Happens all the time—midlife crisis, job pressures, marital discord—in his case, maybe research—"

"Mother," Arlene scolded, interrupting Jordan's thoughts. "Jordan does not need to hear about your funny ideas right now. She has problems of her own."

"No, that's all right, Mama. I understand, and frankly, I'm thinking of maybe moving back to Lokosee, or the area at least. I have to tell you that Lawrence and I are extremely doubtful for the future. Actually," she said and stood, gathering the coffee mugs and wishing they didn't rattle against each other so it was obvious she was trembling, "I'm going to divorce him as soon as I find him, whether or not he's taken off for rest or research. We both agreed a while ago that it's over, and we've just stayed married this last year for financial reasons."

For once, Arlene Hartman looked speechless as she followed Jordan out into the tiny kitchen. "Mama, don't panic," Jordan soothed, putting the mugs in the sink and sloshing water in them. "It's the best thing for both of us. Please try to understand—to be on my side."

Arlene pulled Jordan into her strong embrace. "Believe me, my precious girl, I have always, *always* been on your side."

* * *

Jordan's stomach knotted even tighter as she hung up the phone after her mother and grandmother left. The service manager at their car dealership garage had told her Lawrence had said they could return the car yesterday or today, he didn't care which, and just put the tune-up on his credit card.

Feeling chilled, she went out into the sun, sitting on the steps of the back entrance to her apartment. It was cozy inside, just a one-bedroom, one-bath arrangement with the tiny sitting area and kitchen, but the walls were starting to close in on her. She had the almost overwhelming desire to flee to her home island of Lokosee with its view of the islands, populated mostly by pelicans and porpoises.

Why, *why,* she agonized, would Lawrence have gone off without his car? Or without even telling her? She sat up straighter, gripping the handrail up by her head. Unless, she thought, he hadn't left of his own free will. If foul play were involved, his abductors would not have known the serviced car would be returned soon. And that would explain why some of the wrong things were gone from his closet.

She decided to go back to the condo to search it all carefully again. That had obviously been Marc's first instinct. But as she went in to get her purse and started back out, she saw Lana coming up the stairs.

Lana Hartman Washburn was what Lokosee men called "a looker." She'd always been blond, and she'd inherited Mama's facial bones. But instead of Mama's petite, neat body Lana's was ripe and voluptuous. Jordan was tall and slender like her dad, though where her red hair came from no one knew. Lana emanated not cool control like Mama, but heat and light, whereas Jordan's more muted glow came from within. Though Jordan was only twenty-eight to Lana's forty-four, Jordan seemed a bit older than her age and Lana seemed much younger than hers. Both sisters had porcelain skin and china blue eyes and, they used to say as they laughingly made faces at each other, copycat smiles, down to the white, even teeth. Now Jordan forced a wan smile.

Lana beamed and waved when she saw Jordan waiting for her. "Guess what? I got the lead in a Tennessee Williams play at the Winterhaven Dinner Theater! Maggie in *Cat on a Hot Tin Roof*!"

Jordan gave her a big hug, wanting to cling to her and tell everything as she had Mama. "You'll be wonderful, Lana," she told her. "I can't wait. I'll send every customer and client to see it. Come on in and tell me about it." They went in together, and Lana was soon perched on one of the two rattan kitchen stools while Jordan got two Dr Peppers from the refrigerator.

"I knew you'd understand, Jordan. We just had our first read through of Act One, and I've got to get home, but I couldn't wait to tell you. I still haven't told Chuck or Mama. It's a pretty racy part, at least by Lokosee standards. I spend three-fourths of the play prancing around in my slip, and there's all kinds of off-color language in it, too, as Mama would say. Not to mention adultery, impotence, drunkenness, and a husband who does not give a damn about me."

"Oh," Jordan said and sank on the other stool.

Lana took both soda cans from her and put them down. "Sorry, kid. I didn't mean to put it that way."

They held hands, Jordan's cold from the cans. "I was so upset," she explained, "about having to tell you and Mama that everything is really over for Lawrence and me, but Mama was so great, and I know I can tell you . . ."

She did tell her, most of it, without all her worries about possible foul play, at least until she could convince Yancy, too. Bless her big sis, she had tears in her eyes to match her own.

"Oh, your getting that part reminds me," Jordan added, feeling a bit better as they drank their soda, "wait till you hear who might be my new client. You'll love this. Michelle Merwyn!"

Lana clunked her can down and got to her feet. She looked so surprised her face was devoid of its usual animation and emotion. "Michelle Merwyn?"

"Yes, no kidding!" Jordan said, grinning that she'd really surprised Lana. "Her father owns the SunRay cattle ranch that borders the reservation, the one you pass before the Milfords' spread. I'm going to have lunch with her and, now that you're both officially actresses, maybe I can set it up for you to meet her."

Lana grabbed her purse off the counter. She looked upset, not just surprised or excited. "I think her work stinks," she announced archly. "She can't decide whether to be cute or crazy, and her voice is too breathy. She looks like a Barbie doll reject, same every movie. She can't act worth beans."

Jordan felt as if she'd been slapped. She knew Lana was into heavy drama actresses, but what was wrong with admiring a good comedienne? "I think she's pretty and talented," Jordan said, her temporary elation deflated. "I thought you'd be—excited."

"I have some taste, you know. Go to lunch with her if you have to, but don't get mixed up with those people," she insisted as she shoved the screen door open.

"What people? You're always saying—"

"I've got to run. Call me if you need me—about—the Lawrence thing. Come on out for dinner some

night, just call ahead in case I have an early rehearsal," she called back, banging the door and heading down the stairs, her voice lively again. "Or I could
come in here—I'll stop by to see you ..."

Jordan just stared as Lana's voice faded. What was
that shift in emotion all about? Surely Lana hadn't
become jealous of other actresses now that she had a
part in a dinner theater.

"Hey, there you are! Been looking for you!"

Jordan nearly jumped out of her skin, but—thank
heavens—it was her elderly, silver-haired neighbor
John Hawkins she'd bumped into turning the corner
of her condo.

"Whoa," John said in his Missouri drawl. "Looks
like you're barely keeping ahead of the hounds."

"You don't know the half of it, John."

"Which reminds me. Mary and I remembered something last night after you asked if we saw that van or
anything else strange. In a way, we did. Two, three
times, we noticed a man standing over in what looks
like a vacant condo 'cross the canal," he told her. "We
think he's got binocs looking over here, 'cause they
gleam in the sun sometimes, you know—like cat eyes
in the dark. He was watching when you were out talking to Max yesterday."

"And from there," she whispered with a shudder,
"he could look in Lawrence's—our windows."

"S'pose so. First, of course, we thought it was some
shut-in who liked just looking out, watching birds, but
with no curtains in the windows, must be deserted,
like I said. Maybe he even watches people at the pool,
but after Lawrence left, we got to thinking, like I said.
Maybe the guy's some kind of weirdo. Walk around
the building with me," he said, starting off and wind-

milling one arm at her, "and I'll show you which window he's been in."

Her neck prickled as it had that day the plane had dived at her in the Glades. She remembered the feeling someone might be watching her at the apartment and shop last night. So she talked John into not going out to the middle of the lawn to point out the window.

"That one," he indicated as they peered around the corner of the building together. "Sixth floor, two from the top. Corner place, east end. You just be careful now, if you're going over to inquire. I'd get the police in on it if you find out anything funny."

After thanking John, feeling desperate for any lead about Lawrence, Jordan decided she had to do something now. Though she felt nervous about it, she immediately drove over the bridge to the Villa Club Condos.

Mr. Bigler, the stooped, shuffling resident manager, informed her the condo she'd seen from her place across the way was for sale. She took advantage of the situation—and his offer to escort her to see it.

"Don't mind if Daisy goes along, do you?" he asked, referring to the neon-hued parrot perched on his sloped shoulder. "Knows this place better'n me."

"Isn't that a dog bone you're feeding Daisy?"

"Thinks she's a dog, a watchdog," the old man explained with a conspiratorial wink as they went up in the elevator. "Show her, Daisy. Good dog!"

"Bow-aarrr-wow!" Daisy barked so shrilly that Jordan jumped.

"I'm glad you didn't say, 'sic her, Daisy,' " she told him. He led her to the condo in question and unlocked the door.

"You wouldn't think a place would get dusty just closed up empty, would you now?" Mr. Bigler asked.

"Place just new on the market, though. Things held up by an estate settlement. Takes forever if folks are out-of-state residents when they pass on. A law firm uptown name of Lansing and Mitchell been the technical owners for nearly a year. Mind if I ask you something? You look real familiar."

"Maybe it's because I was interviewed on TV yesterday."

"No . . . Say, aren't you the orchid lady, the one did that nice flower garden for the Royal Palm Convalescent Center's courtyard? See, the wife's in there, been for two years."

"Yes, that's me. I do a lot of retirement and nursing home gardens around town."

While he rambled on, telling her how much his wife liked to look out her window at the orchids, Jordan remembered one of the last arguments she and Lawrence had:

"I swear, Jordan, sometimes you don't have any common sense at all. If you want to do promotion for your business, retirement and nursing homes are *not* the place. America's ill and elderly are hardly big-time consumers, not for what you're selling, anyway. You think that clientele's going to come waltzing into your store? And you're doing it *for free*?"

"It's something I want to do for people, and—I know you won't understand this—for the flowers, too. Besides, I've gotten some customers through people who visit or work there, and I'm making a good profit in other ways. Don't worry we'll have to stay married for more than the year it takes us to bail ourselves out of debt. Besides, you're ultimately working to help others, aren't you? Not only the cats, but all mankind?"

"But that's a *real* investment, Jordan. Beyond self-satisfaction and philanthropy, do you have any idea how much even the hope of such a cure could be worth in megabucks as well as power and prestige?"

It had been the first time she'd realized that the reason for his research could include the pursuit of fame and fortune. When he had disappeared, she had focused first on her emotions, then his motives. But with greed—Lawrence's or, worse, someone else's in the equation—the danger could be deeper than she'd thought.

Mr. Bigler's voice pierced her painful musings. "Just go ahead and look around all you want," he said. She realized she had stopped dead in the center of the living room.

"Oh, yes, thanks."

Without furniture and drapes, the place looked huge, especially with the plush white carpet. Walking the rooms, she thought she smelled faint cigarette smoke, but she knew it could seep up from downstairs or stay for weeks in the carpet. She was overly sensitive to it anyway.

The carpet in front of the large windows in the living area and the Florida room looked tramped down, she thought, as if someone with those binoculars John had described had paced back and forth. When she walked toward the window to check the view, her heel hit against the baseboard and stepped on something crinkly. She bent to retrieve it, while Mr. Bigler fussed with Daisy.

"Drop something?" he asked.

"Found something—just a plastic candy wrapper, probably left by someone you've shown the place to."

He pursed his lips and shook his head in denial. "Nary a soul till you, and the carpet been cleaned, too. Just the relatives of the deceased, then the lawyer—oh, and an assessor."

"It's been locked the rest of the time? Maybe the lawyers or the relatives still have a key."

"The lawyers only if they got one made on the sly, and the relatives live in Madison, Wisconsin. 'Less it's some phantom mighty good with getting keys not his own," he added, his shoulders shaking silently as if he'd cracked a joke. "Now, tell you what. Since you got such a good heart, I'll just leave you be for a while. Close the door tight so it locks and just wave on your way out. Daisy's late for her supper, see, and then we got to go visit the wife."

"That would be fine. Thanks for your help, Mr. Bigler, and I'll be in touch if I decide I want the place," she added, feeling guilty that she was lying to the old man.

"Real good view," he said as he plodded toward the door, with Daisy cranking her head around to stare back at Jordan. "Now you just remember what they always say. Location, location, and location."

She stood in the silent apartment, over to the side of the window. Unfortunately, the location was all too good for seeing directly into their living room and the room that had been Lawrence's office. She left the condo and closed the door carefully. Downstairs, she waved good-bye to Mr. Bigler through his screened door. Daisy perched on the back of the only other chair at the dining table. But she hesitated in the exit to the building, just staring up at her condo. Her sense of security felt blasted to bits.

And then she remembered the pistol under the bed across the way, the one Lawrence had suggested was for protection only. Maybe he had really bought it for himself, but—as much as she hated guns—it might make her feel better now to carry it.

She got her keys out, hurried to her car, checked to be sure no one was crouching behind the back seat. She got in and clicked all the locks closed. Warm weather or not, she left the windows up. It wasn't until she grasped the steering wheel that she realized she still held the candy wrapper. And it had little words printed across it.

She bent over to read in from the thin beam of the tiny flashlight dangling from the end of her car keys. *Feather Fan of Naples,* a restaurant she'd never been to. Like their condo across the way, she'd have to check it out.

It couldn't be, but the gun was gone. She knelt and ducked her head to stare under the bed again, ran her hand over the dusty carpet. She got a flashlight from the bedside table drawer and shined it everywhere under the bed. The gun was only a small one, but neither it nor its box of bullets were here now. Surely, she had not just touched the metal foot of the bed yesterday and thought it was the gun.

She sat back on her heels. Could Lawrence have returned for it and some other things late last night? Or—it was a really wild idea—could Marc Chay have taken it? Surely, Lawrence had never given him a key, but there was an extra one hanging in the kitchen he could have taken to get back in after she left.

She raced to check: the extra key was there, though maybe on a different hook. But then again, Marc could have had a copy made of it and replaced it when he came to look around again. He had seemed so desperate to inspect every nook and cranny last night.

She began to search the apartment, every cupboard,

drawer, under and behind things. Maybe she'd find something Lawrence had dropped, something he had left behind to help her locate him. As she went, she tried to recall if things looked different from what she'd seen yesterday, in case Marc—or someone—had searched since then.

She even tore through the Spanish moss she had put in the base of the plastic palm tree in the corner of his office. The plant had been, she was certain, intended as a subtle snub when he brought it in amid her breathing, blooming ones. He had not even wanted the Spanish moss even though it looked so much better than the fake plastic dirt that attracted dust.

Finding nothing, swamped with frustration and fury, she gave the plant a hard kick. It tipped back against the wall with a metallic thunk. Curious about the odd sound, she reached up and parted the plastic leaves to look closer.

And saw a tiny camera. Nestled in—wired to—the leaves. Wide-eyed, she stared at it like the cottonmouth Daddy had killed before it could strike her.

Feeling sick to her stomach, Jordan turned the camera's lens to the wall. Hugging herself, she stared at it a long time, shaking and confused.

Not only had she not known it was here, but she couldn't even tell if it was running. Or if it was one that took film or fed someone's screen somewhere. Perhaps Lawrence himself had put it here, a security camera for his work. Worse, it could be linked to the man that John Hawkins had said was spying on the condo.

Growing angry, she got a plastic bag and, standing on a chair, handled the camera only with the plastic. It could have fingerprints, she thought, that Yancy and the police could use. She placed the camera in the plastic bag and then in a paper sack.

On tiptoe, she searched the rest of the rooms, looking for cameras high up. She finally found one, perched like a parrot in the swagged valance of the bedroom, its eye aimed toward the king-size bed. With a shout, as if it were a live, she threw a bed bolster at it to tilt its direction, then sank cross-legged to the floor.

Could it have taken infrared pictures of them in bed? No, surely it had not been there for a year, and it would have been at least that long ago she shared that bed with Lawrence. What if he'd had a lover? Some people like taking pictures of themselves like that. But she really didn't believe it. Lawrence's only lover for a long time had been his work.

She stood and backed out of the room. She returned with another paper bag, and covered the entire end of the valance. That's when another chilling thought occurred to her. If this place had cameras, what about her own apartment and shop?

Holding the sack with the first camera as if it contained a coiled snake, she went out, first looking up and down the hall. As she fled, she didn't even reach back inside to turn out the lights.

Chapter Seven

Even in jeans and western shirt instead of full Seminole regalia, Seth Cypress looked the living embodiment of last year's powwow poster Mae had mounted on the wall. The customers in her Patchworks shop that morning looked up, then stared as Seth stood in the door.

He came in, moving on silent feet among the racks and display cases of bright items. He was used to being stared at, even in a suit, in some of the most so-called civilized places: a Collier County courtroom, the state house in Tallahassee, a Capitol Hill luncheon for Native American rights in Washington. He usually felt he could handle any problems anywhere, but this thing with Frank had struck too close to home.

He nodded to customers. Behind the cash register, Velda Bowlegs smiled and poked her head through the curtain to call Mae.

She came out and motioned him into the back room. "Hey, you sure give the place some atmosphere," she said as she held the curtains open for him.

"Put me on the payroll, then," he said as he followed her out back.

"No Seminole men on this payroll. Especially ones looking rough around the edges. I bet you been up all night again over that panther thing. I'll get some coffee."

Mae was right; she had hawk's eyes about his moods. But evidently she knew nothing yet about Frank disappearing and, for now, he'd keep it that way. He'd looked for him almost all afternoon; not only was he missing, but his three buddies he'd wanted to question were gone, too.

Rubbing the slight stubble on his chin, he looked around the small back room where Mae had the door propped open to let in the fresh morning air. He could see the top of Jordan's greenhouse over the wooden fence that separated her property from Mae's. He'd been worrying about whether to approach Jordan yet. Despite their most recent failure to communicate, he needed to ask her about a few things.

"This visit's a real surprise," Mae went on, smiling. "Only second time you came around. We got lots of customers out there, even this early."

"I'll keep it quick. I had some business in town, matter-of-fact, at the law office upstairs, right across the street."

He'd stopped by the police station, too, but he didn't want to tell her about that either. The broken dart gun in police possession looked just like his— probably *was* his. But until he found out if he was intentionally being set up by Frank—or if someone else could be behind it—he was telling no one, including Yancy Tatum.

"Mae, I want to ask you something." Her hands froze with the coffeepot poised in midair for a moment before she reached for the mugs.

"I been dying to ask you some things since Jordan drove out to see you," she said and shot a quick side glance his way. "But reading the Naples newspaper the last two mornings, I guessed why she did before she told me."

"Yeah. She wanted to warn me about what she saw that day. So, is her husband still on the panther team or not?" he asked, stepping closer to her. "I mean—how much of a personal stake does she have in nailing somebody for hurting the team?"

Mae turned to look at him long and hard, making him feel he were Josh's age and had just done something wrong. "Didn't you ask her about her husband?" she said, finally pouring him some coffee.

He silently cursed himself for giving too much away already. He didn't really want Mae to know how much he needed Jordan—or for what reason. "We didn't talk about anything personal," he explained. "Just about the panther team being taken. Besides, she didn't tell me anything about Yancy Tatum being the investigating officer, so she wasn't exactly trusting me with everything. Mae, just tell me. I'm only thinking about the good of the tribe."

When she raised an eyebrow, he felt his cheeks heat. She had always read him too well, especially about Jordan. He might as well quit fooling himself, too. He did feel something for Jordan beyond anger that she'd come back into his life after so long.

"Okay," she said, with a decisive nod. "Lawrence Quinn is—or maybe was—on the team."

"Why was?" He forced himself to take a slow sip of black coffee.

"She told me yesterday it's no secret anymore." She shrugged and shook her head. "She's relieved if people know, though I don't s'pose she meant you."

Putting his mug on the counter, he grasped his sister's shoulders. "Know what?"

"I never told anyone 'cause she didn't want it

around before. Her and Lawrence been strange for almost a year."

"Strange? Strange how?"

"Strange—separated. Living apart."

"You mean *estranged*," he said with a relieved sigh. He felt his tension uncoil only to be replaced by another anxious feeling he could not quite name.

"And so," she went on, "*I* been thinking maybe you got more in common with her than you thought. Divorce. Paula leaving you."

"Is Jordan leaving him for someone else?" He concentrated on asking casually, but when Mae flinched he realized he was holding her arms too tightly. Sheepishly he loosed her. She fluffed at the caped sleeves of her patchwork blouse while he forced himself to wait for the answer this time.

"No, she's not leaving him for someone else," Mae said, propping her hands on her hips, "though she should have. But I'm telling you, with their different asses—*assets,* her getting a divorce not easy like for our people."

"But she is getting a divorce?" He forced himself to sip coffee again.

"Was before Lawrence turned up missing. Seems he just took off, and I'm telling you it might be a blessing for her." She gave him her best sharp schoolteacher-type look. "But don't you go upsetting her. Say, what is this anyway, your fancy law court and I'm on the hot seat?"

"Mae," he said, putting his mug down and holding up both hands as if to ward off her next scolding, "I'm just going next door to see if she recalls anything else about what those so-called Seminoles looked like."

"Okay, but I'm telling you," she said, smacking

quickly at both of his raised hands, "you ever go after Jordan again, it better be for all the right reasons."

Jordan had found no cameras in her apartment or shop, but she was still so upset she lost most of another night's sleep, partly because she thought of checking for a camera in the greenhouse, too. As soon as her shop manager, Sally, arrived after her dental appointment, Jordan hurried out there to search for a camera. If someone had invaded that haven, she would feel really violated.

She surveyed her lush jungle under glass. Since the first camera at the condo had been mounted in a plastic plant, one could be suspended here among her colorful Catts or Vandas, hanging from the rafters to get them the best light. Or among the thick clusters of cool-air-loving Paphs and pansy orchids near the ventilator. The ferns and pepperomias she grew for accent pieces and certainly the big-spiked bromeliads could hide a tiny camera, too.

So, with her watering hose, she started purposefully down the rows of Florida *Oncidium* with their showy, yellow-green flowers. She parted leaves, peered behind pots, big roots and rhizomes, pretending only to mist or water them. By the time she moved to the big ferns, she was seeing camera eyes in each shadow or patch of shade, between each pot on each tiered wooden bench. For once, the plants were not relaxing her.

"Jordan."

She gasped and spun so fast she sprayed Seth across his face and chest. He yelped and ducked, thrusting up a protective hand that shot spray back at her.

Instinctively, she blinked and dodged the sudden shower, then wiped water from her face. "Don't sneak up on me like that!" she cried. He stepped back, then stood his ground, looking both amused and annoyed, before the annoyed look won. "Sorry," she added. "I'm just on edge."

"Your assistant inside said you were out here," he muttered as he, too, wiped his face. He slicked his hair back off his forehead, then slowly bent over to rub his hands on the thighs of his new jeans. His buff, western-style shirt was blotched with darker water.

"She probably didn't mean I could just come out," he added, straightening, "but I need a private word. It's important to us—to the tribe, I mean." He hesitated before he spoke again; she turned off the hose but held it in her hands, waiting. "The newspaper reported the panther team members who were drugged say they saw Seminoles, but they were so out of it they can't describe them," he said in a rush.

"That's true. With that mixture of drugs, you never really lose consciousness, but you can't react or recall much. What are you driving at?" she asked, staring straight into his dark eyes, trying to concentrate on his words and not these strange feelings that doused her like more wild water.

"Let me ask you, how would some Seminoles get hold of that drug?"

"Evidently the drugs were stolen from the panther lab last week," she explained, slowly coiling the hose, looking at it and not him now. "I guess that hasn't been in the paper yet. It was such a smooth break-in no one noticed until they went looking after the fact."

"Sounds like a smooth *inside* job to me," he insisted, turning away to help free the hose when it snagged under a bag of mulch.

She glared at him. "You can't believe that someone on the team—"

"I don't know. I'm just saying it can't be my people," he stated, but it was he who didn't meet her eyes this time. He scanned the greenhouse as he said, almost to himself, "If no one knows exactly when the drugs were taken, the police will be hard pressed to ask anyone for an alibi. But," he added, focusing on her again, "my immediate concern is that the police have been in a lot of the tribe's camps, asking questions and stirring my people up. I know I'm probably the last man in the world you'd want to do a favor for, but can you give me any more information about these alleged Seminoles—age, height, weight—anything?"

She didn't answer at first. His assumption she wouldn't want to help him surprised and saddened her. "I'm sorry, Seth," she admitted, shaking her head. "It happened too fast, and I was panicked to see the team members looking dead at my feet. The police asked me the same things, but I couldn't say more."

"I'm just hoping that's what you told the police," he said, hitting the wooden rim of shelves with his fist. "Especially after you failed to tell me that Yancy Tatum would be out to question me."

She dropped the hose so hard over its metal hook the whole things bounced, spilling out several coils. "Why do all our conversations end up with you throwing accusations at me?" she demanded, slapping stray coils back in place. "I'm used to it but my plants aren't. If you can't be civil, I wish you'd just leave."

But she knew she was evading and disguising her own emotions in that outburst. She was terrified at how instinctively she responded to him after all these years apart. Somehow, she had never let go of the man he had once been, of the passions they had shared. Despite her other responsibilities and difficulties lately, it seemed her feelings for him had always been this close, lurking in the jungle of her thoughts.

"I'd forgotten how successfully you always talked to plants," he said, his voice quieter. "But you knew Tatum was the investigating officer—the newscasts made that clear if you didn't."

"I'll tell you what I didn't make clear to Yancy, but should have," she said. "I didn't recall until later that the Seminole dart gun at the scene was one like *you* used to have. But I'm sure you told him that."

His dark eyes widened, but his face looked carved from stone. She saw she'd really surprised—maybe alarmed—him. His hands clenched to fists at his sides in counterpoint to hers on her hips. For a moment, they stared and said nothing.

"I see," he said, each word slow and deliberate, "that you have decided to trust Yancy and not me, so I will act accordingly. Take care of yourself then."

But he didn't leave; she didn't breathe. Suddenly, he turned away, and disappeared down the aisle of plants as if they'd swallowed him.

She squared her shoulders, trying to stem her rush of anger. Damn the man. He had no right to come crashing back in her life, asking questions or for favors, when she had worries of her own. She didn't want him back causing complications and she was going to get rid of the only remnants of him and their catastrophe that she still had in her possession once and for all.

She walked out the way he had gone. On the narrow brick path between the greenhouse and the shop, she stubbed her toe on a fifty-pound bag of fir bark at the bottom of a stack. At the shock of the pain, she stopped and punched furiously at the top bag of cork nuggets, raining blows on it. The plastic came apart at the seams, and cork cascaded out in a brown river, covering her feet. She kicked at the nuggets, sending them flying everywhere. She stormed upstairs to her apartment. Remembering what she had set out to do, she hurried into her bedroom and yanked open the bottom drawer of the small, antique chest of drawers that had been Grandma Hattie's.

She dug down under the old photo albums and her notes from college botany courses she'd never unpacked. When she pulled out the manila folder from under the drawer lining, she scraped her fingernail and got a splinter under her thumbnail.

Cursing the splinter, Seth, Lawrence, and everything else, she dumped the clippings out and watched them flutter onto the bed: numerous newspaper articles, even *Time, People,* and *Life* magazines. Hattie had saved all these and stashed them where Jordan kept them now. She grabbed the nearest one, a yellowed newspaper clipping. The headline from June 6, 1983, read,

SEMINOLES SEE RED
OVER EXPOSURE OF OLD WAYS

TALLAHASSEE (AP)—Several spokesmen for the Big Sawgrass Seminole Indian Tribe have protested to South Florida newspapers and Governor Graham to stem recent public interest in their private tribal affairs.

What apparently began as a backwoods, two-family feud over a forbidden, interracial Romeo and Juliet romance has blown up into the latest whiteman-redman "battle" in South Florida.

After futile attempts to keep the two from meeting secretly, when a white girl, Jordan Hartman, 17, Lokosee Island, eloped with a Seminole Indian, Seth Cypress, 18, the families got the one-week marriage annulled.

Cory Cypress, age unknown, the young man's father, is a revered *ayikcomi*, or medicine man, in charge of one of the tribe's sacred, guardian, 'medicine bundles' as well as ceremonial, herbal healing. He oversees the secret Winter Dance and Green Corn Ceremony every year where Seminole justice is meted out to wayward tribal members.

According to local sources who have studied the tribe, as recently as only one generation past, the Seminoles decreed death to any Indian girl who cohabited with or married a white man. Her punishment would be to "walk into the sun," or walk west until she died of thirst, snake-bite, or drowning.

What would be decreed for an *ayikcomi*'s son who married white against his father's wishes is not known, nor will the secretive Seminoles say. Dr. Grant Thompson, professor of Florida history, University of Miami, an expert on Seminole culture, said in a telephone interview from his office on the campus, "We actually know less about their [Seminole] ways than we do most tribes.

"The Seminoles of the South Florida Everglades were the only American Indian group to keep their independence and not be forced to move West. Some resented and some admired them for this. But the point is, it wouldn't do a medicine man any good among his people to have his oldest son marry white, especially if he is expected to carry on family and tribal tradition."

Another local source remarked, "Some say the Seminoles have been treated like the Negroes in the Deep South, but this incident shows the Seminoles themselves are more prejudiced than some whites. Not only are they against this marriage, but their attitude toward all intermarriage with whites is obviously hostile. Most of the Seminole elements have never signed a peace treaty with the whites and now we are seeing why."

The *Naples Daily News* has confirmed that "this particular medicine man [Cory Cypress] is the same one who led earlier protests in the area against the way Seminoles were portrayed in the movie *Everglades Victory*, filmed partly on Lokosee, home of the white girl involved in this latest incident."

J.J. (Jordan) Hartman, father of the Juliet of this 'swamp romance gone bad,' refused to give a statement and told reporters "to leave his girl and her people alone or else."

The Cypress family has left their home along the Tamiami Trail near Everglades City and has evidently moved to the Big Sawgrass Reservation to escape further publicity. But the renewed problems of red-white relations deeply exacerbated by this incident is not so likely to go away.

"This *is* going away! All of it!"

She wadded and ripped the pile of articles on the bed. Fighting tears, she went into the bathroom and flushed every last scrap of torn paper down the toilet.

Jordan could not believe she had actually kept Michelle Merwyn waiting. She almost didn't recognize her either, because she had her famous face hidden by a floppy sunhat, huge sunglasses, and a ring-heavy hand holding a cigarette. Sitting under the striped awning on the sidewalk patio of the Picadilly Restaurant, she gave Jordan, coming across the street with an orchid plant in her hands, a jaunty waggle of her crimson-tipped fingers.

"Ah, the lady of the orchids," Michelle said as they shook hands, though she extended only three fingers. Jordan perched on the dark green molded chair across the small round table from her. Ordinarily, she gave potential new clients a single-cut Vanda in a Perrier bottle, but she was hoping for good things here.

"You know, Jordan, you look strangely familiar, but it must just be that hair and classical face," Michelle said with a shake of her head. "I adore those paintings by Christina Rosetti with those red-haired heroines agonizing over some grief or guilt. They're so terribly Victorian."

"And you have cleverly managed *not* to look familiar," Jordan told her, pleased at the compliment. "I'm sure keeping your privacy is a problem. Oh, here—I hope—is only your first orchid plant of many from the Orchid Tree." Proudly, she pushed the painted cachepot toward her.

"What darling flowers—pink-and-white striped, like peppermint."

"A *Phaleanopsis*, but many call it the Moth Orchid because the blooms look like moths in flight. We can do a variety of blossom shapes for you. Orchids can look like slippers, ballerinas, nun's habits."

"Flowers with a thousand faces, just like people."

"I never quite thought of it like that," Jordan admitted, leaning closer with her elbows on the very edge of the table. "And the blooms come in every color but black."

"A black orchid would be bizarre, but some scientist will learn how to make one someday," Michelle said with a wise wag of her head, as if she could see the future. "Nothing's sacred anymore." Then, as if that topic were exhausted, she sighed as she leaned forward to tamp out her cigarette in the seashell ashtray, clunking her thick tortoiseshell bracelet on the table.

"The SunRay Ranch has groundskeepers," Michelle went on, "but they're Cuban, like everyone else around there. Cuban cowboys, can you imagine?" She lowered her sunglasses for a moment and rolled her emerald eyes. "Anyway, they wouldn't have the foggiest about rare orchids, and Dad said I should ask if you'd do follow-up visits."

"I'd be happy to." Jordan smiled, relieved.

"Marvelous. Philanthropist that he is, he could kill plants like this in no time flat," she said with a quick chop of one hand, but she didn't laugh.

They chatted amiably through their shrimp salads and raspberry iced tea, though Michelle did most of the talking. "Imagine—ranching cattle *and alligators*! I tell Dad, not so very different from herding actors his whole life. He was a movie director, you know."

"No, I didn't."

"His work hasn't been in vogue lately, not like earlier," she admitted, shrugging her slender shoulders. "Epic westerns have hardly been big the last two decades. Somehow Clint Eastwood and Larry McMurtry picked up where John Wayne left off, and Dad just didn't make the cut. Neither my brother—really, my half-brother—nor me visit much. He's an actor, mostly Broadway stage and the like, goes by name Michael Raymond, but he's recovering from pneumonia in New York."

It amused Jordan that she had found someone who

could outtalk her mother. Michelle even described the story for her new film she'd be working on soon. How wonderful, Jordan mused, to have a romantic comedy to look forward to instead of the mess she was in. For the first time in three days, she almost began to relax. When she described some possibilities for the garden, she remembered how much she loved her work, saving and sharing her unique flowers.

Michelle snatched the check and handed their crew-cut server—who had recognized her by now—a credit card. She signed the receipt with a flourish, then auto-graphed a napkin for the young man, even though it was a linen one and her signature looked shaky. She leaned over to glance at Jordan's watch, lit a cigarette, and jumped up. "If you have a moment, you can meet my father."

Jordan scooped up the plant and hurried after her.

"He always expects people to be prompt, by the way," Michelle said as Jordan fell into step with her down the busy shopping street. "And he's rather used to having his own way."

They walked by several other *al fresco* restaurants where crowded tables dotted the pavement. More than once Jordan was sure someone recognized Michelle. Ah, to feel one was being watched for good reasons, not bad, she thought.

"See, I'm right on time," Michelle called to a tall, thin, silver-haired man who was looking in an art gallery window that reflected them coming up behind him. Like Michelle, he was dressed all in white. He turned slowly to face them, smiling. Bareheaded, with-out sunglasses, he extended his hand and Jordan shook it.

"A great pleasure, my dear," he said with a hint of

a bow. "I do believe you're the only member of your family I haven't met."

"How do you know my family?" Jordan asked, taking a step back.

"Years ago, you see, I directed a film on Lokosee."

She knew instantly what movie it was, but not that he had known her whole family. "You're the director of *Everglades Victory*?" she asked, hoping she didn't sound too naive. "Michelle didn't mention that. Forgive me, Mr. Rey," Jordan floundered, "but I just assumed your name would be Merwyn—stupid of me. I heard what happened with the Seminoles protesting the film. But that movie started my sister Lana on a lifetime love of acting."

"A love of acting?" he repeated, looking pleased.

Jordan tried not to stare, but she couldn't help but marvel at Winston Rey's tight-skinned, boyishly handsome face. Maybe he'd found Ponce de Leon's fabled Fountain of Youth out on his ranch, because the man must be nearly seventy. Only his deeply etched smile lines and mottled hands told the truth about his age. His gray eyes sparkled with the same vitality in his voice. He seemed to cast about him an invisible net of crackling energy, which, as if emerging from the doldrums, Jordan was only too happy to step into. And just wait until she told Mama and Lana about this. Obviously, Lana had not known her early mentor was Michelle Merwyn's father when she criticized her.

"You don't mean your sister's left the area to pursue her acting dream?" he inquired.

"Not exactly," Jordan admitted with a shy smile. "She's just been cast in a play in a local dinner theater. She's still living on Lokosee, married and rearing three kids. But how did you know a Naples orchid grower named Jordan Quinn is related to the Hartmans on Lokosee?"

"How indeed?" Michelle echoed, blowing a smoke ring skyward.

With a smile and a flourish, from inside his pale blue silk-lined sport-coat pocket, Winston Rey produced Jordan's new color publicity brochure and displayed it to both of them with a little *ta-da!* "In your brief bio here," he said with a wink at Jordan, "you're advertising the family business on Lokosee as well as the Orchid Tree. The island is such a small place, I put two and two together, as the name of the fishing fleet hasn't changed, even if the captain has."

"When my father died, Lana's husband, Chuck Washburn, took it over," she explained.

"Ah, such fond memories of J.J. Hartman taking me and the crew fishing," he said with a smile, gazing momentarily skyward as if actually envisioning former times. "I enjoyed the beautiful water there so much I ended up renting a yacht to live on for the duration of the film. As for this pamphlet," he added as if coming back to earth, "I snagged it visiting your shop a bit ago—marvelous displays in there, so I'm certain the SunRay Ranch orchid garden you'll do for us will be absolutely lovely."

Jordan promised him special treatment as Michelle linked her arm through his. Did the woman know how fortunate she was to have a father like this? It made Jordan really ache for her own father's loss.

"Michelle says you don't have much of a green thumb," she told him, with a little lift of the orchid plant she was still carrying, "and that you'd want some 'preserve our plants' visits."

"You bet I would. A black thumb, that's more like it for me. And feel free to bring family members along to renew old acquaintances. Tell them it's a special invitation for auld lang syne."

"That's very kind of you. Mr. Rey, I—"

"Please, call me Winston."

"All right, Winston. I was just wondering if Lana had acting talent, even that young."

"She surely did," he said with an even broader smile that made Jordan realize how proud he was of his career and the lives he'd touched. "I recall your mother told me once she had named her for Lana Turner, and rightly so. I didn't discover your Lana in Schwab's Drugstore but on a dock at Lokosee. She started as an extra, became a walk-on, and ended up with several lines in two scenes." He seemed to study Jordan's intent face. "That movie was good filmmaking, no matter what happened to it. I recall you weren't born then, but have you seen it?"

"To tell the truth—with all the fallout over it," she admitted, "I've only seen it once when I was at a high school party over on Chokoloskee. Someone sneaked it in as if it were X-rated." She shrugged. "Maybe we thought the Seminoles would go on the warpath again if they knew we were looking at it."

He sighed and shook his head. "I can't tell you how much I have deeply regretted all the fallout, as you put it, from that film. I've donated a fortune to Indian causes since, hoping to make amends, usually anonymously, of course, because I half wondered if they'd throw it back in my face."

"Not bloody likely," Michelle put in with a tiny tug on his arm. "Come on, Dad of mine. I'm sure Jordan's busy, and you said you'd take me riding on the ranch this afternoon."

"Do you ride, Jordan?" he asked, not budging.

"I have, but I don't—not lately."

"When you come out, bring your husband, and I'll show you the spread in a swamp buggy then. Who knows, you might find wild orchids there."

"That would be great," she said, extending her hand to shake his when he offered it. "The brochure did mention Lawrence's work with endangered panthers, too, didn't it? But my husband and I are separated and will be getting a divorce—pretty soon."

"I am sorry about that. Well, revelations here, all around," he said and cleared his throat, loosing her hand, then patting Michelle's, still linked through his other arm. "I understand making missteps in marriage, my dear. I do sympathize. Come see us in a few days to look over the garden site, won't you?"

"Yes, all right. And, Michelle, thanks for lunch."

Michelle sauntered away ahead of him, but Winston smiled and took the orchid from her.

Early that evening, Marc Chay showed up at her apartment door with a fragrant, steaming wicker basket of Cantonese food. He stood on the second-floor outdoor landing, smiling at her as if she'd ordered carryout.

Reluctantly, she let him into the apartment. She had still not straightened it since she'd torn it apart looking for cameras. If he had come here to snoop, though, perhaps he wouldn't mind her doing some of the dirty work for him. "What's all this?" she asked.

"*Tien Shuen Yu,*" he told her with a hopeful smile. "Sweet and sour fish, rice, the works. I made it myself from one of my mother's recipes our family restaurant used to feature. The secret is the fresh white fish fillets. I brought some Wan-Fu wine, too. And," he told her before she could protest, "I also stopped by to tell you I checked out Lawrence's contacts with drug

firms as best I could. I believe, together, we can locate him."

She could hardly tell him she wasn't interested in
his information—or his dinner. He began to unload
woven bamboo containers of food where she made a
place for them on the kitchen table.

She crossed her arms over her chest. "It sounds
ominous when you say *drug* firms, as if there's some
sort of dirty dealing going on."

"I should have said pharmaceutical then," he said,
looking suddenly contrite. "I called the three I knew
Lawrence dealt with," he went on, "but they could
give me absolutely no help on why he might have
gone AWOL, as one guy put it. The fourth one, which
I know he mentioned lately, is in Key West, but I
could not find any address or phone number on it.
Not in the Yellow Pages either—nothing."

"He never mentioned Key West to me. It hardly
sounds like a site for a pharmaceutical lab."

"I know. But the point is, we might be able to pursue it further if you'd just rack your brain for places
he might have left his computer files—a copy of a
disk, anything like that. By the way," he plunged on,
when she said nothing else, "whoever stole the tranquilizing drugs from the lab left no fingerprints or any
other forensic evidence, according to the police."

"I'll bet they wouldn't find one fingerprint on the
cameras if I turned those in either," she said.

"What cameras?" he demanded, looking up from
unloading the food. He froze like a statue but for the
slight narrowing of his eyes and a tic that began to
beat at the base of his throat.

She not only told him about the cameras but about
the missing pistol, too. After all, Marc had been with

him when he bought it. "So—you wouldn't have any idea where it went, would you?" she concluded.

"Absolutely not. But I fear something is really wrong," he whispered. She could only nod; she didn't know whether to believe him or not.

"You know," she said at last, clearing her throat, "despite being put off by advice about Missing Persons before, I'm going to the police for help."

His sleek eyebrows lifted his forehead under his glossy hair. "Let me go with you—a concerned friend, that is all."

"I've got to do this alone, but is there anything you can remember about the missing gun? I know Lawrence bought it when you were with him."

Steam rose between them as he glanced down to open the large container of pungent sauce as if he could read some sort of answer there. He lifted his head, and his narrow eyes pierced hers like lasers.

"I've got to be truthful with you. He did not buy that gun, Jordan. It is one of mine I loaned him. I own several—have since my parents were shot by an intruder in their home one night because he thought they were rich." Despite her sharp gasp, he continued, in a rush, "But they had no ready cash around—every dime they put into their porcelain collection or back into the restaurant."

"Marc, I take it they—that's how they died?"

He nodded, looking down at his clasped hands.

"I'm so sorry! I had no idea. Lawrence never told me."

"I never told him. No one knew—here in my new life."

Deeply touched, she reached over to briefly cover his hands with her right one.

"And so," he said, though she had expected he was

too moved to speak, "I got better with guns when I was out West. I learned how to really shoot, to defend myself and what is mine, if it is ever necessary. I will get you the information so we can trace the gun, just like we will find a copy of Lawrence's work. And I will loan you another if you think you need it."

"I keep changing my mind about a gun, but yes, I'll need the details about the pistol you loaned Lawrence."

"Technically, it is a revolver, not a pistol," he explained, seemingly back to business. She marveled at the flashing shift in his moods; he was making her very uncomfortable now. "Revolvers take bullets," he went on, as if lecturing. "Five thirty-eight caliber bullets, in this case, and pistols take clips. You know, Lawrence didn't want to take it at first because it was called a Lady Smith—so small and dainty—just for women, he said. But I told him it was to protect his lady with his life."

She stared at him, her mind racing while she watched him dish out the steaming food. As if they'd been discussing nothing more important than the weather, he said with a smile, "Come on now, try some of this, Jordan. You'll love the sweet and sour."

Chapter Eight

At the Naples Police Station the next morning, Jordan sat in a small room just outside Yancy's office, waiting for him. She had left the cameras in the trunk of her car until she saw how he reacted to what she had to say. She planned to get some advice from him about how to proceed, then to ask him to file a missing persons' report.

"Excuse me, ma'am."

It was the portly sergeant from the front desk. "I got a call that Lieutenant Tatum won't be in for quite a while, and then he's going to be real tied up today. Seems a man's body washed in on the Port Royal beach near Gordon Pass, so that's first priority— maybe his first murder case, as a matter of fact," he said, almost proudly. She could see Yancy was popular here. "So if you'd just leave your phone number," he told her, indicating the front desk, "I'll have him call you when he has some time later."

"I see. A man's body. Yes, I understand." She scribbled her name and number on the WILL CALL sheet the man gave her and went out into the brilliant sunshine. She stood a moment, uncertain. Then, just in case, by some long shot this had some connection to Lawrence being missing, she headed toward the scene of the tragedy.

She had never been given to premonitions or even female intuition, but her hands shook as she drove down Gordon Drive, following the shrill whine of emergency vehicles, getting over twice and stopping when police cars or ambulances passed. Sometimes, even with a fender bender, it seems they sent every rescue vehicle they had. People were out of their houses, walking, some rollerblading or biking toward the cars clumped along the street lined with luxury homes and parklike estates.

She parallel-parked and left her car. The things in her purse bounced as she jogged around four police vehicles and two ambulances, all with lights blinking in the bright day, parked on someone's back lawn. She spotted Yancy down the stretch of beach under the concrete seawall, bending over a wet body that was sprawled facedown in the sand.

Her insides clenched as she stopped and stared.

Paramedics and officers crowded close, but she could see the dead man wore jeans; his white, bare feet pointed toward land. From this vantage point she could not see his head.

She wove her way through the murmuring crowd until she stood on the seawall above the body. The corpse might be about Lawrence's height, but his bare upper torso was bulkier. Besides, the hair looked too dark. They were going to cover him with a blanket, thank heavens, because she didn't want to look any-more or have people stare. She recalled a friend from college had claimed to have an out-of-body experience when he almost died. Strangely, she felt almost de-tached now, as if she were watching herself watching that corpse.

"Did he drown or what?" someone behind her

asked over the wash of the waves. Pieces of voices pierced her.

"Can't tell from here, but I heard he's shot in the head."

"Suicide or what?"

"Execution?"

"Drug runners in Naples? What do they think this is, Miami?"

"Who knows? Body washed in from somewhere."

Oh, thank God, thank God, it absolutely wasn't—couldn't be—Lawrence, she thought, clasping her hands between her breasts. He would never commit suicide, never be out in a boat. He almost got seasick just swimming in the Gulf. And he'd repeatedly refused to go out with Chuck for good-old-boy bonding, even when the water was calm. Yet she could not stop herself from cupping her hands and shouting, "Yancy! Detective Tatum!"

His head swiveled. He rose to his full height, and with quick strides spitting sand, he walked over to the seawall, whipped off his sunglasses, and squinted up at her. It scared her that he didn't ask why she was there.

"Give me your hand," he ordered, reaching up for her.

"Why?" she said, taking a step back, bumping into people pressed in around her. "I just want to know—"

His face looked concerned, strained. His gaze riveted hers as if the others were not there. "I do too. I was going to send someone to get you to be sure."

"Be sure?" she gasped. Her body stiffened, despite her urge to flee.

"Jordan, damn it, give me your hand!" he insisted, shooting a hand up toward her.

"It isn't him. I can tell from here. Lawrence is thinner, blond. That man's hair is dark, so—"

"Being in salt water awhile makes a body bloat and hair look dark. The guy's a blond." His smooth forehead clenched in a frown, but his voice seemed so controlled.

She bent forward, over him, whispering, "It isn't—can't be him!"

"Fine, it isn't him, but just help me out here, or you'll have to ride with me to the morgue and do it there. Is he still missing, Jordan?"

Wide-eyed, she could only nod.

"Come on then. Lean on me."

Hating him, hating this bright, beautiful day, she stooped and gave him her other hand so he could help her down into the sand.

"Yancy, that can't be Lawrence!"

"Just take a quick look to help out the police—help me," he coaxed, his voice not so businesslike now. She dragged her feet in the sand, but he propelled her on, one hand clamped on her elbow, the other pressed in the small of her back.

"Possible victim ID here," Yancy announced. The little crowd around the body parted. She saw a litter of twisted seaweed and broken shells around the corpse. The wash and hiss of the surf came closer. Yancy's arm circled her shoulders as they leaned down together.

"I'm right here with you. Ready?"

She heaved a huge sigh. "Okay."

He motioned to a man who lifted the sopped blanket away from the upper torso.

"This man's beaten black and blue," she said, keeping her eyes on the bare arms and shoulders. "Someone beat this man up!"

"Or he got bruised washing in. The autopsy will tell."

He pulled her down to kneel beside him next to the corpse. From here she could see the face, turned in her direction. She gasped when her gaze jumped to a big deerfly stuck right in the middle of the man's white forehead. But then she realized it was not deerfly season. It was not a deerfly at all.

"Single bullet hole, small caliber, maybe .22 or .38," a man's voice explained, but that blurred by as she just stared.

At least, she thought, trying to keep control, the sea had washed all blood away from the blank face. And the face ... It was—it was ...

Her knees buckled, but Yancy caught and pinned her tightly to his side. "Jordan, is it him?"

She stared at the dead man again, then shook her head frantically. But she had to tell Yancy that the drowned man looked like Lawrence—a bloated, ruined Lawrence. He was her husband and yet a stranger. But he would never kill himself, and if he had been murdered, why?

"Yes," she whispered, wide-eyed. She reached out to touch Lawrence's shoulder, but Yancy pulled her up and back. She shook herself free of him and, when she spoke, her voice sounded calm. "That is—was—Lawrence Quinn."

"All right, everybody," Yancy announced, "we've got a positive ID here. Come on with me, Jordan," he added more quietly.

"I can't leave him here like this."

"We're taking him to the morgue right now. You can see him later."

He pulled her farther away, but she tugged free and turned back. She watched four men lift the covered body onto a stretcher and carry him across the sand away from the encroaching surf. Another man was already placing yellow plastic tape around the outline of the body. Yancy put an arm around her shoulders as they carried Lawrence to an ambulance.

"I'm going with him."

"There's no point, Jordan. Come with me, and we'll call your family."

She wanted to collapse, but Yancy's hands felt sure and strong. Yancy helped her up the back step of an ambulance and climbed in behind her. They sank side by side on a long, plastic-padded seat.

"This is the widow. I'm Lieutenant Tatum," Yancy told two hovering medics, men in dark blue. "Wait outside and close the door so she can have some privacy."

This *was* happening to her, she thought. Lawrence was gone when he did not deserve to die and had so much to live for. This was real, but she could not believe any of it. Why was everything flying out of control, ever since that airplane had dived at her in the Glades?

"Jordan, I'm so sorry for your loss. If there's anything I can do ..."

This time she shook her head so hard it hurt, or had the pain been there all along? Her voice sounded calm but distant. "I have to call his family and mine. Plan a funeral, take care of things."

"In a case like this, it will be awhile before you can have the body."

"A case like this," she echoed his words. She shook her head to clear it and forced herself to look at him. "You mean someone must have murdered him. Yancy, he would not have killed himself."

Yancy shrugged as he shoved a stray strand of hair off his forehead. "A failed marriage, pressure to find some miracle cure. Maybe he had found out he'd failed there, too, and . . ."

"No!" she insisted, shaking her head in defiance of this shock and horror. "He was on the verge of a great discovery. And the two of us had settled things for good."

"Jordan," he said, his tone imploring, soothing as he leaned so close their shoulders touched, "listen to me. If he committed suicide there will be no investigation into possible suspects—no dragging out people's pasts. You understand me. Just keep calm and let me—the system—work."

She sensed the threat he was implying, but was too stunned to care. Afraid she would faint, she propped her elbows on her knees. Before she leaned forward to press her palms over her eyes, she saw two things. Yancy was scribbling down what she had just said. And she was suddenly certain that even if a finding of suicide put her in the clear, the same someone who had been watching them had abducted Lawrence and killed him. But why? And was she next?

Chapter Nine

"I didn't know you'd *all* be here!" Mae cried, skidding to a stop in her dash around the corner of Seth's mobile home. "I just came to tell you something. Seth, can I talk to you a sec?"

He had been eating chocolate ice cream with their parents, Cory and Wilda Cypress, at the picnic table facing the prairie, talking about Frank. Seth had admitted that he and Frank had fought—physically, not only verbally this time—but not about what. He didn't want to alarm them when he had only suspicions about the dart gun or the attack on the panther team. But he had told them Frank seemed depressed before he and his buddies disappeared. His father said that bunch had just taken off before, maybe to get jobs across the state working at the racetrack at Hialeah. He'd be back. But Seth knew his mother was worried.

Now he saw Mae was out of breath, her hair a mess. She looked ready to burst into tears. Neither of his parents' eyes were good enough anymore to read her expression from this distance; he rose from under the table and hurried over to her.

"Something only for Seth's ears?" their mother called out.

"About their white friends. Maybe that woman who came back, visited him," Cory Cypress put in.

"How did they know?" Mae asked Seth, not budging.

"Does the wisdom of the *ayikcomi* still surprise you?" he muttered, taking her arm, but he breathed easier that, at least, it must not be bad news about Frank. "What about Jordan, Mae?"

"Sally, the assistant from Jordan's orchid shop, came to my shop to say that Jordan's husband turned up on the beach," she said in a rush, her hands fluttering. "Dead—shot to death or drowned. Murder or suicide, the police aren't saying yet."

"It can't be," Seth protested, then cursed in Mikasuki. Another attack on a team member, this time maybe murder? With Frank and his buddies gone at the time? He took a step back, feeling he'd been kicked in the belly. He hated to hope someone had committed suicide, but it sure would help.

"If it is murder, do the police have a suspect?" he asked. "They sure as hell aren't going to try to pin this on the Seminoles, too!"

"I don't know. I haven't seen Jordan yet. She went to stay at her mother's place for a day or two. You know, hoping the press won't find her. But it's already been on the noon news, and tomorrow's papers—"

"—will dig up and drag out *everything* again," he finished for her, raking his fingers through his thick hair. Mae nodded, wiping the back of one hand under her nose.

Seth's mind raced. His worries that the media would tie him to Jordan from years ago annoyed him, but that was dwarfed by his fears about Frank. If only he could find him, talk to him, get him a good lawyer if it came to that. And, if he was guilty of raiding the panther team—or this new nightmare—wring his damned neck for dragging himself and the people into this mess.

"Seth," Mae's voice sliced through his thoughts, "I said, are you okay? You feeling guilty? I mean, Jordan wouldn't say," she whispered so their parents couldn't hear, "but I think you upset her pretty bad yesterday at her shop. Now she's going through all this."

He heaved a huge sigh and leaned stiff-armed against a palmetto tree. "Yeah, I know. I do feel bad about that—her. Did you hear anything about what kind of gun was used to shoot her husband?"

"What's all that matter?" she asked, punching his shoulder with a fist. "Just promise me you'll steer clear of her. I thought you should know what happened, but it would hardly be appropriate—"

"Appropriate!" he shouted, shoving away from the tree to face her. She jumped back. "Nothing between Jordan and me was ever appropriate, was it, Mae? Was it, Mother, Dad?" he demanded louder in Mika-suki, glaring at them.

He strode out of the clearing and into the thick grass and brush behind the house. He kept walking, thinking—and, damn it, *feeling* for Jordan. He'd been resentful and angry when she came out to his camp to tell him about the attack on the panther team—but then his old feelings for her had attacked him, too. In her greenhouse she had made him feel as fragile as the glass walls when she defied him. Now he slowed his steps where the ground rose slightly at the site of one of the Calusa Indian shell mounds left behind from the old days before that tribe vanished. Vanished . . . yeah, the old days . . .

From the first time he had seen her at the white man's school his parents were forced to send him to on Chokoloskee, Seth had needed Jordan Hartman. He still vividly remembered his first impression on her. Her hair was the color of Glades sunsets, her eyes the hue of pools reflecting sky on a cloudless day. She might have been skinny and freckled then, unlike any Seminole girl, but he had been attracted instantly.

The unspoken message at school was that even a friendship with her was off-limits to a Seminole, but sassy and sure of herself, Jordan had not seen things that way. For some reason she was fascinated by him and Mae. Even a bully like Yancy Tatum could not tarnish their shiny new friendship. Then it had seemed that a big wind had blown him and Jordan together and swept them away like a hurricane.

"Ever go sliding down the old shell mound on a tray?" she asked him between classes one day, when they were freshmen.

"That little Calusa mound on Chok?" he'd replied with a shrug. "No, but I been down lots bigger ones out in hammocks in the Glades. On a leaf, not some stolen cafeteria tray."

"I didn't steal it. Got it from my dad's boat. But I never did it on a leaf and on a bigger hill. Bet I'd like that."

"I'd show it to you if you wouldn't tell anybody. On Saturday morning, you could meet me, and it would only take a half hour in a dugout to get there," he said, looking sideways at her.

"Mae too?"

"She gotta help my mom."

"Just you and me?"

"Yeah, so forget it," he muttered and turned away.

"I'll be there," she called after him. "Just tell me where."

Those first hours really alone with her were some

of the happiest and proudest of his life. Accepted, trusted—and by Jordan. They slid down again and again, laughing, tumbling, finally shrieking their joy aloud together, when that was not his people's way at all. They ended in a tangle of arms and legs at the bottom, and he rolled them over once so she would not be hurt. But then she was lying flat on top of him with her legs straddling him like a horse.

He sucked in a sharp breath as the power of her presence racked him. He wanted to seize her, crush her to him, become part of her. But the soft sky framed her face and tousled hair. They both went silent and still. Awed. And then he rolled her beside him, slightly under him, and cradled her chin and pressed his cheek to hers, moving, caressing her only that way.

Her sigh of contentment was so sweet it stabbed deep inside him. He'd heard—even seen—how it could be between men and women; it was as if that sigh had captured his spirit forever. In that moment in the golden Glades, he first knew he loved as well as wanted her.

She sent bolts of lightning through him by squirming slightly against him to lift her head and stare so close into his face. "Is it true the Seminoles don't like to kiss?" she asked.

"You mean—on the mouth?"

"Well, yeah," she said with a shaky nod.

"Kissing like that's not our way," he told her, barely breathing.

"That's what I heard. It's kind of sad. You think you're spreading germs or cooties or what?"

But he didn't listen to what else she said. He leaned closer, toward those deep pools of her eyes. His hand gripped her slender waist as he pressed closer to inhale the flower fragrance of her. He tilted his head and lowered his lips to her pouted ones, savoring, then deepening the forbidden kiss. And he had never come up for air again, even three years later, when their parents and their people had forced them into the agony of separation. And maybe they'd blamed each other for that pain ever since.

Seth shook his head to clear it. He sat on the shell mound out behind his trailer, not on that one from the past. Jordan—he had to see her. And for deep, driving reasons he could not even explain to himself.

Jordan paced back and forth on the long screened-in porch of the Hartman home overlooking Chokoloskee Bay. She stared out at the horizon as if it held some answers. Numerous jade green mangrove clumps and clusters that gave the area its name, the 10,000 Islands, stared back at her.

"If you want to take a walk, dear, I'll go with you," Grandma Hattie volunteered as she rocked back and forth in her squeaky wooden chair.

"I'd like to, Grandma, but I have to wait until Yancy Tatum comes. Do you remember Yancy when he was a boy?"

Still she paced, not listening to her grandmother's rambling recital of various pranks the Tatum boys had perpetrated over the years. Her mother came out, wiping her hands with a dish towel after cleaning up from breakfast. Lana had sat up all night with Jordan and had just left, saying she'd be back soon. Even the minister's visit last night had not settled her down enough to sleep. She had been doing a lot of praying, but she still felt frenzied.

"Can't you light anywhere, hon?" Arlene asked as she walked over to put her arms around Jordan's shoulders to stop her steps. "You're going to wear yourself out when you need your strength."

"I'm running on raw adrenaline and anger anyway, Mama," she admitted. But she didn't tell her she was running on fear, too. In her mother's embrace, she sighed. She couldn't just wait around here, being coddled and comforted.

"I have so much to do," she tried to explain as she pulled gently away. "I need to get everything planned and cared for. I wish Yancy would hurry up." Mentally, she ticked the tasks off again, anything to keep from letting terror take her captive.

She had to complete arrangements for a memorial service next Wednesday at the Methodist Church in Olde Naples, whether they had Lawrence's body back by then or not. He was to be cremated and his ashes scattered over the Everglades habitat of the endangered panthers to which he had dedicated his life's work. She wanted to put the condo up for sale. She wanted to find a place to move into back here, but keep the apartment above the shop for nights she had to stay in town. But mostly, she had to work with the police to find out who had killed Lawrence.

"Good of Yancy to say this visit's an old-time friend's condolence call, not official police business," Arlene said behind her back as Jordan turned to stare out the window again.

"Sunday afternoon visits are very neighborly," Hattie added, continually smoothing her skirt over her knees. "Even if someone's coming in an amphibious plane instead of a car or on foot like normal folks."

Both Arlene and Jordan turned to stare at Hattie, astounded at her occasional flashes of lucidity. They were all, Jordan thought as tears stung her eyes again, making a big effort to help her through this. Lana's kids had been so sweet to her last evening, and Chuck had stormed out front the way Dad had once to tell the reporters to get the hell off the property. Later, Jordan had written a brief statement for Lana to read to the press; she'd been on the evening news, looking as if she herself were the tragic victim.

"I hear a plane," Mama said, peering through the window.

"Let me talk to him first, please," Jordan insisted. She went down the steps and across the narrow patch of grass to the water's edge, then out onto the dock.

The house sat high because, like most in the area, it was built on stilts in case storm tides or hurricanes hit these barrier islands. A typical tin-roofed, old-style Florida home—though built new in '68 after Hurricane Donna—it had a wraparound screened porch and high ceilings to catch and hold Gulf breezes. Once her parents' dream home, it was still one of the largest on little Lokosee Island.

Reached only by a ferry, Lokosee still had the ambiance of a holiday site or fishing camp, while the bigger neighboring island of Chokoloskee boasted an airstrip and causeway to the mainland. But Yancy had insisted he would fly in right to their door because he was pressed for time, working all weekend on possible leads about Lawrence.

Jordan had given permission for forensic experts to comb the condo and explained why she'd torn it apart already. She'd handed over the surveillance cameras. He'd assured her they were working with the Coast Guard to check marinas for a vessel that Lawrence might have either rented or been taken out in. And they were interviewing people at the condo and trying to trace the blue van with Challenger license plates driven by an Hispanic man as well as looking for possible links to the attack on the panther team. Jordan had even explained about the gun under the bed, and Yancy had sent someone to see Marc for information about it.

The cream-colored plane circled once, then coasted in on its pontoons; it putted up to the dock where the family kept a small motorboat and a canoe. Chok Bay was very shallow, especially at low tide, so all bigger boats had to be docked in the dredged area of Smugglers Bay. This area had once all been Seminole terrain, across which they poled their flat-bottomed dugout canoes. She saw Yancy had the window down on the passenger side of the plane; he waved to her and she waved back.

She sent the pilot in to have coffee with Mama and Hattie. But she didn't get a chance to say anything before he hugged her to him, pressing her head under his chin, his arms around her back, and didn't let her go.

"Yancy," she protested after a moment and pushed him away. His arm and chest muscles were as hard as rock.

"That's what I wanted to do at the beach," he whispered into her hair. "Comfort you, help you as an old friend." He dipped his head to look into her face as he finally released her. Even with his opaque sunglasses on, his expression was intense. Quickly, she turned away and indicated the wooden bench on the dock.

He hesitated before sitting beside her, perhaps sizing up her actions or emotions. Dressed in crisply creased slacks and ironed, short-sleeved shirt, he seemed a Stallone or Schwarzenegger in a suit. His spit-polished shoes reflected the sun darkly. When he sat—a bit too close—he put one arm behind her on the bench, turning to her and propping one bent leg over the other knee. He bounced his foot to a silent beat. The moment was unbearably awkward, but she had a big question to ask him before anything else happened.

"Yancy, up front, I need to know one thing. Do I need a lawyer for any reason?"

He whipped off his sunglasses, revealing bright, blue eyes. "Not unless you have something to confess to me."

"Confess to you?" she cried, her mouth dropping open. "You don't think . . ." She bounced to her feet, but he pulled her back.

"Of course, I don't, so why are you bringing it up? Stop acting like you don't trust me," he scolded, frowning. "I think you're innocent of any involvement with Lawrence's death, and I'm going to prove it. Suicides don't always swallow the gun. Sorry—police lingo. You know what I mean, but damn it, Jordan, at least let me help you."

"So I am not under any sort of suspicion for foul play?" she repeated, leaning slightly closer to him. "You know, domestic difficulties and all—"

Pressing his narrow lips into a tight line, he shook his head and held up one big hand. "I can personally give you an alibi for that day he disappeared, at least for some of it. So if you can just explain where you were the couple of hours between the time I got you back to your car and you finally pulled into your condo and talked to that gardener there . . ."

"So you have been investigating me. This *is* to be an interrogation. I saw you write down what I said right after I identified Lawrence."

"It's all standard procedure. No, this is not an interrogation. I understand how distraught you are, but

how many times do I have to tell you that I'm a
friend." She watched him tap his glasses on his thigh.
Pent-up frustration seemed ready to explode from
him. "Jordan," he went on, his voice strained but
calm, "I told you on the phone, I'm here to pay a
condolence call on you, your family—and I often visit
my mom Sunday afternoons. With Dad away and
everyone scattered, she's really alone, know what I
mean?"

"I do, and admire how good you are to her. Thanks
for that explanation and your assurances, but you
won't like where I was after you got me to my car
that day," she admitted and leaned against the back
of the bench to look out over the water. "But I do
have at least three people who saw me."

He sat up straighter. "What do you mean I won't
like it?"

"I didn't want to be the cause of Seminole-white
upheaval like years ago. So I tried calling the reservation to explain what had happened before it hit the
papers."

"Didn't I tell you not to?" he demanded. "And only
for your own good, believe me. When will you get it
through that pretty head that I'm trying to take care
of you?"

She ignored that. She knew she had to tell him the
rest, even if it upset him. "It's just that the tribal chairman wasn't able to be reached by phone, so I drove
out to tell him. His sister Mae and her husband saw
me, too. After I explained things to him, I went directly home and found Lawrence gone."

"Damn it all to hell, Jordan!" he said. He looked
so alarmed and anguished it scared her. "Go ahead,
use the guy's name at least. You think I'm some kind
of moron? Yeah, I never could stand the guy, espe-

cially considering how he screwed up your life years ago. Listen," he went on, lowering his voice again, "I'm only trying to protect you. How does it look when you're having marital problems and sneaking off to see your old flame the very day your husband mysteriously disappears?" She saw his handsome face clench into a sneer before he controlled himself again.

"Those two things aren't related," she insisted, fighting for calm. "The point was not that it was Seth Cypress, but that it was the tribal chairman."

"This is tearing me apart, you know." He hit both fists on his knees. "My boss already asked if he should take me off this case because of my past friendship with you, and I said no. But I don't want to have blinders on here." He shoved his sunglasses back on his face and glared at her.

"I've told you everything now," she said, trying to soothe him. "And I was coming in to see you at the police station when I heard there was a body on the beach. Yancy, I *am* relying on your advice through all this."

He sat up straight again, bouncing the back of the bench. His expression reminded her of a kid who had been punished then forgiven. "That's what I like to hear," he said brightly. "I just get overprotective, I guess. See, if I didn't know you so well from way back, I'd wonder why you were scratched and bruised that day in the Glades and why you ransacked your condo after it was turned upside down once already. Then you—and no doubt Seth's sister—benefit financially from Lawrence's demise. And, unfortunately, a Lady Smith and Wesson—that missing gun Marcus Chay loaned you and Lawrence—is a .38 special, when ballistics shows that was the caliber bullet that killed him.

So I'm just saying, trust me to steer you through this minefield, and everything will be all right. Got that?"

Even as she stiffened at his listing of points against her, she saw him slide closer on the bench. Finally, he pressed a solid thigh against hers. His gaze darted down over her and then back to her face. She squirmed uneasily at the prolonged contact.

"Thanks again for your advice and help, Yancy," she said, and stood, wrapping her arms protectively around herself, because she sensed that's exactly what he wanted to do.

"I'm looking at it this way," he said and stood to drape one arm almost nonchalantly over her shoulder as she started to walk away. "Even though you told me the deceased got seasick, he could of killed himself—one shot, standing on the edge of a rented boat, then fallen in to be sure he did the job. I've got a report of a man who leased a boat out up by Wiggins Pass and never brought it back. The initial description matches Lawrence, and maybe the dock manager can make an ID. Just give me a few days with this, and I'll get everything taken care of for you, I swear I will. Then you'll be able to start your new life free and clear."

"Free and clear?" she repeated, stepping away from him to break his touch. "I don't know if I'll ever feel like that again."

She sensed his irritation at her moving away from his touch again, but he kept it out of his voice. "Sure you will. Anything else you want to know?" he asked, blocking her continued exit down the dock.

"Do I have to stay in Naples? I was thinking about coming back here after I settled a few things."

"Here?" he asked, indicating the house. They saw her mother had come out on the steps. Leaning over the railing, she motioned to them. Jordan nodded, and they started walking again.

"I wouldn't live here permanently," she explained, "but I'll find a place of my own either on Lokosee or Chok, and drive back and forth to the shop weekdays."

"Sure, just so I know where you can be reached at all times. Besides, like I said, I get down here a lot." He took her arm, tucking it through his as they walked down the dock. There was no place to go to break the contact.

"Jordan," he went on, his voice warm as the sun now, "remember the time you and I sat out here kind of late one night when we were kids?" He turned to her with a smile she could not return, but he seemed lost in memories as he gestured with his free hand. "The mosquitoes were bastards despite the smudge pot. I made you one of those glow rings of lightning bug bodies, and I was skipping clamshells, and we were eating popcorn your mom fixed, and we said we'd be friends forever. Remember?"

She didn't. They must have been so young, way before Seth, who had obliterated so much that had come before. "Lots of good memories of Lokosee," she said, tugging her arm free when they reached the shore.

To evade his eyes and touch, she went quickly ahead of him up the steps, her mind racing a million miles a minute. If Yancy wasn't going to call this a murder and solve it, she would somehow have to. For him, it was evidently a chance to rekindle feelings that had smoldered over the years ... flames that could only burn her and she wanted to stomp out.

Chapter Ten

Carefully, quietly, just after midnight, Seth poled the canoe across the inky bay toward Lokosee. He had not taken this watery path for over a decade, but the feelings it evoked simmered his blood: the thrill of the forbidden, the tension from pent-up emotions, the explosive physical ache of soon seeing and touching and making love to Jordan.

But he hadn't come to make love now.

The slice of new moon shone silver as he stabbed his pole in the water and shattered it. He knew what he must do, even if no one else would ever understand him. Frank certainly didn't understand he was not giving up the old ways of the people, just because he used some of the white man's ways and weapons as tribal chairman. His father was more supportive, but he was so steeped in customs—the sacred medicine, blessings, and curses—he sometimes couldn't grasp that there were other ways to live. His stand against Seth and Jordan's elopement might not be so unbending now, and yet his father's final words today stuck in his mind like a well-placed poison dart: *Remember, my son, it saps a leader's strength to be near a new widow. It will only hurt you if you go to her. Let Mae tell the woman you are sorry for her loss.*

But he was going to her anyway to find out more

about Lawrence's death. He had to be sure Frank was not involved. And he felt compelled to see her.

His hands clenched the pole as the Hartman house came in view. All the windows—in Jordan's bedroom, too—were dark. He used to be so careful coming here like this, even when he'd been told to stay away, daring to go inside where she'd left the door unlatched for him, after her father started locking it. But now her watchful, wily father was not alive to stop him. After Mae's visit here earlier today, unknowing of his plan, she had told him that only Jordan's mother, the old grandmother, and Jordan would be here tonight.

He nosed the canoe in and heard its sudden scuff against the low-tide sand. The cries of owl and night heron pierced the night; somewhere a screech owl screamed.

He unsheathed his knife and stepped ashore.

Jordan could not sleep. But, strangely, now that she had decided she must discover who had killed Lawrence, it was not memories of him that pursued her, but memories of Seth.

She wished she hadn't seen him at his Glades camp and in her greenhouse. Tonight, when she knew she faced the future on her own, she hated feeling so tangled in the distant past . . .

They had gone swimming out on Sanibel Island the third day after they had run away together and been married. Both were sore from making love in bed all night, and by day on the couch, or in the tub, or even on the rug with those funny, faded flowers.

The sun on the sand and Gulf had been hot that day at the beach—blinding. But they searched for shells, splashed in the surf, ate the peanut butter sandwiches and sodas she'd packed. Seth's skin had bronzed even darker, and they'd gotten some narrowed looks on the beach because she was so fair. She'd burned because she'd never thought to take any suntan lotion when she'd left home, and they were tight on funds until he got a construction job in Fort Myers. But they'd promised themselves this week first.

Lying by his side, her body molded in the sand, her arm touching his, she could smell his clean, salty skin and the tart odor of his wet hair. He had turned to her, propped up on one elbow with that dark splash of wild black hair in his eyes, and put his hand on her flat belly and stroked her there, his thumb sliding down beneath her bikini. Then they'd gotten hotter than the sun and darted back into the seagrape bushes off the public beach to kiss again and again. But no-see-ums and sand burrs had made even a temporary bed there impossible.

So they'd decided to leave early, and he pushed that rusty rattletrap so fast they got stopped for speeding on Summerlin Drive. At first, they were terrified the cops had been sent to find them and had spotted them by their license plate. When they heard they only had to pay a fine, as broke as they were, they happily complied.

Still, Seth drove fast the rest of the way back, so they could be alone together, to laugh and touch and love ...

"Oh," she sighed and pulled her legs together into a tight fetal position even though she lay tensed, too warm and disheveled with the sheet strangling her body, her T-shirt nightgown twisted up above her hips.

She strained to listen. Yes, again—the distinctive cry of the whippoorwill and a rustling sound.

"It can't be," she whispered. Surely, her thoughts had just made her imagine that. Goose bumps peppered her arms; her stomach seemed to drop away. Again, the two sounds that years ago had meant, *Come out! Come out to me, or let me in!*

She shook her head to be sure she was not dreaming or drugged by the sleeping pill she had finally taken. Lawrence was dead, she reminded herself. This is 1994, not 1983. Seth could not be outside, calling for her. Only Daddy had caught on to their secret signals, and he was dead, too.

Trembling, she tiptoed to the window that overlooked the bay. It was warm, even for January, and she had left her window open. She jumped back when the leafy branch swished against the screen, the second sign so she would not sneak out each time she heard only a whippoorwill's call.

It had to be Seth. But now? Why? He had no right to be here, and now she'd have to go out to send him away before Mama heard him and thought they'd had something going recently—like Yancy probably did.

She did not click on the light or make a sound. She grabbed her pale blue terry cloth robe from the doorknob and padded barefoot out and down the hall, through the living room where the door to the porch creaked. That jolted her because it didn't used to. She hesitated, waiting to be caught. Then she went across the porch and out and down the steps to the bay.

Time stopped and spiraled back upon itself. She felt mesmerized, possessed by the past before all the pain began.

She saw the shadow of his canoe where he always came ashore, but she started when he came out from under the steps.

"I had to see you and couldn't think of a good way," he whispered, staring up at her.

She leaned over the railing. "I can't believe you're

here. I don't need any more of your questions or accusations," she whispered. "You'd better go."

"Not until you talk to me. Jordan," he said and reached up to cover her hand, which she did not—suddenly could not—pull back, "I want to apologize for how I've been acting. And I'm sorry for your pain—again."

She sighed and nodded. Those few words touched her deeply. Tears blurred her vision, momentarily making two Seths. "Okay," she said, tugging her hand back. "Thanks. But you'd better go."

"Come with me, just over to our spot for a few minutes where we can talk. Our voices will carry here—someone might look out," he said and gestured toward the dark house.

She glanced at the house, then out along the dock where Yancy had thrown his fit about her being with Seth after all these years. But she had to be honest with herself: she wanted to be with him. She tried to tell herself that she could use him as a sounding board. After all, he was a lawyer. But she had to admit that was not all of it. When she nodded again, he recaptured her hand to lead her to the canoe. She picked her way after him, her feet no longer hardened to the shell-littered shore.

She sat cross-legged in the bottom of the prow before it hit her that she was out here only in her underpants, T-shirt, and robe. She felt her nipples tighten in the cool night air. She crossed her arms over her breasts and studied what he wore: it appeared to be black jeans and a tight, dark T-shirt. He walked into the water to push off, then climbed in. Looming over her, he moved them out with the long pole, standing, balancing, reaching, thrusting.

Meeting like this years ago, they had never gone far

from the house—just beyond the first small mangrove island. But it had grown huge and dark with the years. So, about fifty yards out, he slipped the canoe into the shelter of the clawlike mangrove water roots and rustling leaves. Even though he sat down about three feet away, she tingled with memories of his touch.

"I know Mae gave you my condolences," he said, not whispering now. "But I had to do it in person, too. With the police and press, let alone your family and friends, I thought I would only make things worse by coming to the memorial service. Besides, I have nothing—of him—to remember."

She sat stone still. "Yes."

"I could hardly send flowers—not to you," he went on as if he'd memorized a speech. "I'll make a contribution to the panther fund, from Mae and me."

"Thanks. Good. I'm asking for that in lieu of flowers."

"Jordan," he said, leaning slightly toward her, one arm across his bent knees, "I wish I could help you— be a lawyer, a friend, bodyguard, anything you need right now. But that would hardly work either, not with Yancy leading the investigation."

"That's the truth," she said, staring at his dark silhouette, silvered by moonlight. "You and the Seminoles don't need to get involved in this, too."

He seemed to jerk to attention. "You don't think," he asked, "there's any chance he'll try to tie this to the alleged Seminole attack on the other team members?" She could see his broad shoulders tense. So that was it, she thought: he was hoping the Seminoles would not be tied to Lawrence's murder.

"He says he's convinced it's a suicide," she assured him.

His shoulders slumped as he sighed in apparent relief. For a moment silence hung heavily between them until she said so loudly her words seemed to jump back at them, "Despite our problems, I know I certainly didn't kill him!"

"Shh," he soothed, holding up a hand. "Of course you didn't. Surely, no one would believe that. But even though you're safe that way, please let me know—call or through Mae—if I can give you any kind of help or support. You seem to be the common denominator in the mysterious happenings with the team, so you've got to be careful."

She nodded jerkily as she gripped both sides of the dugout as if to steady herself. "You mean that about offering help—after everything? Even when our being together could look bad? Yancy wasn't real pleased to hear I'd gone out to warn you."

"That bastard's only grown up from sneaky bully to lawful commando." He hit both fists hard on the side of the canoe, making the wood shudder.

"So I've seen. But I don't want to rile him right now and have him after me—you know, to rock the boat," she added with a little catch in her voice at her choice of words, "while I look around for myself."

Seth was the one who gently rocked the boat as he inched forward, his knees still bent before him. "What do you mean, while you look around yourself?"

"The thing is," she said, grateful to be able to say to him what she had not to Yancy, "I don't agree Lawrence killed himself. Absolutely not."

"Then who? Do you have any clues at all? *You're* not saying it's the same guys you saw in the Glades?" He had come close enough that she could see the planes and angles of his rugged face, deeply etched by shadows. Was he really feeling concern for her—or those alleged Seminoles?

"Seth, I have no idea who or why. Maybe because of something secret with his work. I have to find out, because—I haven't told anyone else this—sometimes I think someone's been watching me as well as him."

"Damn! But you're not sure? Did you share his work—know what was going on?"

"Barely. Especially not lately." Her voice wavered. Did he have to keep moving closer? "But he did say," she admitted, locking her arms around her bent knees, "that what he was working on could mean power and money. Maybe someone thought he had already found the link between panther immunity to feline AIDS symptoms and a cure for human HIV. And they— maybe some big pharmaceutical firm or a rival scientist—thought they could cash in on that by making Lawrence tell them—and then he wouldn't. I just don't know, but I've got to find out."

"Not on your own, Jordan. I can't stomach Yancy, but this is what the police should do, not you." His knees almost touched her feet. Unlike most canoes, Seminole dugouts had no seats. She remembered all too well how much room there was for two entwined bodies to stretch out and how the canoe would rock rhythmically when they loved. She went hot all over.

From some unseen source, ripples lapped against the canoe. Adrift in each other's moonlit and shadowed gaze, they seemed to hang suspended as he touched her. His thumb rhythmically rubbed the palm of her hand and inner wrist, electrifying her skin and hair. She could feel him breathe and sense his leashed power.

"I really appreciate your offer," she said, realizing she'd been holding her breath. "But this is a nightmare I have to get through on my own."

With a low groan that sounded like regret, he loosed

her. He stood easily and bent to pick up his pole. The canoe rocked hard; he ducked under the canopy of leaves to guide them out.

"Are you going to stay in Naples?" he asked as if looking for just conversation between them again.

"I'm going to come back here—somewhere."

"Does your family still own that land with the old lodge?"

She sucked in a breath of surprise. Why hadn't she thought of that, the old hunting cabin? It was not on the islands but close to this bay, on the edge of a prairie that merged with the Glades. She'd taken picnics there, used it for a retreat since her dad's death, though Lawrence had not liked the place at all. As a child, she had lived there for weeks at a time with her father, and Seth used to visit when Dad was out hunting. The cabin was a bit isolated from everything else, but that was good as well as bad.

"It would really need some work, but I've always loved it there," she admitted, craning around to look at him. "It's mine now. My father left it to me."

"I used to think it was a real palace compared to the place we lived then. If you want, I'll come out at night and help you fix it up."

She did not answer, and then the canoe scraped the shore. Hadn't he heard her say she had to proceed on her own—that their being together could be dangerous? And she was not sure she trusted his motives any more than she did Yancy's or Marc's.

He gave her a hand to steady her out. They stood a moment, melded, fingers and palms. He gave a tiny tug. She went into his arms, pressed so hard to him she could not breathe. His chest flattened her breasts; his belt buckle imprinted on her flesh. Her arms around his strong neck, she anchored him even tighter against her. They stood strong like that, one being.

She gave his hard shoulders a little shove with her fists. Because his arms clamped around her waist did not budge, that move only tilted her hips harder into his. She could feel the whole length of him, powerful, ready.

Then he freed her and turned away. Without another word he climbed in the canoe and poled it out from shore and did not look back. She stood watching his shadowy form shrink across the water before she picked her way over the shells and climbed the steps. On the porch, she froze when she heard the creak of Grandma's rocker. Her heart thudded even harder. She saw her silhouette, facing head-on, just watching.

"I can't believe it," the woman said and stopped rocking.

Jordan gasped. It was not Grandma Hattie. "Mama?"

"I heard you come out here and thought you might need a shoulder to cry on, but I see you had one. A Seminole canoe—I guess I can still recognize that. Have you been seeing him all these years?"

Jordan sank on the end of the chaise longue and pulled the robe over her knees. "No. That's only the third time I've seen Seth in eleven years. I wouldn't do that to Lawrence, even when we were apart."

"The only reason I am not carrying on—as you well know I can do—is—"

"Because I'm no longer some scared teenager?"

"Because Lawrence was such a crappy son of a bitch to you."

"Mama!"

"Don't tell me not to speak ill of the dead," she said and shook her finger. "He never wanted the children you deserved and downright ignored you when it suited him," Mama went on. "Lana and I could see that. Then for you to be the one who moved out like he was some ivory tower prima donna, and don't tell me he was smart, because he wouldn't even listen to reason."

"You—talked to him about it?"

"Yes, I talked to him about it. Told him to get himself down here once or twice for a chat," she said, now gripping the arms of the chair.

"He never said."

She started to rock angrily as she spoke, the creaks punctuating her rods. "Either because I told him not to, or it slipped his mind the moment he turned back for comfort to that cold computer and those experiments of his. I certainly hope and pray you haven't taken up with that Seminole again, but I hear he's been divorced awhile—as *you* should have been years ago, I don't care what your money problems were!"

"That was our business."

"Your well-being has always been my business, yours and Lana's. I'm sorry Lawrence died so violently and young with a lot of life ahead of him, but it's good riddance for you, my girl." She suddenly stopped rocking; the silence in the room was deafening as she stood and pointed again. "You've picked the wrong man twice, so maybe next time you'll get someone more your own kind, like Chuck or Yancy Tatum. I told Lawrence the Bible says, 'Better a dinner with herbs where love is, than a whole ox and hatred at the table.' "

Jordan stood, too. "What? Mama, I never hated him."

"I did!"

In a ghostlike swirl of white nightgown, Arlene

stalked into the house leaving Jordan staring aghast at the dark door. Her legs trembling, she sank on the edge of the chaise longue behind her. If anyone else had spoken of Lawrence that vehemently right now, she would have reported him or her to the police as a possible suspect in his murder. But Mama? What other hidden feelings did she have coiled inside her?

Deflated and weary, Jordan leaned over to prop her elbows on her knees and put her face in her hands. At least, evidently by comparison, Mama thought her secret meeting Seth had paled by comparison. But if Mama knew the overpowering allure he still had for her even now, she'd probably go back to hating him, too.

Over the years, Jordan had tried to build resentment against him, tried to convince herself he had never been right for her, tried to be happy and go on with life. But it had never been the same without him, and she wasn't sure she could do without him now. And for Mama to mention Yancy as a paragon of a man for her ... She shuddered and a chill raced through her.

She got up from the longue to turn it toward the sweep of screened windows overlooking the dark view of the bay. Waiting for dawn, she sat there, thinking, planning, fearing.

Chapter Eleven

"Since you never liked it here, Lawrence, you'd better wait in the car," Jordan said.

As she gazed out at her father's old hunting lodge, she put her hand on the bronze canister of his ashes belted into the passenger seat beside her. Lawrence's body had been found a week ago today. She was sure she was going crazy sometimes, talking to him this way—of course out of everyone else's earshot. But pretending she had him to reason things out with did help her to lay plans. Thinking through convoluted theories—that was one thing at which Lawrence had been a master.

"I swear to you, I will find out who killed you, no matter how much Yancy tries to prove suicide, even if he always says that would clear me. As soon as Marc or I figure out what you were on to, I'm going to pass it on to the right sources. Whatever went wrong with us, Lawrence, I will let your dedication and brilliant work be your legacy, and not in the wrong hands."

Turning off the car engine, she slumped back in her seat. She was on her way to meet Marc and two other of Lawrence's colleagues at the Naples airport where they were going up in the panther team's plane to scatter Lawrence's ashes. They had offered her the use of the panther spotting plane for this, and she'd accepted, but she just had to take this little detour away from everything first.

This was the first time—other than in her bed at night—she'd really had to herself. She'd been so busy with all the personal, legal, and police procedural business of Lawrence's death. His grieving mother and sister's family had gone back to Baltimore, and she had told Sally to open the shop today. Life had to go on.

"I'll be right back," she said and got out to walk around.

Made of sturdy pine and cypress, the one-floor hunting lodge had withstood time and weather. It was elevated on concrete foundation blocks to keep out dampness, rodents, and snakes. The double aluminum roof not only shed rain slickly but made the interior cooler in summer and warmer in winter. The air-conditioning and central heating was simply the hearth, high ceilings, windows, and the wraparound screened porch.

Mama, Lana, and Chuck hardly ever set foot on the premises, though she'd brought her nieces and nephew here for picnics. Still, these last years it had been more like an unvisited museum. As a child, sometimes for weeks at a time as Daddy's "chief cook and bottle washer," she'd been so happy here. She didn't like to think about it, but her parents' marriage, too, had its problems, because several times they'd lived apart over some disagreement. Maybe the fact that Daddy was the one who had moved out then had made Mama especially angry at Lawrence lately.

In contrast to the unchanged exterior of the house itself, in typical Everglades fashion, the grounds had quickly gone wild. Shrubs, tall grass, fruit trees—lime, banana, and papaya—and flowers had rampaged and marauded so close they looked as if they would devour the place. But she could handle that with mower, saw, and clippers. She was looking forward to creating her own orchid garden here.

She bent down to grope for the key hanging on a nail under the back steps. As far as she knew, her nearest deep-Glades neighbors were still her father's old hunting cronies, "the Turner boys," fifteen miles through prairie and swamp. They had been her friends, too, and she knew she should visit them someday soon.

As she let herself in the creaky back door, the inside smelled achingly familiar. Morning light slanted in through the dirty windows. With doors at either end, the central breezeway of this classic "dog trot" cabin sliced the interior in two equal parts. Half of the house was a big living area—a "great room" they'd call it today, with cedar beams above. Her rugs and furniture would look fine here when she tossed out the mounted fish and dusty deer heads. Those were the only things about the place she had not had in common with Daddy: she thought fishing was boring and hunting horrible. Yet the walls echoed back their happy times together—and his teasing voice singing off-key:

"J.J. would waltz with the strawberry blonde while the band played on. He'd glide 'cross the floor with the girl he adored while the band played on . . ."

She smiled as she had then, feeling him twirl her while she gave her red, curly head a toss, so happy, so important, so loved.

The other half of the house had a big bedroom and a smaller one they'd called the bunk room, as well as a bathroom, kitchen, and storage area. The generator and septic tank out back worked fine; no phone had ever graced this getaway, but she could use her cell phone until she got a line installed; the well water was still good if slightly eggy, but she could buy bottled drinking water.

Yes, it was where she would come for a refuge, at least for now. Seth, of course, and maybe Yancy knew where it was, but no one else from Naples. It felt safe to her. And she'd been pleased to see she had neighbors down the narrow road now, even if distant ones: two weekend-type cottages and a small store with a crudely lettered sign that read GAS, ICE, BOOZE, BAIT, AND BULL. Typical. This area and place were pure old-time cracker heaven, and she couldn't wait to be back. With a tight smile she went out and locked the door, this time taking the key.

"I don't really want to get a watch dog, Lawrence," she said as she got back in the car. "But I think I'd better, considering everything. I sure miss Micco— Mike to you. What happened to him? Did you take him with you or did someone take you and the cat, too? Oh, Lawrence," she cried, gripping the steering wheel, looking at that small, cold canister that was all of him now, "who took and hurt you? And *why*?"

"Seth," Mae said over the phone as he was getting ready to drive over to see the rancher with whom they had the fence problem, "Frank's back. The kid's got new boots, leather covers for his seats in the truck, presents for Mother, me, and the girls. But before I tell you where he is, you gotta promise you're not gonna get in another knock-down-drag-out with him."

"Are his buddies with him?"

"Nope. Says they're still over at the Miami racetrack sweeping out stalls and polishing tack. You gonna promise me?"

"Unless he starts it first."

He heard her expel a sigh. "He seems in a real good mood, Seth, quiet but not depressed. Even if he starts it, don't you finish it, okay? Wilson just called to say he's out with him by the stables along the north fence. Please, just keep calm and—"

"Bye, Mae," he said and was out the door.

When Seth pulled up, he saw Wilson had Frank helping fix a wheel on a supply wagon. He got out slowly; Wilson greeted him and Frank nodded. He wore green, opaque sunglasses—totally unusual.

"Real fancy," Seth observed with a smile and a nod at Frank's shiny snakeskin boots that had to be custom made.

"Not as fancy as you look," Frank said, eyeing his business suit. "Didn't dress like that to see me."

"I'm going over to talk to the guy who owns the ranch where the cattle been coming through. Thought I'd look official."

"Thought you gonna serve that one with papers," Wilson put in, talking around the nails he held in his mouth. "Sue his ass."

"I'm curious—gonna give him a chance first. So," he said to Frank, wishing Wilson wouldn't try to get him off track, "you obviously got yourself a good job, brother. At the Hialeah track, Mae mentioned."

"Yeah, Danny, Larry, Jack, and me. Pretty funny seeing these range quarterhorses after looking at racing thoroughbreds for a week," he admitted, staring down at Wilson's work.

Frank seemed normal again—at least not broken like last time he'd seen him. But maybe not as defiant as usual, either, and that made him feel better.

"They gave you a day off so soon, huh?"

"See, Wilson," Frank said, "with Seth and me it's always like it's some game show and he's the emcee. But there's never any prizes."

Wilson gave Seth a pointed look, then bent back to hammering nails while Frank steadied the wheel, frowning down at it. Seth knew then Mae had only told him Frank was here because she'd made Wilson promise to play referee.

Seth strolled a little closer and tried to sound nonchalant. "I wouldn't ask if I didn't give a damn, Frank. Maybe I went about it wrong last time. The thing is, the Naples police are searching for four Seminoles who abducted a panther, roughed up the panther team, and left a broken Seminole dart gun—like the one Dad gave me that's missing now, like the one you knew about—at the scene. Worse, another member of the team—Jordan's husband, Lawrence—turned up dead."

"Yeah," Frank muttered. "Mae said."

"So," Seth went on, daring to rest a hand on his shoulder, "it's just I'm real scared they're eventually gonna erroneously narrow their suspects to four guys who were out and about that day—at least one with a rifle—and then took off so they wouldn't get questioned by me or the police. Motive—well, maybe at least one of the guys hates the whites for what some real sick jackasses did to him a couple of years ago. Or maybe he wants to get back at the tribal chairman for coming down hard at him, I don't know."

Frank let go of the wheel as Wilson eased it back to the ground, put the hammer in his tool belt and clapped his hands free of dirt.

"Nice you're just explaining," Frank said, hooking his thumbs in his new-looking leather belt, "not asking me about this—'cause you know me better'n that. I don't hate all the whites. Matter-of-fact, I like the ones that pay well—the joke's on them, you know? But you wanta play big brother and call my new boss or have me get a note I been working hard, not robbing banks, not thieving dart guns and shooting whites with them? That what you want?"

"Of course not," Seth said, shaking his head at Wilson as he stepped between them, pretending to check the other side of the wheel. Seth was torn between desperately wanting to believe the boy and thinking the whole thing was just too much of a turnaround too fast—too good to be true. "The only question I have, Frank, is if you'll have some dinner with Josh and me before you head back across the state. He's missed you—we could shoot some baskets, too," he said forcing himself to lightheartedly make the shooting gestured followed by a *swish* sound.

"Sorry, gotta leave too soon. But next time, why not?"

"Sure," Seth said, jamming his hands in his jeans pockets. Somehow, this time he felt the younger one, like some adult business had been pulled over his eyes but he couldn't quite grasp what. Thank God, Frank seemed to have changed, but so fast—how and why?

When Michelle Merwyn spotted the stranger striding toward the ranch house, she slammed the door of her rented sports car and hurried across the driveway to intercept him. He looked like a real, corn-fed hunk. But, amazingly out here, he wore a dark pinstriped suit and dusty cowboy boots. Mmm, better and better, she thought: the larger-than-life Marlboro man had stepped off his billboard. With a predatory little grin as she stalked him, she wondered if that little bump on his hip was a six-shooter or a beeper.

He obviously saw her coming, but did not break stride. She hurried faster to catch him.

"Hello," she called to the man. "You have business here?"

His eyes—dark in a hawkish face—studied her up and down as he stopped and turned to her. Yum, she thought. At least this was a buff specimen of a Native American. If he wanted to take a hostage, she'd be more than willing.

"Yes," he said, his voice deliciously rough. "With Winston Rey. Is he here?"

"He was awhile ago. Hi, I'm his daughter, Michelle Merwyn," she said and extended her hand with a tentative smile. "Let me take you in to him."

"I'll wait here, but I'd appreciate it if you'd get him."

"You mean you're here without an appointment? You aren't selling something, are you?"

"Just tell him Seth Cypress wants to see him, Ms. Rey."

Oh, damn, he didn't know her with this Ms. Rey stuff, and she was dying to know him. She saw he wore no wedding ring, but maybe Indians didn't. He handed her a card from inside his suit coat pocket. She forced her eyes down to skim it.

"Oh, an attorney and chairman of the Seminoles. So, just make yourself at home on the porch, and I'll tell him you're here."

He did not follow her up onto the Victorian veranda of the sprawling house. Two Burmese cats tried to get out onto the porch when she opened the screened door, but she nudged them back in.

She glanced back at Seth Cypress through the screen, but he was surveying the lawn and the front of the spread. She realized that the guard on the approach road had not stopped him along the driveway or evidently phoned his presence into the house. She had just come up that way herself. So where was his car?

She found her father in his den on the phone with his door ajar and two cats curled on his desk. She tiptoed in, pointed, and laid the card in front of him. Abruptly, he said good-bye and hung up.

"He's here?" he asked, eyes wide.

"I'll say," she said, leaning against his big desk and propping one hand on her cocked hip. "Dressed like this was the set of *Wall Street* instead of *Blazing Saddles.*"

He rose and hurried out. She gave him a good start, then followed him, going into the front sitting room, where she hoped to hear them through the screened windows. This showdown at the corral—whatever it was for—was too good to miss. She sat down on the floor and absently petted another cat as it came up to rub against her.

"What an unexpected surprise," she heard her father greet Seth Cypress. She couldn't quite see them where they stood, but she dared not go peek out the front door. She wondered if they had shaken hands or not. "Won't you come in, Mr. Cypress? Did you arrive without a car?"

"I rode my horse through one of your Cuban cowboys' illegal holes in our west fence around the res— the reservation, which we haven't patched yet."

"Holes in the fence? You mean our cattle were getting out? I've got to admit I'm not a real hands-on owner but just watch the bottom line. I am sorry, especially because—let's face it—you have probably heard my earlier track record with your people is not something I'm proud of in my older but wiser years."

"I didn't know until the fence went down more than once and I started checking that you owned this spread. The word's been out for years it was owned by a California conglomerate."

"My company, but I moved here just recently. But damn those Cubans, even my foreman. Look, are you sure you won't come in? All right then. I assure you I'm appalled at what you've told me, and I'll get someone on it right away. If it happens again, please have your foreman phone me."

"I appreciate your attitude—and, frankly, didn't expect it."

Oh, good, Michelle thought, they had walked into her view. She watched the Indian, amazed at how her father had evidently diffused the situation. Then again, he was a genius at handling all kinds of people, even her, when she knew his every trick.

"I'd like to make amends for old problems and misunderstandings," her father went on. "I hope you and your people will give me a chance over time—to be neighborly, at least. I realize this fence mess is not a good beginning."

She tried to read the Indian's body language since his face was in shadow. Maybe she could even get a dinner party out of this—her, Dad, and Seth Cypress. An intimate approach to at least one local Indian affair was starting to look terribly intriguing.

"Hi, Marc. Are the pilot and Brent late?" Jordan asked as, clutching the urn to her, she walked up to the small airplane where he waited. She was relieved it was a new-looking, bright blue Cessna, nothing like that old thing that had buzzed her in the Everglades.

"Luckily," he said, with a smile, "I can fly it. The pilot's got the flu bug, and Brent can't make it. It's the only time we can get the plane today. Honestly," he went on as he studied the obvious look of dismay on her face, "I thought you wouldn't mind if it was just the two of us—those closest to Lawrence."

"I—well, I guess not."

"It would mean a lot to me to be there—to help say good-bye to him." He lightly touched her elbow, then pulled back and leaned his shoulder against the sleek curved hull of the plane. "I'm really concerned that you've been under so much stress. Jordan, you are looking like you think I will fly like a crazy kamikaze or something."

"They were Japanese, not Chinese."

"And I am American," he said, looking hurt.

"I know, and I didn't mean otherwise. All right, let's get this over with," she said, deciding she could trust him. After all, there was nothing for him to search through here, and she did need to keep on his good side in case he found out anything about Lawrence's other contacts.

"You are dreading this?" he asked as he helped her up into the cockpit where she strapped herself in beside him, carefully cradling the urn. "But we are honoring Lawrence's memory in a way he would have wanted," he insisted and slammed the door as if to punctuate his words.

Jordan only nodded. As they taxied out toward the runway, her eyes skimmed the other private planes sitting around. All had clear identifying registration numbers, however. No, that plane that dive-bombed her in the Glades was not in sight.

While a small passenger jet landed, they waited behind one other private aircraft in line to take off. "You look upset in the stomach as well as the heart," Marc observed and offered her a mint from his pocket.

He unwrapped and popped one in his mouth. She crinkled the paper open, but held it in her hand as they soared smoothly aloft.

"Mint with a hint of anise," she said, when she tasted it.

"Anise is an herb that helps the stomach and heart. And mint is as good as a miracle drug—Lawrence said that once."

She glanced down at the paper in her hand—and gasped.

"What is it?" he asked, not taking his eyes off his flying.

"Oh, nothing. I just thought I was going to choke for a second. I see this came from the Feather Fan Restaurant. I—I heard it's good."

"You will have to try it. Excellent Szechuan."

"It hardly sounds Asian."

"You cannot tell a book by its cover or something like that."

She was really in bad shape, she scolded herself, if she was going to panic because Marc had been to the Feather Fan, along with probably thousands of others in this area.

They flew over golf courses and condos into the fringe of the Everglades. It made her doubly sad to see civilization creeping out into once virgin land, for only half of the original Glades remained already. She realized that not only the panther was endangered here, but all of what had once been best about southwest Florida. Naples was poised to become another sprawling Fort Lauderdale or Miami, and they would all be poorer for it.

The lush canopy stretched away, dotted with jigsaw pieces of water to make one huge, blue-green puzzle beneath them. They flew over ribbons of scattered pines and clumps of hammock islands of oak and cabbage palms that sheltered her orchids and Lawrence's panthers. Here and there, sun blazed off the scattered ponds.

"It's so lovely," she said, her voice breaking. "Though Lawrence spent so much time looking at computer screens with all those equations and theorems, he did it to help the cats, their land, and so much more."

"Mankind too," Marc said. "His work could be worth so much. Have you searched anyplace else for possible copies of his legacy to us—to the team?"

"No," she said, instantly annoyed he seemed to still think she owed him something of Lawrence's. "And," she added, hoping it closed the subject for good, "the police didn't turn anything up when they went through the condo with a fine-tooth comb."

"Have they made any progress on locating the gun that killed him? I am willing to help them all they want—just as I will help you."

"This looks like a good place," she changed the subject gratefully, "kind of shady with lots of trees. I've been talking to him, and now I—we've got to say good-bye."

She slid the window next to her open as they began to circle and slowly descend. She unscrewed the lid of the urn.

"I used to love him a lot, Marc—you know that. The two of us started out happy, hopeful of so much. And I'm going to find who cut off his life and his precious work, I swear to God, I am."

"Tell him," he said, as if he understood. "Tell him before you let him go for good."

For good, she thought. That is what Lawrence—or someone—had written to her in his final farewell note.

But she found she could not really say the last good-bye to him until she got some answers about his death. Biting her lower lip, she tipped the urn out the window and watched the earthly dust of Lawrence Sidwell Quinn sift down to earth. She pulled the urn back in and laid it on the floor.

She bowed her head to say a prayer, then realized they were still circling over the same spot. She glanced at Marc. He was staring at her. "We can go back now," she said.

"Not until I explain something to you. I regret to admit that I lied to you."

Her stomach lurched. "What do you mean?"

"About my parents' deaths."

"That's all right. It was none of my business." She wished he'd pay closer attention to his flying because they were circling even lower than before.

"The thing is the police did not find who killed them. I just told you they did, because I wanted to believe it myself. It used to scare me to think the killer was still out there. I just wanted you to know, I can completely sympathize with you."

"All right. I appreciate that. Now let's head back," she said and pointed northwest, as if he needed directions. But he kept up their slow spiral.

"It's just that people can be cruel," he said, not looking at her. "Some whispered I had something to do with their deaths—to get their money. It was right after that terrible Menendez brothers' trial. I just want you to know I will help you to find Lawrence's work and strive with you to get him the Nobel prize he deserves."

"Nobel prize? I never thought of that." So the stakes were that high—fame and fortune indeed.

"Look, Marc, we're getting awfully low. Can't we head back and talk about finding his work later?"

"Sure." He straightened out and slowly banked the plane toward Naples. "You know, Jordan, if you do locate his work, you'll need to call me, because it would be like reading Greek—or Chinese—to you."

She nodded and forced herself to look at him again. He was smiling, evidently pleased at his little Chinese joke or at her apparent capitulation. But he was wrong: once she got her feet back on solid earth—despite offers of help from Seth, Yancy, and Marc—she would forge ahead alone.

"It's been a rather boring day," Grandma Hattie said.

"Lucky you," Jordan murmured, collapsing on the same chaise longue where she'd spent the early-morning hours watching for the new day. They were alone while her mother ran to the store. "I'd give anything for a boring day right now."

"I do understand," Hattie said and reached over to pat her knee. "Especially after your father passed on just last week."

She looked deep into Hattie's cloudy but still somehow sharp eyes. "I do miss Daddy a lot sometimes," Jordan said, deciding not to explain. "I could sure use him right now."

"You probably miss him more than Arlene does, but she said it upset her that she couldn't even remember his voice after he'd been dead and gone awhile. Wished they'd bought a record player."

"A tape recorder."

"Well, at least you have Lawrence's voice on a record."

Jordan sat up straighter. "I have his voice on a record?"

"A little flat one, the newfangled kind that is square and only has a hole in the middle on one side. I still have it where he hid it. He said I would probably forget where it was, but that was all right, because he'd get it back from me later to put more stuff on it."

It sounded to her like a computer disk. Could this be real or had the old woman somehow imagined this? "Grandma, you have this—this record?"

"Didn't I just say so?"

"Now that he's gone, why don't you give it to me? Then I can hear his voice? I'd really appreciate it."

"It isn't even as big as those old 45s Lana used to sing along to," she said as she got up and slowly led Jordan into her bedroom down at the end of the hall.

Jordan held her breath as Hattie marched right over to her bureau and pulled the top drawer open. She shoved her lingerie and the pile of her ironed cotton handkerchiefs aside, then picked up the corner of the scented drawer liner.

Jordan's hopes plummeted as the floral scent arose, making her want to sneeze. That was where Grandma hid things, not Lawrence.

"He asked me to pick my best place and not let Arlene see it," she said proudly. "I hid it for him just before Arlene yelled at him and he yelled right back at her."

A chill raced up Jordan's spine as Hattie produced a computer disk in a clear plastic wrapper. In Lawrence's bold printing it was labeled simply, BACKUP CATS.

"Oh, dear," Hattie said, squinting down at it. "Maybe I got it wrong. I bet it's just that song from *Cats*, the one Lana sings all the time called 'Memories'."

Chapter Twelve

"That's it!" Jordan cried and jumped up from her cramped position at her computer to dance around the shop and hug herself. "A place to start. Key West, here I come!"

What was on Lawrence's backup disk wasn't, Jordan had realized hours ago, some farewell message to her in case something happened to him, but backup records of his recent work, which he had evidently thought he had to hide somewhere. Even the guardian of it, he'd figured, would not remember where it was. Most was in abbreviations and chemical equations Jordan couldn't follow, but she was able to access a lot of it, including his list—in plain English—of four consulting pharmaceutical firms.

The first three companies Marc—and since then Yancy and the police—had checked out to no avail to be certain no new discovery or contacts could have caused Lawrence trouble. But Marc had said earlier that he'd known nothing about one in Key West. And the fourth entry Lawrence described here as "*new, generous—maybe more big private $s to come!!!—contact Leonard Lewiston again*" was the Radiance Foundation on Roosevelt Boulevard in Key West.

"Yes, yes, yes!" she exulted as she took a fast walk

through the shop. "I will contact Leonard Lewiston in person."

She felt great relief she didn't need Marc's help to get this first break. And no way she was contacting Yancy with this. She didn't want him going along to Key West; besides he was working day and night to get a suicide ruling.

From a photo Jordan had provided, the manager of the marina up by Wiggins Pass had given a possible ID. Yes, he thought Lawrence was the man who had gone out in a rented boat he did not return. He had paid the entire rental and security fee in cash and used another name, Larry Smith. Yes, there had been another man in the shop then—kind of Hispanic looking—but not with him, but Lawrence had done the talking and taken the boat out—he was pretty sure of that.

Even more significant, ballistics tests had shown that whoever shot Lawrence Quinn had rested the muzzle right against his skin to pull the trigger. That MO, Yancy claimed, fit someone attempting suicide: Lawrence out there in a boat on the shifting gulf had pressed his gun against his forehead to steady it. Maybe he had even been too nauseous to try putting the barrel in his mouth. If someone else had shot him, it would probably not be from such close range nor looking him right in the eye. It was also unlikely that someone else would have shot him with his own small gun, but would have used something more—well, as Yancy had put it—more surefire.

But despite the fact that a suicide ruling would clear her from suspicion, Jordan was still convinced that Lawrence had been murdered and that the Radiance Foundation was definitely the place to start looking for information about his killer.

To cover her trail and make certain she was not followed, she was going to rent a car for the drive to Key West and not use her own name to interview Mr. Lewiston. So she rummaged through the shop's lost-and-found box until she found the *Pengate-Smith Insurance Investigation and Consultation* business card some customer had left months ago. She whited out the name, and carefully typed in *KATHERINE WESCOTT,* her roommate from college who had married and moved to Toronto.

She took the card and Lawrence's computer disk and, making sure she wasn't followed, drove to the Copy Place, Ink. She had two copies made of the computer disk and the ersatz ID laminated to help cover her tampering with it. Then she left her car in a grocery parking lot and walked to a car rental place called Rent-A-Wreck, which she figured would not keep good records or check her identity like the national places might. The cars looked fine, though they were older models. She leased one for two days, in the name of Katherine Wescott, using cash.

She parked the car a block away from her shop and walked a roundabout route home, checking to be sure she wasn't followed. After dark she turned out the greenhouse lights and, wrapping the disks in thick plastic, dug three holes in the small backyard to bury them. She filled in the soil, replaced the sod, then built piles of fifty-pound sacks of fir bark and potting medium over the spots.

"Let Marc find those," she murmured when she finished.

Leaving the apartment on foot before dawn, Jordan made sure no one saw her get in the car. Driving a circuitous route out of town—continually checking in her rearview mirror—she took the old Tamiami Trail south through the Everglades toward Miami instead of following the new multilane I-75 that sliced across the state. This was a more familiar drive for her through the deep Glades, and she could keep an eye on the traffic better on a two-lane road to be certain she was not followed.

She passed the Miccosukee Seminole Reservation— the Seminoles had several related but separate tribes—and coasted through Miami just after the main Monday morning rush hour. Soon, she was heading across the first of the series of Route 1 bridges that strung the Florida Keys to the mainland.

It felt so good to be out here with the great, open vistas of sky and sea, the aquarmarine Atlantic on her left, the sapphire Bay of Florida and Gulf of Mexico to her right. Her memories of this area were happy ones: Florida college students of her era would not lower themselves to join in the Yankee kids' spring invasion of Daytona and Fort Lauderdale, so they'd made the Keys their retreat. Twice she and Lawrence—long ago, in that other life—had been down here with friends, and they had honeymooned in Key West. Maybe that's why he had felt so positive about this Radiance Foundation and why she did now, too.

On Key Largo about a hundred miles from her destination, she stopped to have a bowl of conch chowder and use the rest room. She debated whether or not to call the foundation to make a formal appointment, but decided against it. She was better off just walking in than being told no over the phone. She ate quickly, hardly tasting the rich, spicy soup. Feeling she stood out in her tailored blouse and skirt while everyone else sported the local uniform of tank tops and shorts, she hurried back to the car.

She became nervous as she counted down the distance to her destination with the MM signs, those green-and-white mile markers posted all the way to Key West. She sat up straighter, gripped the wheel tighter as she entered the northern, tacky suburbs of Key West—strip malls, chain motels, cheap shops.

She pulled into a gas station and pumped some very expensive gas, then started searching for addresses where Route 1 became Roosevelt Boulevard. Any confidence she had felt now blew away with the increasing breeze.

The Radiance Foundation owned a stucco, hacienda-style building, quite new-looking, with a discreet, carved sign. She parked in one of the two guest spots in the small lot, repaired her makeup and hair, rotated the kinks out of her shoulders, and walked around to the front door, carrying her briefcase with its appropriate-looking documents. Her legs were shaking now, whether from the long drive or nerves, she wasn't sure.

Inside the arched entry, a pygmy palm shaded a sculpted sunburst splashing water from its rays into a green marble basin. The front door, carved with the same radiating sun logo, was heavy, but, she thought, at least the place was open. The chill air-conditioning clung to her inside. She felt she was entering a sealed, walk-in vault.

A handsome man in his early thirties with blond, wavy hair looked up from a desk in a tiled reception area dominated by an Oriental rug. His nameplate said James Randall, Executive Secretary. He seemed surprised to see her, but greeted her with a smile and chatter about the great weather being threatened by possible afternoon storms.

Her heart began to pound as she gave him her fake

name and asked to see Leonard Lewiston on insurance business. He glanced at her card but, luckily, did not examine it. Asking her to wait, he went into a back office and quietly closed the door. She had no sooner sunk into a taupe leather couch than the front door opened and a man entered, whistling and swinging an alligator skin briefcase.

"Hi. You been taken care of?" He had his suit coat slung jauntily back over his shoulder with an index finger. The silk lining of the coat was a beautiful bronze.

"Yes. Mr. Randall was just here. You're not the director, Leonard Lewiston?"

"No, his associate, Andy Kramer. Glad to meet you, Ms ..."

She used her phony name again. He put his briefcase down and shook her hand. He, too, was a good-looking man, maybe late-thirties but prematurely balding, which made him look older. Lawrence had a theory that so many young American men went bald earlier now because of years of blow driers, football helmets, and baseball caps. But then, she thought, Lawrence had theories on everything, and that's partly why she was here.

She explained to Mr. Kramer—call me Andy, please—that she was an insurance investigator from Naples. "Love the place," he said with a toothpaste ad smile. "I get over there to see some clients—you know, our donors—quite a bit. Lot of money in Naples."

"Yes, there is. So your clients are wealthy people who donate for what causes? I don't know what the Radiance Foundation funds."

"Our success demands privacy. We've got to protect our benefactors and benefits. Just call us one of ex-

President Bush's 'thousand points of light,'—a big light," he explained with another smile. "I'll let Len Lewiston fill you in on what you need to know."

In Mr. Lewiston's office, which reminded her of some kind of a posh English men's club, Jordan soon realized he would probably *not* fill her in on what she needed to know. Square-jawed and silver-haired, suave and savvy, he was a good decade or two older than the other men. He, too, was a strikingly handsome man. The entire staff here could have stepped from the pages of *GQ,* she thought as she tried again with her inquiries.

"So, Ms. Wescott, your insurance group is investigating grants given to this virologist—ah, Lawrence Quinn—in regard to his death benefits and estate insurance policy after his untimely death? Is that the bottom line?"

"Exactly. His scientific work brought in grants we are trying to trace and verify, and your foundation was among the donors, according to his records."

"Surely, you cannot produce a copy of those records." That was, she noted, a statement and not a question.

She slid farther forward on her chair. "Only your agency's name and address, your name, and some notes in a listing with the other firms and foundations he was definitely working with. I was hoping you could tell me what grants had been presented to him and why."

"If the nature of his work was as you say, I'm sure the list of grants was potentially extensive," he said with a smile somewhere between charming and ingratiating. His gaze suddenly swept the ceiling as he talked. "Imagine, the hope of being able to link successful panther immunity to a lentivirus to immunity for HIV. I've heard of experiments with baboons, but panthers, no. But perhaps he only listed us as a potential source, because—as I said—we have no records of even speaking with him. But of what nature were his alleged notes on us?"

Ah, she thought, he is worried. "His records clearly list your foundation as new but generous."

"Again," he said with a shake of his carefully coiffed head, "perhaps that was hopeful thinking. Without proof a scientist had made some sort of breakthrough, our board would never have backed him. And frankly, though I don't mean to stereotype anyone, brilliant men dedicated to their quests like some rare breed of Don Quixote tend to be a bit forgetful or even fanciful."

"This brilliant man was neither, Mr. Lewiston," she said so forcefully she instantly regretted it. "And you have said, your foundation gives donations for studies of diseases such as cancer and HIV—"

"But not," he said, pointing a finger, "animal ones unless there is a proved link to human plagues. Do you, Ms. Wescott, have personal knowledge that Mr. Quinn had made this breakthrough? If the next of kin could provide us with proof of this, or copies of his work, even posthumously, then you and I would have more to say to each other, perhaps about lucrative future donations to obtain rights to the information. Until then," he added with a regretful hint of a shrug, "I can be of absolutely no help to you, nor—evidently—you to us, though if you can locate another scientist familiar with the work, who will carry on for him, you might have him make an initial contact with me."

She had the distinct feeling during that dismissive speech that he was playing with her—that he knew

her real relationship to Lawrence or had talked with
someone else from the panther team. But, again, she
had no proof. She didn't want to back off or leave,
but she realized she could soon make a fool of herself
here. And even though Leonard Lewiston's tone
skated on the edge of defiance, she felt guilty about
suspecting a place that did their kind of humanitar-
ian work.

He stood, punctuating the fact their conversation
was completed. Calmly, she leaned over to pick up
her briefcase, but she could have hurled it and howled
in disappointment. To be so certain from Lawrence's
records that this foundation had contributed heavily
to his work and then to strike out devastated her. Was
their foundation's policy never to betray a trust, or
were they just afraid of admitting any link to Lawrence and his work after something shocking had happened to him? As Andy Kramer implied, they'd
protect their rich donors at any price.

"Thank you for your time," she said. She realized
she sounded ready to cry and cleared her throat.
"When I obtain further documents and proof, I assure
you I will be in touch again."

She considered mentioning that the police might be
making inquiries. She'd done such a wretched job
here, hoping to spring something loose by rattling him,
that maybe she should tell Yancy what she'd found or
get Marc to try a contact somehow. But she had decided not to trust them any more than she did this
man. Maybe a lawyer—maybe Seth—would know how
to get more information about this bunch.

Jim Randall escorted her to the front door and
opened it, politely bid her good-bye, and closed it
firmly behind her.

"Damn," she said inadequately as she went to her

car and threw the briefcase and purse in the front seat. "All that for absolutely nothing."

She was even more upset to see storm clouds had blotted out the sun. Quickly, she hit the long road home.

Everything scrolled through her mind as the mile markers and bridges blurred by. Could it be possible that Lawrence had *not* been onto something big? That he had learned he was barking up the wrong tree, or had run out of passion for his work as he had for her, or finally simply wanted to leave it or her? Maybe, just like this, he was looking out over the water and decided to kill himself. So he got the gun and went out in a boat to get some privacy and lifted that little gun to his head and—

"No!" she shouted, slapping the steering wheel. "No!"

By the time she had started west out of Miami, gray clouds were pouring rain ahead. Lightning forked at the darkening horizon, and muted thunder echoed. Eventually, she drove right into the storm.

The downpour swept in sheets across the two-lane road, veiling visibility. The world closed in around her, dark, dangerous, lit only by unexpected jags of light. Vehicles slowed and kept their beams on, but it didn't help much. When she saw the Miccosukee Restaurant sign, she drove into the lot and waited until the rattle of rain on the car roof lessened, then grabbed her purse and darted in. She sat at the counter to get served quickly.

It seemed strange to be among Seminoles and know no one, but anonymity suited her. "Gator tail or frog legs and hush puppies, ma'am?'' the Indian waitress asked, assuming she'd want the specials.

"Coffee and pecan pie, please." In other words, she thought, caffeine and sugar to keep her fueled for the stormy drive home.

She went back out when the rain seemed to lift. Others had the same idea, and the restaurant emptied fairly quickly. To her chagrin, she noted she had left the passenger window cracked several inches and that the seat was soaked. Now, why hadn't she noticed that before? Someone could have gotten in. Nervously, she craned around and checked to be sure the back seat and floor were empty. She was glad she had rented an older car as she swiped water off the passenger seat with her hand.

By now the other vehicles had gone. Good—she didn't want to worry about someone behind her and could go her own speed. She pulled back out onto the slick gray road at the end of the exodus.

She drove way under the speed limit until she realized the rain was increasing again and slowed even more. Several vehicles approached and passed her and another car that had come up behind her. Lots of vans were on the roads these days; she was so much more aware of them lately—at least dark blue or white ones. But she'd stopped obsessing over Challenger license plates since so many Floridians had them. She did see, however, several special Florida Seminole ones go by, because she was in the heart of Miccosukee or "Trail" Indian country on this deep-Glades road about thirty miles from Lokosee.

She knew this stretch of road quite well—at least in daylight. It had a deep canal along this side of it; people often fished there, but a wrong turn could take a car into it. A shallow ditch followed the other side in some places, but there were occasional pull-offs over there.

Another cloudburst turned the early dusk to night. She was just getting used to the double assaults of lightning and thunder, then—she could not believe it—a warning light blinked red on her dashboard.

"Real smart to get a Rent-a-Wreck, Jordan," she cried.

She squinted to read what the light said. H, the engine temperature dial for overheating. In this rain? After she'd just let it rest? But she'd owned a used car once where the carburetor leaked and the engine caught fire, and she wasn't taking any chances. If she were only ten miles or so farther, she could stop and get help from her dad's old hunting buddies, Cal and Rebel Turner, at their place along the Trail.

She slowed even more, looking for a small clearing with a few picnic tables she knew on the other side of the road. Surely, it was right along here. She dare not just stop or she could be rear-ended. Yes, there! Squinting to see lights of oncoming vehicles, she pulled across the road, getting way off the berm.

She killed the lights and engine and sat, hoping the problem would cool down and go away if she just waited a bit. She'd be soaked the second she tried to get out to raise the hood or tie on a white handkerchief—she'd probably have to use her blouse—to summon help.

Sheets of streaming gray wrapped around the metal shell of the car, isolating her from everything. For a while the rain was so dense she could not even glimpse headlights going by on the road, unless others had pulled off, too. The moisture and her breath with the car's blower off had totally fogged up the inside of the car windows.

She rested her forehead on one hand on the steering wheel and hit it with the other fist, thump, thump. How had she ended up here? She thought she had planned so well, had a good lead, but Lawrence's death was still a total mystery.

She sniffed hard and blinked back tears that stung her eyes, already sore from the long drive. As soon as this storm let up, she would try the car again and, maybe with her warning blinkers, get clear down to Everglades City or at least as far as the Turner brothers' place. Local people and tourists were friendly if she couldn't get the car started, so she had no reason to be afraid.

But she gasped and ducked away when she saw a black form pass near her window. Had someone out there tried to look in at her? But who, in this downpour? Maybe someone who had stopped to help and wasn't sure anyone was in the car. Or it was just her imagination. Maybe just a sudden wash of rain down the glass; a tree shadow from distant, passing headlights through the downpour. Undoing her seat belt, she scrambled over the console to the other seat, stepping on her purse and briefcase. Panting with animal fear, she double-checked to see the locks were down.

She steeled her nerves and wiped her hand in a little circle on the misty glass, wishing now she hadn't pulled this far off the road. Should she sit here or try to restart the engine and pull away? And what if back there at the Seminole restaurant, someone had tampered with the car while she was inside? She supposed the hood release was inside the car, but with that window somehow open . . .

Headlights of a vehicle passed slowly, smearing light outside that soon faded. But it had silhouetted two men's figures standing between her and the road.

Their heads were—looked like—the shape of big animal heads. Indians? Seminole masks of some sort? In a flash she saw again those Seminoles stalking their panther prey that terrible day she found those dazed men in the Glades.

Voices. She heard the low rumble of men's voices— or was that distant thunder? Steps. Steps just outside the car. Aghast, she squinted through the murky glass. She didn't see them out there anymore. She was going to get back in the driver's seat and roar out of here. But then someone rattled hard the locked handle of the driver's door. She pressed against the opposite window.

And then her little world exploded.

Chapter Thirteen

Shattered glass from the driver's-side window sprayed inward across the front seat of the car. Instinctively, Jordan covered her face; then, when the clatter and tinkling stopped, she looked. A man's head and shoulders—his face a lion mask!—pushed inside. With his elbow, he shoved out the webbed glass that clung. His hand fumbled for the inside door handle. The locks all clicked up.

Yanking the driver's door open, he leaned in to lunge for her. Beyond terror or thinking, she exploded out the passenger side of the car.

Her instant flight must have taken the other masked man unawares. Her door hit him, and he grunted and fell back. Scrambling on her hands and knees, then up on her feet, she tore into the stinging rain. Both shoes flew off. She avoided the road, which would trap her against the canal on the other side, and veered past the picnic tables toward the shelter of the trees.

"Here! She's here!" a man shouted. The voices weren't Seminole, but who?

Only thunder answered as Jordan raced into the thick, wet brush. Limbs and leaves tore at her clothes and skin. Sopping leaves and limbs whipped her. Lifting her hands to protect her face, she shut her eyes. It was so dark in here it didn't matter.

She heard them thrashing after her, cursing. Her lungs burst for breath. Her mind raced faster than her feet. They had done something to her car back there. Because they wanted to take her or kill her, just as they had Lawrence.

A root snagged her ankle. She tripped and belly flopped in swampy water, making a big splash.

"This way. I hear her!"

That voice sounded familiar, but who? Someone she knew. That's why the masks. Those weren't just to scare her.

Lying in mud and slime, praying this was not a gator wallow, she got to her hands and knees, carefully, slowly. Miles of wild land lay between her and home. She had no fear of the Glades, even at night, but she'd never had to flee human hunters out here before.

She heard them sloshing closer. "We don't need this," the second man muttered.

"Shut up and use that light. It's dark as hell in here."

A broad beam slashed past, just missing her. She sidled slowly into the corridor where that shaft had gone, thinking they would shine it someplace else this time. Her hand groped, reaching for the nearest tree trunk. It seemed a big one, sturdy. She pressed herself behind it as the light swept through again. Whoever they were, they were going to find her and kidnap and kill her, just as they had Lawrence, and for what?

"She didn't get far. I only heard her run for a second. Give me that light."

Then she thought of going up. This felt like a pond apple tree with its contorted limbs, but they were slippery, and she was coated with mud.

She reached for the first limb above her head and heaved herself up. She hung a moment; the soles of her feet slipped against the slick trunk. But then she was up. She twisted herself and got up two more limbs, moving entirely by feel. They'd have to climb for her now, she exulted, and she strained to get even higher.

About ten feet up, she saw them almost below her, briefly illumined in a strobe flash of lightning. The image burned in her brain. Metallic objects glinted in their hands.

They had guns.

She clung tight, so tight, praying they would not look up and see her. But she had seen something else, too. They had masks, yes, but she knew what kind. Not Seminole or Halloween but the elaborate ones like revelers wore during Fantasy Fest in Key West. And the flash of light had revealed the tops of their bare heads, because they now held their masks. One man was balding and one had blond hair.

Leonard Lewiston's two men from the Radiance Foundation!

"Hey, anybody out there?" she heard a new, distant voice, another man's. "Anyone hurt in this here car with the window busted up? I hear voices. You all in there?"

A good, local cracker voice, Jordan thought. She'd scream for help right now if they wouldn't just shoot her during the next roll of thunder.

"Go tell that yokel we accidentally locked our dog in our car," she heard just-call-me-Andy say right under her. "Then, when we broke it out, it bolted in the rain. And ditch that mask!"

She clung tighter to the tree, her skirt hitched up around her hips. Her bare legs felt rubbed raw, her chin, too. Her thighs ached where she clamped them around the trunk. Some snakes, she knew, climbed trees, but she'd rather face them than the snakes down there.

"He says he'd be glad to help us look for our dog!" the blond man's—Jim Randall's—voice called back into the trees. She wondered what he thought of being temporarily demoted from executive secretary to assistant executioner. Had these men killed Lawrence?

Beneath her, Andy Kramer spit out a string of curses. She heard him slog back toward the road. Quickly, she shimmied and scrambled down the tree. She said a little prayer that they would not hurt that Good Samaritan out there. And she hoped Lewiston's thugs spent all night looking for her and got attacked by a snake or gator. She was heading deeper into the Glades to hide until morning when she could circle back out to the road to get help.

Still, she had to fight to keep from panicking. She used her Glades savvy, forcing herself to slosh through water instead of seeking out high ground: rattlers preferred it dry. Cottonmouths were less poisonous, and they were the ones likely to be near this low, swampy, rain-soaked ground. She didn't let herself think about an alligator attack, even if they were more active at night. She'd probably be able to hear one coming at her unless she stepped right on it.

Exhausted and depressed, she hung her head. But she lifted it again when she realized what she had proved today, even if she had done it the hard way. The Radiance Foundation was a front. Without disappearing or turning up dead herself, she had to find out what they really knew about Lawrence and his work that was worth trying to get her, too.

Battered, muddy, sore, and cold, just after dawn Jordan phoned Mae from a little place along the Trail called the Live Worms Bait Shop. Wilson answered, none too glad to hear who was calling this early, but he got Mae for her, and she promised to send Seth. No way, Jordan thought, was she going to call her mother or Lana to come see her like this and have to explain everything. Nor did she want the police—and Yancy—in this, at least not yet.

She had somewhat wiped and dried herself off and was on her third cup of coffee from the elderly, taciturn bait shop owner when Seth arrived in his pickup.

"I know," she said, holding up her hands when he just gaped at her appearance, "I look like hell again."

"You look good to me," he said, surprising her.

"I don't think," the old man said, drawling his words, "many womenfolk could spend a night in a swamp and look that good. You a friend of her'n, buddy?"

"From way back," Seth said. Like Jordan, he knew better than to try to pay the old cracker for his kindness, but he thanked him and shook his hand as they went out. He took off his denim jacket and placed it around her shoulders before he put her in the truck. "Let's get you home," he said. "We can go back for your car later. Instead of traipsing around, you should have just stayed with it, especially in bad weather." When she didn't say anything, he added warily, "You did tell Mae your car broke down . . ."

She nodded and shoved her hair back with both hands, momentarily making a ponytail before she let it spill loose again. "That's part of the truth," she said, not looking at him. "The storm and the car was bad enough, but the men with the masks and the guns—"

"What?" he shouted so loud she jumped. "What kind of masks? Did you see their faces? How many guys?"

As she explained, his jaws and fists slowly un-clenched. Still, rain falling on him now, she thought, would hiss like steam.

"I can't believe you got into that mess," he scolded, "after everything else. I told you to be careful and I'd help. I thought you were just down here looking for orchids or something, and that would have been dumb enough, off on your own right now." He looked re-lieved, though. "At least you know this was different guys," he added.

"From the ones who took the panther, you mean. Yeah, but that makes it even more confusing," she said, staring at her hands clasped in her lap. "I know I made a mess. I thought I'd taken precautions, but I can't just surrender to fear or stop living. I'm going to get answers about who killed Lawrence and maybe who took that panther, too. But maybe those things aren't even related."

"Hang on," he muttered. Checking traffic by cran-ing his neck both ways, he maneuvered a squealing U-turn.

"What are you doing? Where are we going now?"

"To look at the evidence while those bastards' trail is still fresh. Jordan, I didn't mean to yell, but you could have been—"

"Believe me, I know it now."

"Could you positively ID their faces with those masks?" he asked, turning to look at her, then darting his gaze back to the road.

"No, but I recognized their voices and the tops of their heads."

"The tops—oh, great. Panicked, in the dark—that will never hold up in court. It would be about like nailing those so-called Seminoles who took that pan-ther when you didn't see their faces. And we'd have to find that cracker that came along and helped save your life. In the rain all footprints are probably gone—with everything else."

"Gone with what else?"

"Just wait and see. The thing is, since you lied about who you were, maybe they weren't trying to kill Jordan Quinn but Katherine Wescott, you know."

"That hardly matters," she insisted, turning sideways in her seat belt to face him. His concern touched her deeply. "They were trying to kill the woman who tried to link them to Lawrence's work."

She got really nervous as they approached the spot, then went by it before she recognized it from this direction and told him to turn back. The car wasn't there or any signs of men or discarded masks, though they did see shards of glass.

"Here—see," she insisted, carefully displaying several broken bits in her palm.

"It could be some car wreck sprayed glass here. You're sure this was the place?"

"Yes, I'm sure!" she said, stomping her foot like a child in her exhaustion. "Whose side are you on with all these stupid questions? Sorry, Seth, I didn't mean that."

"Then, from now on," he said, as he helped her back up in his truck and stared solemnly at her, "let's say only what we *do* mean to each other, all right?"

Seth listened intently as she requested his advice on the way to Naples. "Sure," he said, "I can look into the Radiance Foundation, but places like that are hard to crack. It could even be a front for something else, a sort of dummy corporation. I can check into those goons, too, but we've got to find some way to make sure they don't come after you again."

"I hate to think I actually need a bodyguard. If I were under police protection, I wouldn't be able to look into all this."

"If you need a bodyguard, I'll get you one from the tribe," he offered, reaching over to momentarily cover her hand before he pulled it back. "But I think I can draft a legal, if threatening letter, to make the so-called Radiance people keep clear of you."

"Even if they find out we're investigating them? Even if they realize I didn't get the police on them for this?"

"They won't know that for sure. Besides, I'll bet somebody as slick as that Lewiston has airtight alibis for his men and himself. They'll say you hit your head when a rock flew up and broke your window, and you're lying or delusional, not to mention falsely representing yourself as an insurance investigator to get privileged information."

She stared at his profile as he drove. Yes, that's probably something like they would say. "Besides," she said, broaching the subject tenuously, "if I did get the police, Yancy would get involved, and I don't need that."

"You sure as hell don't." He narrowed his eyes. His voice and expression had gone hard.

She nodded, but she didn't tell him that Yancy's old feelings for her had apparently not faded. And, now, she wondered—she couldn't help herself—if Seth's once forceful feelings for her—that way—had faded, too. She didn't think so, but she wasn't sure.

"If those men took the rental car," she said, trying to get back on track, "I mean, that wasn't hard, because I left the keys in the ignition when I ran, they got my purse and briefcase, too. So I probably should move to my new, unlisted address as soon as possible."

"The lodge?" His face lit at the mere mention of it. "But if you've got five extra minutes right now, I'll bet I know where to find that Rent-a-Wreck of yours."

"I'll have to pay for it, the window or replacing the whole thing," she said with a sigh.

"That's what I mean—I doubt if you have to." He turned in the opposite direction of her place. "Since those goons have to completely cover their tails, *they* have to replace that car—maybe intact, so your story wouldn't hold up. Rental cars usually have the address of the lot in their glove compartments. The place is along here somewhere, isn't it?"

"One more block—and my car's parked two blocks over."

"We'll get it in a minute, and I'll follow you home."

"But I don't have my keys. They were in my purse in . . ."

She could only point with her mouth hanging open. Though it looked like no one had arrived for work yet, parked under the Rent-a-Wreck sign was a car like the one she had leased. Except no window was broken.

"I'll bet," Seth said smugly as he pulled in facing it, "there's not a shard of glass in the interior, and the overheat light wouldn't come on if we drove it either. They probably drained your radiator while you were in the restaurant, then followed you, just waiting for you to pull over. Stay put a minute."

He got out. Shielding his eyes, he bent to look in through the new window of the rental car, then stood and glanced around the lot, apparently to be certain no one was watching. He opened the passenger door and leaned in.

She was going to call out to him that he shouldn't touch anything to preserve fingerprints, but she knew better now. Her pursuers from the Radiance Foundation had totally outfoxed her except for one thing: they had not caught her—yet.

Seth had her purse and shoes in one hand and her briefcase in the other when he walked back toward his truck. He rolled his eyes as if to say, *I told you so.*

"I can't believe it!" she said as he put everything in her lap. Her shoes felt damp, but they were cleaned inside and out. "Now if I could only get my lost cat back this easily!"

"If it means that much to you, I wish I could help," he said, leaning closer when he got back in the car.

She felt herself blush. She turned to meet his steady stare. "You have already. How can I ever thank you?"

He smiled that slanted way of his that lifted the left corner of his mouth. "We'll think of something."

Jordan let the water from the warm shower sluice over her while Seth made some phone calls in the living room. It felt strange to have him here so close while she undressed, showered, and changed. After she dried off and fastened her bra, she noticed both breasts were sore, too. She pulled on a sleeveless blouse and shorts, then tried smoothing skin cream on her exposed scrapes and bruises. But even that hurt. She washed her arms and thighs off again and went out into the kitchen, deciding she would settle for Grandma Hattie's old-time cure-all of warm water with baking soda in it. Seth hastily hung up the phone when she walked through the little sitting area to the kitchen, then followed her.

"Sore?" he asked, leaning his shoulder against the door frame.

"The shower helped," she admitted, with a quick glance at him, "but I didn't want to make it too hot."

"You should sit in a bath. You always said that relaxed you."

Unless you were in it with me, she thought as she nodded and turned away. They'd had a big claw-footed tub in the place they'd lived the one week of their married life. Repeatedly, she finger-combed her damp, curly hair back from her face.

"Want some coffee?" she asked as she dumped baking soda in a glass bowl of warm water and stirred quickly as it went from cloudy to clear. She took a clean dish towel out of the drawer and soaked it.

"Sure. Your face is scraped, too. Here, let me help. If I'd known you'd be like this, I would have brought a special Cory Cypress herbal wash."

"I'm sure he'd like to have you personally delivering me his secret remedies," she said with a little laugh.

"He's not as bad as you remember, Jordan." He took the towel from her hand to dab her left cheek. The expression on his face changed, and she sensed he had something he wanted to tell her. "Besides, I was thinking that it's beneath both of us to meet in secret anymore. If I'm going to help you or we're going to be friends."

"Yes," she said, nodding. "I agree."

"Good. We're adults, and we're both single. And Yancy can't make any case against us individually or together, so the heck with hiding out."

Not wanting to discuss Yancy, she held her breath. Those words, his touch, one hand on her shoulder, the other tending to her skin, made her feel she was floating. She stared at the throbbing beat at the base of his throat.

"Seth," she said in a breathy, hesitant voice, "the thing is, I am newly widowed."

He frowned and she felt his grip tighten. "Do you feel newly widowed? I know you're being loyal in trying to find out about his death and work, but didn't you really leave him—and vice versa—long ago?"

"Yes."

"It's a terrible time to ask this, but are you still emotionally involved with him—other than mourning his death?"

"My emotions are a mess."

As if she'd slapped him, he splashed the towel in the bowl. Backing away, he leaned against the door with his arms crossed over his chest. "Don't look at me that way," he said. "I wasn't going to do anything."

"Weren't you?" Their gazes snagged and held. She felt the impact of that as if he had crushed her to him. "I only mean," she faltered, "that my emotions are a mess with all that's happened lately—not that Lawrence and I haven't been over for a long time. And—with us just now—I was starting to get that old—a strange feeling."

"Yeah. Me too," he said with a tight smile. "And I was just thinking—actually, Mae put the idea in my head—that you might be willing to attend the Winter Dance next week. You and I might as well announce we are going to be, at the very least, good friends in a big, bold way."

Tears stung her eyes. It showed great respect for any white person to be invited. The gathering was secret and sacred, held way out on Seminole land at a place and time that was closely guarded. Closely guarded—that's the way she'd been with her feelings each time she'd been with Seth these last few days.

"I'd be honored," she said, her voice a whisper. "And very pleased to be among your people. I'm touched you and Mae want me there—after I reported that Seminoles took the panther. Besides, I'm at the point where I don't care what people say as long as I know I'm doing the right thing."

He smiled broadly. The impact of that lit the room, loosing feelings she had fought to control. He shoved away from the door frame and moved closer as if her desire had summoned him. Easily, he lifted her to sit on the counter and nudged her knees to spread her legs on either side of his hips to expose her bruised, scraped thighs. He stared at them; she could see each separate dark eyelash that veiled his eyes.

Then he looked up and their gazes locked. He reached for the towel, but didn't wring it out. Water from his ministrations dribbled down her thighs and dripped away. She tingled in the places he touched and ached where he didn't. It did not cool but heated her.

"Everywhere you're sore or hurt," he whispered, "I could kiss and make it better. Jordan, if—when—we make love—ever again—it has to be permanent between us."

"Yes," she murmured, nodding through her tears. "But I get so scared. We can't do it all—go through it all—again. Can we?"

In answer, his lips touched hers; his tongue tasted, then intruded. She arched toward him, deepening the kiss and caress. This wasn't just physical need after all this time—years alone, years with Lawrence, years emotionally alone again after Lawrence stopped caring. She still loved Seth, maybe always had.

Despite how his jeans rasped her thighs, she clamped him closer as he lifted her into a fierce embrace and feverish kiss that went on and on. Finally, he pressed his lips against her temple. His hot breath tickled her ear. "I need you, Jordan. I always have."

Like an idiot, she began to cry. She tried to stop, just to hold him, kiss him back again, but everything combined—exhaustion, her fears, and fury at things . . .

He held her close while she sobbed silently, shaking against him. His touch was gentle now, comforting. He cradled her against him, rocking her slightly, then shifted her back to sit on the counter.

"There will be time for us in all this," he said, his lips moving against the slant of her cheek and down the side of her throat. "The right kind of time and place. We'll make sure."

She nodded, still holding his shoulders.

"But I gotta tell you," he added, his voice raspy, "I'm tempted to take advantage of all this emotion." He gave her waist a little squeeze. "But I'd hate myself later, wondering if you meant it and needed me for the right reasons."

She pulled slightly away from him and gazed into his dark eyes. "I would mean it," she said, swiping tears with both hands before he untied the red bandana from around his neck and handed it to her. "Just so we're honest and can trust each other all the way," she said, dabbing her cheeks with it.

"How about you get some rest and I'll see you later?" he asked, stepping slightly back, resting his hands on the counter on either side of her hips. "I'm going to write that letter to the Radiance Foundation and get someone from the tribe to kind of hang around you in case they try something again. You game?"

She smiled through her tears. She felt stuffed up, but she didn't want to blow her nose on his bandana.

"Why not?" she said and forced a smile. "I've felt like hunted game lately, so I guess so."

He kissed her quickly. "Keep your doors locked, even in the day," he ordered in a gruff voice, which had shifted back to lawyer or Seminole chairman. He squeezed one bare knee and went out and down the steps.

Chapter Fourteen

The man who stopped Jordan had a gun.

"Sorry to hold you up, Miz Quinn," the gatekeeper at the SunRay Ranch told her as he leaned down to her open car window with one hand propped on his hip holster. "Just wanted to jot down your car make and license so you can drive right through anytime after this. 'Specially with Miss Michelle here for a spell, we're extra careful. Enjoy your stay, now," he said, touching one finger to his hat brim.

"Thanks!" she called to him as she drove on with a shake of her head. This was hardly the heart of Hollywood with tourist buses and paparazzi. But she told herself, Michelle was famous and Rey wealthy, so she guessed she shouldn't be surprised at the armed guard.

In a way, she was relieved to see him. She could tell Seth later she'd gone to a safe place. He had phoned late morning to promise that, starting tomorrow, a friend of his, Bill Bowlegs, would follow her when she went out in her car. But she hadn't remembered to tell him about this meeting when she talked to him, partly because he'd read her his letter. He said he was going to get it notarized and sent return receipt delivery to Leonard Lewiston in Key West:

Should anything harmful, suspicious, or even vaguely threatening happen to Jordan Quinn, it read in part, *this entire affidavit will be handed over forthwith to the Naples and Key West Police departments and released to various mass media in southwest Florida, detailing the hereafter described attempt of the following named employees of the Radiance Foundation of Key West to abduct or murder her . . .*

No matter how vehemently you might deny these charges during their extensive investigation, the ensuing publicity alone would make your influential donors reconsider . . .

She was just grateful Sally had reminded her at the last minute about this afternoon appointment at the ranch. Though still exhausted from last night in the Glades, she would have felt terrible missing her first visit to her biggest clients.

Trying to ease the tension from her body, she rotated her shoulders and took deep, slow breaths as she drove down the long lane. Graceful pines and brown fences kept in a mixed hot-weather breed of Angus and Brahmin cattle dotting fields stretching to the horizon. For the first time, Jordan realized that the sprawling ranch shared a very long boundary with the reservation.

As she parked her car before the large, Victorian-style house, Winston Rey himself came out to greet her with a mottled, silver-gray cat cradled in one arm.

"Welcome to the SunRay!" he said, extending his free hand and shaking hers warmly. As Jordan petted the cat, he told her, "Michelle's out back by the pool, near where your garden will go, so let's join her."

"What a beautiful animal this is."

"Thank you. Sadly, I lost his sister not long ago from pneumonia. Terrible virus, even in cats."

"You know," she said as they walked toward the house, "everything in nature, even orchids, can get a virus. They're very mysterious."

"So I've heard. But we'll make sure Baby Blue here doesn't get sick, won't we?" he said. Hearing its name, the cat gazed up adoringly at its master and flicked its tail.

"Actually, my husband's work dealt with studying certain viruses in endangered panthers and their possible connection to human illnesses."

"Fascinating," he said as he led her into the elegantly furnished home. "I'd be interested in hearing about that, at least as it might affect domestic breeds. Please make yourself at home here at the ranch house or anywhere on the grounds," he said with a sweep of his free arm.

Jordan's idea of a ranch house it wasn't. The interior seemed imported from various Hollywood sets, a rich eclectic mix of old and new, eastern and western. The collection of Oriental porcelain on huge, lighted, glassed-in shelves outdid anything she'd ever seen at Marc's condo.

"Oh, you've got so many of these cats, Mr. Rey," she exclaimed as others appeared to follow them and rub against their legs.

"Winston, remember," he chided with a smile. "Yes, I breed Burmese." He put Baby Blue down amidst the others—six of them here and two were sleeping on furniture she could see. "They're all Torties, short for tortoiseshell because of their mottled coats. I'm afraid no one has informed them that they aren't sacred anymore. You know, servants were once killed for simply mistreating them."

She glanced up to study his expression. She thought he had made a joke, but he seemed so serious. She understood and appreciated anyone who could humble himself enough to get along with cats. "I remember," she told him, "reading that the cats of ancient Egypt were sacred. They even mummified them when they died. I just love cats, but I lost mine—ours— somehow right along with Lawrence. It was a nonbreed, but I really miss him."

"I'm so sorry. Would you like one from a new litter of lilac ones?"

"Lilac? I can't imagine."

He looked suddenly very proud. "They're dove gray with pink tones. I'll show you later."

"About the kitten—that's very generous of you, but I'd better not even look. I'd want one, and I'm not over losing ours yet or ready to take on an expensive cat. But that reminds me, thank you again for the generous donation you sent the panther fund in Lawrence's name, Winston."

"Your lovely note was all the thanks I need."

They joined Michelle at the pool and chatted. Rey took a cigarillo from a gold case that glinted in the sun. His smoke, mingled with Michelle's, made Jordan glad they were outside.

The area between the pool and back lawn where they wanted the orchid garden was extensive, but the trees were mostly smooth-barked royal palms. "Rough bark is best for hanging orchids," she told them, "but I can use wire and netting to mount some plants."

"Order a few rough-barked ones if you like," Rey said, his sweeping gesture encompassing the whole area. "I just want this to be special and unique."

"What about bringing in a few rocks for more landscaping?" Jordan inquired. "Coral or coquina stone?"

"My dear," he said, exhaling a perfect ring of smoke upward, "the sky's the limit."

Jordan tried not to let the obvious wealth of these people affect how she regarded them, but it did make them interesting, even intriguing. She spent an hour sketching the layout and jotting notes to herself. They drank mint iced tea by the pool, and a Cuban maid brought out a plate of *quesadillas*. Though these people were light-years away from her usual clients, she enjoyed herself, and almost forgot about her burdens.

"So, when will you be back to get things really rolling?" Rey inquired as he stood and waited to walk her out.

"In just a few days," she said, getting up from one of the padded, matching lawn chairs. "I'll have the layout diagrams done and bring you a list of choices and prices."

"I'm trusting you on this. Come for dinner some evening, or stay the weekend if you want. I'd love to show you our alligator ranching facilities out on the range."

The idea of a weekend away from everything sounded wonderful, but she still had a lot to do to research Lawrence's tapes. "I can't commit right now, but perhaps later. I'm very excited to be doing something of this magnitude for you."

"Well, just dinner then, if not a weekend yet."

"And," Michelle put in with a yawn, "maybe we can invite that Indian chief."

Jordan's head snapped back toward Michelle. "Seminole, you mean? Not Seth Cypress?"

"The one and only," she said, stretching languorously in a way that thoroughly annoyed Jordan. "He came out to see Dad about some of our cattle accidentally getting through our common boundaries. Too bad Dad's still not casting them in flicks anymore. Indians, I mean, not the cattle."

"Michelle, just drop it, all of it," Rey said sharply.

Michelle shrugged.

Suddenly Jordan was sure that Michelle didn't know anything about her past with Seth, but did Winston? More than ever, she realized Lana's advice not to get tangled up with "those people," might be sound. She'd just keep this all business, however fascinating they were personally.

"I'll be seeing you then, Michelle." Jordan forced the words. Michelle gazed up and shaded her eyes into the sun and gave a three-fingered wave. Jordan sensed that Michelle got very testy when Rey was nice to her, almost as if she were jealous of his kindness.

Walking through the house again, Rey asked Jordan to wait a minute and disappeared down a hall. She hoped he wasn't going to get her a kitten, but he returned with a check for—for eight thousand dollars! She'd been planning to ask for a retainer of five hundred when she had the diagrams done. Her eyes widened as she stared at it.

"For initial buys—rocks, new trees, orchids, whatever," he said hastily and escorted her into the front hall, where he gently shoved cats back from the door with one foot as he opened it.

She walked out, heard herself thank him, and got in her car with the check still clutched in her hand. He reached in to pat her shoulder. "I know you'll do a beautiful job for me here," he told her.

Those encouraging words and his wave and smile lifted her spirits all the way back to town.

"Okay," Mae told Jordan, popping back into the kitchen of Jordan's apartment over the shop late that afternoon, "we got these two loads set to roll. You gonna be all right alone till Seth gets here?"

"No problem. Sally's still downstairs for another half hour yet. I'll just lock myself in the apartment and keep packing," she said, surveying the other half-packed boxes at her feet. Yancy had not yet released the condo to her, so she was taking more things from here to the lodge than she'd originally planned, including the furniture Mae and Bill Bowlegs had loaded in their two trucks downstairs. She walked out on the landing and waved to Bill. He had just come by to introduce himself and say she could call him anytime she had to drive somewhere. That was before Mae corralled him as a second mini-moving van.

Jordan walked Mae partway down the steps. "I don't know what I'd do without you," she told Mae. "You've always been like a second sister to me, through good times and bad."

Mae squeezed her arm. "We were at least sisters-in-law once. If you and Seth ever get to be real close again, can't say it would make me unhappy."

"Your family—especially your parents—wouldn't like us getting back together."

"You'd be surprised," she insisted, then shook her head. "But Frank would pro'bly flip." Jordan could tell Mae was upset and waited for more of an explanation. "Him and Seth always going at it for Frank's rebellious ways. Sometimes I think Frank's too much like Seth used to be. Seth's so sure the kid's gonna get hurt."

"I haven't seen Frank since he was little," Jordan said, going all the way down the steps to walk Mae to the door of her truck. Bill Bowlegs started his just ahead of them. Jordan waved her hand in front of her face as the exhaust wafted her way.

"I *hope* you haven't seen Frank," Mae said. Before Jordan could ask what she meant, she rushed on, "He's as tall as Seth. Least now that Frank got a job, maybe they patched things up a bit, Wilson says. But—see," she went on, leaning out the window, "what I mean is Frank even told me Seth accused him of maybe taking that panther in the Glades, just 'cause he was out hunting with three buddies at the time." She reached to squeeze Jordan's wrist, hard for a moment. She was always surprised at Mae's physical strength, almost like a man's.

"Frank, maybe in the Glades that day? Seth never said . . ."

"But I'm telling you, it wasn't Frank, no way. Those men who took the cat didn't look like skinny kids to you, did they?"

"No. No, not really, I guess," Jordan floundered, but she felt as if Mae was hitting her when she pulled her hand back in and hit the steering wheel. Seth, Jordan thought—had he been helping her, staying close, pretending to protect her, because he wanted to protect his own brother? He'd always asked how much she knew, wanted to keep an eye on her, now even with Bill Bowlegs.

"Good!" Mae exulted. "I knew it couldn't be. I just had to ask you. Too much pressure on Seth, the way he's been picking on Frank. Glad you're trusting Seth and coming to the Winter Dance," she called as she started the truck and drove off.

"Suddenly, I don't know who I'm trusting or where I'm going," Jordan said to herself as she watched them leave the alley.

She went back to the steps and started up. She had a lot of thinking to do before Seth showed up—and that should be soon. She had two bones to pick with him now: Frank and Michelle Merwyn. But as she glanced down, she saw Marc Chay in the shadow of the greenhouse. She had no idea how long he'd been there. And he was standing almost on the site of one of Lawrence's buried disks.

"Hi!" he called out with a cheery smile and a hesitant wave. "I did not want to interrupt your time with your friends. But when I stopped by—and surmised you were moving somewhere today—I knew I could help."

No way, she thought, but she spoke as kindly as she could. "I'm doing okay, really, Marc. Just packing a few more small boxes. You know, personal things. Thanks, but I'll be fine." She kept heading up the steps, hoping he took the hint.

"All right, then. Spare a friend a cup of coffee?" he asked, putting one foot on the bottom step and grasping the railing. "I think I've got a lead you'd like to hear about."

She was torn. He was just trying to help, but she didn't feel comfortable about it. "All right," she said. "But I have a guest coming soon, and it will have to be instant coffee."

"Jordan?" Sally's voice called out the back door of the shop. "I wouldn't bother you but there's an old friend of yours on the phone from Chokoloskee, who says she'd like an orchid garden on some historic site or other. Sounds intriguing."

"Can you transfer it up?" Jordan called down to her and went upstairs with Marc trailing after.

She took the call on the kitchen phone—an old high school buddy, Lynn Smallwood, wanted an orchid garden for her grandfather's historic store, a popular tourist site, on the island. Marc stood on one foot, then the other, glancing around the cluttered kitchen, peering in the half-packed boxes. Jordan quit watching him to write down some information on a pad she scrabbled for on the counter.

"I'll love doing it," she told Lynn. "It's a real honor. Right. I'll see you soon. Bye now."

When she hung up and turned back, Marc was gone. Suspicious—and angry at herself for letting him in against her first instinct—she kept talking for a moment. "No, go ahead, Lynn," she said loudly, as if she were still on the phone. "Tell me more about it."

She tiptoed across the small living area and peeked into her bedroom. Marc was quietly sliding drawers open and closed, feeling quickly along the bottom— and top—of each with one hand. She stepped back, remembering too well how he had been searching a closet the day Lawrence disappeared. Suddenly, she was convinced he had taken the extra condo key and had a copy made, maybe taken his little gun back. But surely he was only looking for Lawrence's work he must be convinced she had. Or could he have actually had something to do with Lawrence's disappearance, too? How far would he go to get his hands on the valuable work her husband had done?

Uncertain whether to confront him or flee, she jumped at a knock on the back door. Thank God, Seth was here. He'd toss Marc out. But just as she turned away, Marc jerked around at the knock and saw her. He looked surprised, then angry to be caught with his hand in the till.

"Seth," she called, running for the door. "Coming!"

Yancy Tatum stood there, glaring at her through the screen.

"Seth?" he said. "Why are you expecting him? And who is that? Oh, Mr. Chay, how are you?"

Jordan breathed a sigh of relief; Marc had followed

her to the door. "He stopped for some coffee, but he was just leaving," she told Yancy. "Weren't you, Marc?" she said as calmly but icily as she could, turning for a moment to glare at him.

Yancy's narrowed gaze also raked Marc as he edged closer to the door. "He wasn't bothering you, was he?" Yancy asked, putting out a stiff arm across the width of the door.

"He just came to tell me he was sorry that he had no further leads about Lawrence's research that would get him anywhere," she said, emphasizing the last three words.

"Yeah?" Yancy said, still staring at Marc, who looked more sheepish than she could believe. "Then, see you around, Chay," he said and lifted his arm.

Marc nodded and, mustering his pride, walked stiffly between them and out the door.

He had no sooner left than Yancy stepped inside. "Why were you expecting Seth?" Yancy repeated.

She read his anger—or was it even possessiveness—on his face and determined to diffuse it. "Yancy, I really appreciate your help but let's not start out like this. Despite your investigating Lawrence's case, you're not in a position to probe my personal life with my friends."

His eyes narrowed and his nostrils flared. "Thanks a lot. As if I'm not one of those friends? I come here to give you some good news that I've busted my butt over and get hit with that."

Her anger soared to excitement. "What good news?"

"Cases can be reopened, but—here," he said, pulling a piece of paper from his suit coat and thrusting it at her. "It will be detailed in the newspaper tomorrow, so I hope that keeps the press off you. This suicide ruling obviously clears you."

"And everyone else," she said, frowning down at it.

He came closer, stepping over boxes. "I can't believe you've always dragged your feet on this. Fought my trying to clear you of all suspicion. Like I said, the whole case can be reopened as a full-blown murder one."

"You're still threatening me with this," she said, leveling a look at him. "You asked me to trust you, then continually held this over my head."

"I have not," he argued and smacked the counter with a fist so her cooking utensils there rattled. "Look at what I've just done for you. You're reading things into it. I come here relieved for you, thinking I could even take you out to celebrate, and I get called by your one-time lover's name. Oh, that's right, he was briefly your first husband, wasn't he?"

"Yancy," she said as patiently as she could, "I could never celebrate an official ruling on Lawrence's suicide, any more than I could for his murder."

He seemed to stand stiffly at attention. "Look, Jordan. I've been working day and night on this. And I haven't let one thing slip by, not even forgotten what you told me about losing your cat. I asked around at the marina where Lawrence took the boat out. I won't give up on it."

He seemed so sincere that she stepped closer and touched his arm before she moved past him to stand by the door. "I do appreciate everything you've done. That cat means a lot to me, and I don't want to sound ungrateful."

His shoulders slumped slightly as his eyebrows lifted. "So we're still friends," he asked hopefully.

"Sure," she said, not wanting to hurt his feelings.

She couldn't help it, but she somehow always felt sorry for Yancy, even when she was frustrated with him. Maybe it was because she understood that the Hartmans had been unfairly on the top of the old Lokosee Island social feeding chain and the Tatum boys on the bottom scrapers' end. "Who says friends don't argue sometimes?" she added with a lame little smile.

"Then I'll see you," he said, pointing an index finger at her. "But I sure don't like your idea of moving out to the boonies, a woman alone like that."

"I'm not afraid there," she told him, putting her hand to the doorknob. She had told him earlier where she was going in case he needed her for further police business. "I'm getting security lights and a big dog."

"Yeah," he said with a sigh as he joined her at the door. "One that barks a lot—like those hounds that got killed by those Seminole darts that day. And I said, *Seminole,* Jordan, so I'd really suggest you don't stumble over the same rock twice. Of trusting Seth Cypress and his kind, I mean."

She opened her mouth to take back everything kind she'd just said, but why rile him again? She was glad to see him thud down the back wooden steps into the thickening dusk.

She double locked the door behind him, then hurried through the apartment, closing windows and curtains, despite the delightful breeze. Two unwanted guests so far and still Seth hadn't come. He was late, and she was worried—for one thing, that something bad had happened to him. But if she could get him to admit he'd faked interest in her just to protect Frank, she'd somehow find the strength to lock him out of her life, too.

Chapter Fifteen

When the phone rang, Jordan jumped so hard she hit her knee on the chest of drawers in the bedroom. She had been doing the same thing she had caught Marc doing a few minutes ago—running her hands above each drawer—just to see what he might have been expecting.

She got the phone on the second ring. "Hello," she said, her heart pounding. She expected it to be Seth or some news about him.

"Jordan, Yancy again. I came over to your condo to sign off on it. You know, take the crime scene notice off the door and release it to you."

She wondered why he hadn't mentioned that before. "Has someone been in the condo again?" she asked, twisting the phone cord tightly around her index finger.

"Just me, but I think your cat's here. Not in the condo but outside in the hall."

"What? You found him? Are you sure?" She couldn't believe it: what a coincidence the cat was where he started, especially after Yancy had just said minutes ago he'd keep looking for him.

"Your neighbor, Mary Hawkins, says it looks like him. It's kind of skinny and sick, so I just had her take it in and didn't want to move it, or I'd bring it right over to you. I'm calling from her place. Can you come here?"

"Yes, yes, of course! Let me talk to Mary."

A pause. Muffled voices. "Jordan, this is Mary. It sure does look like him. He's half starved and maybe sick. He's drinking a lot of water but didn't want canned tuna."

"He loves canned tuna," she said. All the same, she tried to tell herself he was probably just excited to be home. "Does he have his collar?"

"No collar. Maybe, you know, if Lawrence took the cat with him when he left, it found its way here some-how, like those things you read about, *Lassie Come Home* and all. I told Detective Tatum he's a real hero, finding him outside your door and bringing him here for help."

"A real hero," she echoed hollowly. "Mary, please keep an eye on the poor little thing. I'll be there soon. And tell Yancy that I really appreciate what he's done, but he doesn't have to take up his valuable time wait-ing for me, because he's gone way beyond the call of duty already."

She hung up and grabbed her purse, then jerked to a stop with her hand on the doorknob. She'd need to leave Seth a note. She gasped when she saw a big man come up on the landing. Seth!

She yanked open the doors. "Thank God you're here. Yancy just called from my condo to say my cat's back. Can you come with me? Please, we have to hurry. We have to talk about some things . . ."

Her voice trailed off when he didn't budge at first, but put his arms around her when she stepped out to close the door. For a moment she thought he might refuse because of Yancy. Then she remembered his family problems. She wanted to ask him about Frank, but that would have to wait.

"I was worried when you were so late," she said, standing stiffly within his embrace. "Seth? Are you all right?" She looked up into his rugged, tired face when he didn't answer.

"Yeah. Somebody told me he saw one of my brothers in Immokalee. I thought he had a job across the state, so, figuring they were wrong, I drove into town to find him. Turned out several people saw him."

"But you didn't?" she asked, gripping his arm as he shook his head slowly, wearily. "This brother—was it Frank?"

That jerked him from his dejection. His gaze met hers. "Why mention him? You remember Frank?" he demanded, sounding so suspicious that her insides twisted. So maybe all of this resurrected romance was—on his part—only playing a role so he could keep an eye on her and the panther investigation.

"It's just," she explained, pulling away from him and starting down the steps, "that Mae said he has a new job and she was proud of him—something like that. Can we talk about it later?"

"Yeah, sure. Let's go get your cat. We can use some good news."

"Micco, it's you! Oh, Micco," she cried when she saw the bedraggled cat.

"Micco?" she heard Seth say, but she couldn't help it if he knew now she'd long ago renamed a cat called Mike with a word that meant *chief* in Seminole. Yancy's quick intake of breath showed he'd caught it, too. Sitting on the floor, she cradled the thin cat in her arms, rocking it slightly back and forth while Mary wiped her eyes and Seth and Yancy just stared—at each other.

"If only you could tell me where you've been and what you've seen!" she murmured into its fur.

"Right," Yancy said. "It's the best witness I've had yet."

Maybe her luck was turning now, she thought. Maybe getting Micco back was the beginning of getting somewhere in this mess—somewhere good. It did make her feel warmer toward Yancy.

But they were right that the cat was ill. Jordan thanked Yancy for releasing the condo and calling her about the cat, but despite his glowering face, she asked Seth to drive her to the all-night vet clinic, where they did some blood work.

"You're very sure this cat had all its shots?" the vet, a young, blade-thin woman with a geometric haircut asked.

"Absolutely."

"But nothing recent?"

"Not for at least six months."

"It seems he's got some kind of viral infection—and a shaved spot on the nape of his neck the fur covers where it looks like he's had recent injections," she said, showing Jordan the spot while the cat winced and actually turned to hiss. Jordan saw what she meant, but she had no idea how he'd gotten a shot.

"I'm not sure what to prescribe," the doctor went on, "but I'm afraid his condition might deteriorate untreated. I'll have a blood sample tested in the lab tomorrow morning. And we'll keep him here for observation tonight so—"

"No," Jordan said, standing and pulling the cat closer to her on the stainless steel examining table. "Check the blood and then call me, but Micco's coming home. I didn't get him back just to lose him again. Whatever he's been through, it's too much. I'll return him for a shot or treatment if you call me."

In the car, she told Seth, "I don't want to, but I've got to spend the night at the condo. It's the only home Micco's ever known. There's still cat food and his things at the condo. I couldn't bear to throw it out."

"If Yancy hasn't already, as many times as he's probably been in there, fantasizing it was his place and you're his wife," he muttered. When she didn't answer, he hit the steering wheel with a fist. "All right, I admit I still can't stand the guy. If you've got a couch there for me, I'd like to stay with you. I'll head back home before dawn. Besides," he said, "we've got a lot to talk about."

"That we do," she said, deciding to save the argument about his spending the night for later. "That we do."

It seemed so strange to be back in the condo—and with Seth. She was really on edge, especially after all the months estranged from Lawrence and the days the police had kept it sealed as a crime scene. And now to have to have a showdown with Seth here was really making her nervous.

Her first reaction when he said he'd stay was to refuse his offer. Then again, Yancy could still have a key and suddenly appear again. Marc might have made a key. Right now, she'd decided to face down Seth and see how things went. She could always demand he leave, then barricade the door for the night.

While Micco flopped in his old place by the sliding door to the lanai, she futility searched the place for cameras. The cat drank a lot of water but turned down food again. That scared her, for it looked fur and bones.

After Jordan fixed them a makeshift meal of soup and crackers she scrounged up in the nearly bare cupboards, Micco came over to sprawl at her feet in the kitchen while she and Seth talked. She had already told him about the suicide ruling on Lawrence's death. When she said she was doing an orchid garden at Rey's ranch and asked about Michelle Merwyn knowing him, he explained about Winston Rey's Cuban cowboys infringing on Seminole land and water—and how accommodating Rey had been to get the situation corrected. Rey'd had his men mend the fences immediately, he said—he'd seen that from an airplane earlier today.

"I believe it. He told me that he feels terrible about the way things turned out years ago with the Seminoles and that he's been trying to make amends. And apparently actions speak louder than words with him. How about you?" she asked, leaning slightly toward him across the small glass kitchen table.

"What do you mean? Do I trust him?" he said, frowning at her.

"I mean, do your actions speak louder than your words? Should I trust *you*?"

"What are you talking about?" he demanded, sitting up straighter. "I didn't know until tonight *you* were working for Rey, especially when we just had a discussion this morning about your not driving off on your own. Now that's trustworthy of *you*," he added sarcastically. He got up to take his plate and silverware off the table and place them noisily on the counter.

She knew he had her on the defensive now and that annoyed her. "I felt I had to keep the appointment, Seth. In all the rush, I'd almost forgotten it. Would you please just sit down? I'm talking about your not being honest with me about Frank."

He refused to look at her. "That's the second time you've brought him up," he said, turning on the faucet to rinse his utensils, then banging them back down on the counter. "I'd really like to know why."

"Mae didn't mean to spill the beans," she said. "She was only concerned about Frank—and you. She says you've been afraid Frank and his buddies might have been the guys in the Glades, but of course you didn't tell me or the police, did you?"

Looking incredulous, he finally turned to face her. Behind him, the faucet still spewed water full blast. "Why should I bring it up when he had nothing to do with it?" he demanded, his voice rising. "Why should I go around putting ideas in people's heads when there's no proof?"

"So you've proved to yourself it wasn't him?"

"That's right," he said, but his voice and stare wavered.

She recalled he had always argued emotionally when it came to those closest to him—including her. The fact he was a lawyer now, supposedly skilled at interrogation and logic, evidently hadn't changed that. She remembered how irrational he'd seemed—fierce even—when his father had tried to lay down the law to him about annulling their elopement.

She put her chin in her hands and added quietly, sadly, "Now I know why you were shook when I recognized that dart gun. In looking into this—maybe in covering for Frank—you decided to get close to me again, didn't you?"

"Listen to yourself," he said, suddenly spinning back to jerk off the faucet so hard the pipes shuddered. "You're the one who came out to see me first after all this time."

"And you were cold and hard, because you didn't know you needed to keep an eye on me yet—string me along to be sure I didn't recall a better description of those Seminoles or something."

She could see his furious expression only in his dark reflection in the window over the sink. "You'd make a terrible lawyer, Jordan," he goaded. "Assumptions, emotions."

She stood up angrily. "A few minutes ago, you mentioned that the tribe has an airplane. One you take up over the Glades to keep an eye on things?"

"Occasionally," he replied, turning around to face her again, but failing to look nonchalant as he leaned against the sink with his arms crossed. "We rent it, don't own it, Counselor. It's an old, beat-up one. With some of the new money, I may get another."

"So, were you up the day the panther got taken?"

"You're accusing me now? Oh, I get it, I was in the plane that dive-bombed you that day trying to keep you away from Frank and his buddies, because *I was in on it, too*!"

He looked livid, though he was trying to keep control. "I didn't say that, and I don't believe it," she insisted, but her voice caught. She was deeply grieved that what she thought they could rebuild between them was evidently sunk in sand. "Seth," she said, holding both hands up, "I'm not accusing Frank. I'm just trying to find out why you're telling me crazy things like you need me and always have when we can be arguing like this. Now, would you just come over here and sit down? Please?"

She indicated his chair across from her again. He stalked over. He sat up straight, his shoulders so stiff he could have had an iron rod running across them.

"Could it be at all possible," she asked, "that a young, impressionable kid like Frank—I don't really know him except from things Mae's said over the last few years—could be mad enough at white people to actually attack some of them? Maybe because of that time he got beat up? Or maybe because he knows what Winston Rey did to his father and his tribe when he made that Seminole movie years ago? Maybe your father told him about it, so Frank decides to make a move against the whites he feels are tampering with the sacred Seminole panther. I'm not talking about Lawrence but the team in the Glades that day."

At the mere mention of Lawrence's murder, Seth stared hard at her a moment, then shook his head. "I think," he said, clearing his throat, "memories of his beating really screwed him up and stick with him. And yeah, Dad has talked about Rey, and Frank could have picked up on that—but why not then go do something against Rey?"

"For one reason, because he's got an armed guard on the gate."

Seth gave a little snort. "That wouldn't stop a Seminole. We share such a long boundary . . ." He stopped, his eyes widening. He swallowed hard.

"—with fences that could be torn down to let Rey's cattle out," she finished for him.

"That's getting too crazy," he said, but his brow furrowed and his mouth was a tight line. "It's just those Cubans don't have the know-how or scruples of Seminole cowboys—I've seen that. Rey's guys probably knocked down a few fences to let their herd use our water or grass. Besides, Dad always admitted—at least years after his hatred of Rey burned out—that his struggle with him back then led to some good things."

"How?" She only recalled hearing that Rey's *Ever-*

glades Victory movie had made the Seminoles look like bloodthirsty savages instead of a people driven to desperation defending their families and land. So, insulted and furious, Cory Cypress had staged a walk-out of the Seminole extras in the film on Lokosee the year before she was born.

Seth breathed out hard, then explained, "The Seminole protest of that movie got Dad to help start AIM—the American Indian Movement. So that helped jump-start the Indian Militancy movement of the sixties that some people linked to the black civil rights movement. Indians took part in the Poor People's March on D.C. in sixty-eight, and red men from many tribes took over Alcatraz Prison to protest the next year. Held it for nine months to make a point," he said, his voice suddenly proud as he gave a sharp nod. "Native Americans occupied Fort Lawton in Seattle and Mount Rushmore for a while—Dad flew out West for both of those."

"I didn't know all that. But if Frank did, he should have felt good about Rey, not bad. Still—kids, confused, hurt, proud, passionate . . ."

"Like we were once?" he whispered. They exchanged long looks and the barest of nods. "I still think we could recapture that passion if we could just fight our way out of these problems. Jordan, I—"

They both turned toward Micco as he determinedly pawed at the cabinet doors under the kitchen sink.

"You keep his food in there?" Seth interrupted himself just when she was dying to know what he'd say next.

"No. Just some catnip-type stuff Lawrence brought him. Letaria. You know, Glades mint. Is it part of any Cory Cypress herbal cures?" she asked as she got up to open the doors for Micco.

"Sure, but I don't know for what exactly."

She watched the cat nose the musty, fragrant hemp sack under the sink and started licking, then eating some loose leaves. They were everywhere under here, so the police had probably been through the whole bag looking for something.

"If Micco wants this stuff so much, I'll take some in with us and try to get him to sleep," she said.

"Jordan, wait," he said, his face intensely earnest. "Yeah, maybe when I came to see you at the greenhouse, I was trying to learn if you knew or had said anything to the cops that would point to Frank. But then—believe me or not—I started to feel the old pull toward you—between us."

"We'd never get back there, would we?" She heard the emotion, the tears creeping into her voice, but she refused to break down or cry. "I just don't know how I can be agonizing about us right now—when there's so much else I have to do. No," she said, picking up Micco and cradling him like a baby, "please don't say anything else right now. I'm going to bed now. Since I'm not sure others haven't had keys made, if you'd sleep on the sofa, I'd feel better. But if not . . ."

"Yeah, sure I will," he said, standing and nodding. "I'll knock to wake you up if I leave early in the morning. Jordan, I hope I haven't made a mess of things—another start."

She gave a little laugh and shook her head dazedly. "I wouldn't even recognize another mess in my life right now."

She wanted to touch him, kiss him. But she gave him only a shaky smile as she hurried from the room before she decided to stay.

Chapter Sixteen

"I've had horrible nightmares since it happened," he admitted.

Brent Rymer's classical nose and pale, intelligent face always seemed at odds with his crew cut, pop art T-shirts, and gold neck chain. Today he even wore a black leather jacket and kept pulling up the collar as if he were cold. But Jordan realized he was trying to hide the blurred tattoo his attackers had put on the panther team members' right ears.

"The bad dreams are like old cowboy-Indian movies from my childhood, real shoot-'em-ups," he went on. His gaze darted around the restaurant. "I dream the Indians are shooting me with arrows and guns, shooting my horse I want to save."

"I'm sorry. Nightmares from reality—I understand," Jordan assured him, leaning slightly forward over the narrow Formica table. She was touched that he had confided in her, although she hadn't gotten anything out of him that might clear Frank as she had hoped: "Yeah, I guess they could have been young," Brent had recalled. "They were pretty slim, though I really didn't get a good look. But I swear they were really Indians, not just dressed that way. And that's why the bad dreams."

"I appreciate your being so honest."

"I owe it to you. You really saved us out there. Besides, like I said, I'm telling you in Lawrence's memory, too. And I apologize for carrying on about shooting nightmares when you've lost Lawrence—that way," he added, his face showing concern, for her or himself she wasn't sure. "I'm thinking of seeing a shrink if all this doesn't stop. I'm like a zombie during the day from lack of sleep, and that and what happened to Lawrence is playing havoc with my work." He rubbed his eyes with a thumb and index finger as he talked. "I've got an out-patient appointment next week in Fort Myers to have this tattoo removed from my earlobe. Laser surgery. Oh, yeah—in the dreams, the Indians are always trying to tattoo me, too."

She felt terrible for him, though the last thing she needed to hear was more bad news. It was early morning, and they'd met only for a quick breakfast at McDonald's near the panther team office and lab, because Brent was going to put in a half-day's work. He'd told her to stop by the lab, but she didn't want to risk running into Marc there.

She had just dropped Micco at the vet and had to go back for him in an hour. He seemed a little better, but his blood sample tested overnight indicated he had FeLV, a feline lentivirus comparable to AIDS, which was ultimately fatal. Now, over juice, coffee, and Egg McMuffins, she explained about Micco to Brent and asked if Lawrence had ever used domestic cats for experiments.

He shook his head. "They're too different from the panthers, despite what the layman might think. Marc Chay might be able to tell you more about cat AIDS, but he's leaving tomorrow to lobby for funds in Washington. Before he and Lawrence had their falling-out, they were pretty tight on things."

"Marc and Lawrence had a falling-out? Do you know what about?"

Brent pursed his lips and nodded. "Lawrence getting suddenly secretive with his latest research," he said, "on a breakthrough he said he needed to corroborate. I was going to talk to him about it, but Marc's team leader now, so I let him have first shot at it. Then—everything hit the fan."

While he frowned out the window, she waited, hardly breathing.

"And, unfortunately," he went on, "Lawrence somehow took his work with him. Even though Marc's in touch with Lawrence's research contacts now, he says he can only reconstruct so much."

She gripped her hands together in her lap under the table. She planned to turn over a copy of the computer backup disk to the team as soon as she figured out if Marc could be trusted with it. He seemed too desperate to get his hands on Lawrence's so-called breakthrough. Maybe he was now trying to get private funds—and resulting glory—for himself, not for the team.

"So, if Lawrence's records were located, it would take Marc to decipher them?" she asked. "You or the team couldn't?"

"Well, maybe in part," he admitted, frowning. "But Lawrence worked with a lot of chemical formulas and—Marc said—lately in his own kind of code."

"Code?" she repeated.

"I'm more into animal lab and field work," he went on, setting the side of his hand on different places on the table as if to block out separate areas of expertise. "Actually, Lawrence could more easily do what I did than vice versa. The guy was a genius at that stuff, Jordan. It's a real loss to the team, even if he didn't always act like a team player." He cleared his throat. "I guess you knew that."

Especially in his marriage, she thought, but she only nodded. "I was wondering something else, Brent, probably off the wall."

"A lot of discoveries come that way, even in science."

"Was there any chance Lawrence had originally planned to go out with the tracking team that day of the attack? Could there be some connection between what happened to the team and then to him that day?"

"Detective Tatum asked the same thing. No," he said, dumping another packet of sugar in his coffee and stirring it intently. "You mean, someone came looking for him with us, then when they didn't see him, just drugged us and went back to Naples after him? Detective Tatum says the timing's too close for that. It would have had to be two sets of abductors. And I asked him why would someone take the panther we had treed because I had no idea."

She leaned forward on her elbows and lowered her voice. "Unless they thought Lawrence would need one to experiment on after they abducted him. Maybe that's why they took our cat, too—if, like you say, they were laymen and didn't know it doesn't help to study domestic cats."

"*They?* Who is *they*?" he demanded, his voice rising. "It was in the paper he committed suicide!"

"Yes, I know," she said, gesturing for him to keep his voice down. People looked around from the next table. "It's just—even with our marriage over, I thought he had a lot to live for," she whispered. "I just can't believe he killed himself."

He hunched his shoulders and tugged up the collar

of his jacket again. "You know, I had hopes," he admitted quietly, "that his work would help put our efforts to save the panther on the worldwide endangered wildlife map, so to speak. I know it was a long shot—off the wall, like you said before. But there is some as yet undiscovered reason the big cats can live with that AIDSlike lentivirus and not show the symptoms of the disease. Damned cancer and viruses—you think science could tame them."

"Lawrence desperately wanted to."

"He said once he thought the Everglades had everything in common with the rain forest—you know, an Edenic breeding ground for miracle cures from simple, God-given plants that primitive people—even our own American pioneers—believed in." Suddenly, his face looked younger, and his voice became excited. "After all," he went on, "if the herb meadowsweet can produce salicylic acid to make aspirin and the rosy periwinkle can produce alkaloids that treat Hodgkin's disease and leukemia, why not something like that to cure AIDS?"

"But you don't mean Lawrence—a virologist—was working with herbs?" she asked.

"Not directly, but they are the source for chemical compounds and synthetic derivatives to attack viruses, and *that* was his domain. You know, Jordan," he admitted, settling back in the booth, "it could have been a Nobel prize–quality discovery."

"So Marc said. And a fortune in all this."

He nodded. "I read somewhere that the rosy periwinkle drugs bring in around 180 million a year. Can you imagine what a curative, preventive—or even just a suppressant—drug for AIDS could mean? Shoot, that would be enough to get my sweet old grandmother to turn to crime."

She had another question, but it flew right out of her head when she saw who was staring at them through the long glass window as he walked around to the front door. She gave a little gasp, then asked Brent, "Did you tell Marc Chay we'd be here?"

"No," he said, craning around to follow her gaze. "It's so close. Our people come in here all the time, though I thought he'd be packing for his D.C. trip."

"I hope you'll keep in confidence everything I've been asking," she said hastily as Marc headed for them.

"Hi, you two," he greeted them with a smile. "Brent, I thought that was your car—and Jordan. What a surprise!"

She hoped Brent—she was beyond trusting or caring about Marc—was not too surprised when she quickly excused herself and left the two of them together.

"This is the thanks I get for letting you have that store!" Wilson yelled at Mae.

He slapped the empty punch-out pack of birth control pills in her lap, but looked like he wanted to slap her. At least the kids were playing at her sister's so they didn't have to hear this, she thought.

"Found that in the trash, looking for something I lost!" he went on. "I lost something, all right, more than I already thought."

"Wilson, just—"

"You care more about your place in town," he yelled, "than this one with your kids in it. Kids you don't want to get any more from me!"

Her pulse pounded. He never raised his voice unless he was drinking, and he wasn't now at ten on Saturday morning.

"Wilson, please, just—"

"You gonna tell me those pills not yours?"

"No. They're mine." She rose from the couch to feel less at a disadvantage. Poking two fingers in the punch-out holes, she defiantly shook the empty packet at him. "See, the month's all gone, so I got my period now, as you well know. The thing is, the timing for another baby just wasn't right, and you know you don't like that rhythm method—"

"But I do like babies, even if you don't!"

"Maybe that's 'cause you're not caring for them, worrying for them in this crazy world we got. Ours aren't even teenagers yet, and look how messed up Frank and some others I could name been acting. But I love them, ours, really. Let's not argue," she said, holding up both hands. "You know our loving's been better when I'm not worrying about—"

"Loving! You don't give a hang for anything but that fancy white woman store. Always listening to that Jordan Quinn. Not listening to me!" He stomped down the hall, went into their bedroom, and banged the door shut. Then he opened it again, probably when he heard her follow him. "Let me know when you want to trust me enough to be honest again. I thought we were a family. Lies and secrets, like that stupid soap opera you used to like." He slammed the door shut even harder.

She leaned against the wall and, irritably, sailed the empty pill packet into the bathroom wastebasket. *Two points,* she thought, as Wilson always said, triumphantly pretending he'd sunk a basket. She did love him and their kids, but she just couldn't handle all this right now.

She leaned her head back and stared up at the low ceiling. He no doubt expected her to knock and plead, then to vow she'd never take what her Seminole sisters called "the golden nuggets" again. But she just couldn't and wouldn't. He was wrong to blame the store. If she had changed, it was from loving people who were hurting, including Wilson. Frank's behavior, Seth's anger, Jordan's grief and guilt over that snake Lawrence—it was all just too much.

She stormed down the hall and into the kitchen. Grabbing her truck keys off the hook, she yanked open and banged shut both the house door and truck door. Letting the cool morning air blast in, she drove straight out where marsh mingled with prairie along the eastern shell road. Maybe, she thought, she'd fish her guns out from under the seat and set up some pinecone targets to blow to bits. That would make her feel better.

Then, as if she had been seeking him all along, she saw her father's old truck parked along the road out by his medicine fields. Unlike white doctors with their drugstores and pharmacies, tribal medicine man Cory Cypress kept his natural collection of remedies right out here. She pulled up a ways behind his truck, killed the engine, and got out.

In the old days, an "unclean" menstruating woman would not have dared approach an *ayikcomi*, but times were different, even for Cory Cypress. Too bad they weren't different for Wilson. Still, she really didn't feel like talking to her father or anyone right now. Maybe she'd just creep close and absorb the healing power of the songs he sang when he honored the plants by taking them from the ground. It would be like a blessing to strengthen her.

Keeping near the line of shrubby bushes, she went closer as the breeze carried his singsong voice to her. She watched where she stepped because she could see

he was pulling button snakeroot, and her old grandmother had once said that would call the snakes for
miles around. It was a tall plant he would use to make
the purifying black drink for men at the Winter
Dance.

She wondered if Seth had told him they asked Jordan to come. His back still to her, he bent occasionally
to place the herbs on his gathering blanket. Soon he
moved on to hairy-stemmed Indian sage, which the
whites called boneset. It cured colds, but Mae longed
to have it cure the heat of Wilson's anger and mistrust.

She leaned against a twisted trunk and let the old
melody take her back to when her father would do
medicine on someone in the next room, the days they
first came to the reservation because of Seth and Jordan. She could picture how her father looked when
she'd peeked in one time, forcing the power of his
magic song into the medicine by blowing smoke
through a tube of cane, just like the old poison dart
guns the people once used to kill game. She closed
her eyes and drifted—and then jerked alert at the impact of that memory when the next strident song
began.

It was a song of love magic, only backward, different, dissonant. The kind of song that cursed, not
cured. Against Seth and Jordan, like years ago? Or
did her father sense—as he sometimes strangely did—
that she and Wilson were scraping along together like
splintered boards? Or maybe Seth was wrong to think
it might have been Frank who had shot darts from the
ancient blowgun into white men who took *co-wha-
chobee.* Her father would but have to say the word,
and any three Seminoles would follow him anywhere.

She peeked through the rustling leaves of the tree.
Her heart thudded her breastbone, and a sheen of

sweat swept her brow. He came closer, eyes closed, head down, shuffling in steps of a dance she did not know. Now it was a pleading, plaintive song that could make a person ill—or, it was said in the old days, could make a man's gun go off and kill him.

She pressed her fist to her lips, but he stopped dancing to gather another herb, Glades mint now. She could smell it, heady and musty all at once. The old *ayikcomi's* many watches and rings—for people often paid him in gifts he wore to honor them—blinked gold at her in the sun.

But the curse song had scared her. She didn't need that today. It might rub off on her or those she loved. It had come too close when she had only longed for a blessing to wrap around her like a shawl.

Mae Osceola bent low. Heart thudding louder than a drum, she ran toward the road.

When Jordan picked up Micco at the open clinic, she asked the vet more questions. "Why do cats like catnip, Doctor?"

"Actually," Dr. Daye said with a shrug of her narrow shoulders, "we don't exactly know. It just has a powerful, almost narcotic effect on them, and they crave it—most of them. You know, when this cat was diagnosed with FeLV, it looked so bad at first I was going to suggest putting it to sleep to keep it from the suffering to come. But it seems clearer-eyed today—as if it's in remission or something. I've got to tell you, though a lot of researchers are working on it, we don't know a thing about preventing or curing this. Maybe it's just the placebo effect on Micco of being home with you that makes him look better and caused his temperature to come down like this. Is he eating yet?"

"A little. But mostly he's been eating leaves."

"Leaves? From your orchids or something? Some could be quite toxic, you know. Or do you mean catnip? Is that why you asked .."

From the muted recesses of memory, pieces of a puzzle began to click together for Jordan. That day Lawrence disappeared, when she questioned Max about seeing him, hadn't he said he had picked up and returned to the Hispanic man a picture that blew out of Lawrence's things? A picture of a *wildcat eating leaves*? It didn't make sense then, but maybe it did now. And on that plane ride where she and Marc scattered Lawrence's ashes, Marc had said, *Mint is as good as a miracle drug—Lawrence said that once.* Catnip was a mint and letaria was, too. Now, somehow, like a scientist—if she had a theory, how could she test it? How had Lawrence tested it?

"Mrs. Quinn, as protective as you are of this cat, and, with what happened, understandably so, of course," Dr. Daye was saying in her best patronizing, bedside-manner voice, "I assume you don't want to consider sanitization for the animal at this time?"

"What? Sanitization. Euthanasia? No! And it's not catnip he's been eating but letaria leaves. Do you know what they are?"

The woman rolled her eyes as she fingered her stethoscope in her jacket pocket. "Botany was hardly my major, but there are many plants in the mint family," she said. "That's the Glades mint, right? Are you growing those? Cats eat some plants to clean hair left in their gut after grooming. Does the cat vomit after eating letaria?"

"No. Maybe he even gets better," she said, scooping Micco in his towel off the cold examining table. Next time she was going back to their original vet. She wanted no dealings with someone who was pushing mercy killings, even for cats, at least not when there was hope.

"Now, Mrs. Quinn," Dr. Daye said and put her hand on Jordan's arm to stay her flight, "don't get your hopes up. This is absolutely fatal so—"

"Life itself is fatal. I have to go now."

"I'm just telling you that this disease has no cure . . ."

No cure, Jordan thought as she carried Micco down the hall. We'll see about that. Yes, just like Lawrence, she was going to do something about that.

Then something else clicked into place. In Lawrence's morass of chemical equations she had forced herself through, he had repeatedly used an abbreviation that she was sure she had decoded. *Le*, he had written again and again. *Le*. She had thought it must refer to the word *lentivirus*, the particular family of retroviruses that caused AIDS in cats and primates, including humans, but lentivirus had made no sense in most cases.

But could it stand for *letaria*? Why else would Lawrence have brought that herb home and kept it around where he could test it? Micco had helped to remind her of that.

Jordan held Micco close, wrapped in his towel, as she marched into the reception room. One-handed, she wrote a check and hurried out for the drive to the lodge. "Letaria, Micco," she said as she put him in his carrier in the passenger side front seat. "Remember that word because you and I are getting as secret as Lawrence was while we look into it. I didn't get a phone line at the lodge just to talk to friends. We're going online to study your favorite Glades mint, Micco. Letaria."

*   *   *

By early evening Jordan had hit the information highway to research everything she could about letaria and the *labiatae* or mint family—botanical, cosmetic, culinary, and curative uses. She even found that the ancient Greeks had believed Persephone, goddess of the underworld, had cursed one of her rivals and turned her into a mint.

"That's all we need," she told Micco, who insisted on sitting on her lap to help. "A curse from the underworld mixed in with this mess." She also discovered that Florida had many species of this large family, but some, like *labiatae letaris,* were found only in southern states, especially Florida.

"I wonder, Micco," she said aloud, stopping to rub her bloodshot eyes, "if it has to be letaria or catnip cats crave or if some other mints work, too." What if, she reasoned, Marc went out West partly to see if mountain lions ate a comparable mint, or once there, he saw they did and put two and two together? When he came back, he demanded that Lawrence fill him in on letaria, Lawrence refused, because he felt fame and fortune should be only his, then . . .

"It's your big sis, kid!" Lana called from out front as she banged her fist on the front porch door. With an annoyed sniff, Micco abandoned his warm perch. "Let me in 'cause I've got some great carryout Chinese for you!"

As Jordan hurried to the door, she realized she had no desire to eat anything right now, but she was grateful to Lana for thinking of her.

"Just coming back from rehearsal?" she asked as she relocked both doors behind Lana and led her into the kitchen through a path of still unpacked boxes. Lana wore jeans and a red T-shirt with CAT ON A HOT TIN ROOF, WINTERHAVEN DINNER THEATER on it, but as ever, she managed to look elegant, not casual. "So," Jordan asked, "how's the play going?"

"Pretty good. Thank God I'm a fast study, because I've got tons of lines, more than anybody else. Been doing the scenes with Big Mama and Big Daddy lately, a lot of fighting," she said as she put the sack on the corner of the cluttered kitchen table.

"What names for parents," Jordan mused, getting out two glasses and pouring iced tea from a pitcher on the counter. "But I guess everyone feels that way about their folks—they loom *so* big for *so* long. At least ours didn't fight much."

Lana opened her mouth to say something, but closed it and nodded jerkily. "Actually, I'm just going to eat one egg roll with you, since Mama's having us over tonight. We were real sorry you decided not to join us. I suppose you're busy getting—somewhat—settled in here," she added with a sharp look around. "Working on that big ranch project, too, huh?" she asked as Jordan rolled up her sketches from the table so they could lay things out.

"I knew you'd get around to wondering about those 'Hollywood types' you warned me about, Lana," she teased as Lana opened a box of sweet and sour chicken. "They're not so bad, really. By the way, Winston Rey said he knew you had natural talent from the first. Oh, Lana—" she cried as her sister knocked the carton off the table. It slopped sauce onto the peach chair cushion, then smacked to the tiled floor before Jordan could grab it.

"Darn, darn, darn!" Lana said, bending to scoop the sauce back in the carton with her hands.

"Don't burn yourself. It took you by surprise he even remembered you, I suppose." Jordan elbowed her away as she knelt with a spatula and paper towels.

With a huge sigh Lana untied the seat cushion and went to rinse it off at the sink. "And his daughter Michelle is sheer drama," Jordan went on, "seemingly sweet, chatty as heck before she levels a look that could kill."

"Sorry about this mess," Lana said as if she weren't listening. She intently pressed paper towels to the wet cushion on the kitchen counter. "Just trying to do too many things, I guess. But don't let this big ranch contract drive you too hard with all you've been going through, kid. I mean, work's an escape, but only up to a point. People like the Reys can be very demanding."

"They're not putting pressure on me, really. As a matter of fact, it's very relaxed and friendly. I'm going there for dinner tomorrow evening. Lana," she said, straightening to look at her again, wondering if she could be jealous, "is something wrong with the play or at home? Is Chuck still okay with it?"

"Sure. Everything's fine. You know, in the play," Lana said, coming over to the table to pet Micco as he ambled up. "I've got a line that says cats can land on all fours and not get hurt—that's a laugh, isn't it? I mean, even if a cat drops a long ways and survives, it's gonna feel it."

Chapter Seventeen

The place looked a lot weirder than she remembered it.

Surveying the road again to make sure no one had followed her, Jordan locked her car and got out. With small, separate sacks of dried and fresh letaria in one arm and a large bag of groceries cradled in the other, she stood at the entrance to the ramshackle GLADES MUSEUM & WILDLIFE & ORKID H(E)AVEN, ALWAYS OPEN. Smiling, she leaned back against her car to read the other faded, familiar, misspelled signs mounted overhead on the patchwork of weathered cypress boards.

KIDS FREE IF ON A LEESH, one crudely painted sign read. HI, Y'ALL, TAKE HOME A RARE ORKID, ONE OF A KIND, 25 CENTS, her favorite said. THE LORD IS GOOD—REJOYSE AND AMEN TO THAT!!! had always been Seth's favorite. CO-OWNERS OF PARADICE & PARTNERS IN CRIME, JUNGLE CAL & REBEL TURNER, PROPS, held up the sign that read, SEE MAMIE, THE FERCE FL. WILDCAT AND KILLER, THE 15-FOOT (ACTULY 4-FOOT) GATOR—ENTER HEAR.

She did enter here, but it worried her that the place looked and sounded deserted. Not that tourists visited this Tamiami Trail oddity much anymore as they whizzed by. She hadn't been here since she and Lawrence started having problems, because Cal and Rebel always asked how things were going, and she couldn't bear to tell them. Though the two old brothers were getting hard of hearing, she recalled that, when a car stopped, they always sensed someone to talk to. They'd regale their visitors with World War II stories or supposedly true tales of the old days in the Glades, but they always asked people about their lives in the outside world they so seldom visited anymore.

"Cal? Reb? You all here?" she called as she walked the rickety, rotting catwalk over sawgrass-covered ground. In the rainy season this walk sometimes floated. How friendly and familiar this place looked with the tin-roofed house on stilts and the two small so-called museum buildings labeled FLORA and FAWNA. The handrail along the path trembled when she touched it, but at least everything looked intact.

She saw they still parked their rusty pickup truck out here on a platform of cinder blocks, covered with an old tent that was much too small. Rust vied with encrusted salt spray to devour the ragged fringes of the vehicle. A crooked TV antenna and telephone and electrical lines were the only signs the house itself was part of the twentieth century.

The Turner brothers had been her dad's hunting buddies. It was possible to hike hawk-flight straight to the lodge from here, about fifteen miles, without seeing a road or a sign of civilization. Dad and the old men had done that many a time, just as she, Seth, and Mae had years ago. Yancy had his brothers used to like this place, too, she recalled, but Cal and Reb had told them not to come back for tormenting the animals.

As a boy, Seth had always wanted to turn Mamie, their pet panther, loose, because he said she was sacred. He'd almost talked her and Mae into helping with Mamie's great escape one night. But he'd seen the panther had broken teeth and liked being fed, and the old men had taken her on walks with a collar, so he'd tolerated it. Jordan had even gotten Lawrence to stop here once with her to look at Mamie. He'd brought Marc out to sedate and examine her, but Cal and Reb said no, and she'd sided with the old men.

They had once been like uncles to her, and she felt guilty she hadn't been here lately. After college, when she had told them she was going to start an orchid shop in town, Cal had scolded her for going into competition with them. Then they'd filled her car with cuttings and plants of every rare orchid they'd ever found in the Glades. Lawrence never knew she'd sent them a small check each month; as for the stubborn, proud old crackers, she'd told them it was profit from sale of the flowers they'd given her, so they wouldn't refuse it.

"Lookee who's here, Calvin!" Reb screeched and hustled down the walk to hug her, sacks and all.

"I was afraid you two went to Disneyworld!" she teased.

"Why, when we got us a better park here?" Reb demanded.

"Whoo-ey, look what the new day fetched in!" Cal cried as he stuck his head out of the door of FLORA, then quick-stepped down the walk to plant a hard kiss on her cheek. As always, his long whiskers tickled. "If it ain't that gal I'm always bragging on to anyone who'll listen. I tell you, Jordy, you got any business a-tall at that flower shop in town, you can just thank me'n Rebel here for sending you folks that was our overflow."

They all laughed at that. Both talking at once, Cal

and Reb escorted her into the crowded, clapboard house. They dressed almost identically in army-store khaki-colored pants and shirts, but Cal was as scrawny as Reb was stout, Reb bald and clean-shaved while Cal wore a Father Time beard and long hair. They unpacked the grocery store treats she'd brought like kids on Christmas morning, but when she began to tell them what had happened lately in her life, they grew silent, shifty-eyed, and grim.

"Gotta admit we heard 'bout your man dyin', but we thought mebbe you'd tell it your way without us blurtin' it out first," Reb admitted, shuffling his feet. "Might as well fess up how we first heard, Calvin."

"I s'pose," Cal said, giving her shoulder a quick squeeze, just the way her dad used to. "See, Seth stops by time to time. We was kind a surprised he kept tabs on you the last couple years."

"The last *couple* of years?" So that meant Seth had not just become interested in her because he was concerned only about Frank or the tribe.

They nodded in unison; both appeared to be studying her. "Now that your man's gone, God rest him, guess we can say that about Seth," Cal admitted. "Anyhow, after Seth told us, we read 'bout your husband's sad death, from the newspaper somebody brought by."

"Seth brought it by?"

"Not Seth that time," Reb said. "But we figured sooner or later you'd tell us your own way, Jordy."

"More'n once, we done told your daddy 'fore he died," Cal put in with a squinty-eyed glance at their hunting rifles mounted on the wall, "we'd keep an eye on you. Actu'ly, we never liked what your man was doin' with panthers like poor Mamie, a chasin' and a taggin' them. Shoot clean if you're hungry and huntin', but if you're not, steer clear of God's creatures, that's what we think."

"Now, 'bout Seth," Reb said, "that'd be fine if you took up with him again, 'cause we said more'n once that boy's the onliest one for you, didn't we, Calvin?"

"More'n once, yeah."

"He told you I took up with him again?" she asked hopefully. It warmed her to think Seth had cared not only for Cal and Reb over the years but for her.

"Not 'xactly, but said you was goin' to the Winter Dance."

"I had accepted, but things got a little rocky after that."

"No way you wanta set foot there," Reb went on, launching into their next topic as if they'd rehearsed all this.

"That's the gospel truth," Cal added solemnly.

"Why not?" she asked, putting her hands on her hips.

"The thing is," Reb said, elbowing Cal to silence, "Seminoles use those times for passin' out judgment and justice to anybody's crossed their ways a-tall. And their medicine men are the big cheese, and you know who one of them is. Seth might be gettin' over things from way back, but you think his old man is?"

"Seth says so. That punishment stuff is old-time talk. Besides, it only applies to their own people."

"And anyone marries into the tribe, so's we hear," Reb said as the two of them exchanged glances.

"But that's not me, and when I was, it was only one week, years ago," she said, her voice almost wistful.

"Recollect Seth told us he dreams you two still hitched sometimes," Cal said. "And dreams is powerful stuff to those people."

"He does?" she whispered. Suddenly, she had to

admit to herself she had lied to Seth last night at the condo—lied to herself, too. She was not *only* interested in her survival and Lawrence's work. She cared deeply about the well-being of Seth and his people. She wanted to be with Seth and if the invitation was still open, she wanted to go to the dance.

"Jordy," Rebel said, breaking into her silence, "just consider yourself warned. Hey, girl, you still 'mong the livin'?"

"Yes," she said with a guilty, little laugh. "Just thinking of the power of Seminole dreams. Before all this hit, mine used to be strong, too. I've got to get them back again."

"Sure you will now. Those sacks of leaves for Mamie, you say?" Cal asked.

"What? Oh, yes. That's partly why I came. I need to know if she'll eat these Glades mint leaves and if she likes them. House cats do—at least mine. I'm wondering if it might not be a way cats dose themselves or at least that it gives them some kind of chemical high—like catnip or drugs."

"Last thing we need's old Mame on drugs," Reb said with a grin and elbowed his brother, who chuckled. "But she likes her salads, all right. Mebbe there was some of that mint in greens we give her, think so, Calvin? I heard tell all mint's good for the nerves."

"Maybe I ought to start eating it myself," Jordan muttered.

They strolled past the empty cages that had once held coons, rabbits, snakes, and other small animals. No white-tailed deer fed in the little corral anymore. She surmised the Turner brothers would have let Killer and Mamie go, too, but they had become, as people said today, codependent. In his fenced-in gator wallow, big, old Killer looked like a muddy log in a patch of sun. And ageless Mamie was sleeping in her barred cage, so Jordan left the leaves and told them she'd phone them or be back in a day or two. Though miles of Glades separated them, she was happy to have the two—actually, four—old critters for neighbors once again.

"Are you burning trash somewhere out here?" she asked, sniffing the faintly smoke-tinged air as they walked her to her car.

"Naw," Reb said. "Breeze carries from the controlled burns the fancy-pants park rangers do. Took 'em years to figger they should pay attention to the way the Indians used to clear and restore land out here. Smell comes clear from Seminole State Park sometimes."

She hugged them both good-bye and headed back to the lodge. She was going to stop by the orchid shop to tend the greenhouse plants, then, in early afternoon, drive out to the SunRay Ranch for a tour and dinner. Although she hadn't bothered Bill Bowlegs to have him follow her out here on home turf today, she supposed she should request he follow her home from the ranch tonight, because she'd probably leave after dark. Seth had to testify tomorrow before some state committee in Tallahassee, so he wouldn't be back until late.

The smell of smoke was stronger now. She hoped it was just a controlled burnoff and not a wildfire somewhere in the heart of the Glades. A few years ago, winter forest fires had devastated thousands of acres of park and Seminole land, though, like the mythical phoenix, the land always recovered quickly.

She mulled over the fact that Seth had kept closer to the Turner brothers than she had—and that he had "kept tabs on her," as they put it. She had to admit that secretly, almost subconsciously, she had been keeping tabs on him for years, too, reading about him, watching from afar, gleaning tidbits from Mae—and now, if they could just get past a few rough spots, she felt strong enough to have him back in her life.

She sighed as she turned left off the Trail toward Chok and the lodge. "A controlled burn—that's what I feel for you, Seth Cypress."

"It's beautiful," Jordan told Winston Rey as the two of them bounced along in a swamp buggy with huge wheels, heading out into the vast expanse of the Sun-Ray toward his alligator ranching facilities. "It seems so wild and free here."

"Your orchid garden will enhance that," he told her, looking immensely pleased at her compliment. "Like a flowery gate to Eden, a mere step from the civilization of the ranch house to the savage wilds."

She smiled at his grandiose speech. When all this was over, she planned to get some videotapes of his old westerns to see if she could discover this complicated man in his work.

The balloon wheels of the swamp buggy slogged through several inches of a slough. He flipped his cigarette butt into the green-skinned water covered with duckweed. When he turned to smile at her again, she could see her reflection in his opaque sunglasses, even in the shadow of his wide Panama hat brim. She smiled back, enjoying the varied terrain as they plunged through a shallow swamp studded with protruding cypress knees. Finally, they bumped their way down a rutted prairie road toward a widely scattered series of wooden buildings.

It was then she heard a screech, somewhat muted, from that direction.

"You know," she said, craning around and lifting herself slightly from her seat to look toward the buildings, "that sounded like a panther."

"I've thought that once or twice myself," he said with a little chuckle, "but you'll never guess what it really is. And I don't mean Michelle throwing a temper tantrum about how bored she's getting around here. She hasn't been able to pin down that Seminole she's taken a shine to, you see."

Jordan would have laughed at his little joke—until the explanation after the punch line included Seth. She wondered if Winston knew about her past with Seth, but of course he didn't or he wouldn't tease about Michelle like that.

"So what was that if it wasn't a panther?" she asked to get him back on track.

"I've got a flock of peacocks here, among my other collections. They're beautiful, but the price we pay for them sounds like that."

"I was thinking there could be one or more of the endangered cats out here. They're very territorial and give one another a wide berth to hunt, and you've obviously got a lot of land."

"Ah, so you do know a great deal about them," he observed. "Here we are!" He slowed the open vehicle next to a sprawling building. Boards propped up the louvered windows about a foot off the ground to catch the breeze but shade the sun. "When there was heavy pine and cypress logging in the area, this used to be the old crew commissary, and beyond the mess hall, bunkhouse, et cetera," he told her with a dismissive wave of his hand at the more distant structures.

When the motor of the swamp buggy coughed to

silence, she heard music pouring through the windows and screened door. It got louder as he helped her down and led her in—Dolly Parton's bouncy beat song, "Here You Come Again."

"So gators like country music?" she asked.

"We've experimented with different types," he said as he held the door open for her. "Call me crazy, but the little buggers seem to grow faster with country than with pop or opera, and I won't allow that trashy rock. The hatchlings keep calmer and don't bark or grunt as much, though there's no stopping the big boys when they bellow or hiss. I'm telling you sometimes at night we have a regular chorus of tree frogs, gators, peacocks, and birds. You'll have to stay over some evening."

He introduced her to his staff of six men, five of them quite young. Amazingly out here, they wore immaculate white lab coats as if this were high-tech cancer research. The older man in charge explained how, when they had gathered fresh alligator eggs from outdoor nests, the temperature of the nest, simulated here, determined the sex: hatchlings would be female if the eggs were kept medium warm; male, if very warm. Despite the calibrated lights in the egg incubators, he told her they kept this first room of the building in semidarkness. The second one with hatchlings of up to about two feet was dim, too.

"I suppose you're trying to replicate the darkness of their nests in the first room," she observed to Rey. "But why are the striped babies in this dim light, too, when they could be in the sun at this point in their lives?"

He smiled, evidently pleased by her interest or acuity. "We keep them in the dark, so they won't struggle and fight so much, my dear. We don't want them thrashing around and scarring their pretty little hides. Not at $40 to $50 dollars a foot for purses, belts, and boots. And when they're six feet long in two years— you'll see those in the last room and outside—their meat is worth $10 a pound, too. That market's huge in Japan and France. This is a bottom-line business, you know, not something where we're trying to help or save them, like the panthers."

"I realize that. So, from a few inches to six feet in two years? You know, I have friends who have an old gator they've kept as a sort of pet for decades, and it's fifteen feet. I just saw it yesterday, and it looks like Godzilla next to these."

"Really? A gator in their backyard, so to speak?"

"They used to have an old wildlife park on the South Trail, but they're semiretired now—all of them, their old panther, too."

They went into the largest room with thick pens of black-green gators basking under huge sunlamps. She could glimpse pens full of alligators out the back door. She wondered if the dull-looking beasts with those dead eyes cared if they got to be outside or not. Suddenly, she felt very sad.

"I knew better than to serve gator steaks for dinner, after you'd seen all these," he said and elbowed her gently. "I believe, Jordan Hartman Quinn, you have a tender heart." She felt strangely touched he had read her mood so well. "Just remember," he went on, "that all of this is strictly on the up-and-up, controlled by licensing and state regulations. Soon we'll be flying over our land to count nests, and then we'll be permitted to take only a small percentage of the eggs from the wild to restart the cycle of ranching."

"Do you keep a private plane here?"

"A helicopter." He waved good-bye to his foreman

and held the door open for her. She noted it had a double dead-bolt lock. That was odd, she thought. Who would want to break into this place?

"And the chopper is at your disposal should you want to go up and search for wild orchid spots here sometime," he offered, and took her arm as they went out into the slant of sweet afternoon sun. Before they climbed up into the swamp buggy, he turned her gently toward him and said, "Is there anything else you want to ask me—to ask for—Jordan?"

He had not replaced his sunglasses yet. His eyes were clearest, sharpest gray, candid, yet intent. If he had been thirty years younger, she would have actually thought he was coming on to her—and might have responded. She put on her sunglasses and glanced past the pens toward other distant, scattered buildings as she answered.

"If you're not serving gator steaks for dinner, Winston, what's on the menu then? I'm starved."

He shouted a little laugh just as an alligator bellowed from inside. "Come on then," he said, steering her back toward the swamp buggy. "I am, however, serving Gator Lager beer—you know, 'The beer with the bite.' I got it to amuse Michelle."

"We drank that stuff in college," she admitted. "I remember that crazy little gator in sunglasses on the label. Not your or Michelle's style, either, I'm afraid."

He laughed again as he climbed up beside her and turned the key. "My style, my dear, is pleasing my guests," he said, over the engine. Its noise drowned the last strains of Patsy Cline's wailing "I Fall to Pieces," as they headed toward the ranch house.

Chapter Eighteen

"Come on, get in the car," Yancy said.

"I'm really busy," Jordan protested, coming a little closer to the unmarked City of Naples vehicle he'd pulled way up into the gravel driveway of the lodge. Before her like a weapon, she held the electric hedge clippers she'd been using to trim growth away from the house. The continued faint smell of smoke had reminded her she didn't need dry shrubs and grass hugging the place—or providing shelter for anyone out here spying on her. She realized she had begun to feel too complacent these last few days.

"Hey, Jordan, no fair," Yancy said in mock protest, holding up his hands as if she had the drop on him with the huge clippers. "I'm not wearing my gun!"

When she realized how it looked, she smiled sheepishly and lowered the clippers to her side. Their noise had allowed Yancy to walk clear up to her before she heard him. That had scared as well as annoyed her at her own carelessness again, but she just wasn't any good at thinking defensively all the time.

He stood on one foot and then the other, instead of in his usual formal stance. He was dressed, as ever lately, in suit trousers and shirt and loosened tie while she was a mess in her jeans and T-shirt.

"Besides," he added, "those things smell like they're gonna burn up."

"That's smoke from land burnoff along the Trail."

"Oh, right. But then, it could have been my short fuse if you haven't even got an hour to spare to see something special to me. I know, I know, you got a convalescing cat. I supposed you'll have to run in and hold his paw, so you can't take a little drive with me. But if you won't, I'm staying to help so you have some free time *someday.*"

"All right, I'll go. I can probably use a little break." His light mood cajoled her, and he had located Micco for her. "Give me a few minutes, will you? We're not going far?"

"Nope. Just back home. I expected you to be over there on Sunday, but when you weren't, I had no choice but to come here today . . ." His voice faded as she hurried into the house.

She didn't want to go anywhere with him, but maybe she owed him something for his work on Lawrence's disappearance, too, she told herself as she washed up in a hurry and pulled on clean slacks and a peach sweater. She would just tell him she was not going to date him, if that's where this was going. The only real problem with their destination being Lokosee today was that it would soon be all over the island that they were together and in an unmarked police car.

"Promise you'll have me back before it gets too dark," she said as he opened the car door for her.

"Marine Corps honor," he said with a grin and snappy salute. "Besides, I gotta be back in town tonight for an important meeting. You're not the only one who's busy, you know."

She felt guilty for distrusting him before. Obviously,

he'd been under pressure from his new job then. Yancy was a driven man, but with his past, she could see why. And Mama was right that he'd climbed far from where he started, she had to give him that.

They chatted as they went over the causeway to Chok, crossed the island, then drove onto the old, four-car ferry for the ten-minute trip to little Lokosee. The ferryman was Bobby Joe Bender, who they'd known for years, so they talked to him a while before they fell silent, watching the gulls and pelicans soar and skim. The intense colors of the day seemed to seep into the sky as sunset approached. When they entered Lokosee Bay, they stood companionably at the ferry rail, watching the heavens pale from blue to lilac as the sun melted across the watery horizon.

"Didn't see the green flash just now, did you?" Yancy teased as soon as the sun sank.

"No, and you didn't either. It's so elusive I don't believe people who say they see it all the time."

"Yeah, but it's really special when it comes along. Like love."

She had begun to relax, almost to enjoy being with him. But at that, she merely nodded and got back in the car. The only vehicle on this run, their car clattered down the metal ramp at the ferry slip. Yancy started down Loop Road instead of Rim Road; they were the only two choices on the 120-acre island.

"I thought maybe we were going to see your mother for some reason," she observed. "Are we going to see mine?"

"Nope." He went by the prehistoric Calusa Indian shell mound where as kids they'd slid down on trays into the water, past Smugglers Bay with the sports and pleasure boats putting in, including her dad's old fleet, then past both her mother's and Lana's houses in the island's newest, only expensive enclave, The Colony. The car's tires crunched shells and sand as he pulled in on the uninhabited southeast end of the island among blowing sea oats and pine trees. Folks had discussed putting a little park here along the beach, but the land had been earmarked for several luxury lots, which no one had bought yet.

"What?" she asked warily as they got out. "Why are we here?"

"I wanted to show you something, even before my mother." He looked away from her at last, his gaze taking in the piece of land. "Years ago we played here, you know—pirates and all that. Lana buried some fake jewelry she had here just to get rid of us, then we spent all day digging for it. Probably, while her and Chuck made out down the beach," he added with a sly grin and a nod.

Jordan brushed her wind-whipped hair out of her eyes as she slowly turned to face him. "Yes, I remember the so-called pirate's gold you always wanted."

"So I've finally found it here."

"What? Where?"

"I bought this lot, Jordan. Your family and mine are going to be neighbors," he announced grandly with a proud smile. "I'll be putting a house in here with an attached suite for Mom—and Dad when he gets out, but the place will be mine."

As he talked, her eyes had gotten wider and her mouth dropped open, but she quickly recovered and managed a nod and a smile in return. Yancy had the money for this lot? And for a house to go on it? It made her wonder if he'd been taking bribes on the job or if his dad didn't have funds stashed from that drug running he was in jail for—maybe from some foreign drug cartel or something. But she was instantly ashamed of suspecting such sordid things.

"That's great, Yancy. It's a lovely spot."

He tilted his head toward her. "I'm going to start my own family, really put down roots."

She hoped her discomfort didn't show as she took a step back in the sand, then another as her feet slid sideways. "I had no idea you'd bought this." She tried to deflect what she feared might be coming next. "And you know how fast word spreads on the island."

"I have my ways of keeping certain things under wraps when I want," he blurted, then looked like he wished he hadn't put it that way. "But you really mean you're happy for me?" he asked, his face hopeful.

"Of course, I am."

He glanced down at his feet. "A lot of people are going to say, 'What's *he* doing in The Colony, moving Clem and Liddy Tatum in there?'"

"They have no right to say that. My people won't," she said, realizing—at least when it came to Lana— she was probably lying. She could just hear her now: *Liddy Tatum—and Clem, when he gets out of the Stackade at Immokalee—six lots down from my kids!* "You know Hattie and Liddy were friends long ago," Jordan went on, "and my grandfather used to poach gators and cook up white lightning right along with yours."

"And your dad got a windfall, too, didn't he—with those boats that put all of you on easy street?"

"Easy street? It wasn't that way at all. But did you get some sort of—windfall?"

"No way," he insisted with what looked like a ka-rate chop through the air. "I just saved for years. I wanted you to understand—and like it here."

"I have always loved Lokosee." She looked out over the rustling waves to avoid his intense gaze.

"I know," he said, looking as if he'd like to touch her, but not daring to. "I'll admit this is pretty far from my work. I'm gonna start paying on an amphibious plane and learn to fly it. We could commute back and forth to Naples together. And I'd like you to do an indoor orchid garden for me as soon as the house is done." Not meeting her eyes now, frowning, he added, "It's time I get some things I really want."

A plane, too? she thought. Next it would be the whole damned island, so what was going on here?

He took a sidestep toward her in the sand. The tide was coming in; she blessed it and took several more steps away, as if to keep from getting her Keds wet. "Yancy, I wish you all the best. I hope," she said, praying this was pointed enough but would not deflate his joy, "you love living here as much as I'm going to love living at the lodge." Before he could react, she turned and walked back to the car.

Jordan had barely settled back down to her work—final specs of the SunRay orchid garden, when the phone rang. Thinking it would be Seth back from Tallahassee, she grabbed it.

"Jordy, that you?"

"Cal? Reb?"

"Cal," he said and coughed.

"Did you catch a cold? Did Mamie eat the leaves?"

"Loved 'em, but we need some help."

"What's the matter?"

"Brushfire getting too close. Don't know if it jumped from the set ones or what, but the smoke's bad and we gotta move Mamie and Killer—and"—he began coughing again—"ourselves, too."

"Haven't you called the Everglades City fire station?"

"Yeah, but they're covering two other fires farther down the Trail, so our trucks—gotta come clear out—from Naples."

"That grass and brush is dry. I'll be right there!"

She turned on her new exterior security lights and darted around the inside perimeter of the lodge, glancing out each window. She hated feeling she was on-stage after dark and didn't keep them on as much as she had promised Seth. If she heard anything, she always thought, she'd turn them on then to see or scare off whomever was coming too close. She needed to get and train a watchdog, too, but she knew its barking would make Micco nervous. Besides, Yancy's comment that it could get killed just like those hound dogs out in the Glades kept haunting her.

She checked on Micco, then hurried out, carefully locking the door. Speeding down Route 29 from Chok toward the Trail, her mind raced even faster. A fire this late at night could not be a burnoff the rangers—or anyone else legal—had set and certainly not that far down the Trail. No storm with lightning had hit since the night she came back from Key West, so it had to be a cigarette tossed from a car or a campfire someone had not put out.

She noticed a car that had been a ways back moved up and kept up, despite her speed. So what? she told herself. People often drove fast out here, especially at night when snowbirds and tourists were scarcer. But what if someone had been watching the lodge and followed her when she went out? What if she were driving into some sort of trap again—but no, Cal had called, and she trusted them. And surely, just because he was out of town, Seth had not had Bill Bowlegs watch her again without telling her.

As she turned onto the Trail, she could see the bad news Cal had not told her. The fire was downwind, leaping quickly closer to their little piece of land. Orange tongues licked the ground, and crimson jaws devoured pines in a blast of hot breath. How were they going to save Killer and Mamie, even if the old men could save themselves?

When she saw the Trail had fairly heavy traffic, she stopped worrying about the car behind her. Its headlights disappeared, so it had either turned the other way or just joined the line of cars. Wishing she'd thought to bring a wet towel, she parked across the road in a fishing pull-off and ran the rest of the way. Not only did she fear her car could be a fire casualty if she parked too close, but in case the fire engines came, she didn't want to be in the way. From the tail- and headlights of cars, she could see the Trail was still open up ahead, though traffic was clogged.

After crossing the road, she found the catwalk by the silhouettes of signs above. If the rickety handrail had not been there, she never could have kept on the walk. Finally, she saw the lights of the house like beacons in the drifting dark.

"Cal! Reb! I'm here!"

Thickening smoke burned her eyes and scraped her throat. She looked in the house. It was a shambles as if they'd grabbed some things and run. She wished she'd noticed if their old truck was gone. Maybe they'd let the animals go and made it out already.

She ran out and headed back toward the cages, but slowed immediately. For some reason the smoke got worse here. The fire crackled closer as if it came from back in the Glades instead of along the Trail, where someone could have been careless. No one would be creeping through the deep Glades at this time of night.

"Where are you?" she cried, but hacked so hard from smoke she thought she would be sick. The horrid smell of burning—of the death of living things—sat in the pit of her stomach like a stone. Did she hear sirens or were her ears ringing? She backtracked into the house, feeling her way along, soaked a towel at the sink, and went back out with it over her mouth and nose. Her eyes streamed tears. She tried holding her breath until she thought her lungs would burst.

Somewhere, very close, a tree ignited like a giant torch with a deafening whoosh. It lent more light but only to see roiling smoke and a silvery shower of ash. At least she glimpsed that Killer's wallow was empty. The thought that this whole area was aflame—that it might devour land clear to the lodge—terrified her. Micco! And she could be trapped here. But she had to look for Cal and Reb, check Mamie's cage.

As she found the crosswalk that led to the cage, she stumbled and fell to her hands and knees over something large. She gasped in smoke and scrambled away. Killer loose? No, she thought, creeping closer. Another big body—Reb. She turned him over, touched his face. He was sweating. Yes, thank God, breathing. But something sticky—blood on his temple.

Kneeling over him, she wiped blood from her palm to her shirt, panting into the wet towel, sucking in the clearer air nearest the ground. She'd never be able to drag him back to the road. And where was Cal? She'd have to go for help, but she was so close to Mamie now, and she knew how to work the old iron bolt on the cage.

A glowing ember bounced off the walk, then another as she kneeled, bent over, trying to get her bearings. Did she hear Seth's voice? *We'll spring the lock, let it free.* Co-wah-chobee *should live free.*

It was just the memory of that night so long ago— the night he wanted to set Mamie free. They had been drinking beer and acting crazy, and she wanted so to please Seth. This reminded her of sacred Seminole smoke.

She crawled around Reb. Her groping hand touched the rough, shell-studded concrete of the base of the cage. Leaning against it, she stood. Mamie had loved the letaria mint, they said. If only she could keep Mamie with Micco—dose them with letaria, maybe the way Lawrence had been testing cats. Maybe God was testing her in fire to see if she could find Lawrence's answers, find who killed him. To see if she could find her way back to Seth.

She peered into the dark, smoky cage before she saw Cal curled around the corner of the base, almost at her feet. He must have collapsed or fainted. The cage door hung open over him, warm to her touch.

Her drying towel pressed to her lower face, Jordan leaned into the cage. Mamie, sacred *co-wah-chobee*, had either fled or turned to smoke.

"Look," someone shouted, "a girl with a man!" Hands helped her as she dragged Cal down the boardwalk.

Firemen, she thought. "Another man—heavy man—way at the back," she cried and started hacking again. "Turn right on the—the boardwalk—at the back."

She had been holding her breath so long. She'd closed her eyes and found her way by keeping the old handrail along her shoulder, bending low to suck in the less smoky air. Twice she'd stepped off and had to drag Cal back up on the walk, which was burning in places now. The shake shingle roofs of both FLORA and FAWNA were aflame, but the tin roof still might save the house in the cascade of ash, sparks, and embers. At the end, only the flaming signs like fireworks overhead guided her back to the road.

Hands. Hands lifting Cal and helped her. Men with hoses, even an airplane low overhead dropping something cloudy white. She tried to duck. But it was not that plane in the Glades diving at her, chasing her again.

"This way, ma'am. Come on. You're gonna be okay now."

They took her in the back of an emergency squad with its lights above, blinking, blinking. She balked at first, remembering Yancy bringing her here after they found Lawrence dead.

"Here, ma'am, breathe this oxygen." A man sat beside her on the cushioned bench, pressed a plastic mask over her nose and mouth.

"Those two men the only ones back in there, ma'am?"

She nodded, sucking sweet, clear air deep into her lungs. She leaned her head back on the wall, dizzy, light-headed, before he gently tipped her head forward over her knees. She kept coughing, and her throat and eyes stung.

"She gonna faint?"

"She's coming around. Looks like no burns, but her hair's all singed. Nostril hairs look pretty good, so I don't think she's got much in her lungs."

As her head cleared, she saw she was with two medics. They helped two masked fireman lift Cal in on a stretcher, then helped Reb in to sit on the floor at her feet. They put oxygen masks on both of them, and the two medics began to wrap their arms and hands with strips of wet sheets and their heads with bandages.

She pulled the oxygen mask from her face. "Are they all right?"

"Gonna be," the first medic said. "Arm burns mostly first, some second-degree. Gonna have to watch them for concussions because both fell in the smoke and hit their heads."

His hand trembling, Reb pulled the mask down. "No," he whispered, his voice rough. Tears and saliva streaked his smoke-blackened face. He pulled away from the wet wrappings and reached for Jordan's hand. He got her wrist, grabbing it tight. "We got hit on the head—by some kind a—Seminoles," he rasped. "And they took Mamie."

When Jordan finally got her car from the hospital parking lot, dawn was dusting the sky pale gold. She'd spent hours at the Naples Hospital with Cal and Reb. After they'd all been treated, interviewed by the fire inspector and police, and—because they insisted—released, she drove them back home to what was left of their H(E)AVEN: the house, the foundations of FLORA and FAWNA, and a cage, sitting on black, stump-studded land. Someone had moved their old truck. Paint-peeled, its rust spots looking like giant scabs, it was parked forlornly where the grand entrance had been.

The news from the district fire marshal on the scene was sickening, too: "Looks like arson," he told them grimly. He wiped sweat and soot from his face with his sleeve. "It's the same MO for all three Glades fires. We would of been here sooner, but the other two hit first."

To draw help away until it was too late, Jordan

thought, and tried to hug her sudden chill away by wrapping her arms around herself. She still reeked of smoke in her hair, clothes, even skin, like everything else here. She felt nauseous. Not only that someone had done all this intentionally, but that, unless someone held a bad grudge against Jungle Cal and Reb Turner, the cat kidnappers were at it again.

"You look 'bout as beat as us, Jordy." Cal's voice interrupted her agonizing. She nodded. She'd give these old friends a few days to recover, then bring them out a carload of plants and cuttings to start their "orkid museum" again.

"Remember," she told both of them, "you're welcome to stay at the lodge for a while if you'd rather. I've got the room and would love the company."

"God spared us what we're s'posed to have," Reb said, his bloodshot eyes surveying the destruction again. "We're stayin' put. This here piece of land's gonna recover a lot faster'n we will. But you saved us, and we ain't forgettin' it."

Chapter Nineteen

"Seth Cypress. You're under arrest."

Seth stood his ground outside his office. When he'd first seen Yancy Tatum leading two plainclothes men up the walk, he'd feared they had come about Frank or even had him under arrest. But it was obviously worse news than that.

His stomach clenched in foreboding as, squinting into the early-afternoon sun, he studied the badge and identification card the tall man—a federal marshal named James M. Bailey—held out, stiff-armed, to him.

"This is Ken Parma, and you know Detective Tatum," Bailey said, his voice as monotone as one of those computerized ones over the phone. His craggy face and ice-blue eyes registered no emotion or personality as he replaced his ID in his suit coat pocket.

"Under arrest on what charges, Marshal?"

"Killing an endangered panther on national lands, Mr. Cypress."

When Seth just gaped at them, Yancy Tatum put in, "And this time they can prove the gun's yours, so you might as well admit that dart gun was, too."

Seth ignored the final accusation. Fortunately, the marshals did, too. The red-haired Parma shouldered Yancy back, and Bailey said without looking at him,

"Thanks for getting us out here, Tatum, but we'll handle this now."

"I have not killed or even shot at a panther," Seth protested, struggling to keep calm as he saw Parma take out a pair of handcuffs. They were going to treat him like some criminal, here before his people.

"I've been in Tallahassee to testify before a senate committee," Seth plunged on, "and just got back last evening. The panther is sacred to the Seminole. Where did it get shot?"

"It was taken from a two-bit derelict amusement park down on the South Trail," Parma said. "Then—"

"The Turner brothers' cat? Mamie?"

"Knew it personally, did you?" Bailey put in. "And it wouldn't take you long since it was shot on Cypress National Preserve lands abutting this reservation. You know it's illegal to shoot any wildlife there, but, Seminole or not, there's big fines and prison time for killing one of those endangered cats."

"I didn't do it."

"We're not just blowing wind here, Cypress," Bailey said, his monotone cranking up a notch. "It was killed with one clean hit from your .22. Your gun you thought you hid had your name cut in the stock and your prints on the barrel."

That hit him like a blow in the gut. His gun—it, too, had been in the back of his closet just collecting dust. He'd never thought to check it when the dart gun turned up missing. Frank again ... He had to find Frank.

He cleared his throat, but he knew his voice quavered when he tried to sound defiant. "Why would I leave behind a gun with my name and prints?" he demanded of them, staring down each man in turn.

"Obviously," Parma said, "so someone who heard

the shot wouldn't see you with it and you could retrieve it later. The shot was immediately heard and
reported. The bullet in the cat matched. And if any
of this stuff about killing a panther before this secret
Indian dance turns out like Detective Tatum here
says . . ."

Seth glared fiercely at Yancy before he looked
quickly away.

"Read him Miranda, Ken, and let's get him to Fort
Myers," Bailey concluded.

"Where'd you get your information on the dance,
Tatum?" Seth demanded, sidestepping Parma to see
him better.

"A little bird, a pretty one," Yancy goaded with a
grin that Seth yearned to smash down his throat.
"And this'll lead to other charges. Arson, assault—"

"Tatum!" Bailey thundered.

"Okay, okay. Want me to get you a good lawyer,
Seth?"

"You have the right to remain silent," Marshal
Parma began to drone the familiar words of official
warning. Every muscle in Seth's body tensed. He
could have launched himself at Yancy right through
these two men.

"Anything you say can be used against you in a
court of law."

Seth feared he would not have a verifiable alibi.
People saw him when he came in midmorning, but the
cat must have been killed earlier, since they'd done
an investigation already. When he got back last night,
he'd stopped briefly to see his son, but otherwise, he'd
been alone.

"You have the right to talk to a lawyer. If you cannot afford a lawyer, one will be appointed for you.

You have a right to stop answering questions at any-time . . ."

Questions. Someone was spinning a web around him. Surely Jordan would not have told Tatum about the Winter Dance. But as soon as his lawyer arranged his bail, he was going to ask her about it, and a few other things.

A crowd of his people had gathered by the time they put the cuffs on him. In Mikasuki, he calmly told several of his men who stepped closer to stay back, that it was a misunderstanding about shooting a panther and he would return soon. He asked his cousin, Danny Tiger, to call Chet Lansing in town and tell him he'd need bond posted at the Fort Myers District Jail.

"How do you know he isn't saying something to them that could be used against him?" Yancy demanded as Bailey escorted Seth away. When Bailey didn't answer, Yancy hightailed it to his own unmarked car. He didn't want to be left standing with the growing crowd of Seminoles.

When Seth hadn't called or come by as she had expected, Jordan phoned Marc at the panther team headquarters and agreed to meet him for a quick lunch on the Naples Fishing Pier. He had been calling her—evidently both from Washington and now Naples—leaving numerous messages on her answering machine implying again that he'd found a lead about Lawrence's research. She didn't especially believe him, but she had to check it out. And she knew he wasn't going to tell her over the phone.

When she spotted him, she got in line to order their lunch at the food window halfway out on the pier. She studied him as he strolled confidently along, obviously looking for her. He seemed overdressed among the bathing suits and old clothes; he could have stepped from an ad in *Sports Illustrated* with his dove gray slacks, patterned golf shirt, and Greg Norman brimmed hat with a shark embroidered on the crown. He joined her in line while she asked him what he wanted and placed their order.

"You've been putting me off," he said, but smiled at her as if to negate the taut tone in his voice.

"Haven't you heard about the right to privacy in this country, Marc?" she said, keeping her voice low so others wouldn't hear. "Twice I caught you going through my things."

"Lawrence's things," he corrected quietly. "Simply searching for official property of the panther team, which you might have overlooked. My actions were for your own good—and ultimately, mankind's."

"Not to mention yours, if you picked up the ball and ran with it." She glared at him over the top of her sunglasses before she shoved them back onto her nose. She paid for the food before he could, picked up the sandwiches and one can of Pepsi, and started away.

"So why here?" he asked. He snatched his can and hurried after her as she walked as far out as she could on the thousand-foot-long wooden pier.

She could have told him the real reason, that she wanted a public place to get rid of him, a place he dare not protest too loudly. But she wanted to hear what he had to say before she alienated him. "I always liked it here," she admitted. "Despite the people, it goes so far out into the water you kind of feel you've escaped. So what's this big news you have for me?" As they walked, she glanced into plastic pails at various bait being kept alive until their turn on the hook.

"I have gotten ripples of rumors," he told her,

glancing both right and left as if these fishermen would be listening, "that several of the firms Lawrence dealt with believed he was really on the verge of a huge breakthrough."

"In other words," she said, already regretting she'd even come, "you have nothing concrete."

"You have become hard, Jordan—hard on me," he said as they sat on a bench amid open fishing tackle boxes on the deep water end of the pier. Forced to sit stiffly close together, they unwrapped their sandwiches.

She might as well get this over with, she decided. "I don't think you've played straight with me, Marc, so I'm going to have to ask you to just give me a lot of space and quit calling. If and when I really know something, I'll contact the team."

"You can contact me, as team leader," he said adamantly, pointing at his chest. "Or will you be running to Brent again? Or the police? Or some other old friend besides me? But I see you are angry, so let me play straight with you," he added, mocking her earlier words, his voice sharply sarcastic.

"Fine," she managed, but she shivered, even in the hot sun.

"We got a call from the Naples police midmorning," he told her, leaning closer conspiratorially. "More about that amusement park panther where you just happened on the scene again."

"Meaning what?"

"Just that the Seminoles strike again. You know, Lawrence wanted me to examine that cat once, but it was really old and had not been in the wild for years."

"Do you mean you wouldn't have wanted it for study? Because it wasn't in the wild where it could eat whatever it wanted?"

"What? To study what, specifically?" he countered, his mouth half full. He stopped chewing. His eyes narrowed behind his wraparound sunglasses.

"I don't know," she said quickly, trying to cover her slipup. "To see if she had the lentivirus or something."

He swallowed hard, bobbing his Adam's apple. "Where have you learned about the lentivirus?" he demanded so loud several fishermen stared at them. "You did not use that term before."

"From Brent," she said, regretting she'd sunk to lying. Marc could check with Brent and then he'd know it, too. But she'd blurted it out because she could not trust Marc. How far, she wondered, had he gone to get Lawrence's research?

Suddenly, she could not stand to be near him anymore. But when she made a move to get up, his hand shot out to pull her back.

"You obviously do not know something else I do, Jordan."

She hated to take his lure, but the way he spoke so calmly compelled her to sit down again. "Like what?"

"The rest of the story. That old stolen panther has been found shot dead."

She squeezed her sandwich so hard the paper crunched. "Mamie? Oh, no. Where?"

"In the Cypress Preserve. But they got the guy responsible."

"Thank God. Who would do that? Someone stole that cat just to shoot it?"

"Some sort of sacrifice, they figure. They say the chief of the Sawgrass Seminoles did it," he said, watching her intently. "They have his gun, his prints—and his motive, so Yancy Tatum tells me—something about a sacred dance."

"Yancy told you? But how would he know? The Seminoles keep that secret."

"Yancy also told me you used to know him—know both Yancy and most certainly Seth Cypress. You disappoint me, Jordan, hiding that first marriage from me. I'm sure your liaison with that savage, as Yancy called him, must have disappointed poor Lawrence. I keep thinking, what else are you hiding from me, from science, from humanity? Brent admitted he told you how much Lawrence's work could have been worth, and that's your motive for keeping me away, isn't it? You want it all for yourself."

Stunned, she just gasped at his tirade. Then, before she could deny it, he stood, made a stiff little bow, turned his back, gathered up his food, and walked away.

"Yancy's behind all this. I know he is," Seth told his father. Seth had just joined Cory Cypress in the shade of the big banyan tree outside his parents' trailer. "He hated me years ago for having Jordan when he couldn't. He's out to hurt me and the tribe, and he'll use anyone he can."

While his father leaned against the trunk with his arms crossed, Seth stalked back and forth, swatting at the dangling tendrils that would become new roots propping up the heavy limbs. This was his mother's favorite tree, because she said it was like the tribe—separate branches but all connecting and supporting the whole. It unnerved him now that he seemed to be getting so little support from his father.

And it rankled him deeply that he—chairman of the tribe—with microphones and cameras thrust in his face—had been booked and later bailed out of jail this afternoon. He had spent an hour trying to make sense of this mess to his son. He'd have to face the shame and explanations again when he was arraigned next week. And if he were convicted . . .

Finally, the *ayikcomi* nodded and said, "You think Yancy Tatum is using Frank?"

With a huge sigh, Seth leaned against the thick trunk of the tree. Neither of them had said Frank's name before as if to speak it would make it true. Nor had he mentioned Jordan's name, other than to inform his father that she was invited to the Winter Dance. The old man's eyes had widened at that revelation, but unlike years ago, he had made no protest.

So Seth had left a message on both of Jordan's phones, the lodge and shop, that he needed to see her out at his Glades retreat. He was headed there now, but he had to consult his father first.

"Yes, I suppose Yancy could have run into Frank somehow, somewhere," Seth said. "Maybe Frank got stopped by cops for messing around, and Yancy heard who they'd arrested and helped him out—then asked a favor of him in trade."

"Get him the dart gun and your shotgun?" the old man asked.

Seth shrugged. "Something like that. Then bribed him to keep quiet. Maybe that's where the kid got all his mad money lately with that cover story of working at the track."

"But you called Hialeah. That's true."

"Only that some Big Sawgrass Seminole kids had been hired out in the paddocks. I'll have to drive over to get their names, check when they were there. And now, of course, I'm not supposed to leave the area until I'm arraigned," he said, shaking his head. "It would fit, too, that Frank could have tipped Yancy off to when we're holding the dance—given him the information about the traditional shooting of the panther we don't even do anymore."

"It makes my blood cold to think the boy is a traitor to our people and family—to his *micco*. But who else could it be?"

Again, Jordan's face flashed into Seth's mind. He could not believe Yancy that she had tipped him off about the dance. He stopped pacing and turned to face his father.

"Should we cancel the Winter Dance with all this going on?"

"No," the *ayikcomi* answered. "The white man must not tell the people what to do. We must have this time of judgment and justice, purging and prayers." The old man looked upward, his eyes fixed on something more distant than the hovering, thick foliage of the tree that blocked their view of the sky. "But," he went on, "we will make it one day early and one day only—be sure no one can know and defile the ceremony."

"All right. Will you pass the word? I'm taking the airboat and heading out to the Old Camp."

"Be back by sunset tomorrow," he said with a piercing look. "From deceits touching the *micco*'s path, you must be cleansed, my son. And while you are away, build up your strength and do not let it bleed away."

Chapter Twenty

Jordan was glad she knew the way to Seth's camp, because she did not want anyone—even Mae this time—to know she was coming out here. This was strictly between Seth and her. She drove straight west into the sinking sun.

As last time, she didn't see him when she arrived, but his truck was parked by the distant bushes. A finger of smoke trailed into the fading blue sky from down by the canal. Because it would get cool when the sun set, she took a jacket. She had changed to a cotton T-shirt and long, pleated red skirt. Seth had always liked red.

To avoid startling him when she came up over the little rise to the canal, she called out, "Seth, I'm here!"

The familiar scent of burning bay leaves lured her on. The Seminoles knew the power of herbs; perhaps he could even ask his father about the Glades mint.

He sat on the bow of a square, flat-hulled airboat tethered to the fringe of the canal. He appeared to be mending a fishing net and did not rise, but she felt the impact of his intense gaze. She waved and walked down to see that he held a large piece of filmy mosquito netting tumbled across his lap and spread legs.

"I'm sorry about your arrest," she greeted him.

"There's some terrible mistake, because I know you would never hurt old Mamie."

His face was all in shadow, haloed by the sun setting behind his head. When he stood, he blocked it entirely, throwing a huge shadow over her. She swung her jacket around her shoulders. "Thanks," he said, getting up. "Wish you could tell that to the authorities. But on second thought, I don't want you telling Yancy Tatum anything ever again."

She gasped and her eyes widened in surprise. "Yancy's in on this? And he said I told him what?"

"Let's take a ride and talk about it—about everything," he said, holding out his hand to her.

"An airboat ride? You can't talk over the noise of that."

"We'll go out to the Old Camp. I need to talk to you, Jordan. And I need—you."

The fading light seemed to wrap around her as thickly as the net he trailed from his other hand. "Like we used to?" she whispered. He nodded while she came down the bank toward him. The Old Camp was where he had proposed to her, the place they'd laid their plans to elope. They had gone there recklessly fast by airboat from her home one Saturday when her parents were gone somewhere, so long ago.

"Yes," she said, taking his hand, "I'll go with you."

He turned and heaved the netting into the shallow prow, then escorted her to the half plane, half boat, waiting for her with one foot on the side, watching her as she stepped in. He made her comfortable sitting between two duffel bags on the pile of netting. She could tell he was still tense and tightly wound, ready to explode. Yes, he needed her. And she needed him.

He jumped into the elevated seat behind her and started the motor. Its roar blocked out all sounds.

Deftly, he backed them into the canal and turned the boat, then accelerated fast, tipping her back.

The noise and blast of air assaulted her. High sawgrass, cattails, bushes, and trees whipped past. Patches of sky swept overhead, silhouetting V's of birds pointing toward their twilight roosts. The roar and vibration shook her, but not as deep as her own desperate desire for this powerful, angry man.

Jordan knew it would not do her any good to try to shout to Seth. The roar of the airboat nearly drowned even her thoughts. When he lifted his foot from the pedal to enter a smaller river, she managed to sit up straight and craned her neck to look up and back at him.

His hands on the joystick, his eyes on the denser vegetation ahead, he guided them in. He turned again into a narrower channel where he had to lean forward to keep from being whipped by the green chaos of hanging tree limbs, vines, and ferns. Vegetation dragged along the hull. The engine roar softened slightly. When they entered a tunnel of trees, she sat on her haunches and twisted around to look up and back at him again.

"I forgot it was this far," she called to him.

"Hang on." He sideslipped the airboat against a grassy bank and killed the engine. They had come about twenty minutes into the very heart of the reservation. Colors had dimmed to shades of gray, but she saw the silhouette of a raised-floor chickee in a small clearing embraced by foliage.

Before he could climb down, she got out, taking her jacket and purse with her. She watched him tie up the boat, and when he tossed out his duffel bags, she dragged one of them up to the campfire site. Suddenly, it hit her for the first time that he meant to spend the night. He hadn't mentioned that, but he probably assumed she was smart enough to know it. She felt herself blush hot all over, but she told herself it was from exertion as she hefted the second bag. Besides, she would have agreed if he had asked.

His brow furled as if he were deep in thought, he unpacked quickly, hardly looking at her: cooking gear, food, blankets all in spartan, purposeful piles.

"Are we going to stay for a week?" she asked him.

"Would you?" he countered, looking up at her in the deepening dusk. It was, she thought, as if they had now become shy or afraid, alone together.

She swept both the hearth area and chickee floor free of debris with a palm frond. Then, when she saw what he was doing next, she got up to help him gather kindling and small logs for the distinctive spoke-wheel fire the tribe—and hunters like her dad—used in the Glades. But when she stood with two handsful of wood near where he was gathering, he suddenly reached for her, pulling her closer, inches from him, holding her by her upper arms. She could feel his body heat, tension coiled so tightly in him. Her kindling clattered to the ground, bouncing off their feet.

He shifted her slightly in his arms. She sensed he was wavering, perhaps struggling yet against whatever was coming next.

"I couldn't admit Frank betrayed me," he whispered. "If others hate me, that's one thing, but I thought—I wanted him to be like my second son."

This close she could see his face looked ravaged. They didn't move. She knew he had to say more. Only the darkening vegetation around them seemed to breathe. "It has to be Frank, working with Yancy," he choked out.

"Yancy?" she gasped, her mind racing through the

possibilities. "You think he'd do all that—make the Seminoles look bad, maybe even get rid of my husband? That he really wanted me that badly all these years?"

"I can believe that," he whispered. "Because I do."

He crushed her to him, and she cradled his head with her arms around his neck.

Later, when they'd clung together and she'd dared to comfort him, Jordan sliced the bread he'd brought while he caught some frogs and fried their legs. They covered it with salsa and washed it down with 7UP from the cooler, savoring not only the food, but just being together. She stayed put, sitting on the log, watching him as he hoisted their supplies into the trees and gathered dried palmetto fronds to soften the bed of blankets he had brought.

"I take it," she said when he came back, "that I'm still invited to the Winter Dance. Cal and Reb said I shouldn't go because I might get judged and punished for things I've done."

He sat down beside her and put one big hand on her knee, sending a jolt through her whole body. "I think," he mused while she reached up to weave the fingers of one hand through his thick hair, "we've already been judged and punished for things we've done—namely, for letting everyone pull us apart." She saw he had closed his eyes. She could feel him relax under her touch, though his hands hardly did that to her. "Sure, we were just kids," he murmured, "but I think we could have made it if they'd left us alone."

"We'd be different people than we are now. You might not have gone to law school and become tribal chairman, and wouldn't have your boy. And I—everything I'm caught up in now . . ."

He opened his eyes and leaned closer. In flickering firelight his bronze face looked all planes and angles, as if he were carved from wood. Suddenly he lifted her into his lap and held her tight, his cheek pressed to hers.

"I suppose I'd be too much of a liability in your new life," she whispered.

"I'll show you that's not true," he declared, pulling back a bit to look in her eyes. "Beginning at the Winter Dance. Times have changed for my parents, my people."

"For mine, too. When I told my mother and sister I was going to the dance, they hardly made one peep. With everything else I've been through, that must have looked pretty good by comparison."

"But you know," he said, smiling, "I'm finding myself not caring what anybody else thinks lately. It's what *you* think I'm concentrating on. Like you said, if it's right in your heart . . ."

Nose tips almost touching, they both smiled. The deep chuckle rumbling through his chest vibrated through her. She laughed with him, for no reason, but shared joy, the freedom of the moment. She felt, not that time had stopped for them, but that it had somehow fulfilled itself.

"Jordan," he whispered, his face intense, his voice fervent, "I need your strength, need you on my side—our side." His ragged breath moved the hair along her temple as he suddenly sat her back again. "Look at something I brought."

As she perched on his knees, she blinked back tears and stared at the creased, worn paper he took from the pocket of his shirt. A small photograph tumbled out, which he retrieved, almost spilling her off.

"See," he said, his eyes luminous in fireglow, "even

when everything fell apart, for all those years, I kept these."

The photo was an old one of them and Mae, the day they cut the tips of their fingers with Seth's knife to take a blood oath to be friends forever. The paper was their marriage license, issued in Fort Myers eons ago.

Encompassed in the cloud of mosquito netting, she lay in his arms, enflamed by his nearness but not yet consumed. His earlier kisses and caresses had only stoked her passions higher and hotter. She pressed closer, remembering how well they fit everywhere, her softness to his strength. But she felt strong now, soaring high.

The palmetto fronds under them rustled as he moved to press her under him, nudging her legs apart with a knee. Each time they shifted, they tugged at the suspended mosquito netting tucked beneath them. When he pulled her across his body, it yanked loose and cascaded, soft but thick over them.

She sighed. He cursed low in Mikasuki.

He got to his feet, pulling it off of her, fussing with it. She looked straight up at him—an interesting view—as he fumbled to refasten it to the beamed ceiling.

"Seth, if we're certain we're committed to each other, even if we're still both in danger and have a long ways to go—I'm just saying I do love you and want you."

"I was getting that idea. And I'm saying you've got me. I swear to you, nothing else will come between us. Or let me deliver that message another way. The hell with the fact that you're forbidden right now."

"What are you talking about? We're not letting anyone tell us that anymore. If you want to make love, I do, too, so—"

She went silent as he lay back down beside her, propped up on one elbow, even more out of breath than he had been kissing her. His free hand splayed open across her belly, then rode along her curves and contours as she turned on her side facing him to mirror his position.

Upward, his thumb moved under the bottom of her bra, then he reached around to unhook it to free her. His hard hand gently cupped her whole breast, shooting sparkles clear into the pit of her stomach. Slowly, staring into her eyes, he eased his hand downward, across her waist to the swell of her hip, tugging her panties lower. She lifted her hips to help him. Then, when they were naked, his hand moved upward again; her head spun so with desire she could barely grasp his words.

"No Seminole men are to get near a woman before the ceremony, or they will bring curses on themselves."

"Oh, no. Do you believe that now? You mean—"

"I mean, this defiance of that is how much I want and love you." She smiled into the curve of his cheek as he rolled her under him and pressed her down. "I've dreamed you're all mine, this time forever."

"That's what I want, too. Just you."

His mouth descended hot and hard. His hands promised and demanded as she matched him with a joyous abandon she thought she had forgotten. The dark depths of night tumbled into tangled limbs, wild hair, and fierce embraces until they shattered blazing bright against each other. At last, she had come home.

"Thanks for the private piano player way out here, Dad. Great sunset, too," Michelle said and saluted it, then him with the glass of her fourth martini.

"Bringing the musician out from the Ritz Carleton, I'll take credit for," Winston told her as he clicked her glass with his. Gershwin cascaded out from the white grand piano in the sunroom to mingle with evening birdcalls where they stood on the back patio. "As for the sunset—I'm working on controlling that, too."

Michelle merely nodded. She accepted her father's offer of a light for her cigarette, then bounced back much too hard in a lounge chair by the pool, causing her to slop part of her drink on her dress. She just flicked at the drops once and hummed along as "The Man I Love" segued into "S'Wonderful." Despite the raw beauty of this place and her father's knocking himself out to make her happy here, it really *wasn't* wonderful.

"Not to change the subject," she said as Winston perched over the next chair, carefully pulling his creased pant legs up slightly before he sat. She took another swallow. "But at this point in my life, you do realize the last thing I need is a new stepmother. Especially not a take-charge woman more or less my age."

Winston's head jerked toward her. "Wherever did you get that idea? I've sworn off women for a while. But I assume you mean Jordan Quinn."

"Sure as hell do. Quinn, the orchid queen. In case you haven't noticed, I'm not some naive teenager anymore," she declared, flicking nonexistent ash off the end of the cigarette.

"You never were. But about Jordan, you're quite mistaken."

"Really?" she said, drawling out the word. "You don't give a damn about flowers, and you hardly contracted for that exorbitant hanging Garden of Babylon for me. I've seen how you act around the widow Quinn. Your eyes devour her."

"Nonsense, though I must admit I admire her entrepreneurial spirit." With great deliberation he lit one of his illicitly imported Cuban cigarillos, but she saw his hands shook. Though feeling a bit foggy-brained, she decided to circle in for the kill.

"Is that what you ex-movie moguls call sex appeal now—entrepreneurial spirit?" she goaded.

"Look, my dear, I don't need your mockery or distrust. I knew her family years ago when I was here doing a movie and I feel sorry for her. Losing her husband, she's been through tough times financially and emotionally."

"But she hadn't even lost her husband when you had me phone her that first time. And if she's some kind of charity case, I'm Mother Teresa. 'Come to dinner ... stay the weekend, my dear ... sky's the limit, my dear,' Did you two really drive off alone the other day to see a bunch of grunting alligators, or do a little grunting yourselves? Hitting the hay in the outback could be just your frustrated cowboy style."

"Michelle! If you can't hold your liquor better than that, just go on to bed and put both of us out of our misery."

"All right, I'll show you then," she insisted as she smacked her glass down on the table and stood.

"What?" Winston called after her as she kicked off both shoes, then walked fast into the sunroom and snatched one of several ornately framed photographs off the fringed silk cloth on the piano. Unfortunately, the corner of the metal filigree snagged the cloth; two other photos and a bud vase crashed to the floor. She shrugged grandly to the young piano player, who actually made a mistake before he recovered. Hell, for the bucks Dad was probably paying him for this little concert, he should be prepared to play through Hitler's entire *blitzkrieg*.

Winston was standing as she came back out onto the flagstone patio. She thrust the photo at him. "See," she said, tilting the glass to the fading western light. "When I first saw Jordan Quinn, I knew. She's the kind of woman you've always gone for—tall, slender—and that sunset-red hair."

She pointed at the old photo of his grandmother in her graceful Edwardian gown. The styles were all wrong, of course—bustle, corseted waist, huge chapeau with sweeping ostrich feathers.

"Seems delicate but is really tough as nails," Michelle plunged on. "A real challenge to seduce and tame, right? The way I see it, Jordan Quinn is only a new model of your earlier three wives. Worse, you never got over *your* mother's death, did you, because Jordan Quinn, like the others, could be a stand-in double for her. Talk about an Oedipus com—"

She saw her father swing his arm. She tried to block it with the photo. But the glancing blow jabbed the corner of the frame across her cheek, and she dropped it. The glass shattered at his feet as she screamed and pressed her hand to her cheek.

"Damn it, Michelle! I only meant to take the photo. Let me look, sweetheart."

"Is it bad? I'm bleeding? My face!"

"I'll take care of you. It's your own fault. The cut's small, Michelle—hold still! But now we're going to need a plastic surgeon."

Chapter Twenty-one

Finally things seemed to be going her way, Jordan exulted as she fed Micco the last piece of chicken from her dinner plate. Her future with Seth seemed strong, and they were starting to unravel Seth's being set up, despite the fact they had to find Frank and make him tell them everything he knew. She was doubly grateful that her own family was strongly behind her—at least, perhaps until they heard that she and Seth were going to be remarried as soon as they could settle their problems. They had a lot of lost years to make up for.

She stretched her arms above her head and breathed in the evening air. Despite the nip in it, she had decided to eat from a tray on the screened-in front porch of the lodge among her hanging plants. After sleeping in an open-air chickee last night, she felt very closed in today.

She reached up to rearrange the blooms of the cream and lavender clamshell orchid. Twenty of these, among many other plants, were in her greenhouse ready to be put in the SunRay orchid garden. Also, she would be using some of these orchids for the new contract she had signed today, to design and install an indigenous Florida orchid garden at the venerable site of Smallwood's Historic Store and Old Indian Trading Post on Chokoloskee Island. It would be a relatively small garden, so she had promised it would be in by the annual Seminole Indian Festival. Seth said the tribe was looking forward to the good PR it would provide for them in these tenuous times. And, she thought, it would be great publicity for the shop.

As she stood, she stroked the petals of a fragrant night-blooming orchid. She had taken a carload of varied cuttings to Cal and Reb today so they could begin to rebuild their collection. But it was their indomitable spirits to rebuild their lives after the disaster that inspired her. She and Seth must be as strong to overcome their problems as those two old men.

"Me-mer," Micco protested, staring up at her and flicking his tail. The message that she was giving entirely too much attention to the plants and not him was unmistakable.

That was the best news, she thought as she scooped him up in one arm and carried her stacked dirty plates into the kitchen. Micco appeared to be on the mend, or at least in a dramatic and sudden remission of the feline lentivirus. Just another indicator she was on to something with letaria.

When dusk thickened, she closed the place up for the night. She planned to be up late to study Lawrence's notes. But if she didn't batten down the hatches now, she'd forget, and she still wasn't taking chances out here. She spent ten minutes going through her nightly ritual of checking window locks, bolting the doors, and making sure the lights outside worked.

Lana had said when the place was lit with the security lights, driving up to the lodge was like approaching a glowing UFO out in the woods: "You know, like in *Close Encounters of the Third Kind.*" So after Jordan checked the lights, she turned them off.

Reluctantly, she pulled the curtains to shut out the windy night.

With Micco on her lap, she settled in front of her computer screen. Tonight Seth was fulfilling his commitment to the tribe, not as *micco* but as any loyal male member, fasting and purging their impurities for the coming ceremonies. At least he had assured her this morning that he did not really believe their being together would put a curse on him. "I'm evidently under one from Frank and Yancy already and don't have room for two in my life," he said, trying to ease her worry.

Hopefully, Wilson would not protest her presence at the Winter Dance. She was excited to meet the rest of Seth's family and tribe after all this time. "Someday, Micco, we'll have an open house here and invite Seth's people and mine, too."

Then she set herself to the task of laboriously tracking her way through Lawrence's notes. Putting in the word *letaria* each time she saw the *le* symbol, again she tried to make sense of how a wild mint could help the cats. But she knew to really grasp and prove this theory she'd need his knowledge of chemistry, virology, physiology, and who knows what else.

Still, she realized she had dynamite here, and the fuse could be lit for good or ill depending on who got their hands on even this much. As soon as she was certain he would not just hand her information over to Marc, she would give all this to Brent and trust him to take care of it in Lawrence's name.

At ten o'clock, she stretched and gave Micco a little bit of milk. He lapped it up, nuzzled the fresh letaria she kept by his dish, and eventually came back to her lap as she began to print out screens of material she thought might help to prove that the herb was the missing link—the wonder drug.

But something scratched at her concentration; her head snapped around and she tensed to listen through the hum of the printer. Micco turned his ears sideways and jumped off her lap with a low growl.

"Outside, Micco? Was that outside?" she whispered.

The cat started to run, then stopped to stare at the front door. Keeping low, he darted under the desk. Jordan clicked off the single lamp she had on. In an instant only the computer screen bathed the darkened room in ghostly gray. With her pulse thumping, she tiptoed to the fireplace and picked up a heavy metal poker. The sound came again, hollow, rhythmic, thudding against the house.

Someone had been knocking and was now pounding on the front porch door, she decided. Although locked outside and latched in, it fitted loosely, so it made a thud-rattle, thud-rattle. At least someone would have to break it down even to get to the front door. Could it be Lana this late? Someone who had car trouble this far down on a narrow, dead-end road? With the poker under her arm, she cracked the front drapes and peered out as she hit the security light switch.

Blinding light leapt everywhere outside, sudden and sharp as a flashbulb. From blackness it brought color and stark definition. Thud-rattle, thud-rattle: the sounds shook her again. She edged over to see that the man at the door wore a dark windbreaker and a green baseball cap. He raised an arm to shield his eyes from the light. Marc? It looked like Marc Chay.

She fumbled with the latch and lifted the heavy sash of a window that opened onto the porch. She knelt and called out through the crack, "Marc, it's late. Go away! Just call me at work tomor—"

"Let me in! Someone's after me! They might be out here right now. Kill these lights, or so help me God, I will—"

"Go to the police on the Trail at the corner of Route 29. I can't have any more trouble, from you or anyone else who—"

"This is your fault! I found cameras at my place, just like yours. Lawrence got us into something. Damn you, let me in, so we can figure out what to do!" he screamed.

He seemed so desperate—almost demented—that she wondered if he was drunk. As he waved his hand wildly, she saw he had a gun.

That settled the question. She banged the window down, relatched it. She ran for the phone. Like some bad B-rated movie, the line was dead. Had Marc done that—even before he tried the door?

Keeping low, she scuttled to the table to grab her cell phone, then remembered it was out in her car.

She heard a car door slam. Marc leaving? Someone else here? What if someone really was after him, maybe because they thought he knew about Lawrence's work? She tore to another window so he would not know where to find her with that gun. He was standing by his car, but he wasn't leaving. He only got something out of the trunk. A tire iron. He ran jerkily, zigzagging, around the back of the house.

She tensed, fearing he would shatter a window to get in. She heard a distant crack. The computer whirred to a stop and the screen went dark. Everything went black outside, too.

Jordan hit the floor, waiting for his next move. He must have damaged the generator out back. It usually made a comforting noise like a low boat motor, but now silence stretched into the darkness. Still, she could almost hear bullets, feel them. Surely Marc had not shot his parents. And not Lawrence.

Move, Jordan, she told herself. *Do something. Don't just wait for something worse to happen. Get the flashlight.*

She crawled into the kitchen on hands and knees. Keeping low, she opened the pantry door; it creaked. She could not picture which shelf she'd left the flashlight on in here. It could have been shoved back when she had unloaded groceries. As she groped among tin cans and pasta boxes, the side kitchen window shattered.

Glass showered inward, missing her behind the pantry door. It triggered the horror of that night the window of her rental car exploded. Those men in the dark again—rain—masks—guns. She shook her head to clear it, uncertain what to do, expecting Marc to come vaulting through the window or at least stick his gun in. He must have figured she had records of Lawrence's work, the ones that were on the disk in the computer and lying for the taking in the printout tray right now.

For a makeshift weapon, she grabbed something off the shelf—it felt like a ketchup bottle—and darted low back into the living room. Fumbling in the dark, she released the computer disk and grabbed the papers. She stuffed both of them under the corner of the area rug and crawled to get the poker where she'd left it. And then she heard a shot.

But it was outside. Someone shouted. A man, not Marc. Another shot. She rolled across the floor and crouched under the desk, accidentally putting her knee on Micco's tail. He yowled; she jumped again and hit her head. When he quieted, she heard a quick jumble of voices, a car engine, two. Another shot. Tires squealed.

Then absolutely nothing.

"I can't believe it," Mae said to Jordan when she explained things to her at Mae's house just before the Winter Dance. "So what did you do then?"

"Shoved the table upright over the shattered window and propped chairs and things against it, furniture I was shocked I could even move by myself. I barricaded both doors. When I thought the coast was clear, I got my cell phone from the car and called the Highway Patrol. They came and checked the grounds to be sure no one was still out there. Tracks from two cars they said—maybe one a van."

"You could have called Yancy."

"No way. I thought about phoning my brother-in-law, but the Lokosee ferry doesn't run that late, and he'd have to take his own boat, then he wouldn't have a car when he landed. And then I'd have to tell my family everything." She shook her head. "I should anyway. Mama and Lana would probably be thrilled to know I haven't gone Hollywood on them, working on Rey's project."

"But the patrol men found this Marc guy at his condo?" Mae asked, leaning even closer over the table.

"Sitting there, composed as you please. He told them we'd had a lovers' quarrel and that he'd lost his temper and he'd pay for any damages. He denied having a gun or that anyone else was out there with a gun, though he said he thought some drunks might have been following him to harass him, because he was Chinese. Now I'm sure," she said sarcastically, "they could tell he looked Chinese in the dark, passing him on the road. He denied he said he was followed or said he had a camera in his place. The patrol decided not to get a search warrant to check it out, but they are going to look for bullets wedged somewhere around the lodge today while I'm gone. They helped me board up the window and waited until service people came out to fix the phone line and generator Marc had beat in."

"Son of a bitch. The guy's certified."

"You mean certifiable."

"That's it. Seth's gonna chew nails when he hears this."

"I know. Another complication besides Yancy—and maybe Frank," she said, reaching over to squeeze Mae's wrist. "I should file charges against Marc. But we'd have to go to court, and breaking a generator and a window is hardly enough to send him to prison to get him out of my life. But I do intend to warn Brent Rymer. A man that unstable and greedy has no right to hold a responsible position on the panther team, however much he blames me if I get him tossed off. You know," she said, cradling her coffee cup in two shaking hands, "I was just daring to hope that maybe things were getting better, that there were answers out there Seth and I could find."

"At least you're making my troubles look mighty little, that's for sure," Mae said, sitting back and slapping her knees.

"I'm glad they're good for something. Hey, what?" she asked as Mae got up to grab her hand and tug her outside.

Mae hauled her out to her truck, opened the door, and reached way back under the seat. She drew out a red bandana and unrolled it to reveal a square-handled, black pistol.

"You'd better borrow this, girl. You just call it a little housewarming gift for the lodge. I swear I'd lend you my shotgun, too, but I better keep something."

"I didn't know you carried a gun."

"Always did, a little one I could hide. A couple of 'em lately, when I saw Seth might be in trouble. Here, put this in your car, and I'll show you how to shoot it later. This top part recoils real fast, see, and you can hurt your thumb if you don't grip it right."

She scrabbled back under the seat and produced a box of bullets, marked *9mm hollow points*. They jingled gaily. Jordan just stared at her, though since she'd been ready to use the little gun under the bed, she wasn't sure why she hesitated now. It just seemed to her, once she glimpsed a slice of daylight, things kept getting darker. Feeling dazed, Jordan stepped a few feet to her own car to hide the gun and box of bullets under her seat.

"All you been through," Mae went blithely on as if she had just loaned her a pair of shoes, "seeing everybody at the Winter Dance not gonna be a bit hard. I'll call the kids and let's go."

The relentless beat of drums stirred Jordan's blood. Rattles, shuffling, thudding feet, rhythmic chanting, and the jog and sway of the cypress poles dangling sacred white heron feathers made her dizzy as the men passed by, turning this way, then that, in a huge, writhing circle around the big bonfire. Seth had been observing earlier, and now he had joined in, this other Seth, bound to his people she must come to know. She was anxious to get him alone a moment afterward to tell him what had happened with Marc Chay, but she didn't want to upset him tonight. She wanted everything to go perfectly, so he didn't regret he had broken a taboo with her the other night at the Old Camp.

Sweat gleamed on his bronze upper torso, intersected only by thongs around his arms and a corded sheath for feathers diagonally across his chest and back. A crown of feathers bounced in his thick hair. His muscles looked molded; his face intense and austere, as if he were in a trance. In the pit of her belly Jordan felt his thrust when he moved his thighs and narrow hips in the intricate steps of the dance.

Wilson, defiant and proud, danced next to him in the family group with another adult Cypress son, Aaron. Mae had told her the empty space between them was Frank's.

Someone plucked at her sleeve, startling her. "You like that ball game today?" Jenna Cypress asked Jordan. Mae and Seth's youngest sister had suddenly appeared in the crowd of watching women and children. "Neat the women won, right?"

"Right," Jordan told her with a smile. "That's who I was cheering for."

In the afternoon they had held the traditional loud, raucous, lacrosse-type game, with teams divided by the sexes, followed by a big barbecue. Now with light fading, there would be a naming ceremony for men and boys—including Seth's darling nine-year-old Josh, who had grinned shyly at her when Mae introduced them. The events would culminate in the displaying of the *ayikcomi*'s medicine bundle of sacred items and the private tribal court held with only men in the chickee here called the Big House.

Jordan had decided to leave before Cory Cypress's part because she didn't want to take a chance alienating him by glimpsing the sacred items of the tribe and Panther Clan. Still, she was starting to realize she could really use his advice about the herbs.

Jenna plucked at her sleeve again and said in her ear over the drums and music. "I want to work in a shop in town, but Mae's got enough girls. I like flowers real good."

Jordan knew she looked surprised. "You mean you'd like to work for me? What would your parents say?"

"My father," she said, then hesitated, glancing right and left, "he would say you should come see him alone out past the powwow field at dawn tomorrow morning. Not this place, *the powwow field,*" she repeated, and Jordan could just hear the old man's emphasis in her words.

She searched the girl's huge brown eyes, for Jenna was bold enough to look right at her. The resemblance to Seth was strong. Could he have already asked his father for advice about Glades mint? Why was she to come alone then? Surely, she could trust Cory Cypress.

Her eyes sought him out. He stood in the circle of dancing men, barely shifting his feet, swaying a little, holding the medicine bundle in a bear skin wrap in one arm. He kept blowing some sort of pipe that made a screeching sound, an authentic imitation of a panther's scream.

It seemed so real Jordan shivered and wrapped her arms around herself. It sounded just like the cry of the cat she'd heard in the Glades the day this nightmare began. And like the sound she'd heard at Rey's ranch that he had insisted was a peacock, which she'd not seen anywhere around there. Besides, peacocks didn't really sound quite like that, she realized now.

Then, as if she had screamed Cory Cypress's name, he turned. His dark eyes pierced her. She felt transfixed, but she nodded to him before he looked away.

When she turned to Jenna, she was gone. But she saw her moving out of the fringe of chanting, rapt women, heading for the food tables on the other side of the Big House. Jordan told Mae that she'd be right back and started after her.

"Jenna!" she called, but that word, even the louder chanting and the drums, merged with an airplane engine's roar.

Jordan looked up. It was not the same plane that had tormented her, but a bright blue one with clearly painted numbers, somewhat like the one Marc had flown to take her up to spread Lawrence's ashes. She squinted, trying to memorize the numbers as it banked, came back, lower, right over the bonfire and the dance. Someone was actually hanging out the side—with a camera.

Women screamed and men shouted. Drums stopped; dancers scattered, not from fear but fury at the violation of the dance. Jordan could see Cory Cypress had thrown himself over his bundle as if to shield it. Seth started back toward him, then just raised his fist at the sky and roared defiance.

That shout stayed with her as the Winter Dance was broken up early in snatches of whispers amid outraged silence. Daylight was almost gone but the sacred fire was immediately suffocated with soil.

"Who could have told when and where?" she heard some of the younger kids ask. Jordan's stomach clenched. Since Seth had not told people that Frank could have betrayed him, they might think she had told someone.

The adults were almost all speaking Mikasuki. Some of them stared at her, but she saw, it was with curiosity, not hostility, except for a glowering Wilson who referred to her repeatedly as "her" when he asked Mae loudly in English if she would be driving "her" and their kids back home, *right now.*

Seth briefly crossed her path, still dressed in his loincloth with jeans pulled under it and the addition of a sweatshirt. "Looks like I'll be checking all the airports sooner than we thought for an airplane," he muttered. "I only got three of the numbers."

"Me too. Marc Chay flew one like that before, but that wasn't the same one that was after me."

"If I find them, I'd like to kill them," he said and squeezed her wrist before he went back to speaking to groups of grumblers. But she understood. He was the chairman, the *micco,* the *ayikcomi*'s son, and she was still an outsider.

Yet many women had patted her arm—all without making eye contact, as was their way—and thanked her for helping Mae start her shop. And Seth's mother had placed in her hands a beautiful rainbow-hued patchwork blouse; Jordan's voice had caught as she thanked her for it, but the old lady had stepped away with a quick nod.

Since then Jordan had worn it proudly, draped over her own shirt. The sad past with Seth was never mentioned except for a woman she was certain must be his ex-wife, Paula Tommie, because little Josh resembled her. Jordan steeled herself for the worst as the woman approached and spoke.

"You broke his heart, and I could not heal it," she said, frowning, staring at the shoulder of Jordan's new blouse. "Do not hurt him, because his people admire him now. Do not, or something bad could happen."

Jordan had almost laughed at that, after everything else. But she said only, "I admire him, too, more than ever. And his people."

Now she wondered as she bounced along in the back of Mae's truck with her three kids, who looked like they'd just heard there was no Santa Claus, what Cory Cypress would have to say.

Jordan hardly slept that night, still replaying in her mind her partial explanation of events to her mother and sister: about Marc Chay's reactions to Lawrence's death, but not about her and Seth's suspicions of Yancy. Mama, strangely enough though, had volunteered to go out to the SunRay sometime with her, while Lana had nodded, tight-lipped, as if they'd made some kind of bargain on tolerating that as well as Seth in Jordan's tumultuous life.

The next morning she didn't even stop to get breakfast at home, but on the way to the reservation, stopped at a little place for coffee and a Danish. On the front page of the local papers, piled in the wire stand, sprawled an aerial color photo and the bold headline, SECRET SEMINOLE CEREMONY EXPOSED.

She was starting to believe in curses.

Chapter Twenty-two

The sky looked like a polished pearl as Jordan parked her car along the edge of the grassy powwow field just before sunrise. Patches of fog floated here, though there had been none on the roads. She left the newspaper on the front seat, but pulled the Seminole blouse Wilda Cypress had given her over her jacket. The hem of her long skirt and shoes soon became wet and cold with dew as she began to walk across the field. She shivered from the brisk air—and from anxiety. She saw no sign of Cory Cypress.

Perhaps, she thought, after the airplane had defiled the ceremony last night he no longer wished to see her. Maybe he blamed her for that, as well as for getting close to Seth again. Or he knew of her ties to Rey and his ranch. Who knows but he didn't still hold a grudge even if Rey didn't.

She gasped when he stepped from a thick ribbon of fog, stopped, and nodded to her. He was bareheaded, dressed in worn jeans and a red-and-white-checkered western shirt. Though thin and slightly bent, he did not look a bit cold and no dew darkened the ankles of his jeans.

"Good morning, Mr. Cypress. I wasn't sure if you still wanted to see me. I do have something to ask you."

"Ask then," he said with a stiff nod.

She gripped her hands in front of her and took a few small steps closer. "I know you use many herbs for the tribe. Did Seth ask you about Glades mint? Its other name is letaria. My deceased husband worked with it."

His eyes widened with interest. "That important work," she rushed on, "was with the panthers, but it might help people, too. My husband believed he discovered that the big cats either fight off or cure disease by instinctively eating a certain plant—Glades mint. Do you know if this could be true?"

"From ages ago, when *co-wah-chobee* the first animal Creator put on the earth," he said, gesturing with one hand in a slow circle, "that sacred cat possessed the healing power of the plants. So Panther Clan people have the knowledge of making laws and medicine that heals."

"But have you ever seen *co-wah-chobee* eat Glades mint? The same herbs you use to heal people?" When he nodded, she went on, "And could you tell me what these herbs do for your people or the cats?"

"For people, little things, fix stomachache, clean breath. Beyond that, much power to heal. Same for the cats. Power to help the body forces that heal, a gift from Creator through *co-wah-chobee*."

Power to help the body forces that heal. He's describing the immune system, she thought, exactly what breaks down in humans with HIV. A chill of awe raced through her, because the brilliant scientists working on the AIDS problem throughout the world didn't realize that the answer might lie with these Native Americans, this endangered animal, and a simple herb. Now she knew Lawrence's secret and must decide who to tell.

"But still *co-wah-chobee* is sad," Cory Cypress was saying, looking toward the fences that separated the reservation from Rey's land. "Always he is walking closer to death when he is in the white man's path."

"Yes, I see. One more thing, something about Jenna. Could I hire her to help at my shop on Saturdays? Mae could just bring her in . . ."

She let her voice trail off, for he was obviously not listening now. Humming a dissonant tune, he turned away and walked down the middle of the field, leaving his footsteps next to hers in the dewy grass. But it was he who had asked to see her here, so what for? she wondered. Since he had let her do all the asking, maybe Seth had actually set this up by saying she needed advice about letaria.

As she turned to walk back to her car, she glanced in the direction of Rey ranch: from here she could actually see the boundary, a distant double fence, the Indian one of wire running along the familiar SunRay pine. Sad in a way that Cory Cypress had to be reminded of Rey's misunderstanding of the Seminole, even if it was years ago.

Again, suddenly, she recalled the strange pantherlike scream she had heard on Rey's ranch. Had she imagined it as a cry of outrage or pain? Although he'd claimed it was the cry of a peacock and she had let him gloss over it then, she knew better. It had to be a sacred *co-wah-chobee,* and Rey had to know it was on his land.

"And now our lead story from Channel Six On Your Side, Fort Myers," Jordan heard the voice from a television set drift out the door of the ice cream store as she walked by. "Another mysterious tragedy stalks the Naples-based Endangered Panther Team. Stay tuned for Live at Five News, coming up after these brief messages."

Her pulse pounding, she stepped inside the small Ben & Jerry's Ice Cream Shop and stared up at the TV on its shelf above the counter. Did they mean another panther had been taken or shot? Or someone else besides Lawrence had disappeared or been hurt?

Others around her ordered ice cream; voices and laughter buzzed by. The wait during the commercials seemed as endless as her entire day had been.

She often used Saturdays for visits to new gardens to be sure plants were flourishing. Her last stop today had been the Hibiscus Art Gallery here at the Venetian Village Bay Shopping Center. To complement her trademark floral paintings, the owner had leased a collection of orchids for the shop and display windows. From there, Jordan had called Sally to see if things were going smoothly, but she kept wondering about Seth, who had gone looking for the invading airplane at the airport.

As the blond anchorwoman came back on, Jordan jerked to attention. She wanted to scream at everyone to shut up, but she strained to listen.

"In the wake of the earlier Seminole dart gun attack and suicide of team member Lawrence Quinn, now team chairman Dr. Marcus Chay, seen here at the left in file footage, has been killed along with a student researcher, in the crash of the panther tracking plane."

Jordan gasped and pressed her hands to her mouth. Marc, dead? Marc too? She stepped back into a patron. Mumbling, "Sorry, sorry," she kept her eyes on the screen.

"You in line, lady?"

"What? N—no. Go ahead." She shuffled back a little.

She gasped again when they showed the crumpled metal at the scene—grassy prairie with a hammock just beyond. The wreckage—bright blue—like that plane last night. Surely, that could not have been Marc up there taking pictures of the Winter Dance.

"Channel Six On Your Side has learned," the woman's voice droned on, "that Dr. Chay was fully licensed and piloting the plane himself. A distant eyewitness said the plane was flying low and suddenly stalled and nosedived. Dr. Chay had recently taken over the coordination of the team after months of study with a wildcat conservation program out West. The other victim, identified as Bob Randolph, a junior at the University of Tennessee, was helping Dr. Chay track the animal by its radio collar in a joint government-university program. The Cessna 172 was a rental plane often used by the team and had recently undergone a standard inspection at the Naples Air Center. The National Transportation Safety Board will investigate, but the police so far are unwilling to make a statement. More later on attempts to save the panthers and the cause of the crash."

"The cause of the crash," Jordan whispered. Of course, it could be an accident—engine malfunction or pilot error—but maybe not. First Lawrence gone, then Marc. She felt dazed, nauseous. She could picture herself in a plane just like that one with Marc the day they released Lawrence's ashes.

Guilt and blame crashed into her. She should not have turned Marc away Wednesday night. She should have told Brent—the police—someone—that he needed mental help. And he'd said he'd found cameras at his place, a definite link to her and Lawrence's stalker—if he'd been telling the truth.

"You're next, ma'am."

A crew-cut kid poked his head over her shoulder and pointed to the ice cream counter. She saw a line had formed behind her again. She turned and pushed her way out the door. Glancing around, thinking someone evil must be watching, she broke into a little run toward her car. She had to find Seth.

First she tried the Tribal Headquarters Building where Seth had his office, but it was locked. She drove to his home only to find it also deserted. She decided to try Mae's place before going clear out to his shell road camp.

Mae's compound of chickees was ablaze with lights in the evening dusk. She wondered if people here knew—or cared—about the crash. Mae answered the door when she knocked.

"Did you hear about the panther plane crash?" Jordan blurted. "It looked a lot like the same plane last night that—"

"It was. And because Seth was so mad and went to the hangar early this morning asking questions and standing around near the plane, that ass Tatum came out here and took him in for questioning about the crash. Wilson followed him in his truck to get his lawyer friend Lansing and try to bring Seth back home."

"Not again. I can't believe it," Jordan murmured as she slumped against the open door.

"Believe it. 'The revenge of the Seminoles,' Yancy claimed, like Seth knows anything about doing something to a plane so it would make it almost right over the site of the Winter Dance before it crashed. Don't just stand there or you'll let in the bugs. Come on," she insisted and pulled Jordan in by her wrist.

Jordan helped Mae and her sister Ada serve drinks and frybread sandwiches to their assembled family. It was all adults; Mae's other sister Betty kept the kids next door. Both of Seth's parents nodded politely, and Wilda Cypress even stared her squarely in the eye at one point, a compliment and not the challenge it would be in her own world. Jordan studied a picture of the Cypress family on the wall, taken not too long ago. She recognized everyone in it but the one with the angry face; she knew that was Frank.

Jenna came over to insist Jordan take her seat on the couch. "My father says okay I can work for you on Saturdays," she whispered.

So, the old man, Jordan thought, had been listening to her at the end of their strange interview this morning. "Good, Jenna. We'll talk more about it when we get Seth back."

Everyone crowded in the small living room jumped when the phone rang. Silence descended with the darkness outside as Mae took the call in the kitchen, then came back in. "Wilson's going to wait for Seth. His lawyer's there, but they're trying to pin this on him, right along with the panther's death—I don't know what else. Still, no arrest. Wilson says, nobody wait up for them."

Amid grim murmurings and grumblings, people eventually dispersed. "Seth's no killer," Mae muttered, "but he probably wants to kill Yancy about now. Yancy always hated Seth, but he's not too bright—really, never was. I mean, I can't believe he put this whole big plan thing together against Seth."

"I know," Jordan said, shaking her head. "Though I've seen people with ambition and hard work make up for intellect. But Marc was the smart one and—like Lawrence—he's dead. I just don't know. Nothing fits together."

"Guess I better go get the kids back over here and

in bed," Mae said, rubbing her eyes. "Makes me just want to scream. Man, I'd give *anything* if there was something I could do to help Seth solve this damn panther thing!"

"Maybe there is," Jordan said as a hunch hit her. "You know, if someone would ride tonight onto Rey's land to see if there's anything suspicious in his back buildings where I think I heard a panther scream, even if trespassers were suspected or spotted, there's no way Seth could be accused because he's got an airtight alibi right now." She smiled grimly at her desperate idea.

"What? Go onto Rey's land? Tonight?"

"Like you said, all this maneuvering against Seth would probably take someone smart. Rey's that as well as rich. And powerful, at least with all those men who work for him."

"So," Mae said, propping her fists on her hips, "you got some kind of women's tuition about Rey?"

"Intuition. So what do you say? I'm a terrible rider, but I'll make it." She rested a hand on Mae's shoulder. "You can just go to the edge of his land and stay with the horses, because I've seen that layout of the back buildings. If you know the way to get there in the dark—"

"Oh, I know the way all right. Used to range all over the place with Wilson when we were dating. Okay, then. I'll tell my sisters we're taking a little ride and be back soon. But I sure wish we'd had time for me to show you how to shoot that gun if we're doing something like that."

Just before eleven, under a quarter moon, they mounted at the stable nearest Mae's house. They had dressed in loose, dark workshirts of Wilson's over

Mae's jeans. They'd shoved their ponytailed hair up under nondescript baseball caps. Their single saddle-bag on Mae's horse held two pairs of binoculars, her shotgun, and two water canteens. Jordan had not been on a horse in years, but the big beast felt sturdy beneath her as Mae led the way.

They let their mounts walk across the powwow field where Jordan had spoken with Cory Cypress at the start of this tumultuous day. Though thoughts and fears tumbled through her mind, she tried to shove them back. Poor Marc, Lawrence—Seth. But she had to concentrate on this right now. Could Rey have any tie to Yancy? It hurt her to think Rey still might dislike the Seminoles and had been lying to her, but that was *not* a peacock cry. She wasn't reared in the Glades for nothing.

They kept their billed caps pulled low to protect their eyes from pine boughs in the forest. The horses seemed surefooted, but then they were used to herding cattle. When the trees ended, they found a dirt road that eventually lead to a wooden fence, this time without the parallel wire one.

They traced the fence until they found the gate. Mae dismounted to open it and they went through, then she refastened it. "I think," she told Jordan, "there may be swamp water in the grass beyond, if it isn't dry right now."

"How much farther till we're to the clearing for his ranch?"

"From here on out, you're the one knows more'n me, girl."

She saw Mae had been right. The horses slowed to slog through fetlock-deep water in a small cypress swamp. Could this be the same area she had come through with Rey in his swamp buggy just before—

"There!" she whispered and reached over to grab Mae's arm. "See those lighted buildings? That's the gator ranch."

"Crap, Jordan," she said and ripped off her cap to smack it on her thigh. "You didn't mention gators right where we're going. Any loose?"

"Shh. No," she said, leaning closer to Mae. "Well, some are penned up outside, but it's the buildings beyond that I want to peek into."

"You gotta have respect for those things. Can you imagine the feeding frenzy that many would have? And they can run fast 'fore they tire out, and there's no such thing as a dead one. Our Uncle Eddie used to wrestle them, but he'd have to flip them over and rub their bellies to get them to calm down."

"Mae, shut up. We won't be wrestling any damn gators!"

Slowly, keeping back in the trees, they walked the horses along the fringe of the huge clearing. Jordan felt she knew the basic layout, though she saw from this angle she'd remembered a few things wrong. When a big bull gator roared, the horses shied and whinnied and Mae swore under her breath. They dismounted and listened. Nothing else but the usual Glades animal night sounds and breeze shifting branches overhead. Jordan had convinced herself that panther cry she heard around here could not have come from the outlying brush. Besides, a cat running free could scent gators and avoid the area. Now that she saw these buildings again, she was even more sure that the cry must have come from one of them.

"You stay here and kind of cover me," Jordan said, her face close to Mae's so they could whisper. "I'll take my binocs and just peek in a window or two.

Then we're out of here. We'll be back with a full report before Seth and Wilson return."

"Jordan, I don't know about this now. All those windows are lit. Won't that mean someone's in there? And if it's something important, there could be guards or alarms. Maybe Rey himself."

"Don't worry. Stay here and get your shotgun out just to be safe. I'll be back in a few minutes, and you'll be able to see me from here."

She squeezed Mae's arm, took her binoculars, and keeping low, jogged across the grassy clearing toward the first building beyond the ones she'd been in. The old mess hall, Rey had called it. Unfortunately, she was now in the light of the building as well as the pale moon. At least he didn't have floodlights, but what if a siren sounded or an alarm went off? She had figured he did not keep guard dogs, not with his obsession with cats—she hoped.

She pressed against the building and edged to the first window. The problem was that, like the windows on the gator buildings, old-fashioned wooden, slatted louvers attached at the top of the window slanted outward, propped up with a board at the bottom. First, she tried squinting through the slats, but she couldn't see enough of the room. But, if she was careful, she could lift the louver higher and slide underneath it to peek through the panes. Carefully, she hefted it and, taking the weight on her back and shoulder, peered inside.

It looked like a lab of some kind with stainless steel countertops, cupboards, test tubes, a microscope, refrigerator, a microwave-looking machine, maybe a centrifuge. But all that could be part of the gator farm where they studied the eggs and blood samples. Slowly, she lowered the louver back onto its notched

board and hurried to the next window to balance and
lift that louver.

Now she could see two computers, their empty
screens glowing a deep blue as if someone had just
stepped away from them, but a lot of people left theirs
on all the time. A bulletin board way across the room
with charts, graphs, printouts of data. File cabinets. By
the opposite door, a clothing rack with white lab
coats—and several brightly hued Seminole shirts. But
it meant nothing but that workers here liked that kind
of shirt, maybe even bought from Mae's shop. Still,
why would there be several?

The next window was around the corner where Mae
could no longer see what happened to her. Jordan's
heartbeat thumped harder as she slowly, carefully
wormed her way between the louver and the window.
Central counter space—almost like a small, stainless
steel operating table—with hanging lights, a diagram
on the far wall. To try to read it, she lifted her binoculars, then jumped when she clunked the end of them
against the window glass. She held her breath, but
heard nothing but an occasional distant grunt or roar
of a gator in the night air.

Suddenly, she felt pressed in, trapped between the
heavy slats and the window. She fought to keep calm,
but each time she stepped on so much as a stone or
bump in the turf, she jumped.

She lifted her binoculars again, tilting the lever to
adjust the vision. A diagrammed anatomy of an animal
leaped into her field of view, and it was not an alligator. A cat. She could not tell if it was a domestic cat
or its larger endangered cousin, the Florida panther.
But next to that were posted photo after photo of
Florida panthers in the wild.

She shook so hard her field of vision jiggled up and

down. One of the photos was of a panther eating some sort of leaves, though you couldn't tell what. Could it be that photo Max, their gardener, had seen in Lawrence's things that day he was taken? Even if it was letaria leaves, maybe these people—Rey—thought it was wild orchids or something. And that's why he was getting closer to her, to learn if Lawrence's panthers were eating wild orchids. But why hadn't Rey just asked her—unless he had something to cover. But he had seemed so kind, so—real.

She eased that louver back on its notched board and went around the building to the last window. Looking in, she gasped aloud.

A black-haired man sat slumped in sleep over a desk in a small side room stacked with wire cages. Two of them closest to him held sleeping Burmese tortoiseshell cats, the ones Rey bred. The man was not dressed in a lab coat; maybe he was just a guard, one of those Cubans Rey had hired and Michelle detested.

She remembered to breathe, but her shoulder slumped. Rey was probably only using this for a Burmese cat clinic or for breeding experiments. That had to be it. Who knows what a Burmese sounded like when it was in pain? That might have been the cry she heard. He might just be interested in panther studies for comparison, and she was jumping to conclusions.

Despite the risk that the guard might awaken, she stood on tiptoe, her face pressed sideways to the window, trying to peek aslant into the closest cages along this wall.

There she saw living proof that Rey was breaking at least some laws: she could barely glimpse a big, beige panther pacing back and forth. And way beyond that, in the corner, a cage with some sort of—of small ape or baboon.

She jerked her head back in surprise with a little thunk against the wood slats. The noise was not much, but the panther screeched. The guard jumped straight up; his startled face went even wider-eyed when he saw her.

For one moment, each shocked, they stared aghast at each other through the glass. The man—boy—was not Hispanic, but Seminole. And he looked so much like Seth. She knew who it was—from the family resemblance and a photo at Mae's. It was Frank.

She motioned for him to keep quiet, but he shouted to someone and ran away from her through the door before she could get out of her press between the glass and the window.

She let the louver bang down and ran.

Chapter Twenty-three

"*Alto!* Stop! You! I shoot!"

Her brain told her she had to stop, but her emotions drove her on. Frenzied to escape, she kept low, darting zigzag toward the dark woods where Mae waited. Her baseball cap flew off: she panted, sucking in great gasps of air. She heard more than one voice now, men chasing her, but she did not dare look back. Frank had sounded an alarm. Was he with them?

She felt she ran in slow motion. Time stretched out as endless as the distance to the woods. She waited for shots, bullets, pain. Ahead of her, bangs of light exploded from the trees. Mae! Mae, shooting first to hold them back. But what if she hit Frank?

Shouts. Then sounds popped behind her, like firecrackers. Caught in crossfire!

She ducked, jagged, tore to the side. She hit the ground, rolled once, then scrambled up and on. She thrashed into the tree line, then tried to double back through its cover toward Mae. Why didn't she see her and the horses waiting?

"Mae?" she called in a voice as wispy as the wind. "Mae?"

"Back here!"

A horse whinnied. Jordan ran deeper in toward that sound, trying to shut out the men's desperate voices in Spanish and English. No more shots after that initial exchange. She glimpsed the silhouettes of the horses, with Mae already astride, leaning over her mount's neck to keep low.

Jordan grabbed her horse by its dangling reins, reached up to the pommel, and tried to get her foot into the stirrup. The horse snorted and shifted away, turning in a circle, dragging her.

"*Aqui!* Here. Over here, this way!" someone shouted so close that Jordan yanked the reins to pull the horse and ran. Mae knew to follow; they splashed far into the water before Jordan got up on a big cypress knee to mount. She was dripping with sweat and swamp, but the shouts behind them faded.

They had done it, she exulted silently. They had escaped with the knowledge, if not proof, that Rey was tampering with the protected panthers and maybe other endangered animals, too. She'd seen Seminole shirts and the Hispanics who might have worn them to take that first panther and later Cal and Reb's old cat Mamie. But all that was overshadowed by the fact that Frank worked for Rey. And, she was certain, Frank could identify her, unless the baseball cap hiding her hair disguised her.

They pushed on silently. Jordan feared Rey's helicopter would roar overhead, sweeping spotlights to nail them down. She didn't want to tell Mae what she'd seen. Who knows that she wouldn't do something crazy. Jordan's thoughts thudded as hard as the horse's hooves as they found the gate and galloped down the road until they were back on Seminole land.

They reined in at last among the pine trees, side by side. Jordan saw Mae slumped from exhaustion. She reached out a hand to grasp hers on the reins.

"You were great covering me, Mae. And we were smart not to talk all the way back."

"I'm glad they didn't—hit the horses," she replied in such a strange, tight voice Jordan leaned closer. "But they got my good sewing—and shooting—arm."

Jordan lifted her hand to touch sticky, warm blood. "Oh, Mae, no. This is all my fault."

"Just shut up," Mae said through clenched teeth. "I'd shoot—any bastard hurting you. Get me home and patched up—before Wilson and Seth come back."

"Seth, what are we going to do?" Jordan asked, gripping his hands. After Wilson drove Mae into the ER for her arm wound, Jordan had finally gotten to talk to Seth alone, but it was almost three in the morning. Wilson and Seth had been furious with them at first, until Jordan told them she'd seen Frank. Then they'd plunged into desperation and despair.

"I've got an idea," Jordan told him when he just stared and frowned into space. They sat on the couch at Mae's, leaning close and whispering, though no one else was in the place. "We delay getting Rey arrested, until you can talk to Frank. Couldn't you do a sort of covert raid to get Frank back first? I mean, maybe Rey coerced Frank somehow, and we can save him yet if you don't bring charges about Frank's stealing from you. Then you and the family could just straighten Frank out while Rey goes down on his own."

Exhausted and devastated, he shook his head. "Just like with that Rent-a-Wreck of yours," he said, sounding close to choking up, "we'll never find Frank if we go back over there, even if we storm the place right now. And if Rey's been paying Frank, he might be paying Yancy, too," Seth muttered and leaned over to prop his elbows on his knees and put his head in his hands.

"You know," his voice came muted, "new boots and a few bucks for a stupid Seminole kid and a new house and plane for Yancy."

"Seth," she said, trying to drag him from his apparent defeat, "couldn't we just get those marshals from Fort Myers to go out to the ranch, look around, then—"

"Jordan," he said, lifting his head and taking both her hands in his, "everything you saw while you were trespassing might not be admissible or sufficient to put Rey away or maybe even be enough to get him arrested. Come on, sweetheart," he said as he rose and tugged her to her feet, "we've got to get you home."

They walked out, arm in arm to Jordan's car. He had said he'd follow her back to the Lokosee ferry and then return here. She was going to spend the night at her mother's again, where she'd left Micco.

"I admit," he told her, "Frank's the link, but I can't even risk sending someone over to Rey's to look for him, because not only will everything be cleaned out of there, but they'll be waiting."

"I'm sorry—my fault."

He squeezed her shoulders hard. "At least we know who took my guns and told about the timing for the Winter Dance. I'm just praying Rey doesn't get rid of Frank now to cover his tracks."

She twisted back to face him. "Get rid of him? I'm sure he wouldn't stoop to that! Buying information, framing someone for old-time revenge, working toward scientific progress—for greed—that's one thing, but murder? I cannot believe Rey had anything to do with Marc's crash or Lawrence's death. I really think he likes me, and he just wouldn't do that to my husband. And if he was paying Yancy off, why would Yancy have let you go today?"

"Because he didn't have enough evidence to even arrest me—only to harass me. He loved every minute of it. The damage is done—or will be again tomorrow—when the media reports I'm linked to every attack against the panther team—and by implication, perhaps even against Lawrence. Rey's been lying about forgiving the Seminole for ruining his career years ago, baby."

"I never meant we should let Rey—just like those murderers from the Radiance Foundation—get away with everything!"

"We won't. But he seems like a nice guy, remember? He wouldn't hurt you—or anyone else either, right," he reminded her. "I think it's time, Jordan, you let go of your little girl trust of Winston Rey just because he's hired a fancy orchid garden done."

He was right. Still, murder? She had instinctively liked Winston Rey from the first time she met him. There had to be some other explanation—the Radiance Foundation or some nefarious drug firm. Seth had discovered that a Los Angeles-based philanthropist named Blaine Phillips had established the Radiance Foundation, but that had not led to Winston Rey.

"Jordan, listen to me," he said, turning her to face him in the dark yard. "It's obvious you have to steer clear of Rey in case Frank ID'd you to him. Have your assistant call the ranch and leave a message you had to cancel working on his orchid garden today. Go ahead and work on that new garden on Chok, while I talk to my father and we decide how to proceed about Frank."

"Yes, all right. You know, I actually had my mother talked into going along to the SunRay to see the place today—for old time's sake, like Rey said when he invited her and Lana. I'll have to tell her it's off because I have to get in the Smallwood garden before the Seminole Festival."

"That's my girl. Clever and tough as nails." She shook her head and squeezed Seth's waist. She hated to spend these fleeting moments with him agonizing and arguing.

"I'm so sorry," she whispered, "about Frank's betraying you, Seth. I can't imagine how terrible that must be. But no matter what, you've got me now. Nothing's coming between us ever again."

Though it was dark with only pale reflected window light out here, she saw him force a smile before he held open her car door for her. Before she could get in, he pulled her into his arms and tipped her chin up. When he kissed her, she felt a tear track on his cheek.

Arlene Hartman's hands shook as she told the guard at the gate to announce her at the SunRay. When he passed her through, she found herself driving slowly down the lane, dreading facing Winston Rey after all these years. But someone had to do this, and she wasn't letting Lana out here. And she, most certainly, was not going inside.

Suddenly, she was glad she had come alone rather than having to talk to him with Jordan somewhere about. She regretted the conversation they'd had over breakfast this morning.

"I imagine it's dreadful having to work for Winston Rey," she'd said to Jordan as they ate their French toast. "Even as a movie director, he threw his weight around, tried to impress everyone. I'm sure he secretly thought Lokosee was podunk. 'Absolute power corrupts absolutely,' something like that."

"Yes, so I've seen lately," Jordan had responded cryptically, just shoving a piece of toast around in its syrup, like a kid. "But he's really acted very kind."

"Acted! That's a good word for him. Lana's been mooning over an acting career she'll never have just because he told her years ago she could act. And I will never forgive your father for letting him have space for his boat on the dock right next to ours."

She'd realized too late she'd overstepped with that. Jordan's head jerked up; she put her fork down with a clink. "Two things occur to me, Mama. That maybe since Daddy's been dead this long, you ought to forgive him for something so dire. And that it's nice to think you must have sided with the Seminoles against Rey in that standoff and only came to think I was too good to marry one of them later."

She'd never quite forgiven them for pulling her and Seth apart, but his people had agreed, too, Arlene thought even now and hit the steering wheel with her fist.

Then, there he was, standing on the driveway, waiting to greet her himself, when she'd expected to have to deal with a maid or a butler first. He looked handsome and imposing still, but then Jordan had said he did.

She braked carefully, but her whole foot shook like she had the palsy, tempted as she was too just mow the man down with this big car on his front steps.

She got out, walked to the hood of the car, and held up one hand so he wouldn't even walk around. He blanched and stepped back. Perhaps he'd thought for one moment she was pointing a pistol at him, but he recovered instantly, completely.

"Arlene, to what do I owe this pleasant surprise?" he inquired, propping one hand on his slim hip.

"When Lana found out you'd come back here to live—well, let's just say I should have paid this visit sooner. But by that time, you'd already wormed your way into her affections."

"I haven't seen Lana."

"Don't play your games with me, even if you do think we're a bunch of swamp rats! I'm talking about Jordan, and well you know it."

"I'm enjoying getting to know her immensely," he said and dared to smile.

"You'd better not say a thing to her. She knows nothing of it and must not. After you and your kind were gone, we all decided that was best," she said, leaning her legs against the front bumper for support. Her legs were trembling, too.

"I'll bet she'd take the truth amazingly well now that she knows me," he said and smugly lit a little cigar.

"Is that your plan? Don't flatter yourself."

"Oh, I don't, Arlene. I deal only in realities, which I control."

"You're demented," she said with a wave of one hand. "And don't try to buy her. The orchid garden's one thing, but nothing else."

"Like I bought all of you? So, how is the family fishing fleet? I was under the impression that it—shall we say—smoothed the waters considerably. Or did J.J. have second thoughts?"

"He loved her like his own—more than his own," she said, shaking a finger at him before she realized it and snatched her hand down. "But it doesn't mean he forgave himself—or you. Well, I've said what I came to. And several people know I'm here, just in case you think your guard out there can pick me off on the way out."

"Pick you off, Arlene?" he said with a laugh she would have liked to shove down his throat. "You people always were so quaint. No, I assure you that you are free to leave. I know I can trust your—ah, discretion."

She got in, slammed the door, and sped away. If her glimpse of him in the rearview mirror was the last she ever saw of him, so much the better.

"Thanks for coming right in and cooperating with me on this, Jordan," Yancy said as he greeted her at the door of his office. He forced her to shake hands before she could move past him. She felt like wiping her palm off on her slacks, but she just sat.

"I couldn't wait to hear what you had to say," she told him, trying to steady her voice. She'd gotten Yancy's call at her mother's house and, since he'd asked her to come into the police station, she'd agreed. She would never have met him somewhere else.

So, after her mother had left for a doctor's appointment she suddenly recalled, Jordan had taken Hattie to Lana's and driven into town. She was going right back to Chok afterward to put in that orchid garden, but maybe if she just played along here, she'd be able to discern Yancy's next move. She was furious at him for the way he'd treated Seth and for probably being bought off by Rey, but Lana wasn't the only actress in this family. She could surely carry this off.

"So, it sounds like this Chay was a pretty strange guy," Yancy said, sitting across his neatly ordered desk from her. "Anything else you can tell me about him? Background info to help with the investigation on his death."

"It wasn't obvious he was kind of unstable at first. But especially after Lawrence's death, it got worse."

"You should have called me when he showed up like a raving lunatic at your place that night. But, let me tell you what I'm theorizing now."

"You're not going to try to convince me that Seth Cypress had anything to do with Marc's death. That's partly why I agreed to come in—to speak on Seth's behalf. Even if the plane that crashed is the one that reporter leased to ruin the Winter Dance, Seth wouldn't know a thing about tampering with airplanes."

"A smart guy like Seth could learn, couldn't he?" he asked, leaning back nonchalantly in his chair. "Besides, he might have a revenge motive against both Chay and the plane. All right," he added, holding up both palms to head off her protest, "I don't want to discuss Seth. I just want to tell you that your suspicions about a stalker and possible murderer of Lawrence—yeah, I know you never quite accepted the suicide ruling—can be put to rest with Marc Chay."

"Marc?" She sat up even straighter. "Can you prove he—he did all that?"

"Could be." He flipped open the manila folder in front of him, but didn't break eye contact with her. "From things we found in Marc Chay's condo, I believe he was watching Lawrence and may have, at least, been behind his disappearance. Your husband would have trusted him, gone off with him."

She sat farther forward on the padded chair. "Will you reopen Lawrence's case?"

"Without Chay's testimony or admission, the suicide ruling will stand. But just to set your mind at ease, here's the evidence. One, we found cameras at Chay's place of the same make and model as you previously handed over to me from your condo."

"But he told me that night I called the police on

him that his place had cameras, too. That had evidently helped to panic him."

"No," he went on, tapping the folder with an index finger, "these cameras were in the boxes he bought them in out West, not hidden or positioned around his place. Two, that gun collection of his just happened to have two other Lady Smith and Wessons identical to the one that killed Lawrence—guns Chay didn't show us or mention when he was interviewed after Lawrence died. Ballistics established neither of those shot Lawrence, but Marc obviously favored Lady Smiths as an easy-to-hide weapon of choice. Three, we found, just as accessible as you please—no encriptments or key words or anything—that he had a lot of information in his home computer about Lawrence's work."

"But he used to work closely with Lawrence."

"Yeah, but I heard Lawrence wasn't sharing stuff there at the end. Some of this seems to date from long after Chay got back from out West. Like," he went on, glancing down at his folder for the first time, "correspondence with the latest private grant lab to get on Lawrence's bandwagon, ah, the Radiance Foundation in Key West."

Her head jerked up, but she fought to keep recognition or fear from her expression. No one here but Seth knew of her nearly fatal confrontation with those men, and she dare not let on what she'd held back now. But it did prove, didn't it, that Marc was in with those killers or was Lawrence's killer? Or was she being sucked in by Yancy again with Rey pulling his strings?

"No comeback on that?" he asked, his voice suddenly taut. He hesitated, as if he'd been expecting more from her.

"I told you, Yancy, Marc Chay was a very unbalanced man. I deeply regret I didn't insist he get some help, but all this doesn't really prove he had anything to do with Lawrence's disappearance or death. Marc was at panther headquarters that day Lawrence disappeared. He was there when I called in for help, just as you happened to be nearby on the Trail to come to my rescue."

His eyes narrowed. "Which means what?"

"Only that coincidences can happen, and Marc didn't take Lawrence directly from the condo. Brent Rymer told me that Lawrence and Marc argued, but that's not enough for a motive either, though I suppose a good case could be made for Marc's ambition and greed really getting out of control after Lawrence left his work behind."

He seemed to jerk to attention. "So Lawrence *did* leave some work behind with you. That's why Chay was after you."

"I mean *if* Lawrence had left something behind."

She could see he was really angry now. That telltale pulse beat at the base of his throat where he had his tie loose and collar slightly open. "*Semper Fi,* Jordan, that's you," he accused, his voice cutting. "To everyone but me, that is. Hell, you can't even see through your ex."

"You said you didn't want to talk about Seth." She inched forward on her chair, wanting to flee. "It's just I felt sorry for Marc for some past things in his life, which, like Lawrence's, is now ended much too soon. If you're done now, I'd like to leave."

"Actually, Ms. Quinn, I'm done with you—for now. You don't trust me, and you once trusted this man Chay, didn't you? *Didn't you?*"

"Once. Yes. Yancy—"

"And you've been wrong about *not* trusting me when I've done nothing but help you!" he shouted and hit the desk with a fist.

"I appreciate anything you've done in all sincerity," she said in a rush. She got up. "I really have to go now."

She opened the door herself before he could come around the desk. Without looking back, she threw up a hand in a quick wave, but she knew she'd finally made an enemy of Yancy Tatum.

At the front door of the police station, she ran into Brent Rymer. "Oh, Brent," she said, surprised as he bounded toward her, and they shook hands. "This tragedy on top of the others for you and the team—I'm so sorry."

"I knew you'd understand. Losing that student was really terrible, too. I'm flying to Chattanooga for his funeral tomorrow. You know, I'm starting to think we're getting signs from God to keep our hands off the panthers even if they pass into oblivion. Well, gotta go talk to Lieutenant Tatum. Said he needs information on any work Lawrence and now Marc could have left behind. I'm in a hurry," he said, backing away from her, "because we're having Marc Chay's cousin over for dinner at the house tonight. He flew down to claim the body. Marc's parents were both too old to come."

She gripped his arm as he started away. "Marc's *parents*? He told me they were both—dead."

"No, just in delicate health, I guess. Sadly, the cousin says Marc had a huge blowup with his folks and hasn't spoken to them in years. I guess they spoiled him rotten. The only son born late—heir to

their big Cleveland-based porcelain import business
and all that. Gotta run."

She stood in a shaft of sunlight outside the door,
staring at the sidewalk. Had Marc told her anything
that was the truth, ever? Had Yancy lied today? Rey,
from the beginning? Thank God she had Seth. Mama
and Lana, too, even if they argued sometimes.

She walked dazedly to the parking lot and leaned
against her sun-warmed car. Then she smacked the
roof with both palms when she realized she had left
her purse in Yancy's office. Now she'd feel she had
to change her locks at the lodge, just in case. Sometimes, she was sure she just couldn't take any more
surprises and shocks. Quickly, she headed back in to
ask the officer at the front desk to retrieve the purse
for her.

Chapter Twenty-four

"Hey, why you hanging flowers in the trees, lady?"

"Careful up there, now, Jordan. You know, your old man never did like heights."

"So how you been lately since your husband up and—you know—passed on to his reward? And how's old Hattie doing? I ain't seen her for a month a Sundays. . . ."

Jordan called down what responses she could, but she kept hanging orchids in the buttonwood thicket next to Smallwood's Historic Store and Old Indian Trading Post. She had been looking forward to this solitary, simple task to have time to think. Ordinarily the historic site where pioneers once shopped and Seminoles came from miles away to trade was peaceful where it sat at the end of Chokoloskee overlooking the bay and 10,000 Islands. But today it was bustling, and that made her even more uptight. Finally, her friend, Lynn Smallwood, who had commissioned the orchid garden, came to her rescue, holding the ladder and warding off tourists and the locals while she worked.

Lynn was the granddaughter of Ted Smallwood, pioneer and patriarch, who had built the wooden store on stilts about ninety years ago on the southwest Florida frontier. Lynn and her friend Nancy Hollister, who had restored the place inside and out, even repainting it the original rusty red, would oversee the annual festival tomorrow. But just when Jordan thought Lynn had managed to protect her privacy, she saw two men unpacking cameras and sound gear from a van.

Feeling instantly nervous again, Jordan called down the ladder, "You expecting publicity from a TV station, Lynn?"

"No," she said, craning her neck to watch them. "That's a crew from Miami, freelancing for that Arts and Entertainment cable channel from New York. They do that *Biography* series."

"I've seen that," Jordan said between the bangs of her big staple gun attaching netting for the orchid rhizomes. "So they're doing a segment on your grandfather?"

"No, this crew called yesterday to say they're shooting segments on Chok and Lokosee for a bio about that Hollywood director who filmed *Everglades Victory* here years ago."

Though she had a plant in one hand and stapler in the other, Jordan grabbed for the ladder and held on tight. She knew it couldn't be swaying, but it felt that way.

Winston Rey? What a chance to find out more about him, specifically if he ever contributed funds for studying animals or medical research. If she could link him to that L.A. philanthropist who funded the Radiance Foundation, it could really help the investigation she was going to have Brent Rymer pursue. No way she was going to Yancy with any of this.

"You know," Lynn prompted when she didn't say anything, "that guy who started all that old Indian flap. I just hope this film crew is out of here before the Seminoles arrive to set up or who knows what they'll still say about Rey. There's always been bad blood. Jordan—hey! Watch out!"

She had accidentally dropped her staple gun, just missing Lynn, but she managed to hang on to the *oncidium.* "Damn," she whispered. "Sorry," she called down. "You okay, Lynn?"

"By about a foot. And since I'm still among the living, I'd better go say 'hi' to them. This will be great publicity for Smallwood's—maybe for your orchids, too, if you want to talk to them."

She had to admit they were the first media people she'd wanted to talk to in years. She kept an eye on them while they spoke with Lynn. But she didn't have to get down to talk to them; they came over, a gangly, long-haired man and his bald African American cameraman, both in T-shirts and jeans.

"Yo, up there! Aaron Branson here and this here's Marlon Wills," the thin man said. "The curator here says we should tell you we'd like to shoot this site without your ladder, and so forth, while the light's good. We'd be glad to help you move stuff out, then back in when we're gone, it that's cool."

"Well—I really need to get this done before the festival. But if you don't mind my asking a few questions ..." she said, starting down the ladder. Mr. Branson spoke with a definite New York—was it a Bronx?—accent.

"We know next to nothing about breaking into TV, 'less you wanta do camera or sound," he said, as if millions of women must have already asked them how to become stars. That's probably exactly what Lana would have asked them.

"That's okay—it's the last thing I'd want. I'm just wondering what you're going to cover for 'This is

Your Life, Winston Rey'? Are you going to his ranch later?"

"Gonna try, but this is more like an unauthorized biography," Branson admitted, jamming his hands in his back jeans pockets. "Rey's about as touchy as Jackie Kennedy. People are usually honored to be featured, but guess he's afraid the piece will stir up all the anti-Indian brouhaha again. But our researchers said there's ample evidence he's changed his views about all that over the years."

"That's what he says. Do you believe it?" she asked, leaning over to put the orchid down.

"You know him?"

"I'm working for him—just to put in an orchid garden—one much bigger than this. But I've been out to dinner at the ranch and spent some time there."

"That's cool," Branson said with an approving nod. "Wouldn't know if his son's out at Rey's ranch, would you? They tried to set up an interview with him in New York, but he's disappeared."

"I've only met his daughter."

"Michelle Merwyn," he said, nodding knowingly. "But yeah, the son's an actor, name of Michael Raymond. Kid's kinda followed in his footsteps, though not as a director." Jordan could tell Branson was flattered she'd been asking about their subject. "A few of his latest films flopped, but the guy's got megabucks from somewhere. We can't figure what his problem is with our team researching him. We're hardly going to mention his illegitimate daughter. Hey, a show of this caliber ain't no *Hard Copy* or *A Current Affair,* no way."

"Michelle's not really—legally, I mean, his daughter?"

The two men exchanged lightning glances she could

not read. Branson stuck his hands under his armpits and cleared his throat. "So, the reason we want this view of the bay is because Rey filmed one of the pivotal scenes for *Everglades Victory* here and we can juxtapose it with old clips and a voice-over. It wouldn't take us long to help move the ladder and the plants, then move them back for you."

"Then tell me more about Michelle," she said as she began to move several of her plants to help them.

"Like I said, this is no exposé, so if you see Rey, tell him that, will you? The thing is Michelle Merwyn's mother was a starlet he seduced on a movie location in Texas in the midsixties. Hey, so the guy had a thing for ingenue types back when. You know, the old casting-couch approach, because he's had a few May-December romances with some bit-part honeys and sowed some wild oats here and there. He did feature Merwyn's mother in one of his movies, but she was never in films after that."

"But he didn't—do something like that—during *Everglades Victory*?" Jordan heard herself ask. She felt strangely detached from them, even from herself now. Her voice didn't sound like her own. "I never heard anything about that—here."

"The guy never flaunted his affairs and kind of bought people off more than once. It wasn't like today, where people would run right to the tabloid papers and cheap TV shows, know what I mean?"

"Right." Marlon Wills said something at last as if Branson had been talking to him. "But like they say, absolute power corrupts absolutely. So, we'll just help you move your stuff? Ms. Quinn, you okay? We just want to know, can we . . ."

But she just walked away, ignoring his voice and Lynn's as she called to her about having lunch. All

Jordan could hear was Mama's voice the day they drove out to Rey's ranch saying that she didn't like the man because "absolute power corrupts absolutely." She needed to know something right now, and she had a feeling the place to start was with Grandma Hattie.

Jordan drove straight to the ferry to Lokosee, then parked her car several houses down the road from her mother's and walked. She knew it was about Grandma Hattie's nap time, but that wasn't going to stop her and at least she could get the old woman alone. Scared and numb, she felt she was marching on a mission into enemy territory; everything in her life was out of control, and this couldn't be happening to her.

She walked quietly around the side of the house and under the back steps to the deck. She could hear her mother had the TV on above her on the screened porch—the familiar cable weather channel. Grandma Hattie's words leaped through her brain: "Your mother thinks that Hurricane Donna is coming again, and she's got to warn J.J. out in his boat or lodge or wherever he's gone off to this time." Her parents' arguments she remembered so vaguely and Lana didn't want to talk about—what had they really been over?

Stealthily, Jordan went back around the house and let herself in the front door. Few folks locked doors on Lokosee during the day, if at night. She tiptoed across the dim, curtained living room; a glimpse out back through the brighter Florida room affirmed that Mama was sitting on the porch glider, watching TV, her profile visible. Jordan slipped down the hall and went into Grandma Hattie's bedroom. The old woman lay on her side, curled up, a bright blue crocheted afghan over her, but she was not asleep.

Hattie squinted to see who it was as Jordan closed the door behind her. "Arlene? Didn't I just get laid down?"

"It's Jordan, Grandma. Want me to get your glasses off the bureau so you can see?"

"No, they hurt my nose. Just sit close here," she said and slid over to make room for Jordan on the edge of the bed.

"I came to ask you about some things that happened a long time ago. Do you remember when that movie company came to the island once, the year before I was born? Do you remember the director, Winston Rey? He's the one who gave Lana her first acting job."

"She's acting again, you know. But not in a movie."

"That's right," Jordan said, cradling one of her grandmother's parchment-skinned hands in hers. "Do you remember Winston Rey?"

"He brought a lot of changes here. Money, temporary jobs. Everybody was excited."

"Any other—changes, like in our family?"

"That's when your mother finished her change of life. You knew you were a change of life baby. I thought she was through with her monthlies way before you came, but she said no. That movie director changed everything, just like you being born so late in Arlene and J.J.'s life. Changed everything," she repeated and furrowed her brow as if she were trying to remember something.

"It changed where you all lived," she went on, "because to get the boats, J.J. had to move the family to Key West for a while. You weren't born yet when they left. It's only across the state, but they didn't

come back to visit for a while. I missed them terribly. Terribly."

Jordan began to tremble. She knew the four-boat
fleet came from a friend of Daddy's in Key West, but
not that the whole family had moved there for a while.
And, though she'd never questioned it before, she
wondered now why some friend would just leave four
fine boats to her father when he lived in Key West
and Daddy had always lived here, except during
World War II. Yes, it was probably somebody he'd
met during the war.

"But where was I born?" she asked Hattie. "My
birth certificate doesn't say Key West."

"Well, I guess I *am* remembering rightly," Hattie
said huffily and sat up to pull her hand free of Jordan's. "Maybe they just lied about it."

"Yes. Grandma, when Lana got her part in Mr.
Rey's film—when she was sixteen, I guess—why did
he pick her and—"

"Fifteen. She was fifteen because she was sixteen
when you were born. And I'm telling you, your
mother and your father argued about Lana taking that
part and about a lot of things after. I mean, they were
proud of her, too, because she was so pretty and everyone knew it, but they didn't know about Lana and
Mr. Rey and what happened. It broke Lana's heart,
too, but I told her if you live long enough like me,
my girl, you'll see plenty in this life, so you just go
ahead and marry that fine boy when you graduate high
school because he loves you to death. Is that what you
were asking me?" Hattie concluded through a big
yawn that made her eyes water.

Tears blurred Jordan's vision, too. On top of everything else she had been through, could it be? Not that
Winston Rey might look on her as a sort of ingenue

to spoil and seduce like he used to do young actresses. No, he could favor her for another reason, and from the first, she had felt such an instinctive affinity for him.

As much as it had once terrified her that someone might be trying to harm her, she had also wondered lately if someone might be trying to protect her, and at the cost of lives around her. She and Lawrence were having problems and then he was gone; she was left with all their assets and the legacy of his work. Then Marc harassed her and died. Seth was now under increasing attack. But who cared about her so deeply—and perversely?

Her stomach cramped, but she had to face Mama. Why put poor Hattie in the middle of this? If Jordan started quoting her, Mama would just say Hattie was confused. She was, of course, and yet Jordan feared she had told too much of the truth.

"You get some sleep now, Grandma, and I'll see you later," she managed to say when she only wanted to scream. She got up and went out, closing the door.

Feeling sick and afraid, she headed for the porch. She would have to confront her mother about this— even if it alienated her, even if the timing could not be worse. But she dreaded trying to get her to admit anything was wrong. Mama would say she was ready to crack up again over all the strain. And just maybe, she was.

The woman's voice from the television drifted out to Jordan: "A cold front moving in later in the week in the western states, but continued storms in the Great Plains. Locally, fair skies should continue in the Sunshine State, but small craft warnings are out for this evening. Sunset at five fifty-seven. High tide at the Naples pier at six-fifteen p.m. Water temperature . . ."

Jordan stopped in the open doorway. Mama was asleep, nodding over a *Good Housekeeping* magazine lying facedown across her knees. Jordan walked over, intending to shake her shoulder and demand the truth no matter what it was. She looked down at her graceful, limp hands in her lap. On the cover of the magazine, smiling TV personality Kathie Lee Gifford had her arms around her darling blond son.

Jordan spun and ran out the front door. She tore to her car, squealed the tires as she backed around, then U-turned, heading four doors down to Lana's.

When no one answered the door there, Jordan realized the kids were not home from school yet. Thank God, because she could never have taken Lana on about this with them around. That's right—they were to go to Mama's this week until Chuck got home. Because Lana had a dress rehearsal in Naples.

She ran to her car again. The ferry trip blurred by; she knew she drove too fast, passing cars on the Trail into Naples, but at least most of the traffic was streaming out at this dinner hour. Lights were on already; a crimson winter sunset had devoured another day.

It was only then she recalled she didn't have the Smallwood orchid garden hung; she'd driven right by the place without a glance. The Seminole Festival was tomorrow, that serpent Rey's monstrous Garden of Eden was only half done, and she was supposed to meet Seth at the lodge tonight. But now he might never want to see her again.

On Central Avenue, hunched over the steering wheel, she honked slow drivers over to the right lane, but braked when she saw a police car up ahead. All she needed was for one of Yancy's cronies to cite her for speeding. He'd find out; he seemed to know everything she ever did. But she'd bet he didn't know what she didn't want to know from Lana.

She parked right beside Lana's van in the lot of the dinner theater. 10,000 ISLANDS SPORT FISHING was lettered large below a wide-eyed, blue marlin leaping from a wave with the family's phone number strung out from its swordlike nose where the fishing line should be. As she got out, several people came out the side door of the theater and lit cigarettes. Good, she thought, maybe the cast had a break.

She excused herself to get in the door past them and found herself backstage. Lights illumined a set that looked like a bedroom with French doors to a balcony; she heard Lana's voice muffled somewhere in the depths of the rows of curtains on the other side. She strode straight across the stage.

Lana was sitting on a wooden stool talking to a good-looking man on crutches; Jordan didn't know if those were for real or just for his character. She only wanted to know what was real in her life anymore.

"Oh, my goodness—Jordan!" Lana slid off the stool and pulled a white terry cloth robe tighter around herself. "I didn't expect—is everything all right?"

"Your family, yes. It's not that. I need to talk to you."

"Sure, fine. Todd, this is my little sis, Jor—" she got out before Jordan took her by one arm and propelled her toward and out the door on the side backstage that read EXIT.

"Jordan. Hey, I've got a slip on under this robe and the pavement will run these nylons. I'm barefoot. Jordan, *what is wrong*?"

"You tell me. You finally tell me!" she shouted. Lana yanked away and spun to face her. Her arms crossed over her breasts, she stood against the outside stucco wall, wary but defiant as if she faced a firing squad at close range.

"I'm sorry to barge in like this," Jordan began again in a more controlled voice, "but I have to know something now. I've been talking to some men doing a TV biography of Winston Rey and then to Grandma Hattie, and the other day I overheard Mama—"

"Winston Rey?" she interrupted, blanching despite her heavy stage makeup. "About his past? What's he done or said about me?"

"I want to know what *you've* done or said. Why did he give you that role in the film the year before I was born?"

"Who cares about back then? Has he been lying about me? Okay, okay. He saw me on the dock one day swabbing Daddy's old boat, he thought I was pretty, that I'd be good in the movie, he gave me a chance and had a bit part written for me, so—"

"There wasn't even an original part in the film for you?"

"He just wanted—to give me a shot."

"What a great guy!" Jordan exploded and smacked both fists against the rough stucco wall. "Like he gave a lot of other innocent girls parts when he did films on location. A shot, is that what you call it? Did you know he had a string of young, nubile conquests? Michelle Merwyn's mother included, but maybe he bought off her and her family to keep quiet, to raise the kid. Lana?"

She looked stricken. She was hugging herself, swaying slightly, but her eyes were narrowed as if she would leap to attack. Like Mama, Lana could brazen anything through, but not today. Her lower lips trembled; twin tears marred her mascara.

"Oh, dear God, don't let it be true," Jordan murmured. She leaned against the wall, afraid she'd faint, then slid down to hunch over her knees almost as if she were talking to the pavement. "Winston Rey seduced you and bought off Daddy when he found out, didn't he? Was it because you got pregnant. Oh, no, oh, no, oh, no!"

"That's just crazy," Lana shrilled, but her voice shook. She stooped to seize and shake Jordan's wrist. "Have you talked to Mama? Have you?"

Jordan tore her hands away and pressed them to her face. Like a little kid hiding from a boogie man, she just shook her head.

"She'll tell you it isn't true, Jordan. That—"

"Stop it, damn you, just stop it!" she shouted, her hands turning to fists on her knees. "She can't lie for little Lana anymore!"

"They—they forgave me, and you've got to, too. Jordan, please. And I'm begging you, don't tell Chuck, or you'll ruin my entire family."

"I'll ruin *yours?"* she choked out, gaping up aghast. "You know, what you and Mama obviously feared most didn't even happen. Winston Rey hasn't said one damned thing about this. But I'm his—*his.* Not—not Mama and Daddy's at all, am I? You've always jokingly called me 'kid,' because I am, right—yours?"

"I swear to God, I'm sorry if I—we hurt you," Lana sobbed to smear her face and clog her voice. "We did it to protect you, because we cared about you, loved you so much. We could have given you away, but we didn't, so that—"

"Maybe I can't figure out who took Lawrence's life," Jordan shouted, shaking her head. "But I sure as hell can figure out who gave me mine. My real father bought my—my phony father and family off with four boats and all of you were willing to raise me with lies—all lies. At least I was worth four boats to you."

"I said it wasn't like that. We loved you, kept you, raised you. You're mine, but Mama's, too, my little sister, that's what Mama decided. Daddy understood and they just kept it from Hat—"

"He didn't!" Jordan screamed, jabbing a finger at Lana so hard she pushed her back. "He wanted to tell me, didn't he? And all that time they were protecting *you,* their only daughter, the only one they ever loved—"

"No, I said, no, no." Lana stooped to reach for Jordan's shoulders as if to cling and beg, but Jordan scrambled up and away from her.

"And all those years I thought Daddy loved me, he wasn't even my father. The lies protected all of you, even Winston Rey—not me. And you never told Chuck either. Your kids are my half-siblings, and Mama's really my grandmother, and Hattie . . ." She sucked in a sob and kept backing up from Lana, who staggered after her between parked cars with one hand holding the robe together and one arm beseechingly outstretched.

"And my real father," Jordan went on, "is the man Seth and his people used to hate and are soon going to hate again more than they ever hated me—yet."

Lana lunged at her, trying to hold her. "I loved you—always. Jordan, please, please, I beg you . . ."

Jordan shoved her away so hard Lana bounced off a car and sprawled on all fours. The robe split open; she scraped her knees, breasts, and arms, then just pressed her forehead to the pavement and wailed.

"Stay away from me, all of you," Jordan insisted. "I don't have a family. That selfish, cold bitch Michelle

Merwyn's more my sister than you ever were anything to me."

With that, all thoughts, emotion, even words, crashed into a blank wall. Jordan turned and ran even as she heard the stage door open and a man's voice call out, "Hey, Lana, Act Four. Lana, you sick? You okay?"

Darting through the maze of parked cars, not turning back for her own, Jordan just kept going. She ran down the street toward the beach, just to get away, to think. But she couldn't. Couldn't do anything anymore. Not only did she have no past, but this meant she did not have a present or a future. She would never run to Winston Rey. He still might be a murderer. And Seth—Seth would not want her now.

She crossed the street that ran parallel to the gulf beaches. She could hear the water now, reaching out its arms to her. *High tide and small craft warning,* Mama's—that woman's—weather show had said. The waves had washed Lawrence in down the beach, washed him in all white and dead and quiet in his heart.

She climbed up the wooden steps to the beach, then down into the sand. She was so out of breath that the stitch in her side felt like a slash there. Her footsteps were unsteady through the shifting sand until she hit the slick, packed part where the waves washed in. Salt spray stung her eyes; the wind pushed and lured her. Tumbled pieces of foam like soapsuds flew loose around her.

She tried to pray, to ask for forgiveness for them all, but she couldn't forgive them herself, so that seemed a lie. She did not even startle when the first cold wave wet her to her knees. Her hair rippled away from her scalp; her clammy clothes molded themselves to her. Staring into the blowing darkness, she took a step farther out, feeling so alone and small, but suddenly not afraid. Because she could make it all just go away by walking out into the rolling black.

And then, as she reached out to embrace it, a piece of seaweed snagged her wrist. She pulled it loose, holding it, remembering her flowers, hanging under glass, hidden in the Glades, dangling their beauty like jeweled necklaces. Caressing the seaweed in her fingers, she thought of sunny days there with Seth, gentle breezes in the ferns and trees and of panthers strolling their kingdom God gave them before man and his evil washed in like a great, gray wave.

And she knew she could help Seth and his people, the panthers, too, even if it was the last thing she managed to do. She turned away from the Gulf and staggered back up on shore. She had a purpose now. She was going to get the gun Mae gave her from under the seat of her car and go looking for Winston Rey.

Chapter Twenty-five

You can't go home again, some people said. Jordan felt that way now. Even when she saw Lawrence dead, even when those men tried to kill her, she had never felt more alone and afraid.

Seth should be at the lodge waiting for her by now, but Arlene or Lana might show up, and she never wanted to see them again. Until she did what she must, she couldn't face Seth, couldn't bear to tell him what she'd learned, who she was.

She finally pulled over to get gas and phoned Seth on her cell phone. He had a key to the lodge, so he'd be inside. She might as well, she thought, tell him the place was his now because she might never be going back.

"Sweetheart," he said when he answered, sounding excited, "I was just starting to get worried. First of all, I just found out Rey is a friend of the L.A. mogul who founded the Radiance Foundation. And Rey's got an actor son, who has AIDS. Then listen to this," he plunged on so she couldn't get a word in. She hung her head, savoring his voice, letting him talk: "Bill Bowlegs says when Rey shipped some cattle out yesterday, one enclosed truck was riding high on the axles, evidently without much weight in it, and Bill heard a panther scream from inside. Bill tailed them and saw Rey's men let a panther loose in the Glades. That's a little victory, anyway, so—"

"Seth! Seth, just listen. Please feed Micco and take care of him. I can't come tonight. I have some family business."

"Are you at your mother's? What's wrong?"

"I'll explain later. I'm sorry. I—I do love you and always will. I have to go now."

"Jordan, wait. What's—"

She slammed her thumb into the disconnect button so she wouldn't change her mind. Seth must not be at all involved in this. He must not even know where she was. She put the phone in the trunk of her car so she would not be tempted to call him back. Still, when the car idled at a traffic light, she could hear the phone's muffled ringing, ringing behind her.

She drove all over town, aimlessly, mired in mental mud. It was as if everyone she'd ever loved had died. Stopping at last at a fast food drive-through, she ate and drank something. She knew she should get some sleep before tomorrow, but where? Just park her car out on some road? But what if the police found her and that led to Yancy? Besides, she couldn't fall asleep like that; she still felt haunted by the nightmare of men in masks breaking through the window of her car.

But again, as when she stood in the Gulf waves, she remembered her orchids, God's gift of rare beauty, the promise of peace and perfection. They would not betray her. She left her car parked behind the restaurant where she'd had lunch with Michelle Merwyn— her half-sister. Keeping close to the buildings, feeling the criminal she would probably become tomorrow, she hurried to her greenhouse and tiptoed in the back way.

The impact of mingled fragrances staggered her when she opened the door. She walked the familiar aisles in the dark, touching leaves, bending to inhale scents, to stroke satin petals, whispering endearments as she always had. Now, she was saying good-bye. Then, keeping her purse with the loaded gun and bullets close, she piled some rags on plastic under a tiered bench filled with vandas and lay down flat on her back. She made a pillow of a bag of fir bark and dragged several sacks of cork nuggets close to hide herself.

Lying there, staring into darkness, she tried to make plans, but nothing came beyond one thing: get close to Rey, demand answers, make him sign a confession, then take the gun and do what she had to do.

Seth sat up all night, frantic over what could have happened to Jordan. After he'd left the lodge, he'd gone to her shop, banged on the door of her apartment, then come back to talk to his father as he'd promised. Together, they made the hard decision to take what they knew to the police—not Yancy Tatum—through Chet Lansing, Seth's lawyer. In the coming fray, Frank would have to fend for himself.

Seth was going to put in a showing at the Seminole Festival this morning, but he was going to spend most of his time looking for Jordan, starting with her mother and sister. Now splashing water on his face, he bumped his head on the medicine cabinet when someone pounded on the door of his trailer. The whole place reverberated loud as his heart inside his chest. Praying it was Jordan, with his shirt still unbuttoned, his face wet, he ran to the door, then realized he'd better be sure. He looked sideways out the window. Sunrise streaked the sky, silhouetting his visitor.

Frank!

"You alone," Seth yelled through the door, "or did you bring one of Rey's guys to shoot me instead of a cat this time?"

"Let me in before they find me. I just took off from Rey's."

So he was going to tell the truth at last. Seth opened both doors and pulled him in.

Frank slouched with one shoulder against the wall, staring down at about the level of Seth's belt.

"Are they really after you? Right behind?" Seth asked, but Frank shook his head. He looked beaten, not by a person, but by life. Though Seth felt furious toward him, now he almost hugged him. His face was pale and drawn, even dirt-smudged, like Josh's sometimes. The Frank who could spring at him, defiant, and demand to know why he always asked so many questions, was gone.

"I was sick and tired," Frank said, closing his eyes, "of thinking I had to live up to what you done all the time. And you tried to push me—get a job, go to school—so I got madder. Then I met this guy who used to know you on Chok—a cop, no less, a guy first said he admired you and wanted something of yours. You know, to pay me—buy something. But when he heard you weren't my—you know, hero—that's when he told me you used to fight with him all the time and he hated your guts, too."

"Yancy Tatum."

"Yeah," Frank said and slid down the wall to sit on the floor with his knees pulled up almost to his chin. The new boots he'd been so proud of were scuffed and muddy.

"I didn't even care," Frank went on in a near monotone, "when some guys hit the panther team with the dart gun. Yancy got me a job at the SunRay Ranch, night watchman with some Cubans I found out hit the team. My friends—he got them in over at Hialeah. Then I started thinking when I saw they meant to pin it—maybe more on you."

"You took my shotgun, too?"

He nodded. "But then I thought they might tie you to your old wife's husband getting killed. And then I saw her and Mae at Rey's and knew they could of been shot, too. I mean, I didn't have a gun on me, but the other guards did and they shot at them."

"Mae got hit in the arm, but she's all right."

When Frank sucked in a sob, Seth said, "So you recognized Jordan and saw Mae. Did you identify them to Rey's men?"

He shook his head. "Didn't matter anyway. He knows about her—Jordan, 'cause I overheard him say to some white guys in his study—see, I was going to take some stuff from his desk to bring you ..." He sniffed hard and wiped his sleeve under his nose.

Seth stooped to seize Frank's shoulders and lift him to his feet. "Tell me! What did Rey say about her?"

"He told the guys it was time to go get her today. One guy, a bald guy, said she'd been on her own too long anyway since Key West, whatever that meant. And when they left, right after I ducked out so they didn't see me, Yancy Tatum was driving."

"Not in a police car?"

He shook his head, hanging there like a scarecrow held up by Seth's hands. "A regular one. Nice—big gray Buick."

"Frank," he said, setting him back while he buttoned his shirt and tucked it in, "can you go on over to Dad's and tell him all this? Have him get Wilson? I'm only hoping they haven't left for the festival of Chokoloskee yet. Will you?"

"You trusting me? I was thinking I should turn myself in."

"We'll take care of that later. I've got to go find Jordan before Rey does. I'm not sure why he wants her when he's been on her side before, but I've got to go ..."

He seized his keys and banged the door behind him, heading for Chok.

Winter daylight wakened Jordan; when she remembered, depression wrapped around her wet and cold. Tears tracked into her ears and hairline as she lay stiff on her makeshift bed. Last night she had heard Seth pounding on the upstairs door of her apartment, calling to her, then finally thudding down the steps and driving away. How desperately she had wanted to run to him for help and hope, but she had to do this alone. She swiped at her tears, then got up to wash her face and hands from the watering hose.

She combed her wild hair and, using her mirror on the back of the sun visor in her car, applied enough makeup so Rey would not suspect anything right away. She hid her bloodshot, dark-shadowed eyes behind big sunglasses.

Yet dried, white salt water marked her jeans; her shirt looked rumpled and wrinkled, but she didn't want to chance going inside where she had several changes of clothes. Sally would be in soon, Mae might arrive next door early, and Seth could come back. But then she remembered Mae was setting up a booth at Smallwood's festival today and Seth would be there, too.

By nine o'clock Jordan was at the SunRay Ranch. "How ya doing, Miz Quinn?" the gate guard greeted her and stooped to talk through her car window.

"Just fine. I'm going to go do some more work on the new garden. Please phone into the house and tell Mr. Rey I'll take him up on a standing invitation for breakfast first."

"Oh, sorry, ma'am, but he's left with some friends to meet guests for breakfast in town, then he's going with them to some Seminole festival way down on some island, Chuck-something."

"He is? With guests?"

"A film crew doing something on his life, ain't that nice? Something about showing him supporting the Seminoles, his interest in them these last couple years. That's exactly what they had me phone up to the house last evening when they come by. Gonna get some good shots of Mr. Rey at the festival, see?"

"Yes, I see. Thanks!" she called out as she backed and U-turned. She reached over to touch the gun in her purse. It felt cold and hard, just the way she'd have to be when she found him.

After she drove onto the island, she began to shake so that she pulled off the road. Traffic was thick, all heading in for the festival: trucks with the distinctive SEMINOLE license plates, Florida vehicles, lots of out-of-state tourists' cars, even a senior citizen bus or two from retirement centers or tours from Miami.

She decided to park right where she was. Clutching her purse, she walked toward the noise, the music, the drums. She could hear Lynn Smallwood speaking over a scratchy public address system, telling everyone when to see the next sewing demonstration, canoe carving, *sofkee* sampling, and dancing.

Bright blankets and decorated booths circled the store. Clothes on hangers at Mae's stall fluttered in the breeze like bright butterflies. Jordan glanced across the crowd at her unfinished orchid garden; someone had clustered the plants she'd not yet hung around the edge of the buttonwood trees.

And then in the distance she saw Hattie and her moth—Arlene. Jordan bit her lower lip and edged way around them, her eyes searching for Winston Rey.

"Jordan," a woman called and she jerked around.

"Mae. Oh, your arm—"

"It's all right, so don't worry. Superficial wound, they said. But where you been? Seth's frantic and me, too."

"I'm sorry, really, Mae. Have you seen Winston Rey?"

"Can you believe that snake showed his face here? They were over there where your orchids are, him and the film people," she said, flinging her head so her big headpiece bobbed. "Good thing Seth's not here yet, or he would of lit into him. Listen, I'm gonna go inside and call him, 'cause he was looking for you last night and he's late here. I heard he went to your mother's house but she's here. Jordan? Okay?"

"I'll see you later—Seth, too. I'll have something to tell him. Later . . ." she said and hurried away.

"Jordan!" Lynn Smallwood called and put herself firmly in Jordan's path of flight. "*There* you are. People—including me—have been looking for you."

"I'm sorry about the orchid garden being half done. I'll—I'll make it right somehow."

"Your mother just said you haven't been well and to tell her if I saw you. And you didn't mention you knew Winston Rey. He said the garden you're doing for him is fabulous, and I should come out with you and see it someday. He said he'd be stopping by your place to give you another payment—"

"When? Stopping by the lodge when? He knows where it is?"

"Jordan, listen, you look—funny. Let me call your mom over. Oh, now where did she go in this mess?"

"No, don't, Lynn," she pleaded, grabbing her wrist. "I've had a disagreement with her and need some time to sort things out. You understand. I know you're busy, so go ahead now. I'm just heading over to Lokosee and get some rest there, so I'll see my— mother later."

She had no intention of going to Lokosee, but she'd be happy to let Lynn lead Arlene astray. At least Lana hadn't shown her fakey actress face here. Jordan made a quick circuit of the grounds looking for Rey, grateful Seth had not come back. Then she hurried to her car and headed for the lodge. Whether or not Winston Rey had really gone there to pay her or not, she was certainly ready to pay him back for everything.

She drove up to the lodge; she sighed and laid her head on her hands on the steering wheel when she saw no car. She'd evidently missed the chance to confront Rey on her own territory. Now she'd have to drive clear back to the ranch, but at least she'd go in and see Micco first, change clothes, maybe go out back with the gun to see if she could hit even something as big as tree trunk if she had to. But she couldn't stay long, because she didn't want her ex-family or Seth to find her here.

Even the bright sun did not lift her spirits as she unlocked the front porch door, then the main door and went in, locking it behind her, blessing the silence. She tossed her sunglasses, purse, and keys on the couch and started for her bedroom.

"Micco? Here, kitty, kitty!"

"I haven't seen hide nor hair of him, so I hope my presence didn't scare him into hiding."

Jordan gasped and spun around. Winston Rey leaned nonchalantly in the kitchen door with his arms folded over his chest and his head slightly cocked. His mouth lifted in a smile; his expression evoked calm and contentment. She wanted to run for the gun in her purse, but she stood rooted to her little spot of floor.

"How did you know I live here—get in?"

"Someone must have mentioned it. And the back door wasn't locked, so I just came in to wait."

Lies, Jordan thought, all lies again. Unless Seth in his hurry to look for her last night had not locked the back door. Or had Winston Rey been the one who had always had such easy access to plant cameras in places he shouldn't be? Suddenly, she was certain that those clear gray eyes could probe anything.

"Lynn Smallwood mentioned you'd be here," she said, trying to let him know he'd be suspected if anything happened to her here, "but I didn't see your car."

"I drove around in back. Lovely view there with the trees, the tall grass prairie, then the Everglades right out your back door." To her dismay, he came closer and sat comfortably on the center cushion of the couch, right beside her purse.

"Jordan, I thought it's time we really talked prices and costs, so to speak. I want to make you a very rich woman in every way. Come sit down, won't you, and hear me out?" he said, patting the last empty seat cushion on his other side.

She just stared at him. Now she knew where Frank and Yancy got their windfalls. Instead of going where he indicated, she sat facing him across the woven area rug in the straight-backed chair, the closest one to her purse. She forced herself to cross her legs, to lean back as if at ease. Trying just to rest her hands on the chair arms, not grip them, she met his eyes.

"By the way," he said, hunching slightly forward, elbows propped on his spread knees, "I found the backup computer disk you'd hidden under the edge of the carpet. But even with that, which my people haven't had time to study yet, I'd like to offer you the same bargain I did Lawrence."

His direct assault—his jumping way ahead of where she thought they must start—scrambled her thoughts even more. "You—you are admitting you had him abducted and killed?"

"My dear, what outrageous assumptions. How could you ever think such a thing? I simply made him an offer I thought he could not refuse, but at the last, for very selfish, foolish reasons, he did."

"Then you got rid of him."

"Jordan, please. We had a disagreement and he evidently went off on his own and killed himself. We never really know what people are capable of, do we? I have no idea who's been filling your head with these lies about my harming Lawrence, but—"

"Then what is the offer you are making me?"

"I want you to come home. I've done some wretched things in my life, Jordan, but I've learned to value family. Michelle's like the will-o'-the wisp, and—"

"—she's not legally yours. I had a little chat with the people doing that *Biography* segment on you."

"So they told me. I figured I'd better not keep things from you anymore, even if Arlene and Lana try to poison my care and concern for you. I'm done with letting the Hartmans, Seth Cypress, or whomever try to turn you against me. Such a bright as well as beautiful girl, you have finally discovered we are a family, haven't you?"

Jordan just stared. She mistrusted this man, hated him—didn't she?—but he was leveling with her when the Hartmans never did. And he was right; they had poisoned her life with lies.

"Why did you wait until now?" she whispered. "Just because those cameramen told me?"

"Not at all. I've been watching you from afar for years—frankly, ever since you eloped with Seth Cypress and it hit the papers all over the country." He smiled at her, daring to look proud and paternal. "From that moment," he went on, "and not because of bad feelings with the Seminoles, I began to rue the day I'd let the Hartmans keep you. I didn't want you to ruin your life. I was so proud of you when you got the marriage annulled, went to college, to Europe for a trip, started your own business. But I said to myself, *I* should be doing those things for her, and so much more. Even when you married such a clever man, I watched—"

"You watched and not from afar. You watched Lawrence with cameras in our condo!"

"No, it wasn't like that, though I had to watch him after he promised me access to his work I was funding, then reneged on it. And when, of course, I learned he was not good to you, worthy of you, I couldn't bear that because I had been a terrible father and I had to make it up to you."

Although she had known that flat-out admission of fatherhood was coming, hearing him say the words rocked her. She gripped the chair arms and tried to fight back tears, but whenever she blinked, they speckled her flushed cheeks.

"Jordan, as you may have realized, the other aspect

of this was the increasingly desperate need of Michael—your brother." His voice broke. He looked genuinely distressed. "He's dying of AIDS, and I was panicked to find some cure—even a rogue one—quickly before I'd lost him as I did you. Then it all started to come together, that Lawrence might be onto something big. And now, if you have any knowledge of his medical breakthrough, you could help me save your brother, save all mankind affected with this scourge. But, as desperate as I was, I didn't want to push you. I wanted to give you a chance to really know me, before I told you. Then, each time I almost came to it, you'd get another jolt in your life, and I couldn't bear to alarm you. And Arlene accosted me the other day, threatening me to say nothing or else."

"It doesn't matter what she said now. But—excuse me—I've got to get a tissue."

She got up to take her purse, then sat back down in her chair, leaving the purse half open on her lap, slowly drawing out a rumpled Kleenex. The gun was just inside, loaded, ready. But he was so confusing and convincing. Yet she knew, even with Lawrence's backup tape he'd found under the rug, he might not grasp the link to letaria leaves. The updated copy of the disk she'd worked on was still in a plastic bag, wedged under a loose floorboard in her bedroom closet. But if Rey had this place ransacked as he had Lawrence's things, he might come up with that, too. And would her life be worth anything to him then? But how much she wanted to believe his slant on things.

"You know," she said, after wiping her eyes and blowing her nose to stall for time, "I was starting to hatch a theory that someone was not out to get me but protect me. Was that you?"

"As best I could."

"Meaning, get Lawrence away from me for good?"

"I told you, I had nothing to do with his disappearance or death, Jordan. You must believe me. We are going to have to build our trust to be together, work togeth—"

"Or protected me by framing and defaming Seth Cypress?"

"My dear, you're making this reconciliation very difficult, though I understand what a shock it is on top of the others. Seth Cypress has never been good enough for you—you'll come to admit that. Why don't you pack up a few things and come to the ranch with me, just get away from everything for the weekend?" he offered with a charming smile. "We can go over what you know that might help Michael's cure and settle everything between us. Later, I can introduce you to a whole new world of contacts for your flowers, new friends . . ." He ticked things off on his elegant, long fingers.

"You mean you'd eventually try to tell me who to marry or not marry this time, just the way my par— grandparents did with me and Seth years ago," she said, sliding forward on her chair.

"I'd be lying if I said I didn't want you to marry and have some little boys and girls—my heirs."

"But how can I trust a man who seduces girls like Lana, dangling snatches of stardom before their innocent, young eyes?"

"We've all done things in our lives we regret, Jordan," he said and stood, smoothing down his wrinkled white pant legs as if the conversation were over. "And, believe me, she acted older than her age and was very willing."

Though he was hiding it, she could tell he was angry

now; his face looked florid and a vein beat in his throat where the collar of his golf shirt was unbuttoned.

"But I've never regretted," he said with a tight smile, "that you are mine. Unlike Michelle and Michael, you won't let me down about marrying and having a family, will you? But, I assure you, it won't be from screwing that smart-ass Seminole."

She stood and reached for the gun in one smooth movement, standing so the purse slid off her lap. She gripped the handle hard; the gun shuddered, so she put both hands on it and lifted it straight-armed directly at his chest.

"My dear, I'd hoped so desperately you would cooperate and take advantage of all I'm offering," he said, looking annoyed but not afraid. "Put that thing down. Gentlemen, you'd better come in now," he called, inclining his head slightly toward the kitchen.

A dark form blurred in the door. Not moving her body, Jordan glanced sideways. A black-haired man, Hispanic, stepped into the room, and behind him two others: Andy Kramer from the Radiance Foundation and Yancy Tatum. The Hispanic had a needle syringe in his hand. The other two held guns but not pointed at her. Kramer looked grim, and Yancy grief-stricken.

"Don't make things difficult, Jordan," Rey's almost mesmerizing voice went on. "I said I want us to work together, and I'm offering you a rich, rewarding future—family, wealth, the chance to make Lawrence's name great—all for just a little cooperation."

"I can't believe you—anymore. Get out of my house, all of you. Yancy, the hell with your claims of *Semper Fi*, you traitor!"

"You're the one who let him down, Jordan," Rey said, coming slowly closer, lifting a hand toward Yancy to still his protest. "He's always adored you and wanted to protect you. Didn't you know or care that he had always loved you? Yancy, get her things together. Andy, steady, because she's not going to shoot her own father. We'll just give her the same injection we gave the panthers so we can continue this conversation back at the ranch later."

As the Hispanic stepped toward her, Jordan swung the gun at him and pulled the trigger. But she hit Kramer; he yelped in pain, a look of utter astonishment on his face before he doubled over. She darted for the front door, fumbled with the bolt, the knob.

"He's hit, *señor!*"

"Yancy, catch her and let's go!" Rey roared.

She was out the door into blinding sunlight, but Yancy pounded after her across the porch, out that door. She'd never make her car and the keys were back in her purse. Would Yancy shoot her to catch her?

Fury and fear stoked her exhaustion to crazed physical power. Even her deadened emotions leaped to life as she tore toward the heart of the Glades.

Chapter Twenty-six

Jordan heard Yancy crashing through the brush behind her. She could almost feel his breath and hands. He'd always been in shape—he'd catch her. If only it were night and she could hide.

Help—how could she best get help? Try to run back toward the road, but her nearest neighbor was too far away, and they could get her by then. Cut clear through to Reb and Cal's, but that was fifteen miles of prairie, swamp, and sawgrass.

She dared not look back. She thrust branches away, clawed leafy limbs back. Yancy might have cared for her but in the wrong way, just like her so-called family. He had betrayed her, too.

Stop, she told herself. Can't outrun him. Jump behind a tree, plant your feet, and shoot. But these tree trunks were thin, shrubs low. No cover. He had a gun, too. She felt she fled naked.

She ducked and darted, circling, heading back a bit to try to shake him behind the man-high marlberry trees. If he'd just lose sight of her, she could try to hunker down and hide here.

At least she was familiar with this area, or had been once. But everything seemed changed since the days she had hiked here with the man she had once loved as her father; grass and shrubs had shifted since the days she and Seth met secretly here. If only she could make it two miles out to their old meeting place ...

"Jor—dan!" Yancy yelled behind her. "I only—want—to help. I won't hurt you—let him. We'd be rich—with Rey. He'd let us be together—marry you. Stop—just talk."

Finally, because his voice sounded somewhat distant, she dared her first glance back. He slowed, then paused, panting, across a little clump-grass clearing set in a semicircle of the pale-barked trees and buckthorn shrubs. He leaned one stiff arm against a slender tree trunk. She could see both hands; his gun was holstered.

"Stay there!" she warned. She stuck her gun in the belt of her jeans, then kept her hands in plain view. "What?" she demanded.

"Just what—I said. Why haven't you ever let me—take care of you? I can now—finally. We can live in my mansion on Lokosee."

"I'll never go back to Lokosee. My family is not my family."

"All right. He just told me, too. I wasn't sure how you felt. Anywhere you want then, on his ranch, anywhere. You're so lucky he's really your father, but he's been like one to me, too."

"Lucky! And you've done anything he asked," she accused. "You helped him kill Lawrence, then got it ruled a suicide."

"No, I didn't, I swear to God. I never shot anything but one old panther."

"The Turner brothers' old cat, Mamie? You bastard!"

"I didn't want to, but it was a—a necessary step to get Seth away from you. Like Rey said back there, that Seminole's not your kind, never was, big law de-

gree or not. Come on with me now, and I swear I'll
protect you if Rey's still upset. He wants you to be
happy, part of his family. Honest to God, he loves
you."

As he spoke without breaking for breath now, she
realized she'd made another big mistake, though she'd
needed to catch her breath, too. This was Marine
Corps macho man. Though he hadn't touched his gun,
he could probably draw and shoot it before she even
sighted hers. And no way she could outrun him here
and now. She was trapped.

"How is he, Juan?" Rey asked as he drove the four-
wheel-drive vehicle himself. They were heading to the
baseball field at the high school on Chokoloskee
where they would meet his helicopter coming in from
the ranch.

"Bleeding bad for one bullet, *Señor* Rey. In his
middle."

"Just—get me—some help, now, Rey," Kramer said
through gritted teeth. "I'll need—that chopper to get
me to the hospital—and you're gonna take it—after
her."

"Juan will drive you. And you'll tell them you shot
yourself accidentally."

"They'll—see—it—wasn't close range."

"Don't give me a reason to just deposit you somewhere in these mangrove swamps, man. I was tempted
to do something like that before when you almost
killed her. Good—there it is," he cried and turned the
car toward the low-slung school with a painted sign
that read HOME OF THE GATORS. "I'm glad I noticed
this site coming in today."

He stopped the vehicle near first base of the brown-
grass baseball diamond and got out without a glance

into the back seat. He scanned the sky, then checked
his watch, but it had been barely a quarter hour since
he'd called the ranch. They had waited ten minutes at
that ramshackle house of Jordan's to see if Yancy
would bring her back in. But his girl was much more
clever than that redneck cop would ever be, so he'd
have to personally oversee her capture himself. Later,
he'd clear Yancy out of her life somehow, just as he
had the others, because damned if he was going to
have that lout breeding Jordan's kids any more than
that pompous genius, some slant-eyed chink, or inso-
lent Seminole.

"Should I drive him into Naples now, *Señor* Rey?"

"Not yet. I can't be left standing here if the chopper
misses this spot. Just tell him to hold on."

Jordan tried to hold on to her control. If she couldn't
outrace Yancy, she'd have to outthink him. And then
she glimpsed her possible salvation, and thanked the
Lord silently for the first time since she'd found out
her whole life had been built on lies.

Between two low, scrubby buckthorn bushes about
halfway to Yancy, she saw a slight hump in the
ground, and hoped she knew what it was. Dad—J.J.—
had always said just not to bother them, but he'd
poured poison on them if they got too close to the
lodge because they could be painful and deadly.

It was an anthill, a distinctive one, that looked like
it contained fire ants. Now if she could get Yancy to
walk across it, without herself getting bitten, or she'd
wouldn't be able to go another step.

"You swear you'll protect me from Rey?" she
asked, her pulse pounding so hard in her ears she was
afraid she could not hear his answer.

"Yeah, I swear it," he vowed, his face lighting. He

heaved a sigh and raked both hands through his hair in relief. "He doesn't dare cross me because of all my law-and-order contacts and all I know about him—enough to send him to live in a cell next to my dad's if he doesn't toe the line."

You fool, like I once was, she thought. She fought to make her expression seductive, not surly, because she had to position him right. If he didn't walk on the nest or if she'd miscalculated that those were fire ants, she had no illusions what would happen to her in Yancy's hands—or in Rey's.

"All right," she said, forcing a nod. "I can't outrun you, and I never—even in my heart—could escape you."

Those last words made him even more careless. "At least meet me halfway," she coaxed and started slowly toward him, her hands held slightly out as if in invitation.

He came in long strides, right on target between the two bushes, but she had to stop him there or he could step right over it. "Yancy, just take it easy, please. I'm still a little afraid of you."

He halted and smiled. "Then we'll get you over that right now. Let's just seal this deal out here before we go back," he said, his leer almost burning her this close. He reached down to hook his thumbs in his belt. "Besides, I want to know once and for all you really mean it, honey."

He shuffled one step closer toward where she held her ground. She was doubly doomed now, she thought, because he didn't seem to be in the slightest bit affected, so . . .

He went wild. Like a madman, he screamed and doubled over to beat at his legs. He jumped and danced and howled. Jordan knew how it felt, because once they'd bitten her ankles and Daddy had to keep ice packs on her for days, staying with her, helping her . . .

Jordan turned and ran with Yancy's screams like those of her own agony in her ears.

The moment Seth let himself in the lodge through the back door, Micco appeared to rub against his ankles. Jordan hadn't been on Lokosee, and he'd missed her at the festival, but he'd finally cornered Mrs. Hartman—who was so distraught herself that she told him enough so he knew why Jordan was upset. He had wanted to shout at Arlene Hartman for what she'd done to Jordan, but he saw she was suffering, too, and at least, she'd told him the terrible truth just in case he could help Jordan. But how could he help if he couldn't find her? So he thought he'd try here once more before heading back to Naples.

"Where's your best friend, Micco?" he asked the cat, reaching down to stroke his head. "She wasn't on Rey's side before, but family ties bind tight. Is she on his side or not now, baby? If I could only find her . . ." His voice trailed off as he picked up the cat to cuddle him.

On the way to the kitchen he stepped in a spill of sticky red stuff. Micco in his arms, he kneeled to check it. It was blood, drying on the edges. Whose?

As he looked the cat over to make sure it wasn't his, he heard the unearthly scream out back. He tossed Micco onto the couch—where he saw Jordan's sunglasses—and tore outside.

Yancy Tatum, looking like a drunk with the d.t.'s, staggered toward him, nearly naked. He'd torn off his pants and shirt and wore only briefs, shoes, and socks. Red pustules and welts peppered his muscular legs, chest, and arms. Seth had seen that scourge before: fire ants. It could kill a man.

"Help me—help! Burning—needles."

"Where's Jordan? What's happened to Jordan?"

"Water—ice. Hospital."

Seth grabbed his big arms and shook him like a limp doll. "Where's Jordan?" he shouted. "Tell me, or so help me, I'll take you back to those ants!"

"She's—out there."

"Where? Tell me, or I'll just tie you up here till morning. Tell me . . ."

It came out as broken as Tatum looked, the story about Rey coming here, even about Rey being her real father. It enraged Seth even more than when Mrs. Hartman told it. Seth could have pounded him right into the ground. But a deafening, whacking sound from the sky made him drag Yancy under the grape-fruit tree nearest the back door as a helicopter roared overhead.

"Is that's Rey's?" he demanded.

"Never felt pain—like this," he cried, sobbing now. "Help me-ee-ee."

Seth took off his belt to bind him, then realized the man was beyond running farther. He'd call the rescue squad en route. He let him sink to the ground, then dashed for his car, knowing it was no match for Rey's chopper or other forces he might be calling in to find and chase and trap Jordan out there. He knew one place she might go, but there were many others— every hammock she'd probably explored for orchids between the lodge and the Turner brothers' place on the Trail over the years.

He revved the truck and sped down the road, trying to figure a good access to help her. But, once again, where was she? He had two calls to make, and Tatum's would have to be the second.

Jordan heard the helicopter coming and knew better to hope it was the police or park patrol. She dove into the six inches of tea-colored water in the fringes of a shallow swamp, just before the prairie ended. Rolling onto her back, she shoved out a formfitting nest for herself, breaking reeds and grasses to pull them down and over her.

The helicopter zoomed overhead, then returned in a huge, repetitive circle of the area. If they had spotted her, they could land nearby, but they didn't. Or had they radioed her position, and were waiting for reinforcements to surround her? She had actually thought about doubling back to the lodge after dark, but Rey might have men stationed there. Right now, she only hoped the gators were in deeper wallows and no snakes swam by. She never came out here without her snake boots, but what good would they be when her whole body was on the ground in shallow water?

Before the chopper's next more direct pass, she wriggled down to rake grass up over her legs, too. Thank God, it wasn't sawgrass or that would have sliced her to ribbons. Lying in her cocoon, this time she squinted upward to discern forms leaning out the chopper with binoculars just like that day this nightmare began.

"It was you from the first, wasn't it?" she shouted. "Wasn't it, Winston Rey—my fath . . ."

She choked on that. It was the truth, but always, always in her heart, her father would be J.J. He might have lied by not telling her what he surely felt he must, but his love had not lied. He had taught her to know this land, to spot a fire anthill, find orchids, mark a trail, feel happy and loved. And though folks always called him J.J. rather than Jordan James, he had given her his name, maybe to protect her from gossip or to show, if she ever found out, that he loved her, even from the grave.

"I know," she whispered, "that you loved me—Daddy."

Too late, Seth realized he could have summoned his men into a trap—another Seminole War with Rey's forces—by his desperate phone call for help.

"That demon dog chasing Jordan!" Wilson had shouted in Mikasuki into the phone at Smallwood's when Seth had explained about Rey chasing her, but not that he was her father. "Listen, *Micco,*" Wilson said, "some of us go watch that old hunt lodge of hers. I'll take Mae and the *ayikcomi* and go myself, send Bill and some others out on the roads. And you're right about not calling police, since they been on our tails. What they gonna do out in *Pay-hay-okee* but stop us from helping her and go crashing in there where they don't know nothing. I'm gonna go tell Mae and the men."

But now, in fairly regular intervals along Route 29 and the Tamiami Trail, Seth saw Hispanic men he was sure were cleverly posted: lone fishermen, two drivers standing by cars with the hoods up, hikers and picnickers this late in the day. Probably Rey's men waiting for Jordan to emerge from the Glades, looking for help. Or perhaps they were prepared to plunge in after her when they got word from that chopper where she was. At any rate, he didn't need Seminoles taking on Rey's people if he asked his men to do the same kind of surveillance for her.

He reached for his cell phone and punched in the number of Jordan's lodge. Mae answered immediately.

"Mae, stay put, but send Wilson out to gather the men to wait at the old Carnestown Welcome Station. And tell them if there's any trouble, not to handle it themselves, to get the Highway Patrol in on it after all. I'm tired of falling into Rey's bad PR traps for us. We don't need more Seminoles arrested, so let me handle this until I call you back."

"The emergency squad came for Tatum. He was out of it with pain when they took him away. But Seth—Dad already went off on his own."

"Driving? For where?"

"On foot—out the back door. And he's got that old poison dart gun he was showing at the festival. He muttered something about justice for *co-wha-chobee* and the *micco,* and next time I looked, he was gone. You—don't think, he's after Jordan—after all these years—in the wrong way—do you?"

"No. No, that can't be." But sometimes he thought he didn't know his father's heart at all, and if he'd somehow found out Jordan was Rey's daughter ...

Seth clicked off the call. His stomach cramped in fear. He could park at the Turner place and go in from there to find and help her. But now, Jordan might be doubly endangered out there.

As soon as dark descended, Jordan moved on, two miles farther in. Her first glimpse of her planned resting spot, bathed by pale moonlight, quieted her heart. No more roar of chopper blades, Yancy's screams, or her own from the depths of her soul. Here, in the old camp where she and Seth used to meet, silence stretched out to comfort her.

The once clean camp Seth's grandparents had built

years ago, when Seminoles could pole their dugouts in every direction through the river of grass with no barriers of highways or canals, had shrunk. Vegetation had closed in, blocking out the sky—at least from a helicopter, too. As she came closer, she could see the once rich garden had gone wild but scrawny around the fallen chickee and cold-packed hearth.

When her sweat from the hike evaporated and her clothing dried, she began to shiver. Night breezes whispered here like spirits. She wrapped her arms around herself, then realized she was thirsty. The words from some poem she'd learned in high school, *Water, water everywhere and not a drop to drink,* was true in the Glades these days. Once Seminoles and settlers could find good water, but not now with fertilizer runoff from the huge sugarcane farms to the north.

She knelt and dug a scratch well as her adopted father had taught her. As the hole filled, she dipped out the muddy water and let the fresh but warm water flow in, then plunged her hands in ...

She drank ravenously, then made herself slow down. Despite the chill, she took off her clothes and washed, scrubbing herself for warmth with a palmetto leaf. She wished she could wash the entire last year—her whole past—away.

She realized she was hungry, too; she yearned for some of Seth's swamp bread or hoe johnny wrapped around a mangrove root and baked over a fire. But she had nothing to build one, nor could she risk one. Besides, she had one roaring in her head and heart.

Just when they had begun to find each other, he would not love her anymore, even if she lived through this. For she was the child of the man who had brought the Seminoles nothing but years of pain and betrayal and who had personally plotted to destroy Seth.

She could not sleep, so she wandered the still grassy part of the clearing and found a gift from the Glades, a rare, night-blooming orchid. Though delicate and pale, alone in the dark, it was hardy enough to emanate a powerful fragrance.

As she inhaled the sweetness, she recalled certain times of her life had been sweet. Even a few with the Hartman women. She recalled Arlene saying not long ago, "Believe me, my precious girl, I have always, *always* been on your side."

She paced around the clearing until her thoughts began to smear together. Because snakes would stay away from anyplace they smelled a fire, at last she curled up on a bare spot where the old hearth had been. But she didn't sleep or even rest; she had thirteen miles to go before dawn. Her best chance, she'd decided, was to head for the Turner brothers' place, but since Rey's men had been there once before, she must go in warily.

She rose and risked shooting her gun once to see if it would fire; because she'd gotten it and the bullets wet yesterday, it snapped uselessly. She kept it though, stuck in her belt, just in case she could bluff someone with it.

Before she left the camp, she turned back for one more sustaining glimpse of it. Just in case she didn't make it and someone—Seth or his people—ever came here, she went back to leave a message, but not scratched in the ground so rain could wash it away. She broke off some scrubby sugarcane stalks that almost always grew wild at sites of old Seminole camps and spelled out on the ground: LIFE TO THE SEMS AND GLADES. J.Q.

Chapter Twenty-seven

"Hog-tie and gag them, then cover them up in their beds," Rey ordered his two armed men just before dawn. "We can see to them later, because if she's around, I don't want her hearing shots. Cut the phone lines, then hide yourself somewhere in here where she can't spot you until she gets inside—if she's coming. Then turn out the light."

As his men forced Cal and Reb to the floor with guns pressed to their backs, then bound them, Rey tugged the cloth curtains closed in the windows. Anxious for a breath of fresh air, he stepped out onto the new boardwalk the old coots had evidently been building to replace the burned one. Though the fire here had been recent, already green shoots were popping through the blackened crust of earth.

"It will be that way for Jordan and me," he murmured, though he patted his gun to be sure it was in his waistband under his shirt. "She'll learn to forgive me, and we'll start over."

He peeked into the small, clean-planked building these yokels had labeled FLORA with a newly painted sign. The whole place was a ramshackle mess, except for this new shack, the rebuilt boardwalk, and a fairly new truck he'd seen parked a ways from the house near their old rattletrap. Yes, he thought, as he surveyed the plants inside, Jordan might indeed flee here. He'd wait for her among the orchids.

Seth loathed feeling hunted in the Glades, where the Seminoles had once been free. "Damn! Here they come again."

He raced for the shelter of a buttonwood thicket for this pass of the chopper. Both that and an old, unmarked prop plane had begun making passes at first light, and who knew what forces Rey had on the ground. He crouched until the buzz droned away, then went on at a loping gait.

These miles of thick Everglades were taking him longer than he'd planned, though he pushed himself to the limit in the waning dark. Not even waking Cal and Reb, he'd set out in the pitch black, leaving his truck next to their old one. He had to find Jordan before Rey did and he figured she might be hiding out at their old Seminole camp meeting spot.

Now dawn scratched pink stripes across the sky when he was only halfway there. He saw ponds had shifted places since he'd last been through. Not that there ever were actually paths out here, but even if she was heading this way, he supposed he could miss her.

Unfortunately, he was looking for his father, too. If he bypassed both him and Jordan, maybe he should rent a plane himself. He shook his head grimly at a desperate, wayward thought: he'd trail a banner behind a plane the way they did to advertise along the beaches in Fort Lauderdale. And it would say, *Jordan, because of who you are, because of who I am, must we part again?*

Then for one moment, he fancied he heard his father's voice singing a dissonant song. It was that old

chant about love being a curse as well as a cure for
heartache. And the curse—the curse part got louder,
louder. It had to be just his emotion and exhaustion
talking—but—clearer now, it sounded as if the song
were coming from behind him, not ahead.

Seth turned and tore back the way he had just come.

Filthy and exhausted, Jordan sensed something was
amiss when she glimpsed Cal and Reb's property from
the thinning edge of the Glades. No smoke trailed
into the sky from their little Franklin stove this brisk
morning; no lights were on inside. The curtains were
still drawn when the Turners had always been early
risers. Of course, she told herself, that was years ago,
and they'd probably just changed their ways in their
old age.

Still, the hair on the back of her neck prickled and
a shiver chilled her flesh despite the sheen of sweat.
Those two airplanes this morning—especially the one
that reminded her of the unmarked Cessna—had
made her dart and duck all the way here. But the
Turner brothers had a phone; the Highway Patrol
would be her first call and Seth her second.

She walked cautiously past Killer's empty gator pit
and passed poor old Mamie's empty cage with its
metal door ajar. At first, she stayed off the boardwalk
since her footfalls might make a sound. Despite the
muffled hum of traffic on the Trail, it seemed quiet
here. But then, she tried to tell herself, with the bushes
burned and leaves singed off these trees, no birds
would be here now.

She opened her mouth to call out for Cal and Reb
but stopped. Crawling up onto the boardwalk, she tiptoed the last few steps to their door. And then, just
when something told her to flee, she looked toward

the Trail and saw Seth's truck sitting next to the brothers' old jalopy. Seth had come here to find her. They were either inside or close.

"Oh, thank God. Seth! Cal, Reb!"

She heard the door of the orchid house creak open behind her. She spun around, so grateful, so glad—

"You!"

"We meet again, and always shall, my dear."

"No. No!"

She turned and ran down the wooden walk toward the Glades, but he shot twice—either at her or into the air. "Stop, or I'll kill those old crackers we have in there!"

She stopped and, when she turned back to look, saw Rey flanked by two other men with guns raised. Trembling, she stood her ground as he motioned the men back into the house and strode to meet her on the boardwalk, a gun in his hand, pointing down at the ground.

"I'll go with you if you don't harm them—harm anyone else," she said, but her voice shook as hard as her knees.

"You'll go with me anyway, but I'll take your cooperation on Lawrence's work—and on starting to act like a dutiful daughter." He took her elbow and steered her farther away from the cabin, straight back by the old panther cage at the edge of the new walk. "Because, you see, the first time you cross me, Seth Cypress is the first to go, then—"

"You've already tried to smear him and get him locked up."

"Now that, I don't deny. How could you be so blind about him?"

"Blind about *him*? It's you I couldn't figure out. I

can't ever respect someone who lives like you do with perverted power, egomania—"

"Don't you preach to me. We're not only going to save Michael but conquer AIDS together. And, Jordan, I will make it up to you. I've been watching Lana with cameras in the theater. She's still a beauty, flaunting herself half dressed. I'll court her again, get her to marry me, make her famous, make everyone happy. What do you say to that?" he asked with a smile, turning her to face him.

It was only then, looking deep into his eyes, she realized he was not only evil but mad. Not crazy or insane by most people's standards, maybe. He was clever, but so far removed from a sense of morality— from anybody's will or rights but his own. She didn't even protest that Lana was married, because to Winston Rey, a barrier like Chuck Washburn and maybe their children, too, could not keep him from what he desired.

"Agreed?" he asked, giving her a little shake. His gun pressed into her shoulder. "We'll head back to the SunRay and have a real reunion with Michelle. You know, she actually thought I was romantically interested in you because you look so much like my mother and my wives," he said, with a little chuckle. "My mother—your grandmother—had a backbone of iron, too, but she finally realized that I was right, black sheep of the family or not."

She saw her chance then, maybe a last one. No use trying to draw her pop gun on him or grab his. No point in screaming for help or thinking Seth or anyone else could rescue her. And if she went to the ranch with Rey and explained the letaria leaves, would he even keep her alive?

"You must understand," she told him, "this has just

been a nightmare for me. I feel so exhausted, even faint." She leaned slightly against him. His hands steadied her. She lifted her arms straight out over his shoulders as if she would hang on or hug him. He responded, tugging her closer.

And then she reached behind him, grabbed and swung the metal gate of the panther cage as hard as she could into the back of his head.

She thought she heard his skull crack. He grunted, staggered into her, almost taking her down. She let him fall to his knees, then grabbed his gun. But a shout shattered her momentary victory.

Both his men ran from the house. They must have been watching. Now Rey would have Cal and Reb shot; he'd got rid of her for sure. Chancing they would not shoot her because of who she was and what she knew, she scrambled away, darted down then up the concrete of Killer's pit. She had a good start on them. She tore for the brush, but the fire had denuded the area of good cover.

"I'm gonna shoot!" one man shouted, pounding after her.

A bullet scuffed sand at her feet. If only she could reach the sanctuary of the Glades again.

The next shot whanged a tree trunk two feet from her, peppering her face with bits of bark. She would never make it across a grassy stretch before the first hammock. She had outsmarted Yancy, then Rey. Maybe, if she just faced these men . . .

Panting, utterly exhausted and bereft, she stopped and turned back, trying to hide Rey's gun along her hip. "Drop the piece, *chica*," the closest man, a Hispanic, said, gesturing toward her. They both had their guns raised; she threw Rey's pistol as far as she could. "You know," the same man said, shuffling closer, "more'n once I thought of hitting him with something, too, but you're worth more to us alive than dead right now."

"Just like my husband Lawrence was—for a while," she dared.

"*Sí, chica.* Just like that."

At last, she thought, she knew. Though it wasn't exactly an airtight confession, someone had finally admitted Rey took Lawrence and had him killed. Tears filled her eyes and made her stumble. The other man, a blond, grabbed her arm and dragged her toward where Rey propped himself up on all fours on the ground, like a dazed animal. Blood matted his silver hair.

And then, she heard a little thwack, thwack sound. The Hispanic grabbed for his neck, and the other man batted at his back as if something had stung him. She saw tiny darts fletched with down had hit them.

She almost clapped and cheered, but instead, under their guns, she stood very still, holding her breath, waiting. They looked puzzled, then relaxed, then almost silly. The blond thudded to his knees, then facedown next to Rey; the man holding her arm grabbed her as he sagged to the ground and toppled, too.

She scrambled for their guns, then scanned the area to see who had shot them. No one visible—no one, not even in these sparse, burned trees.

She went to Rey when he looked up; she pushed him back against the base of the cage and pressed the gun to the middle of his forehead. Her entire body shook down to her trigger finger.

"Is this how you told them to shoot Lawrence? Right here, right in his brain? Is it?" she screamed. "Get up. Up!"

Still holding the gun, one-handed, to his forehead,

she dragged him to his feet. He swayed; she shoved him toward the open cage. "Get up on that step, up there. You're going to be locked away for the rest of your life, so you might as well get used to it in the panther cage. You had Yancy shoot that old cat, hoping to blame Seth. Get in!"

An adrenaline rush poured through her as she half lifted, half shoved him. He rolled, then sat stupefied against the wall as she clanged the cage closed. She slid the old, rusty bolt shut and ran for the cabin. Within two minutes, she had her friends untied. Because the phone line was cut, Cal went out on the road to flag down a car to go for help, and Reb guarded Rey and the drugged men with his own shotgun from the wall of the cabin.

"Half the tribe coming to see this sight!" Cal shouted as he hustled down the boardwalk toward Jordan and Reb a little later. "Why, if we charged admission today, Rebel, we'd be set for life. Met up with a friend of yours, Bill Bowlegs on the road, Jordy, and he got the rest of the Seminoles waitin' Seth's say-so down at the Carnestown Station. Seth had him just adrivin' back and forth on the road in case he could spot you, but he spotted me instead."

"Bill, I'm so glad to see you! *Che-hun-ta-mo*, everyone," she added, her eyes searching the group for Seth.

No Seth, but Wilson was with them. He graced her with the first smile she'd ever seen from him. "If you're looking for Seth, he's right behind you," he told her with a nod.

She turned just as Seth ran and Cory Cypress walked from two different spots in the distant barren trees. Seth's stricken face softened when he saw her.

Tears glazed his dark eyes. He hugged her hard, then gaped, mouth open, at what was in the cage.

"Who trapped that rat?" he asked. "Maybe *co-wha-chobee* will live free if Rey's behind bars."

"They had him that way when we came," Wilson said.

"Jordy done it herself, din't she, Calvin?" Reb said, but it was Cory Cypress who nodded.

The other Seminoles tied up Rey's men and heaved them in the cage. Everyone just stared at first until Cal shouted, "I'll bet if we kinda just let them loose in the Glades, something would get 'em 'fore the police did. A nice big cottonmouth maybe. We used to have one for a pet, and I know where to look."

Reb shook his fist at Rey, still slumped over with his head buried in his hands. "He burned us out and shot old Mame," Reb said. "So how 'bout we give him a good toastin' or just go find old Killer to settle his hash by makin' hash of him."

The murmurings in Mikasuki sounded even more ominous than that.

"Stop it," Jordan said, letting go of Seth's hand and turning to face the crowd of men. "Someone please, go get the police. This man's a killer, but he is—he is my real—father."

The taunting and muttering stopped. Cory Cypress gulped air like a beached fish, though she could tell from Seth's grim expression he already knew. At least he wasn't yelling or leaving her—yet. She braced herself when the *ayikcomi* stepped forward, and she saw he had something stiff up his sleeve—a dart gun.

"That man not your father," he declared with a steady stare at her. "Your father, I knew. Name, J.J. Hartman. A hard man but good. Hunt like us in *Pay-hay-okee,* much respect to the land. Now you be smart daughter know who is her father. And she know the Glades and the Seminoles her friends, too."

She wondered if the old man had come upon the message she left in the old Seminole camp of his ancestors. Tears almost blinded her, but she didn't cry. She opened her mouth to thank him, but he turned away to the cluster of men. He spoke in Mikasuki, and two of them ran for the road. Others hefted out and dragged the drugged guards and Rey down the boardwalk.

"They'll get the Highway Patrol," Seth said and steered her toward his truck. "We don't take things into our hands anymore. But," he added, tightening his grip, "I want to talk to you alone."

Now, she thought, he'll tell me he's sorry, but we can't go on. Yes, the Seminoles would be her friends, but their *micco* would say that he could never love or trust the daughter of Winston Rey. And she understood that, she really did.

"Jordan, listen, you need time to get yourself together before you face the police. Let me drive you home, and they can come there later. I'll get my lawyer for you, too, if you want. And—if you want—I'll be with you all the way to get Tatum and Rey indicted, investigated, and convicted."

"I'm grateful for the legal help. But personally now—"

"You know, I was actually thinking you might choose Rey over me. I mean, you'd chosen your other parents over me—your other father once."

"But that was because they said I would ruin your life—your family and future. No matter what, I could have clung to you, if they—your father, too—hadn't argued how my love would hurt you."

He shook his head. "They said the same to me that

day. We were wrong to let them separate us even for
one moment. I hated our parents then—especially
your father, but when I agreed to the annulment so
you would not lose all of them, you know the last
thing I ever said to him?"

She shook her head, eyes wide, seeing that scene
like a vision, although she had not been there. "I
asked him to protect and care for you—and he said
he would. He would, no matter what."

His voice broke; lustrous tears glazed his eyes and
spiked his thick black lashes. These moments of final
farewell would be far worse, she thought, than that
first time. She couldn't bear it, but she would have to.

"And now, that you are the *micco*," she whispered,
"you have your future to consider more than ever."

"Not without you, even if I lose all of them, just
like you've lost your parents. But you saw my father
back there—the others—even the new look on Wilson's face. I think we can be together and have my
people, at least."

"Then that will have to do, because I can't forgive
Lana and Ma—Arlene. But, Seth, if you cut me, I'd
bleed half his blood—Rey's, and my real mother's just
as deceitful."

"People under pressure do strange things. But you
are your own woman, not Rey's—and I'd like you to
be mine. We're both different now, sweetheart, so we
can really start over—if you will. I don't want to let
you get away again."

They shared a moment of sacred silence like a vow.
Then she gripped his hand, nodding wildly, then
launched herself against him. Crushing her close, he
felt so strong and sure, but then, she did, too. She did,
too, for the first time in so long and not just because
Seth still loved her. She had come through, she knew

who she was, separate from adopted or real parents
or anybody else. And she chose Seth Cypress, chose
a life with him in this place.

They kissed firmly, then fiercely, slanting their
mouths, moving closer, caressing. He brushed her
cheeks with the backs of his fingers, then cradled her
head in one big hand while she held him closer with
her finger twined in the thick hair at the nape of his
neck. But when they heard the scream of sirens approaching on the Trail, then stop, they stepped a bit
apart.

"Ah, before I was interrupted," Seth whispered, his
dark eyes glazed with tears, "I was going to say that
back at the lodge, Micco needs you urgently, right
now."

"Which Micco?" she asked with a smile no longer
shy or shaky. "Both of them, I hope."

"Yes. *Shon-a-bish,* my sweetheart. Yes!"

"I think we got us enough fry bread and fixings for
the whole tribe!" Mae declared as she carried another
platter out to the round buffet table they'd set up in
the new chickee behind the lodge.

"If even half the people I asked stop by for this
belated housewarming, we'll need it," Jordan said. She
rearranged the spray of pink and peach Laelias on
the long plank table lined with folding chairs she'd
borrowed from the Seminole community hall for the
day. Hands on her hips, she stood back to survey
everything.

"You know, Mae, this is starting to remind me of
old paintings of 'The First Thanksgiving.' "

"Right," she said, as Jenna plunked a pot of baked
beans next to the pot of *sofkee* on her next trip from
the kitchen. "The Indians at peace with the settlers."

"And," Jordan whispered to herself, "thankful hearts for survival and the future."

Seth and Wilson had built this chickee in a burst of energy after the court-ordered psychological testing of Rey established he was mentally competent to stand trial for masterminding and bankrolling Lawrence and Marc's murders. It was an "Everglades Victory" for the Seminoles when he was formally indicted and various depositions exonerated Seth from all pending charges. Yancy was going to trial soon, although he'd only given his own police department the equivalent of name, rank, and serial number at first. The entire SunRay Ranch and the Radiance Foundation had become sealed crime scenes for a while; the foundation was still closed while the men who ran it were investigated and indicted.

Best of all, Frank was living back at home, though he was working two jobs in town and saving money. Seth was not pressing charges against him for his part in all this, but she got the idea the Seminoles had Frank under their own form of probation.

But most important of all to Jordan, she had finally been able to turn over all of Lawrence's work and what she knew about letaria to Brent Rymer, who had passed it on for further study to Florida State University, the FDA, and the Center for Disease in Atlanta. The positive public relations fallout for the panthers had been huge. Brent had jokingly said it might be the first time an endangered animal won a Nobel prize for medicine. Perhaps, Jordan realized, it might actually be awarded posthumously to Lawrence; with that hope, she had buried him with honors in her heart at last.

Yet she could hardly feel total joy, because last week she had flown to New York and stood by a windswept grave next to a trembling, hostile Michelle Merwyn when they buried Michael.

"Can't we just bury all the lies and hatred with him?" she'd asked Michelle that day, but she'd turned her back and walked away. And besides Seth's sadness over Frank, she still wasn't reconciled with her other sister—her real mother, Lana—and maybe not likely to ever be. It seemed neither of them could bear to make a move toward the other.

Now Jordan clapped and cheered as Seth's son made a daring, diving swoop to return a shuttlecock to Mae's boy in a badminton game—something the Seminole kids had never seen before today. Their delighted screeching had made poor Micco take off to hide under the bed inside. Now Josh grinned gap-toothed at her as he got up and brushed himself off. He had "helped" his dad and uncle build the chickee, and Jordan knew she would love him as dearly as her own, even if she and Seth had kids someday.

As she went in the back door, she ran right into Seth. A huge pitcher of lemonade in one hand, he reached out to steady her with the other.

"Someone's here you didn't exactly invite," he said, lowering his voice, evidently so his mother wouldn't hear. Wilda Cypress had commandeered the kitchen, although she kept mumbling to Mae and Jenna, Jordan's new assistant at the orchid shop, that the cooking should have been done outdoors. There the *ayikcomi* had perched on the end of the picnic bench as if to oversee the entire affair.

"What?" she asked. "Don't look at me that way. I'm afraid you're going to say something like Rey or Andy Kramer, even Yancy, have broken out of jail before they could even be tried and escaped to show up here."

"I didn't mean to look so grim. Your brother-in-law just arrived to say that Lana came along as well as Arlene, Hattie, and the kids. He wants to know if she's welcome here after she—she hasn't gone anywhere for a while. He said," he plunged on when Jordan didn't speak or move, "they came early in case you don't want her, then no one from Lokosee will know she went back home."

"In case I don't want her," Jordan repeated in a whisper.

She had managed some good, honest dialogues with Arlene these last two months, but after Lana had given up the lead in the play to her understudy and she and Chuck had been through some rough weeks, she'd been emotionally burned out, as Arlene put it. She'd not come to see Jordan, and Jordan had not made one move to go to her.

"I'll talk to her. Where is she?" Jordan asked, but she didn't wait for an answer as she moved quickly through the lodge.

Lana stood with her back to everything across the road from the line of parked trucks and cars. On the front porch, Hattie already squeaked back and forth in Jordan's rocking chair. Standing in the doorway, Arlene briefly squeezed Jordan's shoulder as she went out; Chuck had evidently taken the kids around the side of the lodge because Jordan heard them greeting the Seminole children. She had hoped to see that, but she must do something else here, once and for all.

Lana was throwing pebbles in the pond fringed with spotted butterfly orchids which the streak of very warm weather had burst into first bloom. The two of them stood shoulder to shoulder, not talking. Lana heaved another stone and the ripples went out, out.

"I'm glad," Jordan said, "you came."

Lana turned to her. The pain in the blue eyes muted her beauty. She had lost weight; little lines edged her upper lip, and frown marks made crazy commas above her nose. It surprised Jordan how much she wanted to smooth all that away.

"I'm glad you came, too," Lana said, her voice wispy. She cleared her throat. "I mean, not just came over to talk to me now—but years ago, despite how—how you got here, came into the world. Jordan, I know I lived a lie, but I always loved you more than a sister and always will, even if you can never forgive me."

Someone moved first; it didn't matter who. They clung, trembling, sobbing, smiling, at the edge of the wild orchid pond.

Author's Note

Because I live part of the year in Naples, at the edge of the Everglades, I am constantly aware that human habitation in South Florida is booming. However, since only half of the original Glades remain, hopefully, the Everglades Forever Act—and the restraint and respect of citizens and visitors—will help to preserve what is left.

It is not fiction that the Florida panther, though protected by law since 1958 and named the state's official animal in 1982, is indeed endangered. The Florida Panther Wildlife Refuge contains nearly 30,000 protected acres, but the current count of panthers living in the wild is less than fifty. Although I created all the characters on the panther team in this novel, the team is a reality that does what it can to stem the losses. Contributions to help the Florida panther survive through habitat preservation and captive breeding may be made by check, payable to the National Fish and Wildlife Foundation at 1120 Connecticut Avenue, N.W., Suite 900, Washington, D.C. 20036, and designed for the Florida Panther Recovery Fund.

Although I have fictionalized that the panthers eat letaria, a mint plant that does not exist, there is some as yet unexplained reason the big cats do not exhibit symptoms of the feline HIV they carry, which is basically equivalent to human AIDS. When this book was almost completed, I read that, "A potion from the rain forest used to treat the AIDS virus is under study in labs." (Mark Plotkin, ethnobotanist and vice-president of plant conservation at the Conservation International in Washington, D.C.) Also, it has recently been on the news that scientists are studying African lions for the same reason as my fictional scientists studied the Florida panther: the big cats carry but do not become ill from Feline HIV. Perhaps truth and fiction will someday merge in this important matter.

Although I completely created Lokosee, Chokoloskee Island is a real and very charming deep-Florida site in the 10,000 Islands. Smallwood's Store may be visited there. My Big Sawgrass Seminoles and their reservation is loosely based on the Seminole Tribe of Florida and their Big Cypress Reservation, although all depictions of tribal members are fictitious.

I wish to thank the following people for information and advice used in the story: Nancy Hollister and Lynn Smallwood McMillin; Jim Krakowski, Florida Panther Refuge manager; fellow author and emergency room nurse, Laurie Miller; the staffs of Gun World in Hilliard, Ohio, and Glades Gun Works, Naples; the Babcock Ranch and Babcock Wilderness Adventure, upon which I partly based the layout and terrain of the SunRay Ranch; Amy at Jackson Electric Company, Naples; and the Library of Collier County, Naples. Also thanks for help with my study of feline viruses to Norma J. Bruce and her staff at the Veterinary Medicine Library, the Ohio State University, Columbus, Ohio.

As always, deep gratitude to my husband, Don, without whose support and encouragement I could not continue to write; my agent—the best!—Meg Ruley; and my very wise editor, Hilary Ross. A special thanks to John Paine.

—Karen Harper

Naples 1996

Watch for Karen Harper's
next exciting novel of suspense

Empty Cradle

coming soon from Penguin

The wait seemed endless.

In the draped cubicle even their small talk fizzled out. Her friend Sandra fidgeted in the chair while Alexis McCall stared at the ceiling from the narrow hospital bed. She heard her stomach growl as if in protest of the coming ordeal.

The nurse, Beth Bradley, appeared, gave her the tranquilizing injection she'd been expecting, and stayed a few moments to take her pulse. The squeak of her crepe soles as she walked away sounded incredibly loud. The distant drone of an airplane high above the surrounding mountains permeated even here, probably a jet out of Kirtland Air Force Base in nearby Albuquerque. For a moment Alex panicked, lifting both hands to press them, one on top of the other, over her mouth.

Sandra jumped to her feet and bent over her like a worried mother, patting her shoulder. "I can get you out of here right now if you're not still okay with this," she insisted in that gravelly voice of hers.

Alex slowly lowered her hands to grip them together on her stomach. "If I'm not okay with this . . ."

she echoed, staring up into Sandra's sharp brown eyes, then beyond at the white acoustical tiles she'd been studying as if she could see that plane aloft, one like Geoff had flown. Her nostrils burned and tears prickled her eyelids, but she didn't cry. Her voice got stronger, a little louder. "I'm not okay, but I'm going to do it."

"Then I'm with you—here for you."

"Hey, after all," Alex said with a forced little shrug, "lots of TV personalities work on air right up to the minute they deliver. Lots of women do a good job as a single parent. But most of them," she plunged on, her voice getting sharper, "weren't single when they conceived, and everybody knew it. The truth is," she whispered, looking back at Sandra and gripping her hand so hard she winced, "I know this is the right thing to do. But I've still never been more scared in my whole damn life."

Sandra nodded jerkily, then stooped to give her a quick, hard hug. She was a stork of a woman, long-nosed, tall, thin, and angular. Though she now wore stiff paper scrubs which crinkled, she usually tempered her appearance with softly fitted business suits and draped blouses, not to mention her tumble of curly hair.

"Alex, I know," she intoned, perching on the edge of the bed and emphasizing each word in her best on-air authoritative voice, "this is going to work. For sure. In nine months you're either going to be spending big bucks for a nanny or hauling diapers and formula to the station."

"Oh, I'm sure M&Ms would love that," she countered, referring to Mike Montgomery, their station manager. Unlike the nickname they used only between them, he was not sweet and did not have a soft center. "Sandra, he said I should be grateful he was only giving me one week's unpaid leave. I wish I could explain to him the real reason I lost it on the air, but this crisis is my personal affair—the last private thing I have."

"I know, I know, kiddo." She looked away, and her gaze became distant. "Funny how we make a career of exposing other people's lives but fight like hell to keep any piece of our own quiet." She bit her lower lip to halt the quiver of her chin, and Alex knew she was remembering her own tragic loss. "I can just feel it," she said as she smacked her hands on her knees, then bounded back to her feet, "everything's gonna go great for you."

In her best moments Alex believed that too. Despite terrible odds against someone with her ovulation and miscarriage problems, she trusted the doctors and staff of this private high-tech clinic to do their brilliant best for her. This just had to work and not only because her thirty-seven-year-old biological clock was clanging. Her husband, Geoff, had been dead for four years this month.

But right now she knew if she didn't get her mind off that, she'd dissolve in tears. Nervously, she wet her lips with the tip of her tongue. "You know," she told Sandra as she peeked out through the drapes before flopping down on her chair again, "that shot I had, Versed, is an amnesiac, but I'm remembering things so far. I think."

Sandra grinned. "I'll tell you everything that happens later, I promise," she vowed, jokingly crossing her heart. "Why, if you and His Holiness," she went on, referring to Dr. Stanhope, "had said I could take a full camera and sound crew in there, I would."

"And I thought you were on my side—you know,

to keep all this a big, dark secret." She sighed so hard she felt physically deflated. Maybe the drug was grabbing hold. Suddenly, she felt so drowsy and limp she could barely move so much as a facial muscle. She did, however, manage to yawn.

"On our way, now," Beth told them cheerily as she whipped open the drapes. The nurse's warm hazel eyes and wide, full mouth seemed to fill her heart-shaped face, framed by a chestnut-hued page boy with bouncy bangs. She had a missionary zeal for her work, which Alex admired. Beth was a short woman, so, over her shoulder while she adjusted the bed and blanket, Alex watched Sandra try nonchalantly to deal with the items Beth gave her.

With difficulty she shoved her abundant hair back into a plum paper cap, then fooled with a face mask she didn't quite know how to tie on. Pale plum, just like the interior of this room and the drapes, Alex thought—designer colors for designer babies.

Two other nurses appeared with a wheeled gurney and helped Beth lift Alex onto it, then disappeared. With Sandra trailing behind, Beth pushed Alex out of the prep and recovery area down the hallway lined with watercolors of flowers blooming in the desert.

" 'We're off to see the wizard,' " Beth sang, " 'the wonderful wizard of Oz. I hear he is a whiz of a wiz, if ever a wiz there was ...' " Alex wasn't sure, but she thought she probably made that little hop step Judy Garland did in her red sparkle shoes. Sandra laughed, but Alex only felt like Dorothy drugged in that vast field of poppies while the Wicked Witch pursued her.

She closed her eyes because the ceiling tiles and recessed lights flying by overhead were making her dizzy. How desperately she wanted to be awake and aware through all this, her last chance to have a baby for her and Geoff. He was lost to her in the long corridors of passing days and the world's daring to go on without him. That last night in bed together, he had been so desperate over their continued failure to have a child.

She could hear his deep, impassioned voice now: *Alex, swear to me, that even if I—I don't come back, you'll still try. Try to have our baby, a precious piece of posterity, someone for you to love and care for . . .*

He moved against her, closer in the cocooned darkness of their blanketed bed that moved and rolled with their lovemaking. *Yes, my darling,* she had vowed. *Yes, I promise you . . .*

"Almost there," Beth sang out to bring her back.

They passed the hall door to the embryo lab and turned into what was called the transfer room in this large, renovated pine and adobe former hotel set in the forest foothills east of Albuquerque. Suddenly, the soaring sounds of Handel's majestic *Water Music* washed over her. Other patients had said Dr. Hale Stanhope always played classical, but his wife, Dr. Jasmine—whose nickname Alex heard was Jazz—played Basin Street's best in her lab.

Oh, good, Alex thought, her mind was working great. She remembered a lot of things . . . maybe too many.

The large room bathed her in dim, greenish light. She floated on her back into a watery cave under the sea. Since eggs and embryos never saw the harsh light of day inside a woman's body, soft indirect lighting, machine displays, and the doctor's high-intensity head-lamp would provide the only illumination of the area during this and other in vitro fertilization procedures.

"Why don't you just stand on her other side there,

Sandra?" Alex heard Beth say, and Sandra swam around the end of the gurney to get out of the way. "The doctor will be right in," she told Alex, then hid her smile by tying her own mask in place.

Beth and the anesthesiologist, Nathan Greene, bent over her, and soon she was wired to machines. That cleared her head, didn't it? By just turning it she could watch the rise and fall of her pulse and respiration tracked in amber and green waves on instruments. Yes, it was wavy like that on their honeymoon, when they went scuba diving on Grand Cayman in that deep sea cave, but now they were waiting for King Neptune to swim in. . . .

Sandra jumped and looked up at the ceiling as a woman's clipped, disembodied voice filled the room: "Good morning, Alexis. Dr. Jasmine here, waiting for those lovely eggs to mix with your husband's sperm in the embryo lab next door. Then, hopefully, in just two days, implantation. Dr. Stanhope will be right in."

Despite their shared last name, only one person at the clinic was referred to as Dr. Stanhope, so his wife went by Dr. Jasmine. The queen of the Evergreen Reproductive Health Clinic reigned only in the lab across the dividing wall from her husband's O.R. The two rooms were linked by a hatch through which harvested eggs from hormone-ripened ovaries, or sperm, or embryos could be passed to be implanted.

Yes, she was ready for this, Alex thought. She had waited too long to try IVF again without Geoff. At least now she had learned to live without him.

Beth gently lifted Alex's draped legs into stirrups and washed her with an icy disinfectant. For the crazy cost of a complete IVF cycle, couldn't they warm that stuff? Several pricks of slightly stinging pain followed—a local anesthetic. She knew the whole drill.

She'd talked things over with the doctor, Beth, the counselor here, and other patients.

Even in her groggy state, she startled when the double doors to the hall opened with a resounding crack. "Good morning, Alexis, ladies, Nathan," Dr. Hale Stanhope's nasal, somewhat monotone voice rang out. He was from Boston and, she thought, always sounded like those old videos of President Kennedy. He said *potly* for *partly* and *idear* instead of *idea*.

People returned a muted good morning; Dr. Stanhope brought a reassuring presence into any room. Alex thought she said hello, too, but she wasn't sure.

He bent over her, his pewter gray eyes framed by thick lashes and raven eyebrows that had not turned prematurely silver along with his hair. Instead of his usual crisp white coat or pale plum scrubs like everyone else, his were baby blue. She hoped the color was a good omen.

"Ready, Alexis?" he asked with a tight smile and a quick nod that seemed to answer for her. "I am, and we're going to do a good work here. Ready in the lab," he ordered, instead of asked, over the piped-in music as he moved away and clicked on his headlamp. He stepped closer again, this time between her draped legs. She was grateful that he hid the long probe with its collection needle from her. Sandra must have seen it, though, because her eyes widened over her mask, and she put a shaky hand on Alex's shoulder.

"Since we have KALB-TV's best-loved noon and early evening anchorwoman and top investigative reporter in attendance," the doctor went on as Alex felt the slight thrust of pressure, "I'll just tell everybody to watch the TV screen, and we'll hope for some very good ratings today."

Alex turned her head to follow the Doppler ultrasound probe on the big video monitor. The black and silver picture shimmered like a rain-glazed window to her womb. No one looked at her now but at the image of her interior. Suddenly, this—all of it—seemed unreal.

Watch the TV screen, the doctor's words reverberated in her head. She hoped her suspension from the station would be the end of the mess she'd made. She needed and loved that job, but the hormonal drug Pergonal had given her such wild mood swings that she had cried on the air while reporting a case of child abuse. How could anyone harm his own child, even a child he didn't want? If that bastard had been in the studio, she could have pounded his face in! He had fled and not been arrested yet, but she hoped the coverage made life a living hell for him.

"Oh!" she cried out as she felt a deep cramp. Tears blurred the screen; Sandra gripped her shoulder harder.

"Just a little prick," Dr. Stanhope announced, his eyes riveted on the monitor. "I'm in the right ovary, first follicle," he called out, evidently loud enough so the embryo lab could hear. "See that follicle on the screen, Ms. Swanson?" he asked Sandra, his voice a bit quieter. "That black sphere the size of a grape. The computer calculates the path for the needle to follow and draws a line on the screen. But it takes skilled disconnected hand-eye coordination, like playing a complicated video game, to control it. See, when I probe the follicle, it collapses and hopefully yields a ripe egg in this vial of fluid—there!"

"Yes, I see!" Sandra cried triumphantly, leaning over Alex's prone form to get an even better view of the screen.

Alex groaned as he siphoned the fluid out through

the small, attached hose. She could hear but not see
him splash the contents into a small Teflon-coated
bowl Beth held for him. But Alex glimpsed it when
she carried it past, proudly and carefully, as if it held
a newborn itself. The bowl had been labeled in bold
strokes of black Magic Marker: MCCALL, A. Beth
passed it through the hatch as Hale Stanhope turned
to his task again. Alex guessed she felt less shaky, less
chicken now, as her brothers used to call her when
they were children. Which came first, she thought, the
chicken or the egg?

"Here's hoping for an egg." Dr. Stanhope interrupted her scrambled thoughts. "Second follicle on the
right . . ."

It went on in a blur and sticks and groans, terse
comments. This really did hurt more than they'd led
her to believe, so maybe it was worse for some patients. But pain—deep, soul-struck pain—was something she had seen close up and survived.

"Egg!" Dr. Jasmine's voice boomed on the inter-
com. Sandra cheered; Beth patted her arm; Handel's
music soared, and Dr. Stanhope hummed along. Even
as that voice from the heavens called out "Egg!" three
more times over the next twenty minutes, Alexis
McCall lay on her back and sobbed silently in relief
and joy.

Two huge eyes stared back at her.

Jasmine Stanhope had a habit of studying herself in
the lenses of her $40,000 new Nikon electronic micro-
scope before she pressed her face to it to peer within.
The darkly mirrored reflection rested her strained
eyes, but mostly it assured her that she was beautiful
as well as brainy.

Her aquamarine eyes and up-swept, layered platinum hair framed a classically oval face. That, as well as her lithe model's body, always startled people when they discovered she was a doctor, an embryologist, no less. At thirty-seven, the very age of the patient who had produced the eggs, she looked in her early thirties. And no way she would give in to that damned, creeping middle-age spread, she thought, shifting in her chair. If she had to spend every spare, sparse free hour working with that *Butt Busters* video to keep the lard off this bottom, that's exactly what she'd do.

"You gonna be awhile?" Max Fox, her young associate embryologist asked over the roll of music—a Creole jazz band's rendition of Gershwin. "Thought I'd eat my lunch outside, maybe take a quick walk through the old town," he added. Five acres of clinic property abutted ramshackle ruins that had once been a prosperous silver mine and its little, long-dead boomtown.

"Sorry, I'm going to be a while, Max."

"Okay. But I packed enough for two here—blue corn tortillas stuffed with sprouts, pinto beans, and chilies. A politically correct lunch, even for the Jane Fonda of the fertility world."

Not lifting her eyes from the lenses, Jasmine automatically stretched and snapped the wrists of her latex gloves. She wore her gold and diamond tennis bracelets under them, which imprinted in her flesh if she didn't shift them around. She adjusted the magnification focus knob; the egg flew into sharp relief.

"A lot of blood, a lot of cells," she observed. "But only four eggs from Alexis McCall today, and I've got to take good care of them." It went unspoken that some egg harvests went as high as twenty eggs, but this one had been really minimal. "She's my age, lost her pilot husband in Saudi Arabia during the Gulf War in that SCUD explosion in a barracks. A real dicey situation to get her a viable embryo out of this with four-year-old frozen sperm."

"You'll handle it, Jazz—if you're not skipping meals so you get light-headed again," he added, not budging. She could sense he was practically breathing down her neck. "I mean, Hale said you need to keep up your strength with the long, late hours you been putting in, you know."

"Yes, mother," she mocked gently. "And when Hale says, 'Let there be light,' all that draw breath must obey. I'll eat when I get done here," she said curtly. "In other words, Max, I've got to get those greedy, wriggly, won't-take-no-for-an-answer little tadpoles you washed and centrifuged to thrust themselves inside this lovely, waiting egg, though it looks real happy on its own."

Even over the hum of the incubators, she could hear he finally took the hint. His lunch sack rustled, his feet scuffed the tiled floor, as he walked out and closed the door.

She liked him, all the staff they'd assembled here these last three years, she really did, but she didn't need someone else watching her closely. And she didn't want to encourage his embryonic—she smiled grimly at her pun—infatuation with her. If Hale could cope with scores of desperate women who adored him, she could handle one man.

She lost herself in the fascinating world that blossomed before her enlarged gaze. Using a micropipette, she swirled the egg around, marveling anew at how every one of the thousands she'd studied resembled a distinct cumulus cloud—just like unique snowflakes, no two alike. She turned up the power of the scope again. The egg bloomed even bigger.

She moved it into a second dish, rinsed it, then added a small drop of mineral oil to it in a third dish. Her neck muscles ached as she rose to get the vial of sperm of—in this case—a dead donor whose future, if not his life, had been preserved in a glass ampoule in a freezing bath of liquid nitrogen. With tweezers she removed the lab's temporary plug Max had put on the narrow neck of the vial. She would fertilize each of the McCalls' eggs separately, this one first, and pray she had four viable embryos to coddle before Hale took over again and got all the glory.

She released a tiny jet of sperm into the dish with the egg, then put it back under the microscope. She watched the battle as the writhing warriors tried to outpace each other to attack the fortress of the much bigger, thick-skinned egg. But the ranks of this army had literally met their Waterloo.

Staring into the microscope, she muttered under her breath, as if it were a magic spell, "The ultimate orgasm—the ability to say no and mean it. The chance to beat them. And they think," she added, her voice derisive, "they're in charge of the whole big world."

She shook her head in disgust if not disappointment. Before the sperm battered themselves into oblivion and she would have to use an alternative plan, she reached for her micromanipulation tools. She did a micropuncture on the egg, selected one lucky, lively sperm, and ejaculated it directly into the egg. It exploded inside with dark, linked genetic pairs of chromosomes instantly apparent. She might never bear Hale Stanhope a baby, but again *she* had created another potential one here.

Smiling, she rose and walked over to reach into the back corner of the incubator where she'd hidden another petri dish, one no one else knew about. She rocked its fragile glass cradle a moment before she went back to her work.

SIGNET **ONYX**

CONTEMPORARY ROMANCE
AND SUSPENSE

☐ **SLOW DANCE by Donna Julian.** Lily Hutton is going home to the close-knit Southern town where she grew up. But along with her past, Lily must face again the heartbreakingly handsome, darkly driven man whom she never forgot, and who is now desperately trying to drive her away. (186710—$5.50)

☐ **RIVERBEND by Marcia Martin.** As a dedicated young doctor, Samantha Kelly was ready to battle all the superstitions and prejudices of a Southern town seething with secrets and simmering with distrust of an outsider. But as a passionate woman she found herself struggling against her own needs when Matt Tyler, the town's too handsome, too arrogant, unoffical leader, decided to make her his. (180534—$4.99)

☐ **SILVER LINING by Christiane Heggan.** Diana Wells was a beautiful woman, a brilliant success, and a loving single mother. Was she also a murderer? The police thought so. The press thought so. And the only one to whom she could turn for help was dangerously attractive Kane Sanders, the lawyer who was her worst enemy's best friend ... the man whose passion threatened the defense of the last thing left she could safely call her own—her heart.... (405943—$4.99)

☐ **BETRAYALS by Christiane Heggan.** Stephanie Farrell appears to have it all, as one of television's most in demand actresses and the mother of a beautiful daughter. But beneath her carefully constructed image is a girl whose childhood was scarred by a tyrannical father and whose one chance at happiness was overturned by a shocking betrayal. "Dazzling romantic suspense!"—Judith Gould (405080—$4.99)

*Prices slightly higher in Canada

Buy them at your local bookstore or use this convenient coupon for ordering.

PENGUIN USA
P.O. Box 999 — Dept. #17109
Bergenfield, New Jersey 07621

Please send me the books I have checked above.
I am enclosing $_____ (please add $2.00 to cover postage and handling). Send check or money order (no cash or C.O.D.'s) or charge by Mastercard or VISA (with a $15.00 minimum). Prices and numbers are subject to change without notice.

Card #_____ Exp. Date _____
Signature_____
Name_____
Address_____
City _____ State _____ Zip Code _____

For faster service when ordering by credit card call **1-800-253-6476**

Allow a minimum of 4-6 weeks for delivery. This offer is subject to change without notice.